I0787974

OPHEIR
Melania Mountains
Deseret's Citadel
Queen's lair
Sadal
Juka
Ken'ar
Zalnazari
Jotun
Mikado
Desarca
Taylor I
Oon k'dahl
Swamps
city
city with portal and
portal

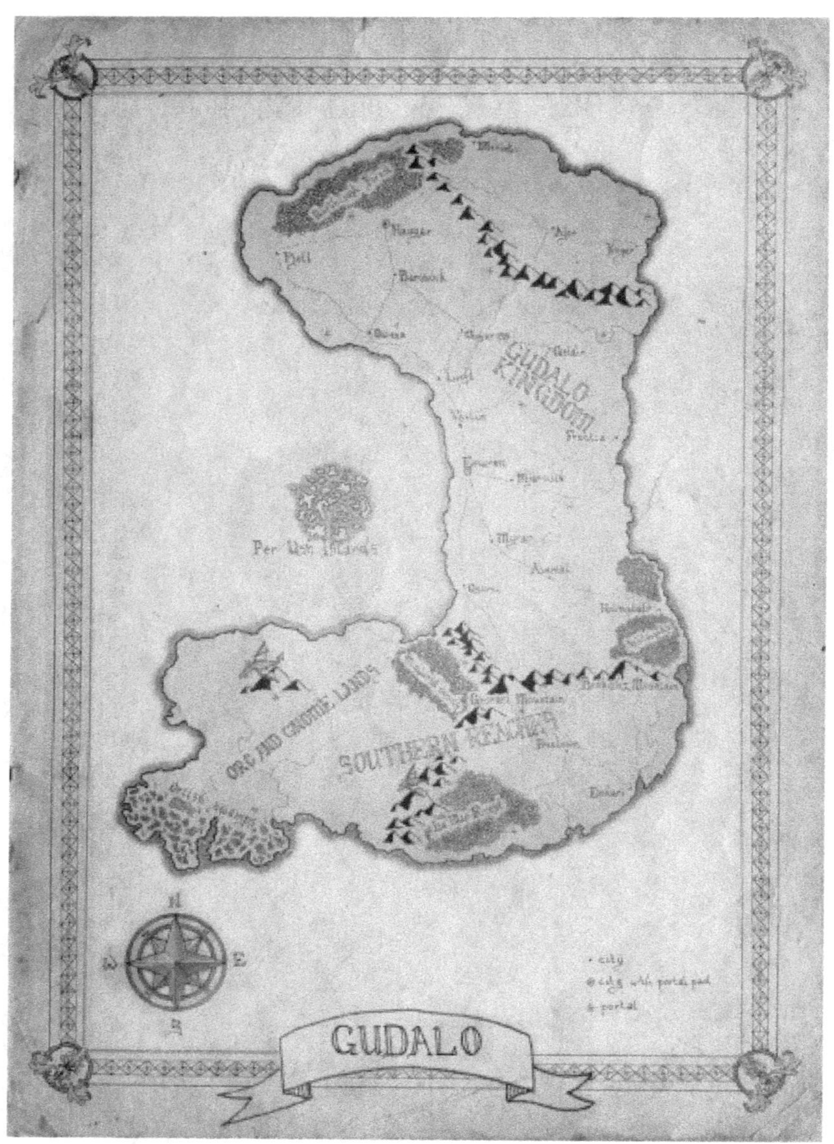
GUDALO KINGDOM
ORC AND GNOME LANDS
SOUTHERN KINGDOM
Per Ileh Islands
GUDALO
city
city with portal pad
portal

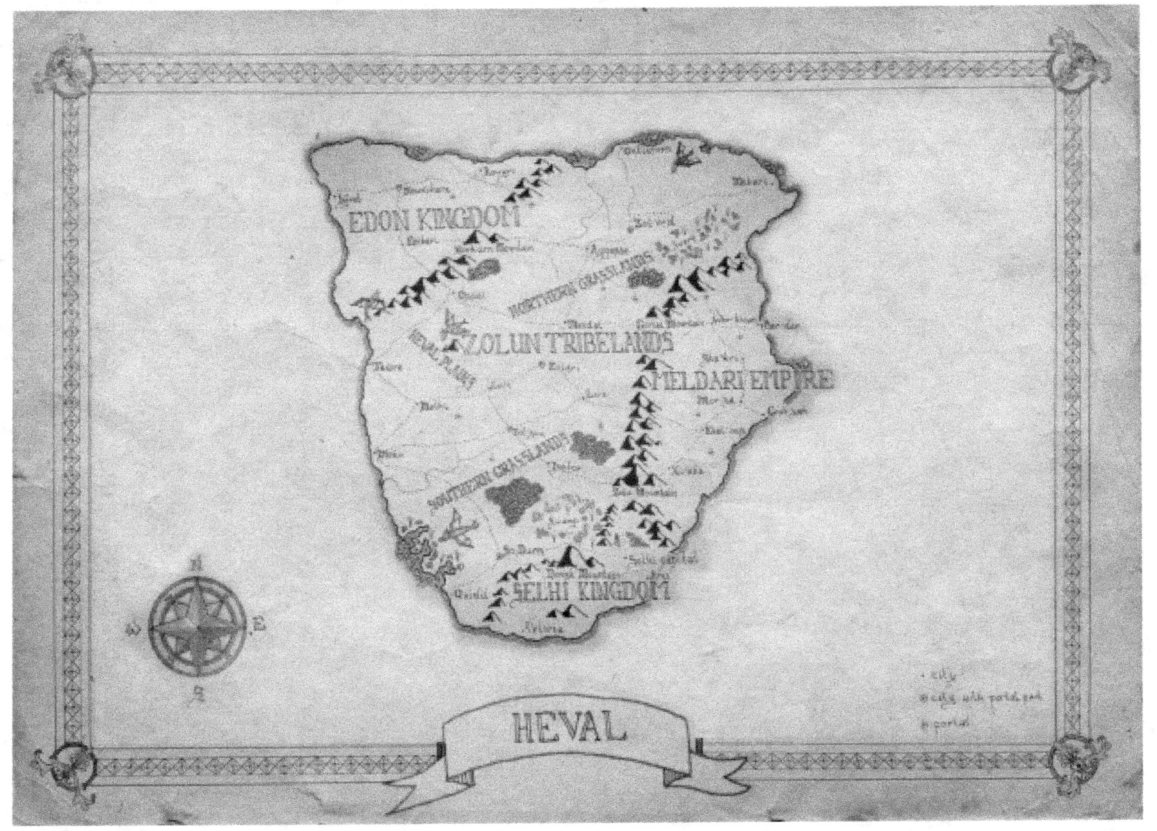
EDON KINGDOM
NORTHERN GRASSLANDS
VOLUN TRIBELANDS
VELDARI EMPIRE
SOUTHERN GRASSLANDS
SELHI KINGDOM
HEVAL

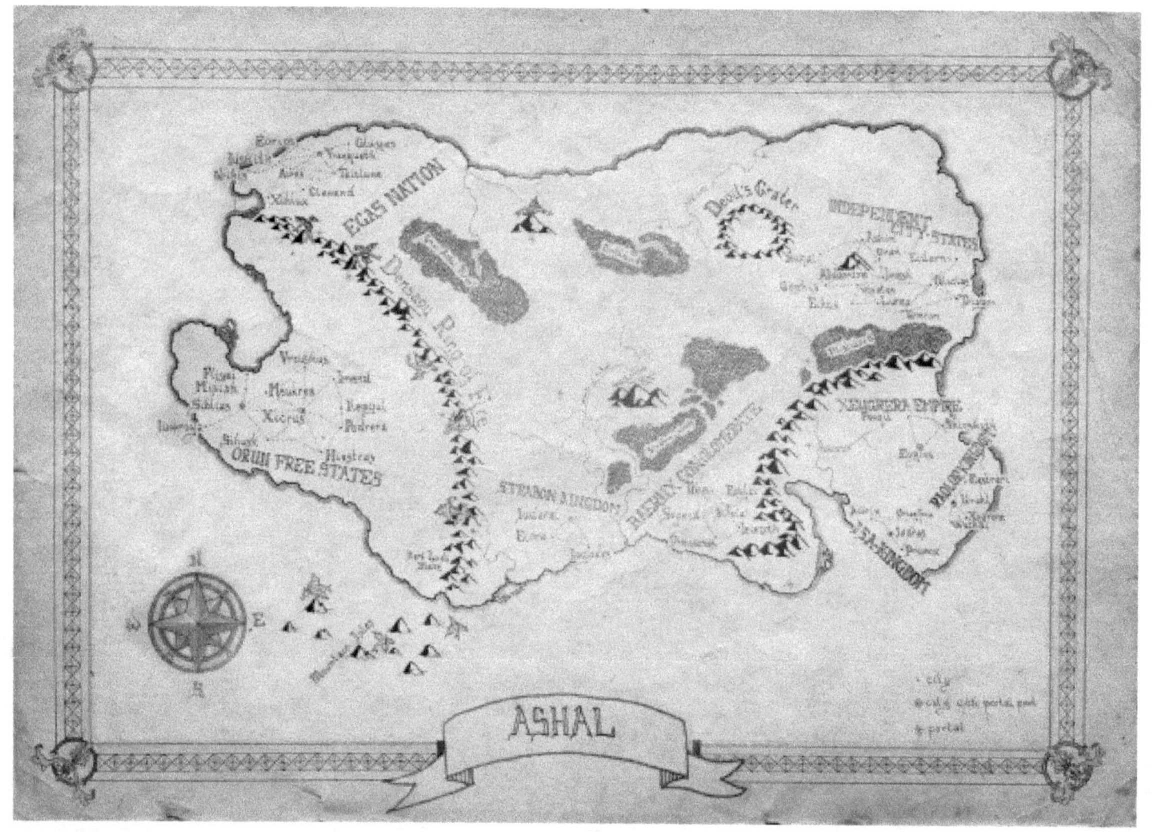
EGAS NATION
ORUU FREE STATES
Darren Range of Fire
STEPHAN KINGDOM
FLEXNOY CONFEDERATE
Devil's Crater
INDEPENDENT CITY-STATES
NEMRERA EMPIRE
JISA-KINGDOM
ASHAL
• city
• city with portal pool
portal

MARKOLM
MARKOLM RANGE

Want a bigger map of Emerilia and the continents? Check out http://theeternalwriter.deviantart.com/

Character Sheet is located in the back of the book for reference.

Emerilia

Benvari Mountains

Prologue

Bob appeared in a cave. Wind howled with a cold that would make any mortal person freeze to death within just minutes.

As Bob walked, his gnomish body changed, growing and expanding until he became Lo'kal and then passed through what looked to be a solid wall and looked upon a massive cavern.

Unlike the previous room, this was actually warm. The room's light was provided by skylights above. A metal walkway extended from the wall Lo'kal had entered through, between the large black boxes extending to either side of the cavern, and toward a silver pod.

Lo'kal took an excited yet scared breath—guilt and warmth of what he knew to be love passed through him. He completely ignored the entire cavern, including the humming black boxes he was walking past, as he zeroed in on the silver pod.

The silver outside of the pod became translucent, showing a woman in her thirties. She had an athletic build to her body; her face was beautiful but serious. Her tanned skin was framed with silver hair that complemented her features.

Lo'kal tenderly touched the outside of the pod. It hurt him every time to see her like this.

"It's time to wake up, Anna." Lo'kal's voice was soft as the black boxes started to pick up their pace.

Emerilia Administrator Command Panel

Do you wish to wake Emerilia Administrator AI 24681 (Anna)?
Y/N

"Yeah." Lo'kal's voice caught with emotion.

The black boxes made more and more noise; lights blinked on the side of the standing pod. They first shifted from yellow to red and then green over several days. During this entire process, Lo'kal didn't move. Days meant little to him as he used his remotes to view Emerilia.

Finally, the pod doors opened.

For a few moments, Lo'kal just looked at the woman lying inside, scared that the procedure hadn't worked.

Her eyes opened, looking around the cavern and falling on Lo'kal. He held his breath as his eyes watered. He'd spent so much time around the Humans that his own reactions had become similar to theirs.

"Anna." His voice was filled with relief and nervous excitement.

"Hi, Dad." Her serious face split into a smile that made Lo'kal's heart jump. She pushed herself out of the pod and wrapped her hands around him.

"Oh, my girl, I've missed you so much." Lo'kal put his hands around her, not wanting to let go.

"I see that from all the records of you sneaking in here to watch over me." Her voice was soft and filled with emotion.

Lo'kal laughed. They pulled apart slightly, and Anna looked down at him. He only came to her shoulder height.

"Something big must've happened for you to wake me," Anna said.

"I found one. I found a bleeder." Lo'kal smiled.

Anna tilted her head, blinking rapidly. "Wow, that *does* change things."

"And I have had my administrator rights revoked for looking over the other Affinities. It's as you predicted and feared. The empire cares little about actually suppressing the other aggressive species. Now, they just want to use Emerilia as a massive life-or-death coliseum. Blood and death to appeal to the masses. They've lost sight of Emerilia." Lo'kal sighed. He was weary and his creation had been turned into a bloody form of entertainment. "They're allowing the

Affinities the ability to have magical creatures and champions, as long as they use their own power."

Anna's hands balled her hands into fists with intense anger.

This anger was the reason Lo'kal had needed to put her to sleep as it had built and was directly aimed toward those who used her people. Unlike the callous Affinities, she didn't just watch the Humans. She'd lived among them for millennia, watching the actions of the Jukal Empire as they introduced the gods, added in more portals, and stopped killing off races that were bent on killing and destroying everything in their path.

She'd countered it, dropping pieces of information and aiding the People of Emerilia and the Players' growth of skills and knowledge.

Every time the empire added in new things, they ordered Lo'kal to change the rules to make Emerilia more "interesting."

She'd finally come to him, asking him to put her to sleep. If she stayed in Emerilia, then she would stop just aiding the Players and People of Emerilia. She would start leading them against those who wished to use them.

Lo'kal was the closest thing she had to a father and family. She trusted him completely and he had abided by her wishes, even if it had left him alone for centuries.

He'd left her systems hooked up to Emerilia so her mind could continue to browse through the information, even while her physical body had been sealed away.

She'd seen the strain it had put on Lo'kal, sealing his daughter away for three hundred lonely years. Anna's analytical functions had been shifted to a quantum computer to assist him to balance Emerilia's forces. Her father was a great man, but he was also an emotional creature and she loved him for it all.

"So, the time has come." Anna looked at her father.

"It has." Lo'kal nodded.

Anna nodded slowly. The cavern felt as if it chilled a few more degrees. She smiled after a while as her data banks caught up with relevant information. "It has been a long time, Father."

Lo'kal's smile was as happy as it was sad.

"Too long, Anna—too long. Though there are many interesting people I must introduce you to."

Chapter 1: Brightest Day

Due to his damage, it had taken three days for Malsour to regenerate all of his Health. Induca had stayed nearby, looking after her own injuries and keeping a lookout.

Malsour shook his mass and moved his wings. They were now fully healed and stronger than ever before. Both of them had increased in levels from fighting at Boran-al's Citadel.

"Are you sure?" Malsour asked.

"I am." Induca's red eyes found his black ones. Induca might be younger and have spent most of her time away from Emerilia in hibernation, but Malsour had always felt close to his little sister. It was why he volunteered to watch over her as she wanted to look for the Lady of Fire's child.

"Very well." A smile filled Malsour's face as he walked to the edge of the cave that they had cut out of the Mithsia Mountains, high enough and far enough away to stay hidden from the Dwarves as they tended to their wounds.

The mountains ranged for miles, so there was plenty of room.

"You almost seem like you want to go and see them again." Induca's voice soured.

"I do. That power Dave was wielding was nearly as much power as our mother." Malsour hid his face as he thought of those who had been lost.

He didn't like getting attached to the short-lived People of Emerilia but without his understanding it, he had become friends with them. He'd come to care for them and he *needed* to know what had happened to them.

"Well, at least one of us can admit that they just want to make sure that they're okay." Induca saw through his bluff. Moving her body past his and leaping from the cave's entrance, she used fire under her wings to shoot herself up.

Malsour jumped off, diving for the ground before his wings snapped open and he curved back up into the sky. He beat his wings, hurling himself upward as they rose into the clouds and headed toward Cliff-Hill.

***

Dave looked over what was left of the citadel.

The bodies had been cleaned away, leaving just the battleground behind.

Deia squeezed his hand.

He looked to her, a sad smile on his face.

Both of their eyes were red from tears and the inner pain they felt.

Dave hugged Deia as the tears she'd been holding back broke through. Dave let out tears of his own.

Deia had been with Lox's warband for ten years. They were as close as family, even closer in some ways. They'd faced death together, drank together, and lived through one another.

While Dave had only known them for just over half a year but he, too, had become attached to them. He'd seen Joko, Tounk, and Max's bodies.

Joko and Tounk had been killed by black lightning and then risen again as undead puppets. Max had been killed by the metal-sheathed tentacles as he lived through his worst fears.

Dave and Deia pulled apart as their tears slowed.

"Fuck the gods, fuck the fucking Affinities Pantheon. What gives them the right to do this? To kill all of these people just to try to get more fuckin' power." Deia's red eyes seemed to glow a bit more with her words.

Dave put his arm around her side as they leaned against each other for support. Dave's mind reeled with pain and tried to understand why the lords of Dark and Earth would bring this down on the people who served them.

It would have been kinder if his mind didn't come up with probable answers.

Death magic was in part a melding of Dark and Earth magic, binding the natural and the unnatural together to raise the dead and pull the life from others. It was a twisted abomination of the two Affinities and took a large amount of power to do it.

The cultists by themselves were tossing around enough energy for a dozen Dwarven warclans and their mages.

If they had been able to kill us all and then use our bodies to start their undead army, then the power would have been immense. Every person the cultists killed and brought back would be turned into their minions. Which, in turn, would make them minions of the lords of Dark and Earth. If the lords who gave them this power asked for a larger devotion of power toward them, they wouldn't have hesitated. With the power of their undead, they would've had nations' worth of power that they didn't need.

Dave shook his head. On Earth, money had been the currency of power; on Emerilia, power came from your abilities. Materials could augment it but pure, unrefined Mana was the currency of the Affinities.

Dave shook his head sadly.

A group of mages were around the pillars that made up the portals.

He wanted to get away from this all; he wanted to just go and explore Emerilia and have his house in Cliff-Hill.

But you know that this is only the beginning. You remember what Bob said about the Pantheon. They're not the type of people to take this and shrug it off.

If I want my friends to survive, then I'm going to have to learn more. I'm going to have to become stronger. My friends gave their lives so that we could bring down this citadel, to protect their people. I might want to just hide in the seeder and play with inventions, to let the world burn itself, but that would just sully their names and their sacrifice.

Dave walked toward the pillars, Deia holding his hand.

"Excuse me, but I was wondering if you could hold off destroying the portal for just a moment," Dave said.

"Boy, this thing is coming down," one of the Elven mages said.

"It will only take a moment and it will make sure that even if they put these spikes together they won't function." Dave looked at the Elven Earth mage.

They looked as though they wanted to argue but they were too tired to do so.

"Go for it." He waved at the pillars and then signaled to the other mages to wait.

"Are you sure about this?" Deia let go of his hand.

"We need to know more about the portals and this is one of the best ways," Dave said.

"Okay." She smiled.

Dave gave her a small smile back and walked up to the four spikes that rested in the center of the black rock square.

A bloody altar rested in the center of the four spikes. Red runes covered the altar, creating a circle around it and then spreading up the four pillars.

Dave pressed his hand to the closest spike.

The ebony that the citadel was made from was filled with magical potential.

Magical Circuits

You have found a complex series of Magical Circuits. Are you interested in trying to learn from them? The Circuits will be destroyed in the process.

Cost: 100,000 Mana (Due to your Affinities, cost is reduced to 78,924)

Reward: Unknown

Y/N

Dave checked the reserves in his armor.

Abscondita Armor

Forged by Dave Grahslagg, this armor is more than meets the eye.

Quality: B

Defense: 523 (Magical shield with enough power)

Abilities: Magical Shield.

Automated Mana Siphon.

Automated Soul Siphon.

Automated Self-Heal.

Increased Agility and Strength (base 10%).

Grows in strength with user.

Manipulation possible (Associated values liable to change due to creator's changes and level of charge).

Armor Link (Users of this armor can share their power and link capabilities. If one armor is fully charged, then it will feed power to the other to charge it).

Charge: 4,537/2,000,000 (Linked Armor 5,888/4,000,000)

Durability: 97/259

4,537 charge points was worth 45,370 Mana.

Dave opened his character sheet with a thought. He had dismissed his notification bar that had been blinking wildly for the last few days. He hadn't wanted to look at the rewards he'd gained while others had died.

Character Sheet

Name:	David Grahslagg	Gender:	Male
Level:	3	Class:	-
Race:	Human/Dwarf	Alignment:	Chaotic Neutral

Unspent points-195

Health:	1,900	Regen:	1.56/s
Mana:	910	Regen:	3.70/s
Stamina:	620	Regen:	2.45/s
Vitality:	19	Endurance:	78
Intelligence:	91	Willpower:	74
Strength:	62	Agility:	49

Dave sighed and looked up to the corner of his HUD. His notifications came into view and he clicked on them.

Passive Skill: Dodge
Level: Expert Level 4
Effect: 71% chance to evade objects.
Passive Skill: Perception
Level: Journeyman Level 9
Effect: 61% chance to find hidden details
Active Skill: Surveyor
Level: Expert Level 5
Effect: 73% chance to see resources within your range sight.
Range: 1,100m
Cost: 5 Stamina/s
Active Skill: Sprint
Level: Expert Level 3

Effect: 69% increased speed
Cost: 5 Stamina/s
Active Skill: Stealth
Level: Journeyman Level 2
Effect: 47% chance to remain undetected (reduced in direct light).
Cost: 5 Stamina/s
Passive Skill: Night Vision
Level: Master Level 2
Effect: 87% increased night vision. 20% increased vision in magical darkness

> **Racial bonus:** Dwarves, even half-Dwarves, are at home in the darkness of mines and their empires dug underneath mountains. +25% increased night vision (+5% in magical darkness).

You have unlocked a Master Level Skill

Master Level skills are different from the other level of skills. Gaining one level as a master is more difficult than any other level. With each Master Level you gain, you will also gain an additional enhancement. Once passing through the Master Level of Night Vision, you will gain increased skills to see through not only natural darkness but magical darkness. Other Master Level skills will gain you different additional bonuses.

Dave read it and continued on to his other notifications.
Active Skill: Magical Circuits
Level: Master Level 3

> **Effect:** 89% chance of creating better Magical Circuits and understanding them. 15% Reduction to cost.

Cost: Dependent

Active Skill: Mining
Level: Expert Level 2

Effect: You cut through rock easily, finding ores and gems beneath. 67% chance to get higher yield of materials from ore vein. 67% faster at mining.

Cost: 10 Stamina/s.

Racial Bonus: Dwarves are the mining powerhouses of Emerilia; +15% Chance to get higher yield of Materials

Active Skill: Lumberjack
Level: Journeyman Level 7
Effect: 57% increased speed and damage to cut down trees and shape wood.
Cost: 10 Stamina/s
Active Skill: Maintainer
Level: Expert Level 2

Effect: 67% chance to restore durability, at higher levels possible to increase durability, quality and gain 4% Sharpen bonus to items that have been cared for.

Require: Dependent on gear; sharpening stone, hammer, anvil. Better maintainer's tool leads to higher chance of increasing stats.

Active Skill: Builder
Level: Journeyman Level 9
Effect: 61% speed and efficiency.
Required: Tools
Active Skill: Alchemy
Level: Expert Level 3

Effect: Combine multiple ingredients together. Creations gain a 69% boost in effectiveness.

Required: Alchemy tools
Active Skill: Sneak Attack
Level: Apprentice Level 7

Effect: When you are undetected in stealth, attacks will hit with 268% increased damage (Massive increase when hitting Critical area). May your aim be true.

Cost: (Attack 50 Stamina)
Active Skill: Cooking
Level: Journeyman Level 6
Effect: Creations effects are 55% higher
Active Skill: Dual Wield
Level: Expert Level 2
Effect: 32 % increased damage. 25% reduced damage with off-hand weapon.
Active Skill: Smithing
Level: Master Level 1

Effect: 85% improved quality of smithing creation. 5% Chance to imbue metal with skill. Able to analyze items made of Stone, Iron, Steel, and Silver.

New Active Skill: Soul Manipulation

One of the freakier skills you can get in this place. The Xelur Demons use souls to power their bodies and magic; you use it in your t-shirt. Well, I guess you are original. Just, you know, try not to go all dark side with this shit. SUPER annoying, and those maniacal laughs, ugghh!

Level: Expert Level 6

Effect: You understand Soul Manipulation 75% better. Tools you make to manipulate souls and their energy are 75% stronger.

Cost: Dependent on creation.

Well, that's new and it could definitely be useful. It jumped right up to Expert Level 6. Must have to do with all of the soul gem work I've done and the understanding I have of soul manipulation tools from my armor to the Daggers of Demons Ruin and soul trap. Dave sighed. If he had gotten the skills at any other time, he would have been excited as hell. Right now, with the deaths of his friends so recent, he couldn't bring himself to do more than be mildly interested.

New Active Skill: Spell formation

> Well, you are one for surprises! Saw you more as an anvil beater, but it seems you've created a new skill. First ever in like—well, that number just makes me feel old. Let's say a long time. Anyway. Go forth and make spells, or fuck them up horribly and blow yourself up. Magic! Who doesn't like fireworks! Seriously though, don't fuck it up. It's messy as hell.

Level: Journeyman Level 5

Effect: You understand magic on a Mana-formation level. Your spells aren't just incantations and messy emotions. They're refined tools. You use 15% less Mana and your spells are 53% stronger.

Whoever is making these damn skills is no less of a smart ass. Must be because I saw and started changing people's spells from the inside. I thought that would be put toward my Perception and Magical Circuits.

Made a whole new skill instead and the benefits are pretty good. If I focus on refining spells even more, maybe I can get it up. It will also make breaking this citadel's Magical Circuits down a lot easier.

Dave closed his eyes as he pushed away the last notification. It was as if a stream of information filled his mind. He understood more about his skills; connections he hadn't made before became clear. It felt similar to opening a skill book and the information taking its place in his mind. Dave stood there, opening his eyes, a little shocked and terrified of the connections he'd made.

Level 58

You have reached Level **58**; you have **275** stat points to use.

Dave barely looked at it as he moved to the next box.

Stat Increase

+5 Strength

+37 Intelligence

+39 Willpower

+27 Endurance

+16 Agility

+7 Vitality

Character Sheet

Name:	David Grahslagg	Gender:	Male
Level:	3	Class:	-
Race:	Human/Dwarf	Alignment:	Chaotic Neutral

Unspent points-275

Health:	2,600	Regen:	2.10/s
Mana:	1,320	Regen:	5.65/s
Stamina:	670	Regen:	3.25/s
Vitality:	26	Endurance:	105
Intelligence:	132	Willpower:	113
Strength:	67	Agility:	65

Affinity Levels

Dark 61 Light 49

Air   39 Water 37

Earth 53 Fire   47

A second notification was blinking, the one that told of loot and other things. Dave disregarded it as he looked at his raw stats.

He put his hand to the spike-portal.

Magical Circuits

You have found a complex series of Magical Circuits. Are you interested in trying to learn from them? The Circuits will be destroyed in the process.

Cost: 100,000 Mana (Due to your Affinities, cost is reduced to 59,924)

Reward: Unknown

Y/N

"Yes," Dave said.

Smoke seemed to drift away from Dave's body, gray light showing across his body. Energy poured from his armor, into his body.

With all the power running through him, it felt as if he was a god. He opened his eyes which seemed to glow silver as shapes of runes started glowing down his arm and into the spike.

He had engraved magical runes into his skin, aiding in transferring his armor's stored power through his body without the energy loss that had been happening before. The cost was what looked like tattoos across his body.

He cast Touch of the Land as he watched the runes light up with his power before being burnt away. He closed his eyes to focus as information started to fill his mind. There were magical runes all across the square, embedded into the stone floor. Magical runes made up magical formations that linked into the Magical Circuit. Its complexity was dazzling.

Dave doubted that the cultists understood what they were doing when building the portals. The language wasn't any that was spoken on Emerilia; it was Jukal.

Runes were words of power that were grouped together in orbits to create laws. As power passed through a magical circle, they went through orbits. Each orbit changed the state of the supplied energy, passing more laws onto it.

One law might turn the supplied power into a fire ball. Another would be to project that fire ball in a constant stream; another might be to direct where that fire ball was going to fire.

As magical circuits got more complicated, then it became impossible to include all of the laws you needed in a single magical circle.

With a portal, there was a need to figure out your location and compute the distance to the other location you were trying to connect to. You needed to open the portal, keep it open, and create corrections so that the portal didn't close mid-way.

Each of these processes took multiple magical circles to figure out. Magical circles were grouped together to work on certain problems, creating a magical formation. They passed on their product to other formations, gradually working until the Magical Circuit could complete its function. In this case, forming a portal between two points and keeping it open long enough so that the Undead Demon Lord was able to come under the cultist's control.

A Magical Circuit could be something as complex as a portal, or it could be as simple as a magical lighter. A Magical Circuit used runes to change the state of the energy that you provided it, whether that was to complete computations or to increase a sword's frost damage.

Dave's own armor paled in comparison to the potential complexity of formations and overall circuits. His runes were, however, pulled from dozens of languages of power. The more runes he knew, the more accurate his laws could be in changing the states of his energy.

He wasn't, however, so shocked that he didn't retain any knowledge. He focused, trying to understand rather than remember. His own saved files would allow him to look at the formations in more detail later.

As the runes and formations were destroyed, red mist seemed to pour toward Dave and Deia, their armor pulling in the magic in the area.

The runes left burn marks where they had been. The latent and stored power flooded toward Deia and Dave. The mental fatigue of pouring out his energy fell away.

Both of them got just over seven thousand points of Mana in their armor and half-full Mana bars.

Dave looked at the battlefield.

Dave didn't gain any levels or stats for understanding the Magical Circuits. It would only be when he created them that he showed his ability and understanding.

"What's going to happen to the citadel?" he asked the Elven mage who was staring at him with a shocked expression.

"We're going to cut it apart. It's formed from ebony and silver." The Elf recovered quickly. "It'll be split up for bonuses and to give those who lost someone or something."

Dave's eyebrows crept up. With his Touch, he'd been able to see the seven-foot-deep ebony and silver blocks that made up the ground.

They had been stored with the cultists for millennia, gaining strength from their raw Mana. That amount of already Mana-treated ebony would change the markets and more than a few people were going to make a lot of money.

Dave nodded. He saw two figures walking across the square. Dave moved to Deia as the two figures met them.

"We're about to move out." Lox looked rough, with dark circles under his eyes and his shoulders hunched—not under the weight of his armor but memories.

Gurren was beside him, his arm in a sling. He looked over the battlefield.

"Let's go home," Dave said, his voice soft, as he clapped a hand on Lox's shoulder.

Lox looked to Dave and nodded.

There was a loud crash behind them.

They all looked back to see the spikes breaking apart as the Earth mages turned the portal into a pile of rubble.

Dave and Deia's hands found each other's as they followed Lox and Gurren.

Chapter 2: The Stone Price

"Sir, the forces at Boran-al were successful," Wrole said.

Fend nodded and held out his hand toward his advisor. He had seen the battle raging through his telescopes. He had sent an entire warclan but in the light created from the great battle, fear and doubt had crept in.

Wrole gave Fend the report and then left him alone. Wrole knew Fend would need time to deal with the information.

He read the complete battle report. His stomach sank as he read through the losses. His eyes became itchy with tears and his sigh heavy with sadness. This sadness and guilt quickly turned to inward rage as he balled up his fists.

I should have sent more! I didn't think that there would be anything more powerful than an A class dungeon in Opheir. Fend shook his head, and went back to reading.

His warclan had gone under his orders. He had desired to be on the battlefield, to be with them, but as the lord of Mithsia Mountains, it was not possible.

The least he owed them was to read the report his soldiers had bought with their lives.

He knew that more stories would come to light as word was passed back to the mountain. For now, all he had was the terse and economical words of Wender. The remaining Dwarven warbands rested under his control.

Just over one and a half thousand Dwarves had survived. Most were injured but they were getting treated by not only the mages of Mithsia and Kufo'tel, but the Players as well.

He read the reports on the Players who had stepped up. That had been the reason that there was any of the Dwarves and Elves left.

Their power was immense and their loyalties true. He made a note to send messages of thanks and a token of appreciation to them—to the Stone Raiders, to the Golden Sabres, their guildmasters and the individuals Malsour, Induca, Dave, and Deia.

Wender clearly doubted they would have been able to fight off Boran-al's cultists without them, and he doubted many of the wounded would have survived as well.

The Kufo'tel Elves had numbered three thousand when they went into battle. Just under a thousand would be returning to their forests.

>After the battle, it is my duty to inform you that I believe this warclan and supporting Elven elements are incapable of going into the field. After the mind attack by the cultists and the loss of so many combat effective units, I believe it would be best to replace our forces with another warclan. While those under my command can still fight, I believe doing so will create irreparable damage to their minds.

Your faithful commander,

Wender Olfson

Fend put the report down and looked to the map that dominated a wall to the left side of his office.

A full ten warbands were halted, awaiting the outcome of the fight at the citadel.

Fend would send orders to them about the success at the citadel and they would continue on. The spring defrost was coming. Soon the lands would turn marshy and wet for a few weeks. The more land Fend could clear now, the less he would have to do later.

A black line traced the area which enclosed the Mithsia Mountains, the Kufo'tel forest and curled around the Cliff-Hill village.

Fend was done with letting creatures get to his door to attack him. Lord Evo'Mael had agreed to the proposed plan.

Over a period of years, mages had been dispatched nearly six centuries ago. They'd walked the forests, valleys, and hills.

Lying dormant under the ground, along the borders so agreed by the Humans, Elves, and Dwarves were battlements, a wall that spanned three hundred miles across. It cut the two groups off from everyone else, going from the northern tundra to the southern tip of the Mithsia Mountains.

The mountain's coffers had more in them than ever before. Sales of goods through Cliff-Hill and Omal were bringing in massive revenue.

Fend hadn't turned Mithsia into a war economy but he had placed orders for artillery pieces, swords, armor, and other supplies that they might need if someone started trying to mess with them again.

The Pantheon had blindsided him once and killed the brothers, sisters, mothers, fathers, daughters, and sons of his people.

"As the saying goes: when a Dwarf stops smiling, it's time to stop laughing and start running." Fend's words were hot as his eyes were hard. His hand gripped the sword at his hip.

They didn't sound like words one might have remembered from a memory. They sounded like a promise.

***

Josh Giles looked at his Stone Raiders. All who had died had run from Omal to Boran-al's Citadel as fast as possible.

Everyone had gained a few levels from the fight.

It had been nothing like what he'd expected. The People of Emerilia might just be lines of code, but to an E-head, someone who lived in Emerilia, they were more real than those who lived on Earth.

That was why he found himself standing on a wagon, looking at his people.

"I ain't one for speeches and too many people died for me to be really happy about Boran-al's Citadel, so I'm going to tell you straight. I want to turn Cliff-Hill into our base of operations. They walked with us right into Boran-al's keep and they fought as ferociously as any of us—even more. But they *knew* that they weren't coming back from battle. They *knew* that they might die and they still went. We drank with them, joked with them, and fought beside them. They might not be Stone Raiders but in my heart, they were. Cliff-Hill can provide us with a decent base of operations. The Dwarves are willing to train us Evolvers. They have the skills and materials to look after our gear. It might not be a central city or even village, but the people of this town, the Dwarves of Mithsia, and Elves of Kufo'tel, stood side by side with us. I doubt we would find many other groups that would be willing to stand with us and defend their homes. That said, this is not *my* guild; it is *ours*. Check the guild forums and vote as you desire on the poll." Josh looked to his people. There weren't cheers, smiles, or laughter—that would come later.

Josh looked at his lieutenants—Dwayne, Lucy, and Kim.

They smiled up at him and he smiled back.

No matter what, they would become stronger and grow from this. The drops from the citadel had been impressive for the magically orientated of the guild.

The raw materials that had made up the square would be dealt with by the Elves. It had been broken down by damage, defensive stats, and so on, Emerilia designating the split.

Josh's eyes wandered over to Malsour and Induca. They had done the most damage of anyone there.

His eyes quickly moved toward Dave and Deia's home. They were the third and fourth biggest hitters. They got the largest portion of the raw materials. Josh knew that Malsour and Induca had given away half of their claim, to be given out to the NPCs who had died in battle.

Another message had come in from the guild's connections in the Endon kingdom. A large raid area had been found and the forces were currently moving out to attack the settlements between it and the city Pundt.

Josh had accepted after his fight for Boran-al's Citadel. He knew that without the Stone Raiders help that more people would die.

He saw gold and Mithril moving toward Dave and Deia's home. He didn't need to use Analyze to recognize Naylor, Bok Soo, and Cassie.

Well, seems that I'm not the only one reading the MVP's sheets.

The poll closed down as everyone had voted, from across Emerilia and even those who were on Earth. Looking at the 95% result, Josh smiled.

"Well, seems that we will be putting a bid in on those golden-plated bozo's place." Josh smiled.

The others smiled and gave a lighthearted cheer.

Josh had already sorted out the details with Cassie. The Golden Sabres were leaving to return to Opheir's capital city, Nadorf. They had some housecleaning to do, but Giles knew it wasn't the last they would see of the other guild.

Chapter 3: To the Ends of the Earth, and Beyond

Suzy Markell pushed herself off the Altar of Rebirth. She looked at her starter gear and the meager funds she had. However, she dismissed all of the extra information and pulled up her map.

She was in the city of Omal, exactly where she wanted to be. Her destination lay to the northeast, in a small village called Cliff-Hill.

She hadn't cared to pay attention to her character during creation; she had one job and she didn't care what her body looked like in here. However, it looked like she'd gotten lucky. She had been assigned a High Elf avatar. It was a bit taller than her normal height but she didn't seem to have any issue in moving around. Her features were the same except for the pointed ears, which framed her face giving her an exotic look. She'd always prided herself on her appearance. It had made more than one meeting turn into a pushover.

"Not bad." She gave a small smile, approving the avatar the game had formed.

The only person who had looked at her as a *real* person and not just Austin Zane's secretary had been Austin Zane himself.

She had been his first hire when he had started mining asteroids. He needed someone to handle his struggles. He had dealt with too many people who were all looks and no brains. The hiring agencies kept on sending pretty people at him without care.

They'd met accidentally. Suzy had gone in to Rock Breakers Corporation, trying to get a floor-level job. She'd seen her ex and trying to hide from her, she'd run in to the bathroom—the men's bathroom, where Zane was sitting on the bathroom sink, trying to figure out how to manage meetings with NASA, investors, a few groups of lawyers, and still keep his own work on schedule.

They'd got to talking and he'd offered her a job. She'd made a quip about him offering a girl a job in a bathroom.

He replied with another about her sneaking into the men's bathroom.

She hadn't been the best at her job in the beginning but she was determined to do her best. Zane was a man getting choked out by what he had made to be a stepping-stone for Humanity to the stars.

She saw the dreamer behind those eyes and she wanted in on that.

There were multiple rumors that they were sleeping together and although Suzy did think the man needed to get laid, she didn't swing that way. She was more interested in the fairer sex.

They weren't just coworkers—they were friends. After a while, they became each other's only friends. It was hard for them both but they had each other.

Her face hardened as she remembered what had changed over the last two months.

Austin had started to make passes at her. She had never advertised she liked women; Austin had still figured it out but didn't care one way or another. Although her parents had ostracized her, Austin accepted her.

However, he started making passes and doing all kinds of things that were out of character for him.

It's like there's an imposter in his body. Most people don't notice it but I've known him better than anyone these past fifteen years. Something is wrong and it began when he started playing that video game.

That thought drove her to look into his gaming habits more. It had taken her months before she found anything.

She began thinking it was all in her head until Suzy saw the images coming from a big event happening in Emerilia. She'd been browsing through various feeds; Austin was always interested in games and his addiction had turned into an interest for Suzy.

When she'd been looking at the headliner event for Emerilia, a raid on a place called Boran-al's Citadel, she'd stopped.

There, standing among the other Players, was Austin. He had a beard but Suzy instantly recognized him. Around him there was an Elven woman, five Dwarves, and two others wearing black and red leather.

She'd surfed and looked on. She hadn't been able to find the character's name but she knew it was Austin. She bought a feed subscription and watched the entire battle live. Austin was right next to a shield wall, diverting Dark energies.

Suzy hesitantly looked up and watched Austin at his desk.

Unable to shake it, she'd bought a VR set and ordered Emerilia. As soon as she got home, she booted up the game.

"Now to go and see what the hell is going on." Suzy walked toward a caravan that had a message floating above it, saying that it was heading for Cliff-Hill.

"Excuse me, could I get a ride to Cliff-Hill? I will pay," Suzy said.

"One silver," the Elf in the front seat of the wagon said.

She knew it was a man but there was an effeminate way to his actions that interested her.

Whoever made this game knows how to make characters.

"Very well. What is your name?" Suzy asked, trying to figure out how to give her money to the Elf.

"Wis'Zel. Are you having some trouble there?"

"I don't know how to access my money," Suzy admitted.

"Well, us People of Emerilia just think of the amount and it appears in our pockets when we pull it out. With you Players—well, I think you can go to your inventory, hold your hand out and pull out a single silver, or you just shake my hand and the transaction will complete. Us people use that as well—easier than fiddling around with coins all the time." Wis'Zel shrugged.

"Ahh." Suzy held out her hand.

Wis'Zel smiled and shook it.

Trade

Wis'Zel will allow you to ride with him to Cliff-Hill for:

1x Silver

Do you accept?

Y/N

"Yes," Suzy said.

Chink

Suzy opened her inventory and she had four gold and nine silver left.

"So, what made you pick a High Elf? Want to be a mage?" Wis'Zel asked as they released hands.

"I just got it randomly generated. I need to check something out," Suzy said.

Wis'Zel nodded, looking impressed. "Few if any of you Players get anything but plain old Human. Obviously not as good as a Wood Elf." He smiled. Suzy couldn't do anything but join in as his eyes sparkled with amusement. "But it will be passable. Jump on up. Let's get the hell out of Dodge!"

Suzy smiled and walked around the horses, getting up onto the other side of the carriage.

Wis'Zel whistled and the horses moved forward.

"So, what's your name?" Wis'Zel asked.

"Suzy Markell."

"Well, it is good to meet you, Suzy. I do like to meet new people. Makes the ride much more enjoyable." Wis'Zel smiled.

New Passive Skill: Trader

Look at you, just entering Emerilia and already hacking a deal together to get an old Elf to give you a ride! You go, gurrrl!

Level: Novice Level 2

Effect: 7% chance people will give you preferential treatment. 2% better prices with those that see you as friendly.

"The hell?" Suzy said, reading the new skill.

"Hmm?"

"Oh, sorry, just had something pop up. It's weird," Suzy said, studying it more.

"Oh, the skills?"

"Yeah."

Wis'Zel snorted. "Yeah, seems that wherever they come from, something makes a new description for every single one. Emerilia, the land of Demons, portals, and smartass pop-ups."

Suzy laughed. It had been some time since she had just been able to have a conversation with someone without either her or them trying to get something from the other. Small talk didn't have much of a place when you were the secretary for the CEO of the most profitable company in the world.

"My friends call me Zel."

"Suzy." She smiled and sat back. She could understand why Austin enjoyed this game so much. "How long will it take to reach Cliff-Hill?"

"With these roads, a few days," Zel said.

"Okay." Suzy settled into her seat. *I think I might come and check this place out a bit more, no matter what I find. Austin was right. It is a nice place to go and just be myself.*

***

Dave sat with Deia on the wooden love seat he'd made. A fur was draped over them to keep off the chill. Spring was coming but it was slow in showing up.

Dave and Deia were making small talk, while Dave laid down with his head on her knees. Her hands idly moved through his hair as they sipped mulled wine.

"Hello, you two." Bob appeared near Dave's feet. With him, there was a girl standing in black clothes that looked too thin and sheer for the early spring weather.

Deia's eyes quickly assessed the woman. She was dangerous and strong. The two-handed great sword on her back wasn't just for show. Deia wanted to be angry with Bob for what the lords of Dark and Earth had done but she knew it wasn't Bob's fault. She also knew that without Bob and Dave's help, then their plans might have succeeded.

"Hey, Bob." Dave made no move to get up.

The other woman smiled at this.

"Bob." Deia nodded, and then looked to the woman. "Who might you be?"

"I'm Anna. I've seen and heard a lot about you, Deia." Anna closed her eyes and bowed. She was mostly a Human. A tail swished from behind her back and Deia saw two ears twitching on the top of her head. As she opened her eyes, they almost seemed to glow green.

"I have not seen a Beast Kin in many years. I thought that most of them were wiped out centuries ago" Deia said.

"Most of my peo...ancestors were killed off some time ago." Anna's tail moved in anger.

"My apologies." Deia bowed her head.

"Thank you." Anna smiled.

"You two can come out. I think you might know more about lords and ladies of Affinities," Dave said.

Deia looked to her left, where Malsour and Induca seemed to appear from the shadows.

Their porch was getting rather crowded and Deia was unsure why Malsour and Induca were there.

"Why would they know more about the Pantheon?" Deia asked.

"Well, they *are* dragons. Your own Lady of Fire made them." Dave looked up at her.

"When did you figure this out?" Fire entered Deia's voice as her eyes flashed.

"Uhh, well, about the time that they came into Cliff-Hill?" Dave tried to shrink into her lap as she stared at him.

"So, for two days?" Her eyes thinned.

"Might have been since they transformed at the citadel?" Dave's voice sounded rather small.

"Next time, let me know before they show up on our damned porch." Deia sighed, knowing that it had probably slipped Dave's mind or he had wanted to be sure before he said anything.

She loved the man, but he was a complete idiot at times.

"Okay." He smiled up at her, making a kissing motion with his lips.

Any annoyance left her as her eyes softened and she smiled down at his face.

"Now that we're all here, we can get down to business." Bob pulled out his pipe. "Chairs, if you will, Dave."

Chairs appeared, with drinks on their armrests. Bob's own recliner appeared as the others took their seats.

Deia had several questions for everyone there but if Bob had something to say, it was best to see what it was.

Bob puffed out smoke and looked to everyone there. Anna sat back in her chair, sipping her drink. It seemed that she knew what was already coming. Her expression did not look particularly happy.

"The lords and ladies of the Affinities Pantheon will now be able to create Creatures of Power as well as pick their own champions as they see fit. The one condition is that these new creations must come from their own power," Bob said.

Deia took in a sharp breath as Malsour growled and Induca took a large swig of her drink.

Dave laid there, unfazed by it all. "Well, that will be a pain in the ass," Dave said.

"Indeed," Bob said.

"I didn't know that you had magical creatures," Malsour said, looking to Anna.

"Oh, I'm not a magical construct like you two. I started off a lot differently than you. Been around a bit longer too." Anna looked over the two.

"You are a Demi-wolf. None of the old ones have lived into this generation," Malsour said.

"There are still a few of them and ughh—Dad, can you just finish what you want to say? I've got a lot of work to do. Being in just one body is a pain."

"Yes, Anna." Bob pat her hand and gave her a fond look.

She smiled at that.

"You've all seen what happens when the lords and ladies of the Pantheon get involved. Boran-al was just a *very* small show of the Dark Lord and Earth's power. Hell, the Undead Demon Lord was something that Boran-al came up with from his own Mana. That is one twisted and pissed off Dark Elf." Bob rolled his eyes. "Now the Pantheon's powers will be unleashed. Some might use them to help the People of Emerilia; others will use it to hurt them. Nearly all of it will be done in a bid to gain more power. The only two who will probably not be in the whole power bartering business are Fire and myself."

"Is she going to take champions?" Deia asked.

Bob shrugged. "I haven't got a clue what she's going to do. I'll have a talk with her later. Right now, I came to warn you of what is coming and to pass on my condolences." Bob's face softened.

"I might be the one who made this prison but I have come to know my captives well. For it, I am happy, but I am also saddened when I see them taken away. I know that you four made friends and met people you cared for and who died because of the actions of the lords of Affinity. I know that you are sad and upset, but a new dawn will come and Boran-al's Citadel is just a taste of what is to come." Bob's eyes found Deia and Dave.

"If you do not press on, then I fear what will happen to Emerilia after this incarnation. With the Pantheon's abilities unleashed well before the portals are supposed to start opening, things can only get worse."

"What happens when the gates open?" Dave asked.

"Think—if you have a species that wants nothing more than to destroy you and everything you hold dear come charging out of a portal, would you not pledge your very *soul* to the Pantheon to be able to do something against them? Would you make massive devotions of your energy for some spell that the Pantheon is holding on to and could hurt the enemy? To them, those spells are as easy as that." He snapped his fingers and a flame appeared above his forefinger.

"How much power will they gain if their champions are not only charging into battle, but their magical creatures? People will move their devotions from one lord or lady to another based on their interest and whims. The people might stay constant, but the Players, the people with the largest Mana pools of any group on Emerilia? It's just a game, and to get a one up on your enemy, you just have to give a bit of Mana away?" Bob snorted, shaking his head.

"Shit," Dave said, his face grave.

It didn't sound good to Deia, but surely, they could make it through this all. They had to.

***

Kol used his senses and his constant sensing Touch to see even better than most who still had eyes. It allowed him to see through the smithy, finding Dave and Deia, who kissed each other good-bye. Dave headed for the smithy and Deia headed off for the Stone Raiders' camp to train.

The losses had been heavy and the battle was the kind of which that hadn't been seen in hundreds of years.

Kol could see it in his grandson's eyes.

Gurren had been fully healed but losing three of his best friends and fellow shield bearers was bad. Other veterans from the citadel had been pulled together, and Lox had retained command. They were getting to know one another but there was still a tension that came from them replacing those who had been lost.

Kol knew that they would get past this, but he didn't know how his grandson or any of those who survived would act. He'd seen that the actions at the citadel had not only changed the People of Emerilia, but the Players as well. The Stone Raiders had been kind to the people; now it was as if they, too, were people of the land.

Kol put down the armor he was repairing and walked through the smithy, intercepting Dave before he got his gear. "Come, boy, let us have a talk." Kol put his hand on Dave's shoulder.

Dave followed him to a bench that was at the rear of the smithy, overlooking the cliff that surrounded Cliff-Hill on three sides.

"I have an offer for you," Kol said.

"Oh?" Dave asked.

Kol sighed and faced out over the cliffs. "This is something that has never been offered before by our race. It is something that is part of our very identity and one of our greatest secrets." Kol paused, letting it sink in.

"The Master Smiths of the Dwarves wish to offer you the opportunity to become a Master Smith."

"I've already broken into the master ranks," Dave said.

"That is quite something, considering that you have still not learned malachite and gold. Becoming a Dwarven Master Smith is much more than learning how to hammer metal. If you choose to accept this offer, you will learn our secrets. Metal will be your instrument and you will make it sing. Being a master at smithing is an incredible achievement and to do it within the space of a year is incredible, but Dwarf Master Smiths are in a league onto their own. If you truly want to come and understand the complexities of smithing and the art of Anvil and Fire, this is the final step."

***

Quest: Of Anvil and Fire
Kol has asked if you wish to undergo the training that would turn you into a Dwarven Master Smith.
Will you accept?
Y/N

"Can I think about this for a bit? I'd need to talk to Deia and well, it's kind of a big change," Dave said.

It was one hell of a chance. No Player had learned the skills of the Dwarven Master Smiths, *ever.* Dave had been shown that to grow, he needed to become stronger, to protect those he cared about.

"Of course, lad. You may use the smithy as you like, but know that your obligations to me are complete." Kol smiled. "You turned out to be a pretty good student."

Dave laughed and shook his head. Kol was a grouchy bastard, hard to those he was teaching and working with, but fair.

"Don't take too long, else I'm liable to forget all of this." Kol clapped Dave on the back and headed toward the smithy.

"Kol," Dave said, turning, making the man stop as he was walking back.

"What is it?" Kol asked.

Dave didn't say anything for a few moments. "Thanks—thanks for teaching me about smithing." Dave smiled.

Kol shook his head but Dave thought he saw the old Dwarf's mouth twitch into a smile.

"You're going soft already!" Kol barked and headed into the smithy.

Dave looked out over the forest below. *Not a bad place to live.* He smiled to himself, taking it in. He turned and walked between his house and the smithy, the furnaces and anvils in constant use as repairs were made and new items were being made.

Going to have to see about moving it sometime soon. The smithy had grown in its abilities. With the Mithsia Mountains and Kufo'tel forest now arming up to defend their lands, they didn't have much production to share with the rest of Opheir. Cliff-Hill's smiths were more than happy to take up the slack but they were going to need more room to expand.

People from all over Emerilia were coming to Cliff-Hill to learn smithing, from Demi-Humans to Dwarves and Orcs. All of them had applied to learn and work at the forge.

Dwarven mountains were secluded spots, but Cliff-Hill bridged that gap.

The gold they were earning from training made Dave think about opening training forges all over Emerilia to educate the general population. Not everyone could make a trip to a Dwarven mountain for a piece of forged metal.

So much to do. He sighed, smiling at the thoughts of expansion.

Heading in toward the compound, off of the main road and through the copse of trees, was a wagon with Wis'Zel driving it.

He waved at Dave.

Dave waved back, seeing a High Elf lady next to him.

Suzy Markell

High Elf

Level 1

"Suzy!" Dave yelled, sprinting over. In just moments, he made it to the side of the wagon and jumped up on her side.

She pulled back and stared at him.

"The hell you doing here, mini-Mom?" Dave asked, confused as all hell.

"What did you have for lunch today?" Suzy fired back.

"What the hell kind of question is that?" Dave frowned.

"Just answer it, Austin." She leaned forward, a fire in her eyes.

"Wolf stew," Dave said.

"And in real life?" Suzy asked, her eyes thinning.

Dave's mouth worked as it was his time for his eyes to thin. "Wolf stew."

"The fuck is going on, Austin?" she demanded.

"I guess the two of you know each other. Who is Austin?" Zel asked.

"It was my name back in the simulation. Mind keeping that bit to yourself?" Dave asked.

"My lips are sealed, boss." Zel smiled and drew his fingers over his lips.

"Come on, Suzy. We've got a few things to talk about." Dave jumped down.

Suzy followed.

Well, this sure as hell made things a bit more interesting. I wonder what my body has been up to all this time.

Chapter 4: Another Offer

"All right—now you've got your funnel, you need your plasma and your push." Induca watched Deia and what looked like four flaming tubes of different colored flames in front of her.

Deia took a deep breath as sweat streaked down her forehead and back. The plasma cannon was a lot smaller than the one that she had created when fighting at the citadel, but it was still draining her Mana and keeping everything together was hard as hell. Even with her ability to manipulate fire with just thought.

She focused, twirling her hand as a cyan ball of what looked to be liquid fire formed in front of her. She guided it to the back of the firing tube. Already she could feel the varying air pressure that was pulling on the plasma ball and trying to pull her cannon apart.

"Hold it," Induca said.

Deia strained and her Mana dropped like a stone. She was already having to use her armor's power reserves to get her to this stage. Deia gritted her teeth and focused. An errant breeze increased the power of one of the inner tubes. Deia tried to correct but overdid it.

She saw it going out of control and the plasma start to accelerate down the tube. She cut off her power. The air seemed to pop as her creation of fire disappeared.

"Good," Induca said as Deia panted.

"Couldn't even fire the thing." Deia slumped onto the grass. She felt spent both physically and mentally.

"It will get easier with time. The one that you used at the citadel was crude but effective. But it was almost an instant cast as you don't have the control or the Mana reserves to control it. I know of plasma breath but adding in the tubes of fire is genius." Induca shook her head.

"I got the idea from the forums and the Internet. I was looking at weapons and the Humans have a lot of them on Earth. They've got these things called tanks and even theories of making other weapons that they call plasma cannons. They also have a ton of information on how the air reacts when it is heated and cooled. I messed around with a bit of plasma and Dave taught me about air pressures and worked with me to make a cannon that would force air through it. I'm still refining it, though."

"Color me impressed," Induca said.

"I said that you should look into more information about your skills," Malsour said from the side of the sparring square, reading a book on his lap.

Induca pouted and looked away from her brother, flicking her hair in frustration.

Deia saw the corners of Malsour's mouth turn upwards at her actions.

"Is there anything else that you learned from this Internet?" Induca asked.

Deia thought of the images and information that had been openly displayed on the Internet. It was no wonder that the Players were so much more advanced than the People of Emerilia. The free access to that kind of information was overwhelming. In Emerilia, knowledge was power. Many high-classed mages and fighters had several secrets that they kept to themselves so that no one could use it against them.

It led to information being lost to the point where many descendants of some of the most powerful people in Emerilia had to try to learn a whole other discipline as their ancestors hid their secrets from the world, and even their families.

The Elves were the worst for it. Different groups of Elves and even families within a community would horde information to try to get an edge over one another. The Elves lived for a long time and abhorred violence but they were paranoid as all hell from seeing so many wars, betrayals, and fights.

"There was one. It was called an F-A-E." Deia felt a presence behind her. Anna might use a two-handed claymore, but damn if she wasn't sneaky.

"Like the faeries?" Induca looked at Deia in confusion. The Fae kept to themselves in their mythical forests. People left them alone and they were fine with that.

"No, it's called a Fuel Air Explosive," Deia said.

"Quite the powerful invention." Anna walked over to them.

Deia looked up and saw a sad expression on Anna's face.

"How so?" Induca asked.

"Deia." Anna deflected the question.

Anna might look as if she were about thirty years old, but Deia had long ago understood that not everyone looked their own age. She sure as hell didn't look a few centuries old compared to the Humans. It was all in the eyes. Anna—the only way to describe her eyes and her aura was ancient.

"A projectile goes toward a target. It releases highly flammable gasses in its wake. They are ignited in stages. The projectile reaches the target, sowing this flammable liquid, and it ignites. It burns all of the air in a massive area, forcing the air around it to be ripped in. Think of it as a reversed air lance. Instead of the air being hurled into the thing you're attacking, it is pulled out of it," Deia said.

"Many defenses can take being hit directly, but what happens when the air inside those defenses is all trying to escape outwards? What happens to the defenders when the air is ripped from their lungs?" Anna said.

Induca looked at the two of them and shook her head. "I never thought about something like that," she said in a quiet voice.

"Negative magic." Malsour looked right at Anna before his eyes flicked to Deia. "Using the properties of your magic to create change within the environment and with elements that are not under your magical control."

Anna nodded.

"I thought that I would find you three out here." Dwayne walked across the yard with a few other Stone Raiders who looked to be getting ready for a training session.

"Hey, Dwayne." Deia waved from her seat. Her Mana was coming back but with her massive reserves, it was going to take awhile for her bar to fill up.

"I don't think we've met before." Dwayne reached out his hand toward Anna. "Dwayne Trebault." He smiled.

"I have heard of you, Mister Trebault." Anna returned the smile.

"How did you get stuck with these three miscreants?" Dwayne looked at the others, who smiled.

They'd all become closer; even Malsour, who was always buried in his books, seemed to genuinely care about the Stone Raiders.

It's hard to admit but all of us feel a connection with them for the way that they stood up with us. Not one of them backed down and as soon as they respawned, they returned to the fight. They might look like a bunch of clowns but under it all, they're some of the most determined fighters I've ever seen. They've turned their own deaths into a weapon. Death is no longer a barrier for them, so they use their deaths to their advantage. They won't die easy and they'll fight with everything they have but they're resourceful, loyal, and kind.

Her thoughts drifted to the invitation that she, Malsour, Induca, Dave, Lox, and Gurren had all been given. The Stone Raiders had done something that no other guild had ever done. They had started to accept the People of Emerilia into their ranks.

Deia was interested in seeing what would happen but if the Stone Raiders could pull it off, she knew that there were enough people trying to make their fame and fortune adventuring with other people. Having a few Players in the mix would only be a good thing. She foresaw big changes, one of them being mixed parties of Players and People of Emerilia.

"I was kind of dropped off and told to fend for myself. They don't seem all that bad, though. Odd but interesting." Anna smiled.

Dwayne chuckled. "Well, it is good to meet you, Anna." He bowed slightly and then looked to the others. "Something has turned up in the Endon kingdom, so we're going to go deal with that. I was wondering if any of you have come to a decision. I know that we would all look forward to having you in our ranks. Even if it meant that you were hanging out in Cliff-Hill all the time."

Malsour and Induca looked to each other.

"We've decided that we're going to stick with Dave and Deia, if they want to party up with us," Malsour said.

Deia looked at the two of them. Malsour looked serious and Induca smiled at her. "Are you sure?" Deia asked.

"You've got a lot to learn and we feel that being around you will be much more interesting that our normally aimless wandering," Induca said.

"Wow, hmm, thanks, guys, and I know Dave will be downright happy to hear that." Deia smiled.

"Well then, that sounds like one hell of a scary party." Dwayne smiled. "We'd be over the moon if you joined us but in the end, no matter what, I hope that we can be friends."

Dwayne made motions with his hands, opening up his interface.

Friend Request

You have received a Friend Request from Dwayne Trebault.

Do you accept?

Y/N

"Yes," Deia said. The others did the same. She wondered how the others had gained interfaces but she guessed it mattered little. Malsour and Induca didn't seem to have access to the Internet, which was, in Deia's mind, one of the most useful parts of the interface.

"Well, I'll be seeing you around!" Dwayne waved to them and headed over to the mixed party that was ready to start their training.

"Well, I think that is enough magical training for one day. I know that you want to whip Dave into shape with his Agility, so have fun with that. I'm going to find Kim and see what she's up to," Induca said.

"Okay, thanks, Induca," Deia said.

"No worries." Induca turned and started to head for the Stone Raiders' camp. "You coming, Mal?"

"Fine." Malsour sighed. He followed his little sister, reading his book the entire way.

Anna offered Deia her hand.

"Thanks," Deia said as Anna pulled her to her feet. The strength in the Demi-wolf made it feel like Anna could've easily picked her up with one hand.

"Do you mind if I walk with you?" Anna asked.

"Not at all." Deia smiled. She was interested in the woman Bob called his daughter.

"So, what made you decide to become a Player?" Anna asked as they walked.

"Going with the easy questions first, huh?" Deia laughed. "Well, I guess that's because of Dave."

"Just because of Dave?"

"No, not just because of him, but he is a large part. If I'm to continue to be by his side, then being a POE will strain things to the point where we can't do anything because he'll be so scared of me dying. He's a good man and he cares for others but I could see that care turning into fear. Becoming a Player makes it so that never comes between us."

"I'm sorry, but what is a POE?"

"Oh, sorry, it's a Person or People of Emerilia. Something that the Players use." Deia shrugged.

"Oh, okay, so what are the other reasons?"

"Well, the sheer amount of information and opportunities I get. There's nothing quite like it. I've lived for over three hundred years and I have never met a man like Dave or these other Players. Sure, there are terrible times and not all of them are good, but Bob was right: Dave and I can act as bridges between the two groups. If we can get them to unite, then the whole of Emerilia will change."

"Old man is stealing my plans," Anna muttered to herself. "What is Dave like?"

"Well, I'm a bit biased on that, but he's a driven man. First and foremost, when he has a goal in mind, he will focus his efforts to attain that goal. Honestly, he forgets to eat and sleep quite a bit." Deia sighed. "He's smart and he cares for those around him. Become his friend and he'll do anything for you. That said, he doesn't just buddy up with everyone. He might be a Player himself but in the beginning, he had a real problem with the Stone Raiders and Golden Sabres leaders because of how they acted. Got Josh to apologize to the people in the smithy and then Kol beat health and safety into Josh for an entire day. Even Cassie, who was..." Deia tried to think of a nice way to say it but shrugged. "A bitch...turned out to be not that bad. When Players just think that you're an NPC, then they get uppity as hell and don't really give a crap.

"After fighting with us, I think we've changed a lot of the Sabres' view on POEs. At least I hope so. She even came over the other day to apologize to Dave, and she offered us both a place within the Sabres. Neither of us is really interested in joining a guild that is so closely attached to the Lady of Light, though Cassie is a nice woman. Even if Dave didn't like her in the beginning, he forgave her for being a bitch and we became friends with her."

"What do you think Dave wants from this?" Anna asked.

Deia laughed and smiled, thinking of her Dave as they walked down the main road that curved through Cliff-Hill on its way to Omal.

"Honestly, I think that Dave just wants to learn, to explore, and to see the world. On Earth, he was one of the most powerful men in existence, yet he had few friends he could call his own and even less people he could trust. Everyone wanted something from him and all those he cared for left him. He stopped doing what he loved—he stopped building things; he stopped striving to move forward. Dave is a man with big dreams, dreams that I can't even come to understand. However, I will do everything I can to make sure that he is never as lonely ever again and be by his side as he reaches those dreams. What does he want? He doesn't really *want* anything. He's got freedom that he never had before, friends—even me." Deia gave Anna a sly smile; Anna couldn't help but laugh.

"With us at his back, I expect that my fiancé is going to do things that no one can really predict."

They walked onto the road that cut through the copse of trees separating Dave's compound from the main road.

"So, what do you want?" Anna asked.

"I want to be able to protect the people I care about. I want to figure out who my mother is. I want to see what the rest of this world has to offer and I want to see the Affinities Pantheon ripped from their towers and made to answer for the crimes that they have committed." Deia's words got more heated and angry as she talked.

Anna simply nodded as they made it to Dave and Deia's home.

"Thank you for being so candid. I think I see now why my father said to stay here awhile. It has been a long time since I met so many interesting people." Anna's eyes drifted away, as if seeing some sad memory.

"Well, anyone who is a daughter of Bob is a friend of ours. Let us know if you ever need anything." Deia smiled.

"Thank you." Anna smiled, nodding to Deia before she walked off.

Deia opened the door to her house, finding Dave and a *gorgeous* *H*igh Elf—wearing clothes that showed her perfect white skin in many places—drinking some of Dave's finer drink.

"Dave?" Deia looked at the barely dressed woman and then at Dave.

"Hi, babe." Dave smiled at her and then frowned at the other woman.

"Sorry, he's a bit of an idiot like that." The High Elf stretched out her hand.

She's even more beautiful standing. Who the hell is this woman? "Hello, I'm Deia."

"It is good to meet you. Zel told me a lot about you. My name is Suzy." The woman smiled.

Suzy—like the Suzy Dave knew on Earth? Deia's eyes squinted and she pulled up Suzy's stats. "From Earth?"

"Uhh, yeah." Suzy's smile faded as she looked away and her face turned serious.

"Dave, what is going on?" Deia asked.

"My damned shell is being a piece of shit, that's what's going on," Dave growled darkly. He took a drink from his glass.

"Dave—sentences. Remember the thing about muttering?" Suzy snapped.

Dave grimaced but nodded.

Who the hell is this woman?

"Now introduce us and pull your head out of development and angry stage!" Suzy snapped.

"Fine! Okay, Suzy, this is Deia, my fiancée. Deia, this is Suzy, my secretary from when I was Austin Zane." Dave stood.

Suzy and Deia gave each other appraising looks.

"Suzy here noticed my face from the battle while at the same time my shell was doing some paperwork. Intrigued, she looked into it some more and finally visited Emerilia. Right now, my shell is making some speech to the people of Japan while I'm here drinking a beer. Now Suzy is in the twilight zone as what is happening right now shouldn't be." Dave sighed.

"I'm sorry." Deia winced at Suzy.

"Me, too. You have to deal with him." Suzy brushed past the elephant in the room.

Deia smiled and looked over to Dave.

"Hey, I am here, you two!" Dave muttered into his cup again.

Suzy and Deia looked at each other, smiling.

"So, are you staying for dinner?" Deia asked.

"Seems like it." Suzy smiled.

Chapter 5: Through the Veil

Suzy looked at her television, which was showing Austin Zane talking at a dinner in Japan. She checked her planner. He was exactly where he appeared. She looked out over her new apartment in Tokyo. She pulled the helmet back over her head and skipped through the menus and started up Emerilia again.

Sitting there on his porch was Dave and Deia, the same as they had been when she left them.

"How?" Suzy asked.

"Welcome to the real world, Suz—that one where we met, it's just a simulation to make us think of this as a game. Who gets PTSD from a video game? Who cares who they kill in a video game? Who would ever believe a game is real?" Dave asked.

"How the hell didn't we know of this?" Suzy asked.

"For centuries, Players roam Emerilia, disappearing for a few decades before reappearing. The new batch of Players are grown, fed the lie that is Earth and they eat it up. Your lives were made to make you more susceptible to play Emerilia and get addicted to it. There are only about four million Players in Emerilia and about five million people who are truly *real* in Earth. Most of them live in technologically advanced places, so it is easy for them to get the rig but their situations are changed so that you are more prone to stay," Deia said.

"Our friend Jules plays this game because she needs to make enough money to keep up her medical treatments. She's a veteran with a limited claim, even though she doesn't have legs.

"The leader of the Stone Raiders was a stock trader who turned to gaming to get away from his life. I was so tired of meetings and just waiting for the next meeting that I went out into the woods and made a house to get away from it all."

Dave pulled Deia close to him; it was easy to see their affection for each other. "I found a few other things along the way, though." He grinned.

"So, how did you figure it out?" Suzy asked.

"Well, I had a bit of a helping hand and I was in here for days. I came out, not being hungry, nor tired. As my body here rested, I would gain energy in the simulation. I took more and more time between waking up. Until I started waking up and my body wasn't in the chair anymore. I was in the middle of a meeting, or at my desk. It's not possible for me to do that, unless it was a simulation."

"Uggh, this is a lot more complicated than I thought." Suzy slumped into her seat.

"So, what kind of magic are you thinking of specializing in?" Dave asked.

Deia hit him.

"Ow. What?" Dave rubbed his shoulder.

"First, we'll work on your Agility tomorrow—you're getting slow. Second, she just found out that Emerilia is real and you're asking her about magic?"

"What? I'm curious!"

Deia pinched the bridge of her nose.

Suzy couldn't hold her laughter anymore at seeing Austin—no, Dave—that happy and with a woman who was clearly putting him in his place. She was clearly a strong-willed woman and exactly what Dave had needed.

After a while, her laughing died down.

"So, what you thinking, Suz?"

"What makes you think I want to live in another reality with you?" Suzy asked.

"Aww, don't be that way Suzy-suz. We make a good team and come on, look at this. We're on another damned planet. We might have been running Rock Breakers, but we both knew what our ultimate goal was."

What do I have left on Earth but parents who hate me because of my sexuality, a boss who is now trying to hit on me and isn't the real guy, and a work life that doesn't allow me to do anything but work constantly? Whoever made that simulation was pretty damned good. There's pretty much nothing that I would like to go back to there. Even Dave's beer ain't bad and Deia is a fair hand at cooking. Was always interested in checking out one of those all-natural diets.

"I think summoning," Suzy said.

Deia looked over. She seemed a bit shocked but also impressed. "Why is that?"

"Well, he never plans small and I have a feeling that I'm not going to be much good at fighting on the front lines. But I sure as hell can get a group organized and facing the right way. If I can summon me a few useful characters, then, coupled with Dave's conjured creations and your fire power, then we're going to have one hell of a fearsome party," Suzy said.

"Someone's been doing their homework, I see." Dave smiled.

Suzy rolled her eyes. "With the amount of damned video game information you were spouting all the time, some of it rubbed off on me." She grimaced.

Dave laughed and winked while Deia looked amused.

***

After talking for a few hours, Suzy went off to wander Cliff-Hill while Dave and Deia retreated into their house. Night was coming and it was getting chilly quickly.

They sat on the couch, lying next to each other and watching the dancing flames. Dave looked down at Deia, tracing his finger over her shoulder and down her neck. She shivered slightly and turned to him.

In that fireplace glow, with her red eyes, Dave drank in the sight of her face, that moment of peace. The more she used her fire and gained a greater understanding with it, her eyes seemed to become more flame-like.

How the hell did I get this lucky?

He tilted her chin up, kissing her lightly. After a few kisses, Deia pulled him closer as their lips and tongues melded together. Deia pushed him back a bit, her face flush.

"Well, seems I still have it." Dave grinned.

She rolled her eyes and snatched a quick kiss. "Before we move this to the bed, I felt it's time that we talked about what we're going to do now. Do you want to join the Stone Raiders?"

"I wouldn't be against it. They showed that they are good people and I've even heard that they plan on making this their base, training with POEs and accepting them into their ranks."

"I was thinking much the same thing. So tomorrow, shall we make it official? I would feel a bit better if we had a guild backing us and when we're done training, then we know that they're going to be in the middle of the fight."

Dave nodded. "Also, Kol did give me a quest to become a Dwarven Master Smith. I haven't decided if I'm going to accept it or not."

"Why didn't you tell me earlier?" Deia hit his arm.

She might have smaller arms than his but her strength was up there. She'd been fighting for centuries; he was just slowly picking things up.

"Sorry, babe. I meant to, but with Suzy and everything..."

"Who is Suzy to you?" Deia asked.

Alarm bells rang around Dave's skull, telling him that he had indeed walked into a woman's minefield.

"She was pretty much my only friend back on Earth. I think of her as a sister and she's like Jules and Esa toward her taste in partners." Dave hoped that he had covered most of the main points.

"Though, she's kind of sensitive about that. On Earth, her parents cut off all communication with her when they found out that she liked other women. Both of us don't really have a family, but we had each other to get through the hard times."

Deia's face softened as she hugged Dave. "Well, you've got a lot more people who care about you now," she said into his chest.

He kissed her head. His heart swelled at her words.

"Will she stay here?"

"Well, that is the million-dollar question." Dave scratched his head in thought. "I think so. Suzy is common-sense smart and over the years, she's gained a lot of technical smarts from all the projects that she's worked on.

"She might not be an engineer, but she's definitely a planner. With all the evidence, I think we can expect to have another bleeder hanging around."

"So, then, when does your Dwarven Master Smith training start? Also, where is it going to be?" Deia asked.

"I didn't accept yet—thought that I would run it by you first. What do you mean, where is it going to be? Wouldn't it be at Mithsia?"

"I knew I didn't just go out with you for your looks." Her hand ran down his shirt and across his groin.

He turned to kiss her more.

"Plan first, fun later," she said, a wicked gleam in her eyes.

"Damn tease."

"Makes it *all* the more fun. Dwarven smiths are trained all over. To my knowledge, they go to another Dwarven settlement to show their skills. This is to make sure that there is no one getting coddled and they're worthy of the Master Smith title. So, will you accept the Dwarven Master Smith training?"

"If you agree. Kol was vague on the details."

"I do. Your conjuring was the support that we needed to cut through those cultists' defenses and tear them apart. I know how much work you have put into learning smithing. If you stop here, I know that you will regret it. Knowing the secret ways of the Dwarven Master Smiths coupled with your conjuring ability, you will only grow in strength. And I know you're not the kind of man to leave things half-finished."

"Oh, is that a fact?" Dave's eyes traced over her body and back to her eyes.

She was trying to look serious, but the upturned corners of her lips failed to obey her.

"Now, Malsour and Induca want to join us, and I think that Anna might for a time as well."

"Well, it is rather nice having those two around. Haven't really had much interaction with Anna, but she seems nice enough and she is Bob's daughter." Dave thought about that little factoid for a moment.

"Very well. Then, once you've got your Master Smithing thing sorted out, I want to head for the Mages College of Per'ush."

"Oh?" Dave asked.

"Malsour, Induca, and I have talked about it. If you want to learn more about Magical Circuits, they are the place to go. They are the oldest and the most knowledgeable mages college in all of Emerilia. If Suzy does join us, then she should have a grip on the basics enough that the information at the college won't go right over her head and she can use it to alter her own spells and casts. It is, also, one of a handful of cities that holds a known working portal."

Dave thinned his eyes accusingly.

"You know me too well." She simply smiled at his accusation.

"I want to get my smithing higher, but then I don't want to ruin everyone else's plans."

"Don't worry. I have talked to them already. Malsour and Induca are used to waiting and they have other things that they are interested in. I'm not sure about Anna but then I don't know what her aims are. Suzy, well, just like you when you first came here, she needs to build up her skills more. The good thing is that you can conjure tools for all of us to improve ourselves with as we work."

"Well, it does seem that you have this all planned out." A mischievous smile crossed Dave's face.

"What?" Deia dragged the word out.

"So good, in fact, I think that you should be the leader of our little party."

"What? Why? You should be—you're the one doing the support," Deia said.

"Deia, you talked to everyone and are starting to plan out our next moves while I'm still just reeling. I might have led a massive company but that is not much use here. Here I'm the guy who makes weapons and armor and supports from the rear. Malsour and Induca don't have the temperament for being our overall party leader. Sure, in some situations either of them would be good. The day-to-day running of it?" Dave shrugged. "No one knows Suzy or Anna enough yet to make them our leader. So, that comes to you." Dave's voice was soft but firm.

He knew it was the right choice. He had picked out the leaders of those who would work on the moon and run his various departments. He knew that he wasn't built to be the leader of this group. He was completely fine with Deia taking over. She'd been in more battles than Dave and he trusted her completely. He knew that the others would agree as well.

She didn't look totally convinced.

Dave moved so that he wasn't on his side but above her. He made to kiss her.

"Dave, this is a serious discussion," she said as Dave started to kiss her neck, his left hand moving to her shirt.

"Da-aave!" Her eyes fluttered.

"As the other..." He slowly kissed where her neck and jaw connected. "Person...in this discussion...I do believe that it is over." His hand had undone her shirt as he moved from her neck to her chest.

"Uhhnnnrgggh." She moaned and pulled his face closer.

Dave grinned as her fingers found their way into his hair.

Chapter 6: Onward and Forward

Dave tapped the doorway into the bunk room.

Two Dwarves playing a card game looked up at him. "Who are you?" one of them asked.

"I'm looking for Gurren and Lox," Dave asked.

"Dave?" Gurren called out, getting up from his bed.

"Well, it isn't exactly going to be a sweet maiden. I Think you scared them all off with your ugly mug." Dave grinned.

Gurren let out a barking laugh and embraced Dave.

"Look at what the damned wolf dragged in. You sure you don't use something to make yourself look uglier every time I see you?" Lox moved the separating curtain from his bed and small table. As a warband leader, he got a few more luxuries.

"I swear, every time I see you, your beard is shorter. It's like you're reversing your puberty," Dave shot back. He clapped Lox up in another hug.

"I heard that you've been offered a position as a Master Smith," Gurren said. The others in the room looked on in interest.

"Yeah, that's something I wanted to talk to you about." Dave looked at them nervously.

"You took it?" Lox asked.

"Yeah." Dave winced, expecting them to be displeased. They had all lost Joko, Tounk, and Max less than two weeks ago, and now Dave was planning to leave with Deia.

"Good! Seems that Deia is actually able to get something in your thick skull!" Lox grinned.

He saw some sadness in there, but he also saw the pride and happiness.

"Let's go to the common room," Gurren said.

They walked out of the bunk room and headed down to a room with a few chairs here and there, as well as a fireplace.

"So where are you going?" Lox asked.

"The Benvari Mountains." Dave slumped into his seat.

"Some good Master Smiths there. Kol talks of them highly," Gurren said.

"He hasn't said much to me other than I'd be reporting to someone called Jesal."

"Jesal, huh? That woman can bend metal with her damned hands. She's one of the strongest Master Smiths in Benvari, if not *the* strongest. Makes sense." Gurren stroked his beard in thought.

"Why?"

"Because you're the first person who's not a full Dwarf learning what are the Dwarven race's biggest secrets." Lox held Dave's eyes. "The Master Smiths are not just a new tier of smiths. It's easier to think of them as a sect. Their skills bring them together but they do much more than just hammer metal together. I've only seen Master Smiths truly at work maybe a few times. Their creations are not only magnificent but powerful. Everything that Kol has done in your workshop has been done to a master's high degree of quality, but none of it has been a master created piece."

"When Grandfather Kol makes even a simple knife or piece, then he is unable to do anything but his highest quality. His standards won't allow him to do any less. A knife made by him could cut through steel as if it were butter. He is not one to use his skills unless it is absolutely necessary and then they are only needed if he is making something. He can add bonuses to items that he works on, even though the original piece, if not created by him, is not to a master's tier of work." Gurren leaned forward and looked around. "Grandfather said that when you become a Dwarven master that you not only learn all of the skills that come with the forge, you learn your true forming."

"Forming?"

"The way that you were meant to create pieces. People are always better at one thing over another. Each smith has their own way of creating their products. Master Dwarves come to understand their method of creation and focus on using the skills that they are best at. They can become masters of multiple different skills but that takes time. You usually only get one or two when you are first given the title Master Smith. It is another reason that the Master Smiths work so closely together." Gurren sat back in his chair.

Seeing Dave's confusion, Lox snorted. "Well, it seems that you know near to nothing about all of this. You'll learn it with your time with the Master Smiths. The Master Smiths are spread all across the Dwarven kingdoms. Outside of the Dwarves, no one knows who the Master Smiths are. The smiths move from one Dwarven land to another, sharing their skills and teaching other Master Smiths as well as building their own skills. The Master Smiths are constantly moving around and there might be three different Master Smiths in one Dwarven kingdom but none of them actually hail from that kingdom."

"That is rather smart. Keeps them as a moving target and even eliminating all of those in one location means that there could be a dozen others spread over others or on the road. You lot are paranoid as all hell, but it makes a certain amount of sense." Dave smiled.

Deia walked into the common room, sending a breeze through the room.

"Well, seems that the old ball and chain has appeared." Gurren smiled broadly.

Deia walked over. "These ears aren't just for show, Gurren, you hairy stump."

They all rose. Lox and Gurren embraced Deia. Dave got a kiss before they settled back into their seats.

"So how long until you leave?" Lox asked.

"Four days," Deia said.

"Makes sense. I'd want to get out of this damned cold weather as soon as possible if I could!"

"You and me both!" Gurren chipped in.

"What did you decide to do about that Stone Raider guild asking for you to join their ranks?" Lox asked, his hand around his beard.

"We're going to see if the invite is still on the table and if so, we'll take it," Dave said.

"They seem like a good bunch." Lox nodded and looked to Gurren, who shrugged.

"Might as well tell you that Gurren and I will not be extending our contracts with the warclan. Those Stone Raiders also offered us positions to teach theirs how to fight properly. They also mentioned a bunch of opportunities —we might get to learn something of our own and go and see the world a little bit."

"I know that the warband was training them while they were here, but I thought that you were just going to do it on the side?" Dave said.

"Well, we were, but now we realize that there is probably something coming. A lord of Affinity doesn't just do it and everything goes back to normal. Something like this only happens once every few incarnations of Players. With the power that the Lady of Light gathered and that which the lords of Dark and Earth lost, there's going to be a power shift happening," Lox said.

Deia, Lox, and Gurren had dark expressions on their faces.

"When the lords and ladies of the Affinities find an imbalance, they will do anything to topple the weaker, and the weaker will do anything to gain back their power. Since their power comes from Emerilia, their struggles break out onto the lands as Players and POEs fight for those they believe in. Think of a holy war but with six different gods and all of them vying for power while using every trick they have to gain more power," Deia said.

"That sounds rather unpleasant." Dave sighed.

"Putting it mildly," Lox's voice rumbled.

"Well, that's enough of that. We have something to celebrate. Let's get over to that new shiny compound that the Stone Raiders swindled away from the Golden Sabres and sign on the dotted line. You know, because nothing ever went wrong for doing *that,*" Gurren said.

"Pessimist," Dave said.

"What? I joined up and I had to see your face. I think that was a big mistake!"

Dave rolled his eyes as all of them grinned. Their losses were still recent, but not so fresh that they could no longer smile, laugh, and joke around.

If they were here, they would've been doing the same thing. Dave stood up with the others, a sad smile on his face as he remembered those he'd lost but focused on moving forward with his life.

He opened up his active quest log.

Quest: Of Anvil and Fire

Kol has asked if you wish to undergo the training that would turn you into a Dwarven Master Smith.

Requirements: Reach Benvari Mountain

Finish training in all metals

Finish training to be Dwarven Master Smith

Failure: do not make it to Benvari within 3 months

Opt out of training

Reward: Dwarven Master Smith Class

Access to Dwarven mountains and forges

Will you accept?

Y/N

"Yes."

Quest: Of Anvil and Fire

Go to the Benvari Mountains and find the Dwarven Master Smith Jesal.

***

An explosion rattled Josh's room.

In seconds, he was up and out in the hallway. Smoke came out of Kim's room.

She came out coughing and sneezing. More smoke came out as she closed the door behind her.

"Hey, Josh." She waved, coughing.

"We just bought the bloody place. Can you try to not blow a hole in it?" Josh yelled.

Kim's face scrunched up as if she was trying the best way to let him know something.

Josh felt his eye twitch. "You blew a hole in it?"

"Well, it does add better ventilation to clear out the smoke!" Kim smiled.

Josh's eye twitched more. He turned, muttering to himself. "Damn wizards, playing with alchemy sets."

"Josh?" Kim asked his back as he walked back toward his room.

"What the hell did I do in my last life to deserve this?"

"Joshie?" Kim sounded as if she was getting worried as Josh reached his door.

"All experiments are to be done *outside* of the apartment. Mikal was a lab tech once. Get him to design it—you build it!" Josh yelled.

"But—"

"No more experiments in bedrooms!" Josh slammed his door shut. The sun wasn't even halfway in the sky yet! Josh got back under his covers.

"Something the matter?" Cassie said as he got into bed.

"Kim blew up her room," Josh growled as he pulled a pillow over his head.

Cassie giggled and moved closer to Josh.

"Aren't you supposed to be with your people, heading for Nadorf?" Josh asked.

"Saying you don't want me here?" Cassie gave him a coy smile.

Josh put an arm around her and dragged her to him. "On second thought, who needs 'em?" He grinned.

She laughed before she kissed him, her body rubbing on his. She smiled at his reaction to her touch.

"With Grif, I think I've got a few more days before I have to ride for Nadorf." Cassie winked.

"You sure you aren't some kind of closet succubus?" Josh peered out from his pillow.

"Well, if you wanted to give me your soul, I might have a soul gem lying around," Cassie said. Even through his shirt she was wearing, he could feel her nipples on his abs moving up to his chest as she pulled the pillow away.

"Yeah, you're definitely a succubus." He grinned, pulling her to him and kissing her. His hands moved over her body as she did the same with his body.

There was a knock at the door.

Josh pulled a dagger from the nightstand and threw it into the door. "Fuck off! I'm busy!"

Cassie chuckled, biting his lower lip and grinding her groin against his.

"Josh, it's Dave, Deia, Mal, and Induca," Dwayne said.

"You sly guildmaster, keeping me distracted with your charms while you pinched those four?" Cassie moved her groin slowly, exciting Josh more.

Josh held up his hand, not really wanting to say the words.

Cassie laughed and kissed him again. "Well, hurry up, or else I'm going to have to look after myself," Cassie teased.

Josh bolted up. "Gimme a minute!" Josh looked around the place.

"Pants, pants, where the fuck are my pant—" They hit him in the face as Cassie threw them at him.

"Tuck up." She dragged her eyes from his groin.

"Succubus." He pulled on his pants and walked out of the room.

"Don't take too long, though this is quite the view."

Josh turned to see her looking at his butt.

She bit her lip and moved the sheet so he could see her wearing nothing but panties and his shirt.

You lucky, lucky bastard! He shut the bedroom door and ran to the door to his apartment.

"Fuck! Shit." He slammed into a desk in the way. "Who put that fucking thing here—stubbed my bloody toe!" He opened the door to find everyone staring at him. "Hello. So, what's up?"

"We wanted to accept your invitation into the Stone Raiders, though we need to go to the Benvari Mountains," Deia said.

"Oh?" Josh asked.

"I've been offered a chance to become a Dwarven Master Smith," Dave said.

"Wow, okay then. I don't think that there are any Players with that offer," Josh said, impressed.

"We also desire that we be formed into a singular group," Malsour said.

"We can do that. Best to have people group together, though you're going to need someone to hold the line and be proper fighters if you go into combat. I know Dave and Deia are good fighters with their weapons but their magical powers make it so that they should stay to the rear in a support capacity, like you two," Josh said.

"We are working on that and we might have others who are interested in joining the Stone Raiders," Dave said.

"Okay, but either me or one of the lieutenants or recruiters will have to vet them before we extend an invitation. If we start asking everyone to join, then we're going to be no better off than those other guilds that got killed from the inside out."

"We understand," Deia said.

"Okay, well then, you'll be Party Zero," Josh said.

"Party Zero?" Dave asked.

"You've got the most magical strength out of any other four parties combined. You're kind of our hidden weapon. If you agree to join the Stone Raiders, remember that in times of emergency—even if you are training—we will band together to deal with any major threats. It hasn't happened yet but if we have something else like Boran-al's Citadel, then I'll summon you all."

"Understood," Deia said.

"So, who is the party commander?" Josh asked.

Everyone looked to Deia.

"Well, good luck with keeping them in check. And send me a report every so often to let us know how things are going. Dwayne can sort out the details," Josh said.

"Thanks, Josh." Dave smiled.

"Welcome to the Stone Raiders, you bunch of miscreants!" Josh grinned.

The others smiled, even the stoic Malsour.

"Do you think it will be Golden Raiders or Stone Sabres?" Dave asked, a grin on his face as he looked over in the direction of Josh's bedroom.

Josh went a bit red as Dave winked at him, as if to tell him "your secret is safe with me."

"Come this way. We'll get your patches sorted out and the rest of the details." Dwayne led them away.

Josh shut the door and ran back to his bedroom.

Cassie was propped up on some pillows, her hands kneading her shirt and panties. She bit her lower lip and looked at him. "Well, you just going to stand there or help me out? You got the four most powerful Players—I feel that I should get something for my loss," Cassie said.

"Abso-fucking-lutely!" Josh closed the bedroom door and advanced on Cassie.

Chapter 7: One Becomes Two

Suzy logged off of Emerilia. She had spent three days in-game, the equivalent of a day on Earth. She had a number of meetings that she was supposed to have attended but figuring out what was real and fake made her stay.

Also, listening to Zel's stories, admiring his artwork and having a drink had led to her having a rather enjoyable time.

She blinked her eyes. Instead of her living room, she found herself in a ballroom. She looked around. She was in the middle of one of the dances that was made to meet and greet Japan's most powerful figures.

Shit. She looked around the room.

She'd held some doubts. Austin-Dave had nearly convinced her but she needed more information and a clear display of Emerilia being real. *Well, this is it. I just woke up in the middle of a ballroom, not knowing how I got here.*

She thought of logging out, the feeling that passed over her body as she entered Emerilia.

The ballroom disappeared and Emerilia appeared. She stood on Dave's porch. There were all kinds of noises coming from the house as he and Deia packed up for their trip to the Benvari Mountains.

"Well, you're back rather soon," Induca said. Malsour sat in a chair, reading his book and looking out over the new day.

"I...well, fuck, is there a beer around?" Suzy moved to the chairs. Dave must've heard as one appeared on an armrest. She grabbed it and took a big swig, looking around Cliff-Hill.

"So, I guess your eyes have been opened." Dave walked out of the cabin.

"Yeah, this is honestly screwed up," Suzy said.

"Yeah, a bit." Dave put down his bag of holding and gave Suzy one.

"So, what now?" Suzy asked.

"Now we go to the Benvari Mountains and we train you so that you can look after yourself here. If you want to join us..." Deia came out and closed the door to her home.

"Well, sounds like a good enough plan to me. Austin was always talking about his games. I think it's about time I started learning a bit more about it all." Suzy smiled.

She was scared as hell of the future and knowing that this was reality kind of made her look at everything differently: Doubts of her childhood crept in. Fear that she was something less because she'd been grown in a vat to provide entertainment for an alien race that had destroyed all other signs of Humanity because they could've disturbed their status quo.

She looked over to Dave, who smiled at her, and Deia, who stood behind him with a hand on his shoulder. Dave was like the brother that she'd never had. The only true family she had left. She'd come to know Deia a bit better. The Elven woman was driven and passionate but also level-headed. She had the strength of will to rein Dave in and keep him focused, but also didn't feel the need to be the center of his attention. They were strong people together and apart.

Induca was flighty and a bundle of energy, constantly smiling and joking around unless she was training. Malsour was stoic; he reminded Suzy of so many engineers and scientific people she'd dealt with. He was a bit distant from the world due to the way that he looked at systems in a way that others couldn't even start to contemplate. Society wasn't all that interesting to him, but give him a juicy and interesting piece of information and he would lock himself away trying to figure it out.

All four of them had agreed to let her join their party if she decided to.

"Well, fuck it, what else am I going to do—mope around here? Might as well go and see the sights, even if that is the inside of some dingy Dwarven mountain." Suzy smiled.

Dave broke into a wide smile and the others seemed excited as well.

Deia moved her hand through the air.

Party Request

Oson'Deia would like to invite you to "Party Zero."

Do you accept?

Y/N

"Yeah," Suzy said. The side of her screen showed the four other members of the party with their Health, Stamina, and Mana bars under their names.

"Mind if I join?" A half-wolf, half-Human woman came around the porch.

"Well, we do need someone skilled with a blade," Deia said.

Anna's name appeared under the other four names, with her own bars under her name.

"Thanks. Sorry we haven't talked more—just been busy walking around and getting to know Emerilia once again. It's been a long time since I saw the place with my own two eyes." Anna smiled but there was a sadness to it.

"Well then, let's go on a journey." Dave rose with a grimace, looking at Suzy's feet. "Deia, you got some better shoes?"

"Yeah." Deia pulled out a new pair of shoes and handed them to Suzy.

"They look like running shoes," Suzy said.

"Well, after a while, the Players got annoyed with messing up their feet so much. It led to a revolution in shoe creation. So, while not everything is that advanced, shoe wear is one thing that competes with Earth's own, kind of like how toilets aren't just a hole in a ground but those Magical Circuits turn it right into odor-free fertilizer," Dave supplied.

"Players don't even need to use toilets."

"Yeah, but all the POEs do. Smelled terrible." Anna grimaced.

"So, anything that was kind of an inconvenience to the Players was given some pretty high-tech solution?" Suzy asked.

"Pretty much. Players who make something and then register it with the traders' guild get a royalty every time their product is made. Whoever made the magical toilet would never have to do a quest again. The POEs have them in every house. The Players aren't the only people who buy and sell goods," Dave said.

"What have you been selling them?" Suzy dragged out her words as she studied Dave.

"Muskoka chairs, screws, some minor magical equipment to help with smithing, and I'm working on central heating and cooling. It's hard to make a Magical Circuit that warms or cools the house without turning it into a bonfire or an ice cube." Dave tapped his chin, his mind drifting.

"Which is why I said we are not trying it out on the house," Deia said.

"Well, it would give me more information and I could always build a bigger house. I'm thinking that we could use the room, maybe make it two stories," Dave wheedled.

"Maybe, but first of all you need to move all of this compound to the new industrial complex," Deia said.

"Yes, well, the kilns have already started moving; the long houses are going to stay. As soon as the repairs and work are done, then the smithy will start moving over," Dave said.

Suzy had looked into Dave's various enterprises in the area. It was clear that there was little to no room for the kiln and the smithy to grow in.

Dave had been hesitant but now with his right-hand woman, she'd gone through all the information and basically beaten him around the head with reasons he should move the kiln and the smithy.

She had also looked over the contracts with the Mithsia Mountains for materials. They had plenty of material now, making the materials cheaper than anywhere for miles. She'd got Dave to buy a good stock of it, more than he currently needed but enough so that his smiths always had something to work with.

The smiths who had come with the warclans were also talking about leaving, so Suzy had talked to them and started the very first contracts that dealt with not only their work but also health benefits.

Dave's property that overlooked the edge of Cliff-Hill remained in his possession and although all of the changes were going to make him lose a bit of gold and building the new facilities was going to be hectic, Dave had already done the first part—he'd moved his portable smithy so even while he was gone everything could continue.

Wis'Zel would continue to run the ceramics factory and kilns. Kol would command the smithies.

An excited shiver ran down her back, thinking of how even his screws were changing the way things were built.

What will happen if he stops just playing with small things and goes onto bigger things? There are a lot of mechanical and electrical wonders of Earth and Dave has the mind to create them. It might take months, maybe even years or decades, but what else do we have but time?

Suzy smiled as she put on the running shoes.

"What's so funny?" Dave asked.

"Well, I was wondering how Emerilia is going to change with all of us working together. Just the lack of boundaries, the ability to innovate, create and do *anything*—it's intoxicating."

Dave laughed. "Well, we certainly are going to push a few boundaries."

"It's not like we aren't already," Malsour said.

Deia and Induca smiled at each other as Anna looked over them all.

Suzy's eyes met Anna's in that moment; it was as if they could read each other's minds.

No matter what the future brings, it's going to be interesting with this bunch.

Chapter 8: Ye Olde Dusty Trail

Dave made sure that the house was secured, turning around to see his party and those who had gathered to see them off.

The Stone Raiders were making their way out of the village in their parties. A large number of them were staying behind to learn a trade, to continue training or act as the support element for the guild.

Josh, Dwayne, Kim, and Lucy were off on the path that led from the compound out to the main road. Before them were Kol, Wis'Zel, Wender, Gurren, and Lox.

The others had already said their good-byes and were waiting off to the side.

"All right, make sure the transition goes smoothly and don't burn it down," Dave said to Kol and Zel.

"Try not to." Zel smiled and shook Dave's hand.

"Look after yourself, lad. Don't start hammering out crap or I'll come down there to try to hammer something useful out of you!"

Dave laughed at Kol's words and grasped his arm.

"We'll see each other in the future—I can sense it. Look after yourself." Wender again clasped Dave's arm.

"You too."

"Well, it has been quite the time seeing you grow up into something of a use." Lox brought Dave into a hug. "Look after our Deia and keep yourself safe."

"I'll try my best." Dave smiled, his vision getting blurry as he thought of those who hadn't made it. They had been his first true friends in years and his first ones in Emerilia.

"Good. And you can tell us the stories over a beer afterwards, though you better be buying!"

"I've seen you drink—there's no way I'm paying for a mountain wolf-sized keg for you to get a buzz on!" Dave grinned as Lox laughed. He shook his head and moved to Gurren.

"I'll see you later. Though you might not be blood of my blood, you're a man I would call brother always."

"You soft bastard." Dave's voice was gruff as he tried to get over the emotions clogging his throat as he embraced Gurren.

They'd gone through a lot and somehow made it out on the other side. They clapped each other on the back before they separated.

Dave looked at them all, taking strength from their faces, their shared memories and experiences.

"Till later." Dave jogged over to the rest of the party.

They started to jog as well, heading down toward the main road. The Stone Raiders leaders headed out of Cliff-Hill.

"Suzy, you got those potions?" Deia asked.

"Yeah," Suzy said warily.

"Good. Put them on your quick menu. Once you do, let's see how fast you can sprint."

"Okay," Suzy said.

Dave smiled; Suzy was not going to be happy by the time they stopped. They needed to get her trained up quickly; having a higher Agility and Sprint could only be useful later on.

The Stone Raiders had taken that to heart, their conjured traveling animals being stored away as they ran.

Suzy took off at a sprint a few moments later.

The party moved to match her speed.

"Once your Stamina gets to twenty percent, start drinking the lower-leveled potions. It's going to hurt, but your Agility is going to go up quite a bit faster than just riding a horse," Anna said.

"Bunch of sadists—prefer to run rather than just sit back and relax on a wagon." Josh sighed.

***

By the time they'd reached the part of the road where it split off to meet up with Boran-al's Citadel, Suzy had stopped cursing and was working on her breathing as Deia instructed her.

Deia talked Suzy through it as the High Elf drank her potions and kept soldiering on.

Dave put his hand on her shoulder, pushing his healing magic through her. She groaned in relief as he put her back to perfect condition.

They all slowed, looking down the road that led to the citadel.

It's hard to think that not even a few weeks have passed since we were there.

Dave looked at the plaque mounted on the side of the road with the names of the groups that had cleared the citadel, listing those who had died underneath and those who had done the most damage underneath that. Once the citadel had been cleared, the stone had simply risen from the dirt.

The dungeon boards also displayed information on the victory at the citadel.

Dave tracked Suzy's body, making sure that she wouldn't pass out or hurt herself from her exertions. To enhance his own training, he upped the weight of his own breastplate. Adding new runes or creating a high-classed sword took a hell of a lot of Mana. Adding a few runes that reversed the Agility and Strength enhancements was a lot easier.

The citadel had shown Dave that there were much more powerful things out there, especially since Opheir was only regarded as a starter continent. Guilds were moving to other continents because solo Players by themselves weren't strong enough to survive long in the stronger lands.

Stone Raiders had been on three of the other continents, each with races much stronger than that of Opheir's, yet the rewards had been incredible. One day, Dave wanted to go and check out those lands; he still had a lot he needed to do in the meantime.

"So, I have been thinking about what you were saying about the magical creations you were seeing in people's spells," Malsour said, not sounding out of breath even though they had been running for hours.

"How they were all weird and messed up?"

"Something like that." Malsour smiled. "I think it reflects back to word association and mental projection."

"Too many words and not enough numbers for me."

"Well, think of it this way. If I say tree, we're both going to think of a tree—yes? But I might think of an Elven wood and you might think of a pine tree. With Magical Circuits, you spell out with words what you want to happen. In Magical Circuits, Mana gives life to the runes which, through their combination, create a law which bends the power to its will with more laws or runes grouped into magical circles, changing the state of that power until you have a final product."

"Okay, yeah, with the more words and knowledge you have, you can refine down those magical circles to just a few runes, which are more accurate. It's like how a kid might say that the hot chocolate was good. Though an adult, knowing more words, might say that the hot chocolate was good due to the combination of the rich hot chocolate mixed with powdered hazelnut and whipped cream. The more words, the more specific you can get."

"Quite, but when you are creating magic yourself and not with your Magical Circuits, then people use incantations to give their spell structure, like writing on the lines in a notepad instead of on a piece of slate without a line in sight.

"When people cast a spell, the fewer words they say, the more thought they are using. With their minds, they are giving shape to the Mana within them. Higher Affinities allow it to be more malleable in their hands and they can better understand the effects of their actions. Higher-level mages' spells are more powerful as they have such an innate feel for magic that they can cast higher level spells without words but by their connection to their spell. The more control they have over their mind, knowledge of their spell, and the Affinities it is created from, the more powerful it will be and the more power that will be used on their target instead of keeping it stable."

"So, you're saying that people casting spells is nowhere near as refined and clean as that of someone using Magical Circuits?"

"Yes and no. Magical Circuits are certainly very good at doing complex things, but words are fallible. Within your mind, you can picture the perfect tree, but imagine trying to explain it. No one is going to have the same idea, even if you give every damned detail, down to the bark and the roots. Everyone is going to see that tree as different in their mind. Take that to magic and if you have a high enough Affinity and understanding of the magic that you're using, your mental image becomes reality. It's why people who use voiceless incantation are so damned powerful. The only constraints on our power are our minds and our Mana reserves."

"Well, that is something I'm working on." Dave tapped his breastplate that was sucking out all but twenty percent of his Mana reserves. "So, what was that I was seeing in people's spells?"

Malsour was quiet, hesitant to continue on. "I think that your Touch of the Land has been altered to such a degree that it could be called its own spell. As you've come to know the elements around you and altered your Touch to observe and understand all around you, you've come to create a kind of arcane sight. Working with

Magical Circuits and creating magical circles and magic while using Touch of the Land refined your abilities."

"Okay, so I went from seeing what was in the dirt, to seeing everything around me in a big sphere or really focusing it and seeing the details of my circuits and magic to get a better understanding."

"With your knowledge of the Affinities and your skills with Touch of the Land, your mind converted the central aspect of the spell. You could perceive the core thought or thoughts that were able to control the spell and you viewed them in rune format."

"A little dumber, please? I can talk astrophysics all day, but magic is still new to me."

Malsour cracked a smile. "Those thoughts that turn raging Mana into an actual spell—I think that you saw them and your mind translated them into runes. When you conjured your Mana into those spells, you were changing the very core of the spell. With the spells attacking you, you overloaded them or spent their power elsewhere. With those you reinforced, you altered their very structure to strengthen them. You've studied multiple languages of power, more than probably anyone else. That gives you more words, more ways to bend the powers of the universe to your will."

"Wow, so I can mess with some spells that people need incantations for and even those where people have a good Affinity and decent Mana pool. If I fight someone's spells and they have a higher Affinity or they've supercharged their spell, then it's going to be more difficult to defend against it?"

"Yes, though the more words of power you come to understand, the higher the Affinity and Mana pool of your own, the stronger you can become."

"I can already feel a headache coming on from trying to think of doing that and then being in the middle of a battle with fewer people around to keep me safe."

"And so, you should," Malsour said with a severe look. "If someone casts a spell just feet from you, you're not going to have the time to counteract the spell."

"So, don't get cocky and put my shield down as I'll get my ass rolled by my attacker—gotcha."

The silence fell as each thought to themselves. The others talked about different things. Suzy kept grunting onward as Deia watched over her.

Well, it is the fastest way to level up her Strength and Agility. Dave felt sorry for his best friend as he turned to Malsour. "It seems the more I learn, the more I figure I have so much further to go." Dave snorted.

"Something amusing?" Malsour asked.

"There's something of a saying back on Earth. A wise man knows he knows nothing. A fool thinks they know all."

"Maybe you Earthers aren't as dumb as you seem." Malsour's face split into a wide smile.

"Just 'cause you've been alive for a few centuries, you think everyone's as dumb as a rock. I'd call that an unfair advantage."

"It's all biology to me." Malsour shrugged.

"Damn beings of power," Dave said under his breath, rolling his eyes and smiling.

Chapter9: To Indal We Go

Deia watched Suzy as she ran. She was faster than she had been on their trip to Omal.

"So, you really just need to have a soul gem or some kind of gem holding power and then form your creation around it. I'd need a few supplies but I think I could get you some decent-sized rechargeable soul gems."

"What's...the...difference?" Suzy asked, panting.

"Well, with a normal soul gem, it's made as a disposable one-shot wonder. You can charge them again but the amount they hold degrades until the soul gem disintegrates. With the rechargeable, they won't degrade for a few thousand charges. As long as you have the power in yourself, you can feed it into your creations, or you can pull it from the soul gems to increase your Mana supply. That's what my armor is. It siphons off my Mana, storing it, so that I have it for later. Your Mana reserves are only a certain amount; you can't hold more in your body, but if you bleed power into your body, you can use it to power spells well beyond your natural Mana bar."

"Can you siphon off other people's power?" Induca asked.

"Any wild energy such as broken spells or Magical Circuits or a soul's energy is automatically absorbed. For souls, I have to cast soul trap, though there's a Magical Circuit that I'm working on that will auto-cast soul trap on anything classified as an enemy combatant."

"Though is there any other way to take power from a willing participant?" Induca pressed.

"Well, with the right magical rune, say on a necklace? Or if I made another set of armor. Deia's and my own armor have a function where we can transfer power to each other."

"Well, make me up one of those necklaces," Induca said.

"Why?" Dave asked.

"Using your Mana increases your ability to make more of it and have larger reserves. With you constantly pulling it away, my body will fight to make more, just like running."

Dave was silent for a while.

We've been doing that with the armor and the results have been great. It keeps our energy down but our Intelligence and Willpower have been climbing up steadily. Deia felt a little annoyed with herself to have not brought it up sooner.

"Only makes sense. Pretty boneheaded move by me." Dave scratched his head as they continued to run.

"Make ones for us, too," Kim said.

"Would be useful to have some stored power lying around if we need it in an emergency," Lucy agreed.

"If you can make those necklaces and make it so that it draws people's power and we can alter how much and then allow them to pull it from one of your soul gems by request, then I'd be happy to pay," Josh said.

"You—paying? Where was this kind soul back in Omal when you left me with the bill?" Dwayne asked.

"What? I said I had a call to take." Josh jumped out of the way of Dwayne's hand.

"Was it from your girlfriend?" Kim asked, a glint in her eye.

"Maybe," Josh said.

"Josh and Cassie sitting in a tree, K-I-S-S—"

"Shut up, Kim!" Josh said.

"I-N-G."

"Is this because I banned you from doing experiments in the apartment?" Josh asked.

"Maybe..."

"YOU BLEW YOUR DAMN WALL OFF. IT TOOK THREE DAYS TO FIX IT AND WE HAD TO SLEEP OUT-SIDE!"

"Well, I doubt that you were getting much sleep with Cassie anyway!" Kim put out her tongue.

Deia pressed her lips together as the others chuckled or outright laughed at Kim and Josh's argument.

"Come here, you damned wizard!" Josh ran after Kim.

"That's mage to you, Shadow Pervert!" She laughed, throwing spells back at him as he dodged them and chased her down the length of the Stone Raiders' caravan.

"Who you betting on?" Dwayne asked.

"Kim," Lucy said.

"Same," Dwayne grunted.

Deia saw that the rest of the Stone Raiders were betting on their two leaders as they yelled at each other, smiles on their faces as Kim threw spells and Josh dodged out of their way.

"Looks...like...hell," Suzy said.

"Don't worry, we'll soon get a game of tree tag going," Deia said.

Suzy gave her a look that Deia might expect a Demon's torture victim might show.

It was all Deia could do to stop herself from laughing.

"I fucking hate trees," Dave said darkly.

"This sounds like a good story," Malsour prompted.

Dave kept his silence as Deia snorted.

"First time he tried to run up a tree, he slowed down too much. Panicking, he grabbed a tree branch. Unfortunately, the tree branch wasn't all that strong, and there was another right underneath him.

"He tried bartering with the tree branch and gravity, but gravity won out and he landed on the branch right below—landing right on his jewels."

The males in the group winced and shook their heads in amusement; the women just snorted at Dave's misfortune.

"Swore I busted a nut. Hurt for two days," Dave complained.

***

"Good, good—now just think of the creation as a balloon. Fill it with Mana to inflate it. Not too much that it becomes unstable, but not too little that it can't support itself. Starting out, it's better using less." Anna watched Suzy as she concentrated on what looked like a gray amorphous blob.

Suzy put her hands to it. Anna could see with her arcane sight as Suzy pushed power inside the creation. It wasn't much and it stuttered a few times but after a few seconds, it settled down and continued to flow more uniformly.

These bleeders are rather impressive.

Anna watched as the amorphous blob started to move, four non-uniform legs connected to a body. It looked like a kind of squid.

"That's good," Anna said before Suzy put too much into it.

Suzy cut off her Mana and watched the blob that got to its feet awkwardly.

"So what makes it move? Or, like, follow commands?" Dave asked.

"Well, essentially it's part of Suzy, a combination of soul and Mana energy turned into a form. Otherwise known as Willpower and Intelligence stats. Making the body is about the hardest part of it, once you get into customizing it. But the center of the creation, what makes it go—act and react—is Suzy. When she makes something, her mind is sort of printed onto the creation. Suzy, think of it jumping,"

Suzy did as the squid thing tried to jump. It was quite cute.

"How?" Suzy asked.

"Well, your mind resonates with your creation. As you think of something, your imprint understands what you mean and carries it out. While I might say fish and we both think of different fish, when you say fish to your imprint, you're both thinking of the same fish.

That is, unless you've gone through a mental shift. The best way to fight a creation summoner is through their mind—hit you with a few psychic tricks and your whole army falls apart as they're all linked to your mind."

"Is there any way to take control of the creations?" Dave asked.

"If you are a creation summoner as well and you have a greater affinity for the type of medium that the creation is made from—so in this case, Earth and water because we made it from mud—and your mind is stronger, then you can override the creation, destroying Suzy's consciousness within them and replacing it with your own. Also, distance plays a factor. The closer the creations are to Suzy, the greater control she has over them."

"Hmm." Looking satisfied, Dave nodded and went back to working on the simple black necklaces.

"Okay, now let's see how far your range is," Anna said. "Push your creature out as far as possible and we'll see when it falls out of your control."

"Well, here goes nothing," Suzy said.

Anna glanced at the girl's Mana. She was at around twenty percent for just filling the creature with power. It had taken Suzy two hours of meditating and casting to build the creation.

The creature walked toward the forest, its movements wonky but workable.

Few can get their first creations to do more than twitch a limb. Maybe it has something to do with the fact that they know Emerilia is real. They're obviously putting more effort into their training and they're both pretty driven, something that they're passing on to the other Players and even the POE. Anna looked at Suzy and Dave, wondering just where the two bleeders might take them.

"Babe! Can you heat something up for me?" Dave asked Deia, who was a bit away from camp, talking and training with Induca and a few other Fire mages from the Stone Raiders.

"How hot do you need it?" Deia yelled back.

"Blue flame, right out of the campfire would be fine!"

The flames of the campfire turned from red to blue, focused in a single flame.

"Thanks, babe!" Dave said.

Most people took some time to get used to the magical properties of Emerilia. Dave treated it as if it was just another tool. Few people had the strength of magic as Players, but Dave seemed to have been surrounded by it or adjusted to it so that it was his new norm.

Dave placed some silver in the fire. "Let's see what you've got there, Malsour," Dave said.

Malsour tossed him over a rune that was no bigger than a copper piece.

Dave inspected it. "Nicely done." He tossed it back to the Dragon.

"It's harder than I thought it would be," Malsour said.

"Just takes practice and determination. If you ever get interested in hammering a bit of metal, let me know. I'd be happy to show you the basics."

Suzy grunted a bit.

Anna looked over to the wobbling squid. It was still going but from Suzy's expression, it was getting harder and harder to send signals to it.

It got another meter and then collapsed.

Suzy rubbed her forehead. "Well, now I've got a headache to add to my body feeling like it just got rolled over by a bulldozer."

Anna laughed. "That's just your body telling you that you're out of Mana and that you've done something that was previously hard for you. As you do more complex spells and magic, then you'll get worse headaches. It's a sign that you're stretching your limits."

"Sounds like a great time."

"Well, your creation made it about a hundred and fifty meters. That's really good for your first try. Now I'm going to teach you how to circulate your Mana to help get rid of those headaches."

"Then what?" Suzy asked.

Pretty smart one. Anna smiled. "Then we see if you can make two of them, and try to get them to go the same distance."

"This sucks," Suzy muttered.

It might for now, but I have a feeling that just like Dave and the others, you're going to advance much quicker than anyone else might be capable of.

Anna only had to look at the Stone Raiders, who were practicing their various skills around the camp. While the POE saw it as a chore to raise their levels, the Stone Raiders focused on raising their stats and pushing their limits in a way that the POE never would. With no need to fear death if jumping between trees or dodging arrows was a good way to level up, they'd try it out.

The people I knew when I went to sleep might all be dead, but there is still hope in their descendants.

Chapter 10: Indal

"Well, seems like the locals are friendly." Dwayne kept his voice low.

"Well, not everyone is going to like Players because of the way that they treat the POE," Josh said. "I've never seen anything like this kind of level of AI. It's so life-like, even their reactions to us."

Dwayne nodded in agreement. As they had become E-heads and Emerilia became their land, they'd come to respect and interact with the POE more. It was hard to treat them as just simple AIs there for their enjoyment. If they hadn't felt that way before, Boran-al's Citadel had solidified it in their minds.

Indal was a farming community and just another stop on the way to the northern cities. There were more people coming through the city than when Josh had made the trip up from Nadorf last time. Their farms and fisheries helped to supply the north with food throughout the year. Winter might be ending but the majority of people were still in the city, waiting for the ground to defrost more, so that they could get to planting this year's harvest.

Omal and Milheilm were both large starting areas, which put Indal right in the middle of them.

If early Players were into something that might be not viewed well in the eyes of the law, then they usually drifted to Indal to carry out their murders and other atrocities. More than one villager had disappeared due to a Player trying out a new spell or making a sacrifice to the Pantheon.

Certainly, won't make things much easier here.

"I think that we'll get supplies and then be on our way. We've still got a few hours of daylight left and I don't feel all that good about staying here tonight. Not only will they gouge our wallets—I'm wondering if they won't gouge something else to make up for those who died by other Players," Josh said.

The other four nodded their heads and Josh put out a message to the rest of the Stone Raiders. There wasn't as much disagreement as he was expecting. It seemed that they had clued into the odd vibe coming from the people and were happy to keep going. They were only two days from Komo and six days from Nadorf, if they continued at their pace. Everyone's Strength and Agility were increasing so Josh was betting they could slim that down a bit.

An alliance between us and the POE would be awesome, but stuff like this is only going to make them not trust us. It might be an idea to get out ahead of the other guilds and Players, and start sending some envoys to the different lands to see what is going on and do a bit of scouting.

"Lucy, I have a job for your mice," Josh said.

Lucy raised her head from her book and cast a shroud around them. People would hear them have a normal conversation and even see their lips talking but it wouldn't be their actual conversation.

"They are currently underused, just hanging around trying to get information," Lucy said.

Josh could see the pride and eagerness to prove her people's worth. "The more I think about it, the more I want to know just what is happening in the other lands and to see what kind of situation we might be getting ourselves into if we go over there. See if you can't have our people go and check it out. Also, get the word out that we're looking for POEs and Players. I'm going to leave the figuring out if the POEs are going to be loyal to you."

"Well, that'll certainly be a challenge. I think I should have a talk with Malsour. He might have an idea about some kind of spell to see if a person is lying."

"He certainly has a lot of knowledge." Josh nodded.

"Yes, and he said that his solution probably looks at a person's very soul. At that level, it's impossible for a person to lie."

"All this soul business makes me wonder if there really is an after-life," Josh muttered.

"Oh, don't worry, there isn't—we only get power from a soul because when a person dies then all that potential disappears. It's as if you disappeared, then due to displacement, air would rush in. Creatures, Players, and POEs all have a power potential. When we die, that power loss creates a vacuum that for a second ejects the power that made up a person's stats. It's all rather odd but interesting. Though there isn't anything after death, in my mind. Though, at least in Emerilia, you get to respawn when you die." Lucy smiled.

"Well, thank you for that little bit of information. Not sure I really understand it all, though." Josh rubbed his head.

She snorted and snapped her fingers, the spell around them breaking apart.

***

Dave shifted. His eyes opened as he looked for what had disturbed his sleep.

"Mmmm," Deia murmured, not fully awake yet.

Dave continued to search, expanding out his range of his Touch.

He passed those who were on watch and then farther out. Emerilia might be a game but it had taught E-heads that it was always a good idea to have a sentry posted. If not for the animals, then the other Players.

"We've got company." Dave opened his interface.

Group Message

Dave > Got a group of forty or so people sneaking up on our camp.

Josh > Which direction are they coming from?

Dave > From Indal.

Josh > Deia and I will scout. Everyone else, get into a line and be ready for them. We should be able to deal with it ourselves. Kim, let the other party leaders know what's going on.

Deia stood and pulled on clothes. Dave did the same.

"So, what weapons are they using?" Deia asked.

"Most of them are using bows. All of them have daggers. There are seven with swords. Five with shields and swords," Dave said.

"See you in a bit." Deia pulled on her boots before she kissed Dave.

"Stay safe."

"I will. I love you."

"I love you, too, firecracker."

Deia snorted, grabbed her compound bow and headed off into the night.

Dwayne was in command as he put people into place. Stone Raiders got up from their sleep, not a single fire or light showing as they moved to their positions. Those without good night vision were helped by those who did. They worked silently.

Dave had detected forty people but they weren't going to just go back to sleep and hope there weren't more.

*****

Deia pulled an arrow from her open bag, notching it onto her compound bow. She was halfway up a tree with her legs wrapped around a tree limb as she used Earth magic to wrap other limbs around her waist.

The forty-three people moving through the forest weren't fighters but they were trackers and hunters. Even farmers out here had to know how to use a bow in case they needed some food in the winter or to drive off animals on their lands.

Now it seems that they're determined to use those weapons to attack us. Deia understood their reasoning but she didn't want to have to kill them.

"I'm going to try to talk to them. If they don't listen, then take them down," Josh said.

Deia knew that most Players would've just killed the POE and be done with it. For the Stone Raiders, they were easy targets and clearly aggressive. They were also some decent levels, so they could get some good experience from them. Maybe a few bits of coin and some equipment to sell off to a town later on.

The Stone Raiders didn't even bat an eyelid.

He was a decent rogue as he moved through the shadows. He appeared a few hundred meters away from the man they had identified as the group's leader. Although Josh had worked on his night vision, the Humans from Indal hadn't and it showed as they cursed and wandered through the dark night.

"Hello, do you mind if I ask what you are doing tonight?" Josh asked.

"Kill them, lads!" the leader said. All of them charged forward.

With regret in her heart, Deia drew and released her arrow. By the time the first arrow hammered its target into the ground, she'd already released a second.

The hunters became the hunted as they cried out in pain and gave their dying breaths.

"They've got Demons!"

"Run for your lives!"

Deia cut another's scream short as her arrow buried itself in their chest.

None of them had reached Josh but over half of their number was dead or dying on the ground.

Josh waited for a few minutes, listening and making sure that the hunters didn't try to come after them again. "Let's head back." Josh sighed, upset.

No one said anything as they moved from their positions, turning away from the battle and back toward their camp.

Deia noticed something odd: the Players weren't happy about having killed the hunters. They seemed to understand that they'd taken lives.

It's almost as if they were becoming POEs and actually care about what impact their actions will have.

She found Dave as she was putting her bow away. He pulled her close, as if sensing her own sadness. She put her head on his shoulder and breathed in his scent. He kissed the top of her head, rubbing her shoulder and reassuring her as they made their way back to their bedroll.

Deia doubted that she would be able to sleep much that night.

Chapter 11: Komo

Komo was the largest town Dave had seen in Emerilia so far. Its roads were shaped into a *Y*, with the prongs leading to Roun-Tuk and Indal and the bottom leading toward Nadorf. It was a large trading hub connecting the north with the south. Raw goods were funneled down from this point to feed, heat, and supply Nadorf and the southern cities.

There was a tension in the air as they arrived.

Malsour guided them to a tavern that he and Induca had stayed at in their travels. They were the last of the Stone Raiders to arrive. Suzy was slower than all of the others. She'd only just started out on Emerilia and couldn't keep up with the hectic pace of the rest of the guild.

Dave cast her a glance as Deia helped her in. She'd pushed herself hard today and she needed rest. Dave had a proud smile on his face. He knew that Suzy would push herself harder than anyone to not only get on the same level as them, but to surpass them.

Inside the tavern, a couple of people were having a drink but it was by no means busy.

"Hello, good to see you. Wish it was under better circumstances," a burly barkeep said from the bar as they approached. "What can I do you for?"

"Four rooms and meals, please," Dave said.

"What's happened? Everyone seems nervous," Induca said.

"I can do the rooms and the food—one gold and two silver."

Trade

Gar Jorkn has four rooms and food for:

12x Silver

Do you accept?

Y/N

Dave accepted and the money seemed to disappear from his pouch.

"I'll have Olai take you up." Gar raised his voice. "As to why everyone's all shook up—well, a Dragon moved into Endal Mountain."

A teenage girl walked out of what must've been the kitchen.

"Olai, show these fine people up to their rooms—four of them."

"Yes, Papa." Olai waved for them to follow her.

"I'll be up in a minute." Dave smiled.

"Okay, I'm going to take a nap." Deia smiled.

Party Chat

Deia > Let me know if he says anything else interesting.

Dave squeezed her hand and she headed off for the stairs. Malsour, Induca, and Dave stayed.

"So, what is this Dragon called?" Dave asked.

"Quindar. Everyone saw him come in down through the sky—never seen anything move so fast! Then he just moved into one of the dungeons that was up there. A group of hunters said that he called himself Quindar and that he wanted to be left alone. A few groups of Players have gone up there since his warning. All of them were revived at the Altar of Rebirth.

"Apparently, he's really powerful to kick the Player's asses." Gar shook his head.

Dave looked to Induca and Malsour.

"That isn't even the worst part! The mountain keeps on shaking and people are swearing that it's growing! It's been bad for business. No one is moving from Nadorf to Komo for fear that he might take it as a slight and attack."

"So, nothing is going down the road?"

"Nothing. People are too scared. There are plenty of traders looking for Players who might be interested in providing security. Though they want a freight bond," Gar said.

"Freight bond?" Dave asked.

Gar squinted at Dave. "Sorry. Thought you were a few levels higher. The way you hold yourself, I could swear that you're a bit stronger than your level," Gar said, apologetically.

"No worries." Dave smiled, happy to have Gar underestimating his skills.

"So, a freight bond is basically an insurance policy. If someone is moving freight or protecting it, then they need to get a license that if they lose their freight that they get something in return. They're backed by the traders' and fighters' guilds. Some kingdoms like the Per'ush also offer them. There's nothing as binding as an agreement with a Per'ush trader."

"I didn't think that many people would want to leave Per'ush. It sounds like quite the marvel," Malsour said.

"Oh, it is. The smartest and brightest go there. Biggest and most revered mages guild in all of Emerilia. It's turned them into a center of magical innovation for centuries. Now, if you've got all that smarts hanging around and you're stuck on some floating rocks, you're going to have a few people experimenting with different things. Those experiments have requirements.

"The mages guild has a bunch of people who need materials and everyone needs food. They've got traders who span the world, selling Per'ush's magical wares and buying up the world's delicacies in food. The fact that they have the mother gate makes them the most powerful continent. It's why all of the other powers play nice with them. No one wants to piss off Per'ush and their mages' or fighters' guild."

"Fighters' guild? I thought that they just had the mages college there," Dave said.

"Well, they did in the beginning, but after getting their asses kicked by a bunch of fighter Players a few years back, they started thinking that just casting spells left them weak. Now *all* of their students train in the martial skills *and* the magical. There aren't many spellswords, but they might be able to hold their own in a bar fight." Gar shrugged.

Dave waved the skill away by making it look as though he were scratching his beard. He felt that Gar was a talkative guy and not having many people around had made him get a bit bored.

"So, this Dragon—when did *he* show up?" Induca said.

Dave's eyes slid to Malsour and Induca. *Seems that they might know the angry Dragon.*

"About nine days ago. It was really bad timing. It was just as we got the timber from the Asha-moor forest."

"Hmm, well, our guildmaster might be interested in talking to these traders who want protection. Where might we find them?"

"Best place is over at the traders' guild. They're debating whether to go to Milheilm with their load, which would double or triple the time it would take. Those roads in the early spring aren't the nicest—more mud than gravel." Gar winced.

"That doesn't sound like a good time at all." Dave shook his head.

"Do you want a drink? We've got a decent selection of beers and even some Elven liquors if you've got the silver for it." Gar smiled.

"I'll take a beer—they'll take some of that Elven stuff." Dave nodded to Malsour and Induca. "Might as well make that three since Deia will want some as well."

"A man who thinks of the lady is a smart man indeed." Gar laughed, quickly selecting a beer for Dave, filling it and passing it back before he moved to the rear counter, putting ice in three glasses and pouring some amber liquid out of a silver-looking flask on top.

"Do you want to start a tab?" Gar asked.

"I have a feeling that you know the ways of my group a bit too much." Dave grinned, taking the beer and saluting Gar with it.

"Ahh, I've seen the Stone Raiders a time or two and you are a rowdy bunch." Gar laughed as Dave took a drink.

"Ohh, now that is beer!" Dave looked at the contents of his mug.

Gar laughed again. "Well, we aren't going to give you that pig swill that other places might have. Make that stuff right here on the premises."

"Hmm, well, I've been doing some experimenting with my own alcoholic concoctions. Would you mind trying a few? I'm trying to get a certain flavor but I haven't *quite* figured it out."

"Thanks for the drink, Dave. I'm going to retreat somewhere far away from this brewing discussion!" Induca grabbed Deia's drink and headed for the stairs that led up to the second floor.

Dave, Malsour, and Gar turned to one another and shrugged.

"Okay, so first I've got this kind of lager here." Dave reached into his bag, not actually pulling anything out but conjuring one of the many beers that he had put into the cold storage he'd made inside the seeder.

Gar smelled it. He took a sip and moved it around in his mouth before he spit it out into a sink.

No light bulbs but they've got some kind of sewage. Hopefully the new pipes hitting the market will sort out that whole running water issue as well as the heating box. I miss taking showers.

"Not bad. Didn't warm the hops enough and I'd go with an Adurn-made cask instead of the Gorla—less of an overpowering taste and would nicely complement the other flavors in the beer," Gar said.

Dave nodded, looking through his notes on brewing as well as other information on the things that he was talking about.

"Hmm, okay, what about this one?" Dave pulled out another mug.

"How many beers do you have in there?" Gar laughed.

Dave smiled. It was hard not to with Gar. "'Bout fifteen beers and seven liquors. Though five of the beers are just working proto-types to try to get my final product."

"He's been trying to make this dark beer from his homeland; been working on it for months, but he's not there yet. His attempts taste pretty good, though. Oh, and his fiancée made him move all of his distilleries out of the house."

"I am truly sorry for your loss," Gar said solemnly, snorting and taking another swig of the next beer as he chuckled at Dave's misfortune.

Chapter 12: Job Opportunity

Suzy was just drifting off to sleep when there was a knock at the door.

Nope, you didn't hear anything. It's just your imagination. Just go back to sleep and everything will be fine.

The knocking continued as Suzy moved in her bed, making annoyed noises.

"Suzy, need your business mind!" Dave said through the door, his words a bit slurred.

"It's four thirty in the afternoon!" Suzy yelled back.

"Come on, I'll buy you a drink afterwards and make you one of the rune necklaces to train up your magic!"

Suzy tossed the sheets back and pulled on fresh clothes from her bag. She opened the door and gave Dave a dark look. "What?"

"Okay, so, there are a bunch of traders in town. They want to get to Nadorf, but there is a Dragon in a big ole mountain that doesn't want people annoying it.

"I have it on good authority that the Dragon just meant that it didn't want people on its mountain. Now someone needs to talk to the traders and see if they would be interested in hiring our services for the trip. I talked to Josh, Dwayne, and Kim. They like the idea but then they're not the best people for making trading agreements. They're more the kind of people you talk to if you need a dungeon or raid area cleared."

Dave burped and Suzy let out a frustrated noise in response.

Quest: A road through Dragon Lands

Traders want protection and guarantees that their freight will reach Nadorf. They're scared that Quindar, whose lair is near the road, will attack them.

You have it on good authority that Quindar will not attack the traders.

Requirements: Make an agreement between the Stone Raiders and the traders to protect them and their goods.

Failure: Get the traders killed or their goods damaged

Rewards: Whatever's in the contract you come up with

Increased standing with the Traders' Guild

Do you accept?

Y/N

"So, then you volunteered my services?"

"Something along them lines." Dave smiled.

As much as she wished that she was still having her nap, she couldn't stay annoyed at Dave for long. "All right, you goof—where are they?"

"Down at the traders' guild. Induca is interested, so she'll go with you."

Anna came out of her room. "Sounds interesting. I'll tag along."

"Damn, those ears are good."

Anna rolled her eyes at Dave's words, smiling a little.

Induca and Deia came out of Dave's room, both of them sipping on a drink.

"Babe, we're going to get some supplies. You got some extra gold?" Deia asked.

"Some things stay the same no matter which planet I'm on," Dave muttered, passing Deia his pack.

"Thanks, babe." She kissed his cheek. She pulled out a small number of coins and put them into her coin pouch on her hip. "Once we're done with all of the trader talk, I say that we go on a little shopping trip. I don't know about you all, but I need some new clothes!"

Suzy watched Dave's smile, his eyes on Deia. It showed his happiness at seeing Deia happy. It was a smile of his that she'd seen a few times when someone had made a breakthrough and Dave left to leave them to their victory.

She laughed and Dave pulled her close, giving her a kiss.

Suzy hadn't seen him that way with anyone else. The two of them just clicked, their eyes shining as they looked at each other.

"All right, boss lady. Well, you girls have fun. Malsour and I are doing some taste testing." Dave grinned.

"Well, don't get too drunk. I have to carry your heavy ass to bed," Deia chastised him, hitting his chest.

"I'll try, dear."

They moved to leave and Dave tapped Deia's butt. She pouted but continued on, Dave grinning the entire time.

"Does anyone know anything about this whole thing?" Suzy asked.

"Ahh, well, Quindar isn't a he, but a she and she's also *really* pregnant. I'm thinking that she came and made Opheir her home. Fornau is probably on the mountain too, and by the earthquakes, it seems that he is expanding the mountain and making it more comfortable for Quindar. He's an Earth Dragon; she's an Air Dragon. In the later stages of being pregnant, a Dragon cannot change their form to Human so they need somewhere to be away from Human eyes to birth and raise their young." Induca looked around to make sure that no one was listening in.

"So, what does Quindar's pregnancy have to do with the traders?" Suzy asked.

"Well, she told everyone to piss off of her mountain and the people in the area took that to mean the entire area. The mountain is really close to the road from Komo and Nadorf. Now people are scared to move their goods down the road. With you Humans, fear can quickly turn into anger and rage. So, it's in everyone's best interests that we show them that it is fine to walk down the road and that Quindar isn't going to mess with them.

"We show them that Quindar is just living on her mountain and that if you don't piss her off, then you're completely fine."

"So, it might not be good to gouge the traders so heavily that afterwards they're angry for paying us so much to go down a road that was completely safe," Suzy said.

"Ehh, that's all your business, though Gar did mention that they would want a freight bond for their goods," Induca said.

"Makes sense. On such a risky thing, I'd want some securities as well. Deia, could you ask the leaders and see if we do have one? Otherwise I don't think we'll even get to really having a conversation."

"I'll send them a message," Deia agreed.

They wandered around the town, taking a long route to the traders' guild.

"Damn, Anna—you need to relax," Induca said after a while.

"Just checking around. Not all of the POE or Players are that friendly." Anna's eyes swept around the area.

"Yeah, but with us three to back you up, anyone who messes with us is in for a nasty surprise, and well, I bet me and Deia can barbeque them faster than you can swing that big ole hunk of metal." Induca smiled.

"Some have said that the Dracul are the most powerful with their mouths," Anna said.

Induca snorted while Deia shook her head.

Suzy felt a flush reach her cheeks.

"Ah look, you made Suzy think all kinds of naughty things! Come on, Anna, aren't you the oldest and most mature of us all?" Induca put her arm around Suzy as if comforting her.

"Don't let the she-bot make you all scared about what our mouths can do. I know that many Dracul have had quite the praise for how our mouths work." Induca gave her a wink.

Oh God.

Anna laughed, deep and hard. Induca joined in as Deia chuckled.

"So, Suzy, how come you were never interested in Dave?" Induca asked.

Deia turned around and glared at Induca.

"What? She's a good-looking girl and they've known each other for years but it's clear as day that there's nothing going on between them," Induca said.

"Well, uhh, I don't really..." Suzy felt her fear rise at the secret that she'd kept for several years. Austin had been her shield against others' prejudices. Coming to Emerilia, she had come to not only meet his friends but become friends with them as well.

Now or never. Either they are grossed out and leave or not. Better that they accept you for everything than just parts.

"I don't really like men," Suzy said awkwardly, looking away and expecting their disgust and confusion.

"Okay, well then," Induca said, a smile spreading across her face.

Suzy felt even more nervous, her cheeks turning red as she looked away.

"Women are *much* more fun than men," Induca said with a saucy wink.

"Be gentle, Induca," Anna said.

"But what if she likes it rough?" Induca smiled into her drink and looked to Anna. It was now Anna's turn to go red in embarrassment before laughing.

"Dwayne just got back to me. It seems that they do have a freight bond for fifty thousand gold." Deia sounded impressed.

Suzy was thankful for the break from Induca's teasing.

"Okay, so let's go and talk to the traders." Suzy turned up a street to take the most direct route to the traders' guild.

Suzy hadn't ever been to Komo, but the other Stone Raiders had. They routinely shared their maps with one another. Suzy had a map of all Komo as well as some of the surrounding area. Another good thing about those who were off training was that they were building up maps of other continents and different cities.

Suzy had originally thought of the Stone Raiders as a bunch of jokers. Now that she saw their inner workings, they still were a bunch of jokers, but they were smart jokers. It was as if she joined the Rock Breakers as they were starting to get bigger. There was an excitement that filled her, thinking of what the Stone Raiders might become. How it could grow and how she could be a part of that.

She walked into the traders' guild. There was a notice board to the right side of the wall, broken up by different kinds of jobs. Tables were all over the place, with booths against the left wall. Stairs led to a balcony above and rooms for passing traders. Underneath the balcony were a bar and kitchen. Suzy saw to the left there was a large doorway that led into a warehouse.

The traders' guild provided jobs, food, drink, lodging, and storage at a discounted price, and had multiple contacts within the towns they were based in. Being part of a traders' guild wasn't a necessity but it was strongly advised.

Suzy walked up to the bar, where a strong-looking lady was pouring beers and putting them onto a waiting tray before a server whisked it off to a group's table.

"What can I do you for?" The woman wiped her hands on her apron as Suzy approached.

"Hello, my name is Suzy Markell. I am representing the Stone Raiders guild. I heard that there were people looking to move their goods toward Nadorf and looking for some protection," Suzy said.

"You think you and your pixie club friends can defend a bunch of traders against a Dragon?" the Elf asked, clearly not impressed with Suzy and her party.

"Miss Potts, we're but one party of the Stone Raiders. There are over a hundred members of the Stone Raiders in this town heading for Nadorf. They fought alongside the Mithsia Dwarves and Kufo'tel Elves against Boran-al's cultists, masters of necromancy and the black arts all above level one hundred and with an Undead Demon Lord and won. I think providing protection for some traders would be an easy job," Deia said, using her analysis to find out the woman's name.

Potts seemed to weigh Deia's words and look her over. "You're not a Player, are you?" Potts asked.

"I am Oson'Deia of the Kufo'tel Elves," Deia said.

Potts's eyebrows rose, apparently impressed. "You related to Oson'Mal?"

Deia's eyes thinned. "He's my father."

Potts's face split into a grin. "I heard he had a daughter but I haven't seen the old codger for some time. I wouldn't think of him to raise an idiot and I've heard about the citadel." Potts looked around, leaning closer, and lowered her voice. "Is it as bad as they say? Did the Earth Lord really band with the Dark?"

"It is worse. The Dwarves and Elves took high casualties. The Players lost nearly three-quarters of their numbers." It was Deia's turn to look around. "The Dwarves are raising their walls."

Potts leaned back, shaking her head. "Messy business, that. I still remember Asha-moor. After that, no lord or lady of Affinity is going to get my devotions." Potts shook her head. "You're going to want to talk to Jaek. He's the jaguar-looking fella over there with all the piercings."

Suzy saw the man soon enough. He and those with him wore some rather exotic clothes that looked better suited for a warmer climate.

"Thank you," Suzy said.

"Just make sure you get them there in one piece. They've already spent a ton on storing their wares." Potts turned to a server with another order for drinks.

Suzy turned and headed to the table where Jaek and his three companions sat.

"What brings you to our table, High Elf?" Jaek looked to her. He looked to be a Demi-Human, like Anna. His eyes slid over to Anna. A frown crossed his face.

"Miss Potts said that you might be interested in an escort down to Nadorf," Suzy said.

"I might, but I need a freight bond. I'm not going to take my goods down there without some guarantees." Jaek's head turned to Suzy; his other friends looked over Anna.

"How much of a freight bond do you require?" Suzy asked.

"Twenty-five thousand gold at least."

"What goods are you transporting?" Suzy asked.

"How do I know you're not raiders?" Jaek fired back.

"While we are called Stone Raiders, it's because we go on dungeon raids. We are one of the most well-known guilds in all of Emerilia. If we were to take your goods, then it would spoil our reputation," Suzy said.

"Why would you care about your reputation?"

"Kingdoms send us a message to ask us to clear out their lands of monsters and clear dungeons and raids that they can't deal with. If we want others to ask us the same, we're not going to start raiding people who are just looking for some added protection. If we took your wares that are worth a possible twenty-five thousand gold, then we're just shooting ourselves in the foot for how much gold we can make off of raids and dungeons that kingdoms inform us of," Suzy said.

Jaek held her eyes for a few minutes before he nodded slowly.

"Very well, come with me. I will show you our goods then we can talk bonds and expenses." Jaek stood and headed for the door. His fellows followed behind the four ladies.

"Deia, could you send a message to Josh or the higher-ups? If they want to do more protection details, then it might be an idea if they were to join the traders' guild and then we could put some postings on the walls here for people to contact us if they need protection down to Nadorf," Suzy said.

"Well, Dave is already part of the traders' guild—Wis'Zel and Kol talked him into it. I can use his reputation to put up a posting," Deia said.

"Ahh, I forgot about that." Suzy opened up her interface's notepad, going to the tab about Dave's businesses, and entered a note about asking the Stone Raiders whether they wanted to do their interactions through Dave's position in the traders' guild.

"You mean Wis'Zel, the ceramics factory foreman?" Jaek asked.

"You know of him?" Suzy asked.

"Yes. I come from Heval's plains. I came here gathering frost giants fat and skins." Jaek led them toward the warehousing district.

"I thought that the plains of Heval were extremely warm?"

"They are. The frost giant's fat is a great insulator and actually cools a home. Their skins also have a chilling effect. I was passing through Omal after trading in For-Dohl and I met up with Wis'Zel. We got talking about building materials and how he had bricks and these shingles that allowed a home to be airy and bright instead of having to make out homes from thick stones. He also talked of the heating and cooling systems that his boss was developing. We became friends and I hope to visit there again when I can. If it is as he says, then I will not need to go to the southern cities of Opheir on my next trip."

"Why are you going south?" Induca asked.

"Well, we got a large amount of timber for cheap and are going to take that down to trade in Nadorf. Our spices and fruits can fetch a good price down there. We sell and move cargo till we reach Zeleheam and then we will chart a ship back to Heval. Taking foods, frost giant materials, some of those ceramics and fabrics found in Mikaow," Jaek said.

"That is quite the journey," Deia said.

"It keeps things interesting, though with a Dragon all pissed off it is costing us dearly." Jaek signaled to two lizard Demi-Humans who stood in front of a warehouse.

Both of them were bundled up in furs, with their weapons clearly visible. They nodded and opened the doors as Jaek walked through with the party in tow.

Suzy looked over the wagons that were stored in the place. There must've been thirty or forty packed into the warehouse.

"We have twelve carts filled with lumber, eight with spices and rarities from my lands. Seven with frost giant parts. Three with tiles and the rest have an assortment of personal trading goods and trinkets for sale." Jaek waved at the groupings of carts.

Suzy looked over the goods that were on display. She pulled up her notes, referencing them to the stock market tracker that tracked all of the markets across Emerilia, from the smallest town to the biggest major cities. Using that, she could start to figure out what price they had bought the materials for and what kind of profits they would be expecting.

"Well, I could understand the need for lumber. It seems that Nadorf got a rather cold winter and they are all very low on fuel. The spices I don't see being useful until maybe Mikaow; their crops went in late this year due to the rains. Must be nice to be butting right on the tropical zone," Suzy muttered.

"Wow," Suzy said, looking at the latest information.

"What?" Jaek asked.

"Well, it looks like some people have got word of the tiles and bricks in Nadorf. Seems that it has started something of a trend. Since Dave is the only person with all of the blueprints to both the factories and the goods, most of the people haven't thought about building a factory due to cost. So, they're buying up all of the materials."

"How do you know this?" Jaek asked.

"I'm looking at the stock market." Suzy bit her lip in thought. *We're going to have to make a factory down there—with the demand and the cost, it would be idiotic not to. Even Earth mages are buying a single brick for up to fifteen gold just to understand how it works and then paying the fees to replicate it to make homes from the material. Having to pair up with Dark and Fire mages just to make the bricks.*

"Stock market?" Jaek asked.

"Yeah." Suzy continued to study the different goods. Something clicked in her mind as she looked to Jaek, who looked utterly confused. *No, it's not possible. How could that be possible? He's a trader but he doesn't have access to the stock market?*

Suzy looked at her interface, her eyes going wide.

Jaek was a POE. She'd checked the forums to see how there were Players working as merchants and making an absolute killing off it. Now she understood why. They had a massive advantage: they could see the trend and check on reports from the various cities around them in real-time. Having a Player working with a group of traders was worth their weight in gold, maybe even Mithril. Constantly updating the markets, knowing what to buy in one town to sell in another. Not just making wild guesses based off their experiences the last time they went through a town.

Jaek was working on four-month-old information.

"Uhh, sorry, just have people I know in the other cities who are passing me information." Suzy smiled.

Jaek nodded. "How much are those tiles and bricks going for?"

"Now that would be telling. Potts might know someone in the city who could give you a better estimate." Suzy turned her attention to the goods. She focused on them, checking her stock market prices against the different materials. Her notifications started blinking and she opened it up.

New Passive Skill: Trader

Level: Novice Level 3

Effect: 9% chance people will give you preferential treatment. 3% better prices with those who see you as friendly.

New Passive Skill: Evaluator

After spending time looking at stock markets and looking at different goods, you're starting to understand the real value of the goods in front of you on an almost instinctual level. Maybe later you can look at a good and you just *know* how much you could get for it in different towns. Might even be able to predict the market. Who knows?

Level: Novice Level 2

Effect: You can roughly estimate the price of some goods that you have background information on (+/- 25% of object's value). The higher quality an item and the less information you have on it, the less accurate your guess.

Suzy read the second notification again and scratched her head. She swiped it away, continuing to look at goods. A faint glow surrounded the spices she was looking at.

Akamaran Spice

29 gold per ounce (Limited information +/-65%)

Origin: Havel Plains

"Well, that might be useful." Suzy scratched her head and looked at another object. Another information screen showed up.

After twenty minutes, she had an estimate.

"All right, we'll do it for twenty thousand bond and three hundred gold," Suzy said.

Jaek rubbed his chin. "Twenty-one and two sixty."

"Twenty-one and two hundred," Suzy shot back.

"You said that you're traveling with Dave, the owner of the ceramics factory. If you get me a meeting with him, then we have a deal."

"Done, though I don't know how lucid he's going to be. He's been drinking for a bit." Suzy looked to Deia, who shrugged.

Chapter 13: Dragons and Driving

"We should see if anyone is into a game of tree tag," Deia said as they jogged. They had a caravan of nearly two hundred trader wagons making its way down the road with all of the Stone Raiders and their guards out and checking the area.

"Yeah!" Induca agreed as Dave shook his head.

The caravans moved slightly faster than walking pace but it was significantly slower than all of the Stone Raiders could now travel.

Dave knew that Deia was going a little nutty just waiting around. He'd been expecting the game to come up in the last two days. A smile crossed his face as he thought of the energy she'd had after coming off of watch last night. *Maybe it's not so bad going slow.*

Deia looked at him, staring as if she were trying to understand his thoughts. Dave just smiled back as her look became suspicious.

"I'll see if Josh is game." Deia looked forward again.

"Okay, just work on putting some more power into it," Anna said.

Dave turned to see another one of Suzy's creations start moving and writhing in her arms. This one looked like some kind of freaky doll made from dirt mud and a few sticks. Dave shivered. "That is just unnatural."

"I think it's kind of cute," Induca said.

Dave and Malsour shared a glance and shook their heads.

Then the damned thing started *moving.*

"I think I'll go and ask Josh personally," Dave said, leaving the freaky-deaky doll behind him.

"What's up, Dave? You joining in on the tree tag?" Josh asked as Dave made it up to the Stone Raiders leader.

"Yeah, as long as it gets me away from that damned doll thing Suzy is playing with." Dave shuddered.

Kim started to laugh. "Getting freaked out by an animated doll."

Dave could feel it coming close before he saw it. "Well, look for yourself."

"Oh, that is weird as fuck." Dwayne looked at the kind of awkward stick and mud figure that was quickly waddling toward them.

"Just like a mud baby." Kim patted the thing as if it were some kind of adorable puppy.

"It's like Chucky turned to mud and left his knife behind," Lucy said, getting as far away from the thing as possible.

"Okay, let's go play some damn tree tag." Josh peeled away to go talk to the other parties.

"I second that." Dwayne followed him.

"I'll see you in the trees!" Dave snuck around the wagons and went back toward his group.

"You have fun." Lucy's carpet appeared; she jumped on it and sailed away from Kim and over the wagons.

***

Tree tag was a game that the Wood Elves had come up with due to their high Agility and need to constantly challenge themselves and one another to be the best that they could be. The Elven rangers were some of the best at tree tag. It was simple: You touched the ground and you were it; you were touched by someone who was it, you then had to go on to hunt for the others.

There were five people who were "it" and then twenty who weren't.

"Go!" Josh said as Deia, Josh, Dwayne, and two other Stone Raiders ran up toward the trees that ran along the caravan's route.

Deia jumped from tree to tree, using branches to swing herself forward, chasing the people who were racing away from them. She saw Dave and Induca run toward the wagons, jumping on them before jumping into the trees on the other side. Four more Stone Raiders followed them, one hitting the ground.

They cursed, dusted themselves off and ran back up into the trees, now chasing their previous allies.

Deia jumped off a tree, rolling over the top of a wagon and planting her foot as she rolled up and threw herself toward the other side of the road.

She used Earth magic to bend a tree's branch into her reach. She grabbed it and continued the chase. Her smile turned predatory as the group she was chasing split up.

The rules for tree running included the ability to use magic, but it could only be on yourself, unless there were people who didn't have magical abilities. With the Stone Raiders, all of them had at least one magical ability and they were using them constantly.

Deia jumped, narrowly missing a runner who dropped three feet, pushed off a branch and moved as fast as they could away from Deia and the now two tagged Players. Deia moved closer to Dave, who was running full out. He had improved his Agility and Strength greatly over the last couple of months and he was doing a lot better than the Stone Raiders.

Though the teacher doesn't teach the student everything!

Deia jumped past Dave, igniting the air to her side, which changed her trajectory, right onto Dave.

He yelled as she tapped his butt.

"Not fair!" He turned and swung around, landing on a tree limb.

Deia grinned and jumped onto a branch higher than him.

"So, who are we taking out next?" Dave looked around at the tagged and the runners.

"That one?" Deia pointed at an Air mage who was laughing and escaping two other people who were it.

Dave grinned and looked to Deia. "Looks good to me!" Dave jumped from the tree. Deia moved with him, keeping pace easily.

It was exhilarating to chase people down one by one, but working with Dave made it all the more exciting. They quickly closed on their prey, working together with little need for words.

Dave jumped early, making the Air mage dodge, only to have Deia drop out from the higher limbs and brush their shoulder.

"You're it!" Deia said.

"Damn it!" the Air mage muttered.

"Sorry!" Dave laughed; Deia grinned with the thrill of the chase. They watched their party chat as people relayed where groups of untagged people were.

***

A golden light descended on Bendel as he and his hunting group moved away from their prey, a group of goblins that had been playing bandits on the road from Nadorf to Iska.

"Bendel, what the hell is going on? You get some special loot?" Gillie pulled down her rogue's hood and looked at him.

"I dunno." Bendel turned his hand to check out the golden light as he shifted the large axe over his shoulder.

Quest: Dragon Hunter

You have felt the touch of the Lady of Light. She believes that there are dangerous dragons in the area. You have proved yourself a worthy fighter and follower of the Lady of Light. Gather your party and anyone you wish to join you and clear the threat of the dragons from Opheir.

Rewards: 1,000 gold per Dragon

Increased Affinity with Light

Stat point increase comparable to efforts

One piece of Light gear from rank Rare to Legendary

Do you accept?

Y/N

"Damn," Bendel said, linking the quest to the others.

"Shit, I say we keep him around, damned glowing lucky charm!" Justin sat on a log with his bow.

"Ha! He looks like a damned glowstick. Think you can do it again for us?" Helen quipped, tightening the wrappings on her hands.

"Where's your super awesome quest from the Lady of Light, monk?" Bendel asked.

"I don't believe in any gods out of this—I sure as shit ain't gonna think of them here. I got faith in my fists and my healing. The monk thing is just to keep the heretic part low-key." Helen winked.

Bendel snorted.

"Soo, now we're done with the dick measuring contest, what we going to do?" Gillie asked.

"You have a dick?" Justin looked shocked and stared at Helen. "It explains soo much!"

"Come here, bow dweeb. I'll show you what it feels like to have none of that useless low-hanging fruit!" Helen moved for Justin.

He laughed and jumped away, dodging her hits as they moved around the clearing.

Bendel sighed. It was to be expected; their farming hadn't gone the best and the two were looking for a better fight. With the Dragon hunt, it seemed that their boredom had turned into play fighting out of excitement.

"So?" Gillie looked at Bendel.

"I think we can safely assume it's this Dragon Quindar that we've been hearing about for a while. Also, see if anyone has any more information on it. Let's go through our friend lists, see who's in the area who can get to us in a few days and would be interested in the quest. Let's see if we can't get a good-sized party of twenty going at this thing," Bendel said.

"Okay," Gillie said.

She and Bendel took a seat, waiting for the other two to calm down and come back.

***

After a few hours, they'd done some research on the different gear that they might get, looked into the Dragon, and then contacted anyone they thought might be useful in the fight. Everyone they talked to was excited to give the quest a go.

They made a rally point with the people from Nadorf, grabbing supplies that they might need on their trek. It would take just over two days in-game to link up and head for the mountain that the Dragon was resting in.

Bendel summoned his riding bear with a whistle; it materialized in front of him. The rest of the party grouped together and got on their mounts as well.

"Well, let's go and kill a Dragon," Justin said, the last to get up on his ride.

"From the sound of it, there might be multiple dragons," Gillie said.

"More gold for us!" Justin fired back.

"I'm looking forward to the armor more," Bendel admitted.

"Just want to be all gold and shiny. I'm pretty sure we can find you some paint, Bendel," Helen said.

"Uggh, why did I agree to party with you lot?"

"Think of how bored you'd be without us!" Justin laughed.

Bendel kicked his bear into action, getting it to move forward and head for the mountain.

Chapter 14: Dragon's Potluck

Malsour watched the group return from the trees. They'd been playing tree tag all morning. It was an impressive sport; it promoted Strength and Agility growth while also working on the Player's coordination and communication. Many of them were still using incanted spells but when the game was going full tilt, many of them forgot their incantations and were using their spells on pure reflex.

Malsour wondered whether they knew what they were doing.

Using magic without incantations showed that they were highly proficient within the spell, or their Affinity, or both.

"Endal, mos'kun," Suzy said. Another doll came to life. This one was made out of mud, sticks, and rocks like the last ones but instead of being about thigh-high, it now reached the bottom of Malsour's chest.

"Good. Now another," Anna said.

She was a good teacher. And with the magical runes around Suzy's neck, the boost she was getting by being linked to a decent-sized soul gem helped immensely. Everyone in the party except Dave and Deia wore a rune engraved necklace that acted as a Magical Circuit, draining a portion of their Mana pool and charging the large soul gem that Malsour carried in his bag.

Malsour bent to his work on the back of a wagon, finishing off the last rune and imbuing the necklace with some of his power to activate the Magical Circuit before he tossed it in a pile of completed necklaces. He grabbed another necklace and got to work.

When Dave wasn't playing tree tag, he joined Malsour on one of the wagons, making more necklaces and soul gems. The gems were made in crystal form and took some time to make. A good number of them didn't form properly, so the few soul gems had multiple groups charging them.

All of the lower-level people had the rune necklaces first. Malsour would have thought that they would have given it to the higher-leveled people.

It was clear that the Stone Raiders were proud about their strength, but they also wanted to make their weakest members stronger in order to strengthen them all. Mages were the only ones who were given the runes no matter their rank or proficiency.

Now that every mage had one, they were moving to spellswords and then finally onto the melee-only groups.

Private Message: Fornau

Malsour > Hello, Fornau. We are traveling the road from Komo to Nadorf and heard that Quindar told no one to come down this road. I wanted to check if that was true and also ask if you were able to see a few visitors? If so, Induca, myself, and a few friends would like to visit.

Fornau >Hello Granduncle,

Fornau >A visit would certainly be nice. We are both going a bit round the mountain with just the two of us. Quindar is nearing her birthing time and is getting increasingly antsy. I would be interested in meeting these new friends.

Fornau >Quindar might have gone a bit overboard with her announcement to those who were on the mountain. We are fine with people using the road. We just want to be left alone while Quindar lays her eggs.

Fornau >If you could get some food on the way, it would be greatly appreciated. Quindar has been eating everything so fast that we don't have much left now that she is moving into her laying egg stage. Do not argue with a pregnant Dragon.

Malsour chuckled at his grandnephew's words and caught Induca's eye.

"What's up, Bruv?"

Malsour shook his head. "Some of the Player's words are interesting—others just shouldn't be repeated."

Induca just smiled.

I have a feeling that she's using half of the words just because I find them so aggravating.

"I have talked to Fornau. He and Quindar would like to see us if we have the time. Also, seems that Quindar ate all of their supplies, so they need some more food or else Fornau will have to go out hunting while she lays the eggs," Malsour said.

"Woo! Great great-grandnephews and nieces!" Induca smiled.

Malsour rolled his eyes.

"I heard something about eggs," Deia said.

"Well, my grandnephew and niece Fornau and Quindar have extended an invitation to us to visit them, though they need us to gather them some food before we get there. I know it is a detour so I don't expect any of you to accompany us. However, if you do want to, you can," Malsour said.

Quest: Feeding Dragons

Quindar has eaten most of the supplies that Fornau squirreled away. Fornau is asking for your help to gather more food so that he can keep protecting his wife.

Requirements: Gather 30x large animals and deliver them to Quindar and Fornau's Lair.

Failure: Do not bring enough meat within a week.

Reward: Fornau and Quindar's gratitude

Do you accept?

Y/N

"Should be okay if we run there, then run back. We move a lot faster than the wagons so we should be back in time." Dave looked to Deia.

Even without a reward, they're more than willing to help. Malsour smiled, the tension leaving his back. He would have helped anyway, but having his friends with him once again reassured him of the trust he had placed in them.

"I'll have to ask Josh, but I don't see him having any issue with it. It will also give us a way to say that we know that Quindar doesn't care about the road, just don't mess with her and Fornau's mountain."

"Quite." Malsour looked at the merchants around them. Having this many people witnessing their leaving would allow their words to carry more weight.

It might also allay their fears of Quindar, Fornau, and their brood. Fostering a good relationship with the people will give them more privacy and stop them from doing anything dumb, like trying to attack them.

"So, whoever wants to go, put your hand up," Deia said.

Everyone, even Anna and Suzy, put their hands up.

"Good. I'll talk to Josh." Deia ran off toward the leader's group.

Suzy continued to form a new doll. She was funneling Mana through the soul gem and herself in order to keep the first powered and give the second strength. It was hard work as her body wasn't used to that amount of power usage for that long. But in small amounts, it pushed her limits higher, faster.

Malsour hadn't much cared about levels and stats before, but now among the Players, he saw their rapid growth and couldn't help but get swept up in the interest and challenge of growing levels. It was hard with his high levels, but he was making slow but definite progress.

"When we come back, you should play with us, Malsour. It's really good training," Induca said.

"You mean good fun." Dave grinned.

"Well, that too." Induca laughed.

Malsour had only left his libraries and books to look after his younger sister. He didn't think that he would've had this much fun.

Or made any friends. He looked at the others covertly, a small smile on his face.

***

I HATE *running*. Suzy chased after the rest of her party. Induca was at the rear, making sure that she didn't lag behind as they ran through the forest. Her Agility and Strength had increased in leaps and bounds over the last couple of days but the others were still looking to run off of trees and over fallen trees.

While they seemed to glide through the forest, Suzy felt as if she were barrelling through like some kind of slow cannon ball.

"Just breathe and keep going. Don't worry—you'll get tree running easily enough. It's a lot of fun," Induca said.

Suzy spared her a doubting glance, keeping up her breathing as her Stamina bar slowly crept down. Not even the tea and meal before were able to keep her Stamina regeneration high enough to counteract all of her running.

"Look how much you've improved already now. It's all a matter of putting your mind to the task and then driving for that goal. Doesn't sound that fun, but afterwards it's really useful!" Induca jumped over a tree and off a tree, coming back next to Suzy. "So, what is Earth like? I've heard that they don't have magic, but technology, the kind of pre-magic systems that allow you to change the world around you."

"Wait, you said that technology was around before magic?" Suzy said as she ran.

"Well, yeah," Induca said.

"How?" Suzy took a drink from her water bottle. Those few words had made her thirsty.

"Well, technology was used to form us dragons as well as create the magical fields in the planet. While we might call magic magic, it's actually nano-machines in your body connecting to your internal power source and your mind controlling the power flow of that energy and making something out of it. At least, that's what Malsour says." Induca looked thoughtful as Suzy's eyes went wide.

I just thought that magic was some innate kind of skill or something, but it's actually technology in our bodies responding to our input.

"Wait, then what happens when I get a higher Intelligence stat? What happens to my body?"

"Well, after training so much with it, then your body adapts and grows. The more you use something, the more it grows. The more you use your Mana storage, draining it all, then the more you can store in it." Induca shrugged as if she was repeating words and only half-understanding them.

It's like a rechargeable battery but instead of it getting less charge each time you charge it, it gets the ability to store more. It makes sense the more I think about it. If these are our real bodies, then there needs to be a way to have our interface and our HUD. Our bodies must be filled with them. Then...does that mean the Jukal might have a system in there to destroy us?

Suzy fell into silence as her brain turned over with the new information as she gained a higher understanding of just what "magic" was.

***

Dave led the group, using his Touch to plot the easiest path through the forest. They'd taken down a number of deer, rabbits, and other animals that they'd found. They'd cleaned them up and stuffed them into their bags.

Suzy, upon seeing the dead animals, had quickly left and released her last meal over the back of a tree.

Anna made sure she was okay and brought her back.

"Sorry about that. Guess, I've never really seen an animal being killed." Suzy looked a bit pale.

"No worries. You Earthers are usually like that when seeing your first kill. I'm surprised Dave wasn't," Deia said.

"How do you know what my first kill was?" Dave looked up from the buck he was cutting up to put in his pack.

"Well, I don't know when your first kill was, but I know the first time that you cleaned out an animal was with that elk," Deia said.

"Wow, you were watching me then?"

"Little bit before then. Thought that you were going to miss horribly and waste the elk. Was prepared to go hunt it just so that its body wasn't wasted. That was a good shot with your bow."

"Thanks."

"Good for an amateur." Deia lowered her voice so only Dave could hear her.

"I heard that." He thinned his eyes at her.

She smiled and continued to pull the doe apart in front of her.

"Do you think that this will be enough?" Dave asked.

"I hope so. Quindar, however, is pregnant and it seems that she is not one for much reason, especially after eating all of the stores that Fornau laid in." Malsour sighed.

"Probably a good idea to get some extra. Pregnant dragons are a pain in the rear," Induca chipped in.

"Never thought about having children?" Anna asked.

"Heck, no. Love kids but damn if I want to have some of my own. All the dragons I know are fun, sure, but not someone I want to raise a brood with." Induca shook her head.

"Malsour?"

"I've thought about it once or twice, but again there are not many dragons around that I find more interesting than my books."

"Well, guess you must like us for not running off to the nearest library." Deia smiled.

"It certainly is entertaining." Malsour smiled.

Suzy ran off again to throw up. It was clear she couldn't easily handle cleaning her kill.

"I really hope she doesn't go all vegan on us. Kind of hard to eat nothing but veggies," Dave said.

"Well, there are plenty of herbs to find all over the place," Malsour pointed out.

"Yeah, but they all taste like damned weeds. Meat is the way to go," Anna said.

"Ah-greed," Dave said.

"Nothing like a nice steak and some good ole-fashioned barbeque sauce!" Induca grinned, making quite the sight as she had blood all over her cheek.

"You have barbeque sauce here?" Dave asked. It hadn't been long since lunch, but he loved himself some ribs.

"Well, of course!"

"Wooo hooo!" Dave's excitement had some birds flying away in shock. Dave got into a heated discussion on different meats and ways to cook them in Emerilia with Induca. She was an expert cook, apparently!

Chapter 15: Quindar's Lair

It took some time to get up the mountain, even with their speed and strength.

They came to a door made of stone. It was the size of two school buses on top of each other.

A man wearing simple clothes and a brown leather cloak with a green underlayer stepped out from a smaller door built into the massive one.

"Uncle, Aunty!" The man embraced Malsour, who looked awkward with the affection before turning to Induca, who hugged her nephew and grinned.

"Hey, nephew! How's the wife?"

"She's..." Fornau scratched his head. "Well, I think that she's within the last days of egg laying. She says that her body is starting to push."

Dave could see that Fornau looked a bit worried as he glanced back to the cave.

"This is Dave, his fiancée Deia, Anna, and Suzy." Malsour pointed to everyone. They shook hands with Fornau and smiled.

"So, they know?" Fornau asked.

"That you're all dragons and that you sometimes like wandering around as Humans so people don't crap their pants outright?" Dave asked.

"I like this one." Fornau snorted, his face sporting a smile. "Please come in." The door within the door opened for them.

"We also brought some food. Where would you like for us to put it?" Malsour asked.

"Well, we've got a cold room. I'll give you a tour and take you to Quindar. Something else to focus on other than laying her eggs might do her some good." Fornau smiled.

The hallway they entered was still as massive as the gate that covered it. Light holders across the walls illuminated it in warm light. The walls were smooth, with almost a polished feel. Dave could sense residual magic and odd formations in the rock.

"Did you make this all yourself?" Dave asked.

"Well, Quindar used this as her home before we were banished from here. When we were stuck on the other plane, she talked about this place a lot. When we were allowed to leave that alternate plane, we started out toward Opheir immediately.

"We didn't want to draw attention but with too many delays, Quindar felt herself unable to use her Human form anymore so we rushed to the mountain. Initially, it had a number of mobs and different creatures hiding in it. I cleared them out and Quindar told everyone to leave us alone," Fornau said.

Straight ahead, there was another small Human-sized doorway that led into an area. Fornau led them through the curving large corridor, deeper and lower in the mountain. It was still a bit chilly but Dave felt the air was warming up slightly.

"What about the mobs and the other creatures? Won't they come back here?" Suzy asked.

Dave had been having similar thoughts but she beat him to it.

"Ah, you must be a Player—interesting. I've never really seen any of you. Many of you tried to kill some of my older ancestors. Some actually succeeded. But that is an old history now," Fornau said. "To answer your question, once a creature or something makes claim to an area, they have to clear through multiple waves of the various mobs that would be found in the area; then they are able to claim it. That said, if we were to leave, then other creatures could come upon this mountain and make it their home, with Emerilia seeding it once more with different mobs and creatures."

They got deeper and deeper; the air grew from cold to warm and rather pleasant.

Fornau, Induca, and Malsour talked while Dave looked over the walls and stretched his senses outwards. He was able to create a map of the mountain within his mind as he marveled at the work that it must've taken to turn a series of caverns into a truly massive home.

A massive white Dragon looked down at them with her white eyes as she shook herself, rising her head to greet them.

The domed room had a few other massive tunnels leading downward. Otherwise, there was a Human-sized doorway and a few balconies and windows in a structure to the right of the corridor/ramp they had come down.

The biggest feature of the room was a large sandy pit, which the massive Dragon was lying in.

"Hello, Aunty and Uncle. It is good to see you," Quindar said, a tired but happy smile on her face.

"Well, you're looking mighty bigger than when I last saw you, little niece!" Induca said.

"Thank you, Aunty." Quindar snorted.

"These are our friends." Malsour waved to the others. One by one, they went through their names.

"I did not think that you of all people would be interested in going on an adventure." Quindar looked at Malsour.

"Well, he couldn't leave his darling sister behind. Mother would be rather angry with him if he just off and left me with a bunch of strangers," Induca said, hanging off Malsour's arm.

Quindar let out a barking laugh as Fornau smiled at the two's antics.

"We brought some food, though this time I hope you refrain from eating all of the stores," Malsour said, obviously taking on the elder role.

"I was so hungry and it smelled so good," Quindar complained.

"Between the laying of your eggs and their hatching, you are at your most vulnerable. We brought a good number of animals with us so you will hopefully not need to go hunting."

"Thank you, Uncle." Fornau sounded relieved.

Dave could understand. There were plenty of beings who wanted to harm and hurt other creatures. Killing a couple of dragons would go a long way in growing someone's skills. He didn't even know the kinds of things that one might be able to sell from a Dragon's body but he hoped he wouldn't find out.

"Show them where the cold storage is. I will be fine with Induca and Malsour," Quindar said.

"Are you sure?" Fornau asked.

"Yes," Quindar said, sharing a smile with Fornau.

"Very well."

Quest: Feeding Dragons

You have supplied Quindar and Fornau enough meat for them to look after their new brood without needing to leave their lair.

Reward: Your standing with the dragons of Emerilia has turned from **Friendly** to **Ally**

+6,500 EXP

"Pass me your packs," Dave said.

Malsour and Induca did so without hesitation. Giving someone the ability to take and use their soul-bound satchels was a pretty big show of trust.

"Thanks," Dave said, knowing that the two of them thought nothing more of it.

Fornau guided them out of the large room and through another one of the tunnels.

"This place is massive. How long did it take you to make it?" Dave asked.

"A few weeks, though I've been working on extending it and growing the mountain. We're going to need more room for the kiddos and it gives me some time away from Quindar when she's not too happy." Fornau smiled at the party of six.

"Smart man," Deia said. The other four women smiled and nodded as Dave gave Fornau a commiserating look.

***

"Well, that is one big ass damn door!" Justin said. A few people rolled their eyes; a few others snorted in amusement. "Do dragons even need doors?"

"Well, do you like to leave your door open all the time?" Wallace asked.

"Depends how warm it is or how many honeys are walking by. Easier than having to open the door for all of them."

"The only *honeys* you get around your house are the ones trying to steal your damned game pod, or trying to get back at you for cheating on them," Helen said.

"Hey, I'm a nice guy once you get to know me!"

"I know you and you aren't," Gillie said.

"Well, I think that we should dismount. Let's get those buffs going and everyone check that you have those potions and weapon classes ready on your hot bar. And Justin?" Bendel looked to the archer as he jumped off his horse.

"Yeah?"

"Shut the fuck up," Bendel pleaded.

"Ahh, sorry—my Internet connection just went weird. Can't understand what you said. The oddest thing." Justin grinned.

"That works with radios and cellphones—not Emerilia, dumbass," Jocelyn said, dismissing her mountain lion.

"So, what's the plan, Bend?" Wallace walked up beside Bendel.

"We find the Dragon, kill it, soak in the rewards," Bendel said.

"How powerful are dragons?" Wallace asked, his voice low.

"No fucking clue, but we've got twenty people level 60 to 83." Bendel shrugged.

"That's true. Well, I hope like hell that this works," Wallace said.

"It better. That Light gear stuff is some of the rarest shit around. It's why the monetary reward was so damned low. Hell, I'd forgo all the other rewards just for a higher chance to get Legendary armor."

"Damned heavy armor freak!" Wallace chuckled. "You been giving your devotions to the Lady of Light?"

"Always. I think it's part of why we got this quest. I made sure to give her a bit more today—hope it raises our chances for higher level gear."

"That whole devotion system is weird. Give some floating blob some power so that they might give you rare quests, gear, and all the rest? Sounds screwy as hell to me."

"Ahh, you are just not a believer in the great Lady of Light. If you have a few moments, then I would love to tell you more about our great lady."

"Fuck off, Jehovah," Wallace deadpanned. He snorted and rolled his shoulders before he hefted up his axe on one shoulder. "Well, how about we go and ask this Dragon if they are interested in hearing more about our great Lady of Light?"

"That's it! For Christmas, I'm going to send messages to every damned Jehovah's Witnesses missionary around your home and say that you are having a crisis of faith."

Wallace winced. "Well, good thing you don't know where I live."

"IP trace, fucker!"

"You don't know how to do that shit."

"Well, I could find someone who does!" Bendel laughed and shook his head, looking around at everyone. "All right, let's get a move on!"

People talked as they made their way toward the massive stone door. The heavies moved to the front line. The rogues moved in behind them, the mages and ranger attackers in the rear.

Buffs were applied; different symbols appeared on everyone's status bars while their bodies were covered in myriad colors. The side panel with the party's members showed the same symbols under their names.

Thank God I just have to worry about hitting things. Never been one for the support class, watching status bars, thinking of spell combos and all that.

They got to the door. Bendel moved to the door that was within the large gate. He pushed it but it didn't budge. It felt as though it were part of the door.

"Knock, knock." Bendel activated different skills, bringing his axe across.

A few chuckled at his words as he slammed his axe into the door. Cracks ran out for two feet.

Bendel hit again. Others added in their powers, working to break the gate without wasting all their power. It took five minutes and then the gate started to fall apart. Its stone collapsed, making everyone run for cover. The dust settled and people moved back to their original positions.

"Anyone home?" Justin yelled, turning and putting his hand up to his ear to try to hear for anything below ground.

"Well, shit, sounds like they didn't even hear us knocking. Might as well go inside and check out what's going on." Justin grinned.

"Damned circus clown," Wallace said as they walked over the door now turned to rubble.

"Hey, I'll let you know that is a very prestigious occupation!"

A roar, inHuman as it was powerful, rushed to meet them.

"Well, seems that someone is home and they're not too pleased about our being here." Justin looked at everyone.

Bendel secured his grip on his weapon. He'd be lying if that roar hadn't just made him a teensy bit anxious about what he was going to face.

Chapter 16: Uninvited Guests

Dave, Deia, and Anna were pulling out the various meats and food that they had caught, putting them onto different racks and cleaning them.

Fornau was also helping out and talking away. It seemed that he was a bit nervous about the fact that Quindar's laying was coming so soon.

"Really, thank you for all of this. This is great," Fornau said.

"No worries. Happy to help out." Dave smiled. He'd gotten a lot better at skinning and cleaning his kills after the elk from a few months ago. He'd been inside Emerilia for nearly ten months now but it felt as if it had been much longer. As if his life as Austin Zane was just a memory of someone else's life.

There was a cry of pain, distorted and made odd by the sealed room they were in.

"Fornau!" a voice bellowed from below.

Fornau rushed forward, his face pale. Dave was barely able to track the man's speed.

The rest followed.

"Well, looks like we came just in time for the messy bit," Induca said.

Quindar gave her an annoyed look but didn't have the time to say anything as her body shook once again.

"Dave, stay here. Deia, do you have any herbs that might help her out? Induca, you've helped with this before—guide her if you need to." Malsour snapped into action. "Anna, we're still going to need that meat later. Could you make sure that it isn't ruined?"

Deia might be the leader of their group but he knew more about this than any of the others, so they snapped to it.

"Sure." Anna turned and left quickly.

"What do you want me for?" Dave asked, feeling not at all pleased with the situation.

Fornau moved from his Human form into a large green Dragon. He put his neck over Quindar's, talking to her and comforting her.

"I want you to use your sense to make sure that the eggs are good to go and make sure that Quindar doesn't get hurt in the process. Might need you to heal her up," Malsour said.

"Cool. Dragon wet nurse—got it." Dave shook his head and closed his eyes before he extended his Touch *into* Quindar.

Extending it into animals that were not magical was kind of difficult. If something even had a glimmer of Mana, then it became a lot harder, their inner strength creating a natural protection, kind of like an organic Faraday cage. The more magic, the more problematic it was to see through it or inside it.

He cranked up the power and focused it as much as possible, getting a faint understanding of what was happening.

"Whoa, there's four eggs," Dave said.

"Look at that—only four. Much easier time than Xendai's brood!" Induca said, trying to stay positive.

Quindar groaned. Apparently, she didn't like Induca's positive statements.

"Okay, so it looks like the pointy end is pointing down," Dave said.

"Good, that's how we want it," Induca said.

There was a banging noise from somewhere. Dave didn't pay it attention as he focused on watching what was happening. *Why the hell didn't he keep this little trick a secret?*

Then there was another noise—a number of them.

"What the hell is that?" Dave asked this time, watching Deia give Malsour a bunch of herbs.

Malsour grew into a Dragon, using his front hands to give the herb to Quindar.

"Chew and swallow," Deia said.

Seems no one is interested.

Dave did something he hadn't done with his Touch before: he focused on one area with it, right into Quindar's stomach, letting the rest of his Touch spread out normally.

"Looking good." Dave's eyes flickered over Quindar's belly to check on the eggs there before he looked inside. Something pulled at his senses, as if there was something wrong. It wasn't in the focused area of the Touch. He searched for the irregularity.

"We have guests, twenty people outside the front goddamned door," Dave said.

There was a crashing sound.

"And the door just collapsed."

Quindar swallowed the herbs as everyone looked to Dave and then the long winding corridor that separated them from the cave's entrance.

"I can see the tip. All right, Quindar, you've got to push!" Induca said, breaking the silence.

Quindar let out a roar that made Suzy, Dave, and Deia duck slightly. Dave couldn't hear too good out of his ears.

"How can people get down here?" Malsour asked Fornau.

"The living quarters or through the tunnel," Fornau said.

"Fornau, cover the tunnel. Induca, tell me if you need anything. The rest of you with me. We'll go through the living quarters and stop them from getting any deeper," Malsour said.

"Anna will meet us," Deia said.

"I'll lead." Dave ran for the Human-sized apartment that stretched up into the ceiling, connecting to the doorway he'd seen when entering the mountain.

They ran through the spiral staircase, going up the dozen or so levels it took to reach the entry hall. Everyone checked their armor and gear as they ran.

They fanned out, Dave and Deia holding their bows. Malsour was in the rear with Suzy and Anna was up front, pulling her massive blade from her back.

Her change was the biggest. She wore steel that had been blackened with ebony and Mithril hammered into it in designs of wolves. The details made her look as if she were a complete wolf, with its paws and detailed claws. Dave was impressed with the quality of the work and could tell that the armor was not just simply rare.

The twenty Players were making a ton of noise as they walked forward, clearing the hall that was now filled with dust.

***

"I know the developers pride themselves on realism, but seriously, this dust shit is driving me nuts." Justin coughed.

Bendel didn't disagree with him as he tried to wave the dust away with one hand, holding his axe over his shoulder with the other. He came to a stop as he realized his party wasn't the only one in the hall. "Huh, well, are you here to kill the dragons as well?"

"Is that why you're here?" one of them asked, a woman by the way her armor was shaped. Bendel couldn't see her face within the hood over her face. Just two twin red eyes.

"Damn, that's some cool ass looking hood. Where did you get it, Oson?" Justin asked.

Bendel squinted and used his Analyze.

Oson'Deia

Wood Elf

Level 67

David Grahslagg

Half-Dwarf

Level 3

Suzy Markell

High Elf

Level 1
Anna'kal
Demi-Human
Level 127
Malsour Dracul
Human
Level 98

All of them are high levels except Suzy and that David fellow. Why the hell are they such low level? How the hell did they even get down here?

He guessed that the others must've helped them to get into the higher-level areas and protect them against the monsters in the area. It was the only thing that made sense to Bendel. He was surprised a stiff breeze wouldn't knock them over.

"I am sorry but we must ask that you leave," Deia said, apologetic but firm.

"I'm sorry, lady, but we were promised some good loot for this. We can't just leave because you want to take the bounty all for yourselves," Wallace said.

"We might be willing to band together but we're certainly not leaving this all to you," Helen said.

"We're not trying to fight the dragons. They're our friends," the one called Dave now said.

"Boy, haven't you heard? This creature said that it would kill anything that came near it! That ain't exactly friendly," Justin said.

"Of course, she did. She's pregnant. You want someone wandering around your house if your loved one was pregnant?" Malsour asked.

That made Bendel and his group pause.

"Eh, it's just a game. Seems that they just got all wrapped up in it." Helen shrugged and looked to Bendel.

The others seemed to agree. Taking down the Dragon while she was weak was the best way for them to get their loot while they could.

Bendel looked at the large hallway just a few feet from where he stood. *Must be where the Dragon is. Definitely, can't fit in the small door behind this lot.*

"Please, don't do anything rash," Dave said.

"Well, unless you can get us all suits of armor from the Lady of Light, then I'd say there ain't much you can do to stop us." Wallace shrugged with his sword and shield.

"Well, if you do attack, I can promise you that you will never be able to get into a Dwarven mountain, buy their goods, or get your gear repaired by them," Dave said.

"You've got some balls for a level 3. I'll give you that, but there ain't no way you can do that," Bendel chimed in, rolling his eyes.

"Well, I warned you." Dave shrugged.

Right then, the tunnel that led down into the large corridor seemed to shiver before earth, roots, and rocks caved in, filling the entire area. The path through the corridor had been blocked but the one behind the other group was still open.

Bendel looked to those around him. He didn't like PK'ing, but these guys were in their way and nothing was going to keep them from that reward.

With a yell, they charged forward at the other party.

***

Anna deflected a Mana bolt with a flick of her sword. A red skull now appeared over the opposing party.

Malsour and Dave cast buffs, increasing speed, regeneration, and strength and linking everyone to the soul gems.

Dave gave power to his first conjuration. An arrow appeared in his hand as he pulled it back. Identical arrows in a quiver were on his and Deia's back. They let loose with the arrows as Malsour turned the floor from dirt and stone into dangerous spikes. Three were impaled by the spikes. Malsour quickly expanded the spike that had caught them, up and through their body. Metal trees ripped through the attackers.

Suzy closed her eyes, moving her hands and talking to herself. Using the spikes and materials Malsour had been so kind to raise from the floor, she combined them with the power of her Mana. Her rune, sensing the change in the output of Mana, went from taking it to restoring it. She went well beyond her limits as her eyes glowed with magical intent.

Tentacles of dirt whipped out, grabbing those who were trying to dodge the growing field of spikes or giving Dave and Deia the opportunity to hit them with arrows.

Party Chat

Deia > Hit the lowest level targets first and work higher. Dave, as soon as they get closer, move to the front to assist Anna. Suzy, be ready with Health potions and keep up distractions.

Dave let loose an arrow into a man with a shield and mace. He'd studied everyone's weapons as they'd traveled. He pulled out a new arrow, closing his eyes and concentrating on the two-handed sword that Anna was using.

He focused; his pre-set runes flashed into existence on the blade. They were blue runes and a faint frost covered the blade. Anna swung and connected with a bear of a woman who was using her shield as a battering ram. The woman's shield was dented badly as she was diverted to the side.

Anna turned, using momentum and the weight of the sword. The woman made to deflect the blade, but it wasn't the real attack. Anna kicked the woman's shield, sending her back a few feet.

Party Chat

Anna > Malsour!

The shield maiden fell. A metal spike branching off the moving sea of them drove into her neck and then up through her brain.

Dave saw it out the corner of his eye as he watched a thin man teleport behind Anna. Dave and Deia's arrows were there to meet him. Deia's arrow worked its way through the unarmored rear of his knee as Dave's hit the man's back.

"Are you fucking kidding me!" The man used his good left leg to try to get out of the way. "I took a fucking arrow to the knee!" The man might be injured but he was still mobile and out of Anna's range.

"Dave, go!" Deia said.

Dave put his compound bow away; he grabbed his twin axes and conjured Magical Circuits on them.

Two more had fallen to Malsour's spikes. Yet the others left were using any method they had to get closer. A man with a massive two-handed axe clashed with Anna. A dull golden light surrounded him.

Anna turned and weaved away.

Dave felt strength surge through him as he brought his axes high and low. His shoulder faced the other party as a man sent a spell at him. Dave hadn't been idle. Armed with the information that he had gained on spells, the lightning bolt disintegrated, the errant power adding to Dave's reserves.

The caster looked shocked but Dave didn't have time to study them more as a man with a sword and a dagger closed in with him. Dave turned the initial attack, his axes moving out of reflex and training. He twirled his blades to deflect hits. His opponent was good, but then he used a skill.

Dave saw the positioning. With his increased Intelligence, it felt as if his mind could remember everything in his life. It was easier for him to make connections between things. In battle, one might not think that was useful.

Right now, Dave remembered watching the same skill being used in the tournament held in Cliff-Hill just a few months ago.

Dave weaved out of the way of the attack. Getting behind his opponent, he threw his axe backward and turned with it. The spike on the rear of the axe slammed into the attacker's helmet but their armor was too high to allow Dave's axe entry.

I'm making new damned axes when I get to Benvari.

Party Chat

Deia > Get down, Dave.

Dave had been too focused on the fight and not using his Touch. A rogue used this opportunity to get behind him. Dave rolled to the side. Deia's arrow slammed into their breastplate. Malsour's spikes rose up to catch them but the rogue dodged out of their way and moved in on Dave.

Dave stood up and into a fight with the dagger-wielding rogue. Dave created a Mana shield, sending it at the rogue's feet. They fell forward. Dave's point came down on the opening between their helmet and cuirass.

Dave left the axe there, jumping back and out of the way of his first attacker's long blade. Dave conjured a new axe in his hand, this one leaking gray smoke as he moved in with his attacks.

His opponent seemed to have blood on the side of his face. It looked as though Dave had hit him hard enough to wound, but not enough to put him out of the fight. Dave sensed that Anna was now fighting three people, holding them all at bay while a second was moving for Dave.

Probably think that I'm pretty easy, being a level 3 and all. A smile formed on Dave's face.

Deia came in, a maelstrom of twin blades. She cut down one of Anna's attackers, taking them out at the knees before she drove her blade up and through their armpit.

Dave conjured her a new blade as the woman she'd stabbed fell to the ground.

Anna didn't spare them a second glance. The golden glowing axe man was going for all he was worth. Anna was able to hold him and another off but the rest of the opposing party was now getting through the field of metal spikes.

Dave dodged a blast of fire, putting him right into the path of his melee attacker. Dave increased his buffs, activating his magical shield as he fought off his attacker's quick melee. Magical attacks soared between the parties and slammed into Malsour's shield.

Dave slammed his foot down on his opponent's, making them yell. The conjured axe turned into a sword; Dave extended it as fast as a spear through the attacker's neck and out the other side. Dave dismissed the sword as the attacker made weak attacks, their body already failing.

"You're pretty strong for a level 3." A woman attacked Dave with a flurry of punches and kicks that seemed to meld into one another.

"Well, you're pretty good for a bunch of Action users." Dave found the rhythm of her attacks and pressed back.

The woman's confident sneer turned into a serious frown as she found herself attacking, only to have Dave counterattack into her weaknesses.

He wasn't getting much of her Health per hit as her passive defenses were good, but he was still taking them down quickly.

She found herself on the defensive, but then her defenses were focused to block against direct attacks.

Dave slammed his axes into her armored forearms. She backed away, getting closer to the mages and archers who had been focusing on the others but now turned to Dave.

Dave slammed an axe into her arms and let loose a stream of fire from his hand as it passed over. The flames got inside the woman's open helmet, ruining her face. She fell to the ground, rolling in agony.

Dave dodged an arrow without really thinking of it and brought his boot down on the woman's head, twice.

The second time, her helmet deformed and her body started to fall away.

Dave now had the full attention of the seven mages and three archers who stood close enough to the fight that Malsour couldn't use his spikes, but far enough away that they weren't a hindrance to the five remaining melee fighters.

Dave sensed Malsour behind him. Dave ran to Deia, getting out of the man's way.

Javelins of metal fired past him. An archer fell to the attack; two of the mages' shields colored slightly with the impacts.

Malsour fired dozens of metal javelins at his two targets. They went from offense to defense quickly.

Suzy got hit with a slash of wind. It broke her barrier and sent her tumbling.

Dave looked over. She was missing her leg and arm, and her face was mangled. She was letting out painful keening noises, but there was nothing he could do.

"Deia, torch them." Dave slammed into one of the two who surrounded Deia. He watched Anna take off another Player's leg and then head in a single motion, turning it into a block that tore through another's defenses and brought a claw across their face and kicked them backward.

Dave took the attention of the Players as Deia weaved out of their attacks. She sent a blue stream of fire right through the attacker Dave wasn't fighting, melting their armor and insides, and boiling them from the inside out.

They dropped dead as Anna stopped the man with a big axe's attack with just one hand on her great sword and punched him in the face. He rolled back and then Anna was the one attacking. She came in, her attacks fast and hard, chipping away at his Health instead of trying to get through all the heavy armor he wore.

Dave focused on his fight.

"Dave, move!" Deia called.

Dave did so. A lance of plasma took off his opponent's head. Dave turned to look at Anna taking out the last melee fighter.

Two mages fired an attack at Anna. She turned; energy came from her blade and slammed into the spell, tearing it apart as she rushed forward. Malsour cracked the two mages he was working on. New spikes erupted from the ground, piercing the attackers and taking them apart.

Four mages remained. Deia created four streams of blue flames that crashed into the two remaining mages' shields.

Anna moved in on one of the last archers. Dave went for the other.

They tried to run but Suzy's creations were hiding. It tripped the archer and Dave jumped, flipping his axes around, and conjured bigger and sharper spikes on the back of them. He slammed into the archer and his axe's spikes went through their head.

He turned to advance on the two mages Deia was lighting up, only to see Deia and Malsour's spells overwhelming the mages' defenses and drive through the two casters.

"Well shit, that was pretty damned impressive," the hopping rogue said.

Anna moved toward him.

"Whoa, don't worry. Everything's sheathed and I'm the only one left. Plus..." He paused, a big grin on his face. "I took an arrow to the knee." He broke out in laughter, looking at the arrow and then everyone else. "Will you look at it? Right through! Can't make that shit up! Oh God, ah, laughing so hard I'm crying!"

Dave looked at the others and then back to the single remaining fighter. A red skull with a five-minute timer counted down above his head.

"Well, thank you for the fight. Not many people willing to go toe-to-toe with our group anymore. Guess I shouldn't underestimate you lower-level ones. Oh, and if you are going to take our gear, I'll give you three hundred gold for my gear. Kind of like the old get-up. Anyway, hope to see you again sometime! Keep my offer in mind—the name's Justin. See y'all!" Justin smiled, his hand a blur as he grabbed his dagger and slammed it into his forehead.

He dropped to the ground, his stupid smile still on his face.

Dave moved to Suzy, who was a bleeding mess at the rear of the cave.

"Hey, Suzy." Dave healed her wounds but couldn't do anything for the stumps.

"Can't repair that damage with magic," Anna said.

"I'm sorry." Deia put a hand on Dave's arm.

"Ah, no worries. We'll just kill her and then she can do a move to the party's location." Dave shrugged.

Deia, Anna, and Malsour looked at one another.

Dave created a simple dagger, putting it in Suzy's hand.

"All right, stab me and then I'll kill you. Don't want to be a PK but if you attack me and don't kill me then I attack you—it's all self-defense."

"Damn game dynamics," Suzy complained as she stabbed Dave's left hand.

A lance appeared from Dave's hand and drove through Suzy's head before she had time to say anything else.

"Dave, what are you doing?" Anna's blade moved higher.

"Well, Suzy will respawn in six hours without all of her body messed up. Then, since she's in a party with us, she can just warp to us. Sure, it'll cost her quite a bit of gold to warp that far. She'll lose some overall experience and thus levels for dying, but she earned her higher attributes instead of using her stat points at every level so she won't lose more than a few unclaimed levels that she can get back after some quests. Me killing her just put her out of her misery. It's much easier than trying to heal those wounds or deal with them. She gets a brand new body right away," Dave said.

"What will happen while she is respawning?" Induca asked.

"You just get kicked out into this place called your home. You can design it as you like, interact with a game and play with the markets. You can even re-organize your gear, sleep, shower, watch TV, and send emails. It's a bridge between Earth's simulation and Emerilia," Dave said.

"The more I think about it, the more I see how Player's dying turns into a certain tactic. Even that other one with an arrow to his knee." Deia pointed to where there looked to be a blue crystal floating. An icon showed that there was loot to be had.

"Well, let's get this all cleaned up." Dave looked at the blackened hallway filled with metal spikes.

The spikes disappeared into the ground as everyone moved to gather up the loot. Dave stored Suzy's gear in his own bag.

"Well, that could've ended a lot differently," Deia said as they worked.

"Nearly all of them were using actions. After a while, it gets easy to read which actions they're going to use, making it simple to move through them. Have to watch out though—after some time, Players will mimic certain movements but they will have complete control of their bodies, trying to lull you into a sense of comfort before they bring a hammer down on your head," Anna said.

"That has to take some coordination to know all of the movements by heart to trick someone into thinking that you're just using actions," Dave said.

"Yes, but when it's Player against Player, in the later stages they start to be the only challengers that the Humans have. Especially when the Jukal start closing the portals to the other realms and the POE have been diminished greatly due to the loss of life and subsequent loss of knowledge."

"Huh, well, I hope we don't get to that stage. Hopefully we can divert people's attentions away from fighting one another and towards fighting these damned gods. I'm getting annoyed with all the little quests and activities that they're giving their people, as if it's easy to just slaughter a bunch of POEs to disturb the power balance in their favor."

"I don't think this was about disturbing the power balance, at least not directly," Malsour said. Everyone looked towards him. "Dragons are the most complex Creatures of Power that have ever been created. It took thousands of years for the Lady of Fire to accumulate enough knowledge in order to create us. In the beginning, we weren't even able to become Human. She worked and worked until finally getting us to this stage. With, I think, a bit of help from Anna and her father."

Anna shrugged, admitting that she and her father had a role to play in their creation.

"Anna, how old are you?" Deia asked.

"Haven't you heard that it's rude to ask a lady how old she is?" Anna smiled before she sighed. "Technically, I am three years older than when Emerilia was first created."

"Huh, I think dinosaurs were still around then." Dave tapped his chin in thought, with a mischievous grin.

"Not that old. In fact, I'm about eighty years younger than Father."

"You said technically you're that old, why?" Deia asked.

"Because I went into hibernation. I placed this body into stasis, using my circuits to continue helping Father run Emerilia but keeping my emotions contained," Anna said.

Dave could see the sadness in her eyes. "Then why did he wake you up?"

"Well, that is a question for later." Anna smiled. Her eyes fell on Dave and twitched to where Suzy's corpse had been.

Dave made a thoughtful moue with his lips, his mind working over the information.

"Well, I think that it would be best if we went and saw how things are going down below," Malsour said.

The light from outside was slowly cut off as a new gate of metal rose out of the ground, with all kinds of inorganic materials weaving into the solid structure. There was a muffled noise from down below.

Dave turned, filled with more questions than when he had entered the room.

***

Deia's mind was filled with questions, as well as new realizations, she was having from fighting the Players. All of it fell away as she saw Quindar with a clutch of four eggs by her side as she curled around them.

Dave got to her first and put a hand on her side.

Quindar looked to him lazily before she looked away. She was tired from her work.

"All's looking good, momma Quindar," Dave assured her and Fornau, who was placed between her, Induca, and the corridor that led to the entrance.

"Damn! Got to have all the fun without me! So how did it go?" Induca asked.

"Well, they were some well-leveled Players, but they relied on their actions too much." Deia knew that they needed to work on fighting together; this had been their first battle and she had seen more than a few issues with it.

"Where is Suzy?"

"She got badly wounded, so Dave killed her. She should be back with us in six hours or so," Anna said.

"Wow, Dave. Cold-hearted much?"

"Better to die and get a new body, than have one that is missing a leg, arm, and half your face," Dave said.

"Remind me to not get on his bad side if I get injured," Induca said behind her hand but loud enough for everyone to hear.

Fornau moved to Quindar, putting his head on hers and giving her a reassuring coo.

Deia looked over at them. A sad smile passed over her face. She looked to Dave, who was also watching them, and put her hand in his.

He looked and smiled to her. Dave squeezed her hand and pulled her close, both of them looking at the new mother and father, focused on their clutch of eggs, their bodies warming them.

"Maybe someday that will be us," Dave said.

"After all this fighting is done and we can find somewhere safe, we'll spread kids all over Emerilia," Deia said.

"How many kids you think we're going to have?" Dave demanded.

"Well, twenty would be nice." Deia nodded, as if it were a normal number.

"You baby-crazed Elf!" Dave squeezed her hand and pulled her closer.

Deia laughed and turned back to the two new parents cleaning and checking their new eggs.

"Well, I say we give this lot some time to themselves and we get finished up with that meat! I'm hungry," Induca said.

Deia and Dave turned, and followed Induca out. Anna did as well.

Malsour looked over his great-grandnephew's and great-grandniece's eggs, as well as his grandniece and grandnephew cooing over each other and their growing family. A happy smile crossed his face before he followed the others.

I wonder what Father would look like if I were to bring a grandchild home? Where are all of these thoughts coming from? Ugghh! He shook his head at his mental ramblings.

"Well, I hope that Nadorf is a lot quieter," Deia said.

"Oh, I don't know. Heard their beds are right squeaky." Dave pitched his voice low.

Deia looked around to see whether anyone heard that. "Horny bastard."

"Who said they wanted twenty kids?" Dave grinned.

She shook her head and rolled her eyes.

Chapter 17: Not Everyone Gets Their Way

The Lady of Light slammed her fist down on her chair. Ripples of light scattered away. Suddenly, a presence started to fill the room. Light looked to the single point that it came from, watching as a flaming portal appeared in her hall.

Servants who had been walking around, attending to the small garden off to the side or walking through the gold and silver room, looked in shock at the portal.

Nothing exited the portal but you could see into it. Another woman sat in a volcano, with a black wall behind her.

"Do not deem it within your abilities to touch my children, *Light.*" Fire's eyes burned with power.

"Oh, get over yourself, Fire. You have no power here." Light dismissed the other woman, throwing away her companionship as the trivial matter that it was against her pursuit for control over the Pantheon.

"No, but my family does." Fire's face twisted into a smile that made Light's eyes thin. She noticed the shadow moved behind Fire. A head came into view, easily four times Fire's own height.

A shiver ran down Light's spine as she saw the coiled fury within the Dragon's fiery eyes—the same color as its mother, Fire, who patted it calmly.

Instead of saying words, the Dragon growled, the power of its anger making Light shiver.

The Dragon's power, even through the portal, was more than enough to rival her POE champions. The Players that Light was nurturing for the role of her champions of Light were nowhere near the stage she needed them to be to face one of these magical beasts.

With her limits gone from her champions and her beasts of power, she was lacking in her knowledge of beasts of power. Killing one of them while it was birthing would have provided her with the materials her people needed in order to create some truly powerful beast of power.

The Dragon snorted and pulled its head back. "Your time will come." The Dragon's voice spoke of power and strength.

Light looked at the Lady of Fire, knowing that she had made a grave mistake. Fire never seemed that strong because she kept on using her power to increase the strength of her dragons as well as teach those who followed her faith. She didn't take their energy but she provided guidance to them.

Fire just looked at Light, and then nodded to the Dragon. The portal closed.

For once in her life, Light saw a new kind of strength: a strength in family. Although at times it was also a weakness, if given time to grow and prosper, it could turn into something truly formidable.

The dragons had not died, but moved to another plane. Now that they were back, they were stronger than ever. Light had underestimated them. It hadn't been Fire who opened the portal; it was the Dragon. Light had never put much attention into the leveling system—she was already naturally powerful.

I wonder how many levels that Dragon has grown while it was stuck on that other plane? I wonder how many all of them have? Would it be enough to challenge even our true servants?

These troubling thoughts moved through her mind as she looked at the information that her Light follower was sending her now that he was revived. She looked at the names closely. A part of her mind remembered seeing them somewhere else.

The citadel! They were the four who did the most damage! How the hell did they get in the middle of this?

***

Bob smiled and looked to the Lady of Fire.

"Thank you for guiding your followers there." Fire bowed her head.

Denur also inclined her head to Bob.

"Oh, stop that, will you ladies? I didn't do anything. I was ready to push them in the direction but Malsour and Induca both wanted to go see Quindar and Fornau. They went of their own volition." Bob waved it away. "Oh, and they're not my followers—just my friends. Well, I guess Anna is kind of my daughter and it's too soon to tell about Suzy." Bob tapped his chin in thought.

"Well, at least let me thank you for hiding my daughter," Fire said.

"Ah, that." Bob smiled. "I thought as much."

"You didn't know that she was mine completely?" Fire's eyebrow raised.

"Well, I kind of put the mirages you were sending to the meetings and the time period of when you were pregnant together." Bob smiled while Fire paled.

"Do you think any of the others noticed?"

"No. I added in my own illusions to bolster the whole thing up and well, even if they do, I kind of like her so I'm going to do my best to see that they don't mess with her. That said, she has stepped on a few people's toes so it wouldn't be that unlikely that one of the lords or ladies starts gunning for that particular little party. She is rather like her mother in that way."

Denur snorted in agreement as Fire looked between the two of them. She shook her head as an amused laugh escaped her lips.

"Well, thank you anyway, my old friend," Fire said.

Bob bowed his head, feeling the real emotion in her voice. "Well, you can repay me by going and talking to her."

"W-what? No... I mean, she has probably forgotten everything about me... She uh...she...might, probably won't need me." Fire looked flustered as she tried to figure out what to say.

"One of these days you'll meet and if you wait much longer, I think that she might end up kicking your ass across Emerilia for being such a wuss."

"If she doesn't, then I will." Denur's big red eye looked at Fire.

"Crap!"

****

The Dark Lord looked over his preparations and the creature that lay in front of him. It was an Alturaran, made from the crystals of the planet. The once organic creatures had attached its soul to the very inorganic material of the planet in order to survive. In their past, they used to spread themselves across the stars with massive machines, taking new planets by force.

Now their machines no longer left their atmosphere and the only way to expand their territory was to use the portals into the realm called Emerilia. The Alturarans were focused; another land for them to take over and to make their own drove them with a new vigor and made them a terrible enemy to behold. If they were able to get a hold in Emerilia, they could craft machines with their abilities that would decimate the planet.

With a wave of his hand, the Dark Lord dismissed the parts of the Alturaran before him. He felt the budding power within him.

Boran-al's Citadel had released power that had been stored for centuries. That power now filled him with new vigor and strength. Enough strength for him to carry out the next part of his plan.

Now to wait until the right moment.

****

Lord Fend looked over the massive wall that extended from the frost plains to the north across the Kufo'tel forests down to the Mithsia Mountains.

"It will take one mighty force to try to attack us now," Wrole said to his lord as they looked over the massive emplacements.

Fend grunted as he looked at the walls that rose in the distance, meeting up with one another to make a complete defensive wall.

"Since my grandfather's time, we have kept these walls a secret while adding runes to them—protection, strength. Countless mages have touched these walls and made them powerful. I just hope that it is enough to keep out the forces that wish our downfall." Fend leaned on the battlements and looked out over the forest.

"High King Rean has asked that we be ready to take on more people if other mountains are attacked," Wrole said.

Fend nodded. He had been moving with his forces while Wrole had remained in Mithsia, doing his bidding and carrying out his orders. Fend's sons were still too young for the responsibility and they respected their father's orders.

"I feel that this is just the beginning—the opening moves have been played. Our will was tested and we spat in their eyes. I wish that they would leave us alone, but I know that they will not. The lords and ladies of the Pantheon are loathe to do much more than act like bickering children."

"Was it so long ago that you and your brother were so different?" Wrole's eyebrow rose in question.

"That wasn't bickering—that was good-hearted discussion! Plus, he's off being a metal banger anyway. Try to get him to come back here for family events is like building this wall from pebbles and leaves!" Fend muttered under his breath as he noticed Wrole's amused grin. "Oh, shut up, damned advisor. Feels like you're just there to make me look like some bumbling ape."

"Well, if you didn't make it so easy..." Wrole's face split into a smile.

"Why you!" Fend chased his advisor, threatening to beat his backside as Wrole laughed down the wall's line.

A few of the Dwarves looked at the commotion; a few laughed and others shook their heads at their lord's and his advisor's antics.

Chapter 18: Nadorf

Josh looked out over the wall, to look down the road they came from Komo.

The traders had been most thankful for the protection to Nadorf. They'd come across a few decently leveled monsters but they weren't much compared to the creatures that the Stone Raiders usually dealt with in their raids.

"Maybe they took a bit of a detour," Dwayne said.

"Well, I kind of bet that they did. It was a detour going to the mountain instead of coming right here, though they said that they would be here soon," Kim said.

"Ah, I think I see something." Josh saw six people run out of the forest, traveling at some speed now.

Josh walked down from the wall. Before, he would've jumped, using someone's house and the other items scattered around to break his fall. After his fight at the citadel, he kept the POE in mind as he moved around.

"Well, at least we've got trade moving again and people will stop fearing Quindar," Dwayne said.

"Well, I'm still hoping that the damned thing didn't eat them," Kim said.

"Knowing that lot, they're probably having dinner with the damned thing!" Josh snorted.

"Well, whatever it is, people are pretty happy that we cleared up Quindar's demands. Also, the fact that the dragons have said that they will be keeping the area clear of high-level mobs is pretty good," Dwayne said.

"You know how much money we're *not* going to get for having the dragons keep those roads clear?" Kim asked.

"Well, there are always bandits." Dwayne shrugged. "Plus, we're raiders, not bodyguards."

"This is true, but a bit of diversity didn't hurt. Some of the ideas that Suzy had about starting to consider trading sound like they might generate some revenue." Kim shrugged.

"You sound like Lucy now," Josh muttered.

"Did any of you look up who she and Dave are?" Lucy asked lightly, continuing to read her book and only half paying attention to the conversation.

"No. How the hell would we find out? Their faces are probably the same, but we can't really go around doing facial recognition on them. We aren't bloody coppers," Josh said.

"Hmm," Lucy said, not feeling it necessary to elaborate.

"Well, you going to tell us why the heck you just said that?" Kim asked.

"Suzy Markell is the secretary of one Austin Zane—you know, the richest guy in the world. The one who mines asteroids; has settlements on Mars, the Moon, and Earth. You know, richest man in *history*. Find it odd that she is spending so much time in here and how that she and Dave get along really well? Now, if you have a look at pictures of Suzy Markell, you notice that there's this rather dapper-looking guy—black hair, goatee, nice suits?" Lucy looked at everyone with their blank expressions. "What the hell happens in those minds all day? How the hell do you get ideas? Just hope like hell a neuron *hits* another?"

"Hey! I'd like you to know that they don't hit one another—they smash one another out of the ballpark!" Josh said.

Lucy gave him a flat stare. The others looked at him for a few moments.

"Boss, I think you just said you're even dumber than we thought," Dwayne said.

"W-wha? No! I was saying that my ideas are so good when they come together that my neurons would probably explode if they were anyone else's!"

"Yeah, still think that makes you pretty stupid," Kim said.

"Aren't you supposed to be my minions? My yes-people? Comrades in arms? You know?"

"Wow, I wish I could mentally bleach this moment from my memories." Lucy shook her head and looked away.

"All right, so what you're saying about Suzy being Austin Zane's secretary—that's pretty crazy, but whatever." Kim shrugged.

"Kim, he's one of the richest and most powerful human beings on Earth," Josh said.

"Ehh," Kim shrugged again, clearly not bothered.

Lucy didn't say anything; instead, a picture appeared in all of their inboxes. There was Suzy and Austin Zane, wearing sunglasses as they talked about something.

"Heh, kind of looks like Dave," Josh said.

Silence fell as everyone slowly looked at Josh. He looked at Dwayne and Kim.

"Lightbulb," Lucy said.

"Miss us much?" Deia asked as she and the rest of her party slowed down to meet them.

Josh just stared at Dave; Dwayne and Kim did the same.

"Do I have something on my face?" Dave rubbed his constant stubble beard.

"Ah-h, no, sorry. We were just talking about something, completely somewhere else." Josh smiled.

How the hell didn't I see this before? Josh looked to Suzy and back to Dave, his brain unable to really understand what he was seeing. Dave was definitely not like some of the billionaires he knew.

But hell, dude, this guy is a trillionaire! Fucking countries could take loans just from him instead of other countries. Fuck, I don't want to know what this guy's taxes are like.

"Sorry about them. We have an inn with everyone in it. We're going to be leaving through the teleport tomorrow but we thought we might as well have a few drinks tonight to celebrate. This lot are off in la-la-land for some reason. Oh, and Josh wants to talk to you about business, Suzy," Lucy said.

"Thanks." Deia stared at them all with a confused expression.

"Ahh, sorry—just figuring something out," Kim said with a half-smile.

"O-okay then." Dave gave them all peculiar looks before they moved to follow Lucy.

"What the *hell*?" Kim asked in a low voice.

"Guess he likes video games. Sure, it's weird but..." Dwayne shrugged.

"I've got to agree with Dwayne on this one. In here, we're just Players. Nothing more, nothing less," Josh said, ending the matter.

***

Justin whistled as he wandered over people's rooftops.

The POEs yelled at him but what could they do?

Call the guards and tell them that there's another Player wandering the rooftops. Might as well set up a café and a few shops up here, there's so many of us here. Though, that one time I jumped onto that roof and landed in that couple's bedroom—well, that was awkward. Didn't know Humans could bend like that. Maybe they were bored with all their other positions?

Justin continued to whistle as he moved across the houses. Nadorf was the largest city in Opheir and it showed. It had originally been built on top of a hill. The main castle still was. Now the original city had been turned into government offices and other boring things that Justin didn't really care about.

As the city expanded, circular walls rose in waves around it.

There were five different districts, all of them with nicer houses the farther in you went. In the Fourth District, there were the teleportation pads that the higher-ups of the country and the Players used to get from country to country. Some of the more powerful countries even had multiple hubs so people could move between cities.

The lore said that it was for soldiers so that allies could assist one another.

Justin doubted it. Although the Human kingdoms were at relative peace with one another, they were by no means the most amicable.

Justin looked out over the city's walls. There were massive fields around the city. To the southeast, massive marshes hid the unsociable gremlins; to the west, there was the Benvari Range with the Benvari Mountains lying to the southwest.

Justin was out wandering in his starter gear. He got his pack back with everything that was in it, but his armor and weapons had been left behind when he died.

Things had been kind of dull over the last few days with the rest of his friends. They were all still annoyed that they had been killed so easily. Bendel looked relieved that he hadn't been made to kill a bunch of Dragon eggs, even though he thought he hid it well. Helen was actually pissed, which just left Justin confused on how he felt.

This was a game but he didn't think that he felt too good about killing dragons in their eggs. When they were roaming around and causing mayhem, well, then he could understand it. Otherwise, it was just a pain in his mind.

There was little fun in killing an opponent before they got interesting. Once the playing field was level and it was Justin's mind against his opponent's—that was where he had fun.

He moved continuously, whistling a tune before he came across the northern gate of the Fourth District.

The Stone Raiders had moved into town. They had brought goods down from the north and assured everyone that the passes were clear and that the dragons were not a threat to anyone unless they disturbed their mountain unannounced.

Justin had put the dots together. The party that he had been fighting had to be the Stone Raiders. He'd heard about them in passing but he was not one for gaming news all that much. Now, however, he'd looked into the decent-sized guild and was surprised by their exploits.

They were true E-heads, so into the world that they in fact defended the POE. It made sense that they would look after a Dragon as well. It made Justin wonder what kind of quests they got for being nice to the people. By the gear that they were sporting, it was not low quality and they all seemed to be a rather fun group.

Justin looked at a decent-sized group of ten people headed down the street.

As Justin had stuck to scoping people out and trying to understand how hard it would be to pickpocket them, he had developed a skill called Risk Sense. He used it on the ten people; they ranged from white, to gray, yellow, and four reds, and one just tinged with purple.

The Risk Sense didn't just come from what the level a person was; it was based off their gaming skill and their stats, which were not necessarily equivalent to a person's level.

A slow smile stretched over Justin's face as he looked at the party moving into the city.

"Well, it seems that we did indeed mess with the wrong kind of people." Justin crouched down and looked at them, pulling an apple from his bag and eating it absently.

If the others are still all pent-up and thinking about revenge, I think I might need to find a new party. Bendel and Gillie are good, but Helen's a bit too hot-headed when it comes to these things. We did attack them first, after all. It's why they got no penalties for killing us.

Justin shook his head and looked out over the city. A thought struck him.

The Stone Raiders are fighting their way across Emerilia and looking to make POE allies. Why don't I just do the same, but with information? We're already a higher level than most of the POE within Opheir. We could look to helping out here, get a few extra quests, maybe build an information network. People are always looking for information. If we get in a position to sell it, then I can try to get out of my parents' place, maybe even get one of those E-head pods so I can be in here all the time.

Justin thought on his ideas as he saw the Players head into a trading house.

An alert pinged on Justin's interface a few minutes later.

Private Message

Hello, Player. It seems that items meeting your requirements are for sale in the trading house.

Goods: Any

Place of Sale: Nadorf, Opheir

Cost: 300 gold

Justin smiled, putting in his bid, and walked away, whistling again.

It might be an idea to make a few Stone Raider friends in the future. Seem like a pretty interesting bunch.

***

After putting the various items that the party had gathered on their adventure up for sale, they split the rest.

Dave didn't really care for the weapons and gear; the weapons might be nice but he already had an idea of what he wanted to build himself.

The Stone Raider leaders went off to start the celebrations.

Deia made sure they gathered supplies they needed for their trip to the Benvari Mountains before meeting up with the rest of the Stone Raiders.

"Woohoo!" a Stone Raider said. A group of five of them was inebriated and was running around the inn's roofs.

The POEs seemed in a joyous mood as well, many thanking the Stone Raiders for what they had done at Boran-al's Citadel. Many others were enjoying the multiple rounds that the Stone Raiders had ordered. After the boring walk, watching over the trader caravan, they were excited to be doing something else.

Dave laughed and clapped as the POE started a quick melody that went with the rambunctious atmosphere.

Josh was in the middle of it, running off on roofs or in drinking games.

Dwayne looked more reserved as he sat with Lucy, who read her books while he drank his beer.

Seems like those two are being the responsible ones. Dave smirked as Kim floated off the second-floor balcony of one of the inns that the Stone Raiders had rooms in.

"Come on, you lot—got plenty of booze in this place and it's almost as good as that Dwarven stuff!"

"I think we'll just have to test this out for ourselves." Dave looked to the rest of the party before he followed Kim inside.

It was as crazy inside as it was out. The barkeep had a massive smile on her face at the Stone Raiders' antics as they had drinking games, sang along with some of the songs and caused general chaos. Yet, they weren't trying to break tables or use powerful magic that might mess the place up.

"Beers, please!" Kim said, getting to the bar.

"How many?" one of the bartenders asked.

"Seven!" Kim chugged what remained of her beer.

"Having an easy night, huh?" Dave looked to her mug.

"This stuff is much better than the crap we get on Earth. It's damned well palatable!" Kim yelled back over the noise of the place.

"Where can we get a room for the night?" Deia asked.

"You've got rooms here. Double bunked, though—so that's three of them." Kim pulled out three keys and gave it to her. "Now let's party!" Kim grabbed the beers as they arrived in front of her and handed them out to the others.

***

Dave didn't try to open his eyes, instead pouring Mana through his body to fix all the damage that he done last night.

Even through his eye lids he could see the morning light.

Dave groaned, trying to get out of the way of the light, finding Deia moaning about his moving. He settled back down, using her hair to block the sun.

Dave felt a poke in his cheek, he moaned, looking over to Deia.

She had cracked an eyelid and looked up at him with a *"you're really hiding in my hair?"* expression.

Dave just grunted back. He wrapped his arms around her more fully and pulled her up higher on him. She made a happy noise and snuggled in closer to him.

Well that was one hell of a night. Dave glanced around the room through Deia's hair, finding clothes, armor, weapons, and gear leading to the bed.

Dave smirked at their trail of destruction before he let himself drift back to sleep.

"Wake up, you lazy bastards! Breakfast is downstairs!" Dwayne knocked on doors as he went.

Both Dave and Deia hid from the noise, hoping that it would just go away so they could get some more sleep.

Others got up and started to move around, fumbling through their rooms and creating a racket on their floor and then the floor above them as Dwayne reached it.

Dave groaned as Deia tried to tuck herself into Dave's chest. Her eyes found his, a pitiful expression on her face. *Why did this have to happen to us?*

Dave just rubbed her head and poured healing magic into her, clearing away the effects of the hangover she was probably feeling. Although Dave had a taste for beers, she seemed to be a wine and spirits drinker. With her Elven metabolism, it was the only thing that could even start to get her drunk.

"Why didn't you do that earlier?" Deia complained, her voice sleepy.

"Sorry, was just trying to go back to sleep." Dave's eyes closed as he got comfortable on the pillows.

"Mmm," Deia said as the noise around them continued.

"We're not going to get back to sleep, are we?" Dave asked.

"Probably not," Deia muttered, not sounding all that pleased with it.

"Five more..." Dave's words were interrupted with Suzy knocking on the door.

"Get up! You two are like damned horny teenag—" The door wasn't locked and only half closed; her knocks opened it. She found Dave and Deia staring at her as her fist was raised to knock again. "Wow. So, tattoos, huh?"

Dave looked at his body, seeing the runes that covered his body. Usually they were hidden under his long-sleeved shirts and pants. "Er..."

"Well, looks like you're up! See you at breakfast." Suzy looked completely unapologetic.

Dave conjured a pillow above her head and dropped it on her grinning face.

"And, shut the door!" Deia yelled.

"So cute." Suzy smiled, looking at them both, and closed the door.

Deia glared at the door and then Dave.

"What did I do?"

"She's your friend."

"Saying you and Suzy aren't friends?"

"No, but you knew her first and I wanted to sleep in!" Deia pouted.

Dave laughed and pulled her to him; her face melted into a smile as he kissed her. "Morning, babe."

"Your breath smells horrible!"

"Jackass."

"But you looove me." Deia grinned.

"How old are you?"

"Old enough," Deia said with a saucy wink, getting out of bed as Dave admired her body. She grabbed her underwear slowly, making a show of it. "Unless you don't want any of this?" Her innocent voice was at odds with her lustful body and seductive look in her eyes.

Dave got out of bed and moved toward her.

"Hey, get dressed! We have breakfast!" Deia said as Dave moved behind her and wrapped his hands around her, one traveling north and the other south.

Her voice caught as his hands found their targets. She melted back toward him, arching her body and pressing her backside against his groin.

"Too true. I could do with some food." Dave released and grinned.

"Damned tease." Deia's face flushed and her eyes went wide in anticipation.

"Learned from the best." Dave looked to her.

Her eyes and mouth thinned but the corners of it turned up in clear amusement.

After a few minutes and some more grab-ass, they made it down and into the actual inn. There were Stone Raiders, POEs, and other Players in the place. The Players just talked to one another or the Stone Raiders, thinking the POEs beneath them. The Stone Raiders, however, talked to everyone as if they were a Player. There were several people with POEs who looked as if they had spent the night at the inn with them.

Healers were going around, curing hangovers. A few went and grabbed a beer right after getting their hangover cured.

Dave and Deia found the rest of their party hanging out at a table with two more spots at it. The food had already arrived, with Suzy ordering for Dave and Deia.

"Oh Suz, I don't know what I did without you." Dave grinned. She had not forgotten his preferences: bacon, eggs, grits, fried tomatoes, and proper hash browns.

Deia smirked and shook her head. She'd come to understand and accept Suzy and Dave's relationship. The two were more brother and sister than coworkers.

They both dug into the food, talking about the antics of last night and small stuff for a while as they ate.

***

"All right, well, until later then. Make sure you send Kim her reports and let us know when you want to go on a bit of a raid." Josh smiled at them.

"Look after yourselves," Deia said.

"And try to not get into too much trouble," Malsour said.

"Fat chance of that." Induca looked away.

"See you later." Dave waved to them.

The Stone Raiders turned and headed toward the teleport pad. It had cost a lot of gold for them to keep the teleport open as the guild wandered through with their wagons and gear.

There were smiles and a bit of joking but their eyes looked around as they entered, ready for any threat they might find on the other side. The teleport pads made for fast travel across Emerilia. They cost some gold, more than a POE might have, but to the Players, it was easy to get.

They were being transported to the Endon kingdom on the Gudalo continent. If Opheir was a level-one continent, Gudalo was a level three due to the high number of ex-POE adventurers who had left Heval or Ashal, or people who were trading goods with the Per'ush islands that floated between Gudalo and Ashal.

Opheir only had the one teleportation pad; however, other continents that were richer or more powerful had multiple teleport pads.

The Lokma Empire on Ashal supposedly had a teleportation pad for every one of their cities. Every single island within Per'ush also had a teleportation pad. Depending on how people were allied, people could transport between kingdoms. Opheir and the Endon kingdom didn't really care for one another and the teleport was usually locked between the two.

Though, with the Stone Raiders messages, they could secure transport over to the different location with a key that they had been given. A key was linked to a Player's interface, so as long as they were on good standing with the kingdom they wanted to go to, then they could.

If that standing went down, however, then their key wouldn't work anymore.

Josh and Lucy moved to join the other Stone Raiders. Dwayne and Lucy had gone ahead to make sure that the other side was clear.

As people stepped onto the teleport pad, they simply disappeared while the runes of the teleport pad hummed with power. After a few minutes, the last of the Stone Raiders walked through and the runes stopped glowing. The rings around the teleport pad started to move as a new group of traders moved up, ready to go through the teleport.

"Well, let's get going." Deia led them away from the teleport pad.

"Yeah." Dave looked to Suzy and Anna's shoulders. Both of them now wore the guild crest of the Stone Raiders, given to them in the middle of the booze fest that was last night.

The two of them talked summoning and different things as Induca started bothering her brother about different sights she saw. Malsour sighed and tried to rein his little sister in.

Dave grabbed Deia's hand as they made their way through the bustling city, heading toward the Benvari Mountains in the distance.

Chapter 19: Benvari Mountains

Dave watched as they exited the forest, finally able to see the mountains in all their glory.

"Those mountains are massive!" Suzy said.

From afar, it was hard to think that anyone lived in the mountains. They still retained their natural beauty. Hundreds of wagons traveled to and from the mountain range. The approach was covered by vast fortifications and concealed artillery.

The actual mountain had a gentle road leading up and into it. A curtain wall covered a town that had formed outside of the mountain's trading entrance. Only a few people were allowed past the inner defensive gates and defenses that extended before the mountain's different entrances.

Dave and the party passed through the small town. Once they got to what Dave was thinking of as the inner sanctum, he showed his necklace to a Dwarven shield bearer. A mage checked it and then bowed and waved for them to continue.

They passed through the Dwarves' first true defensive line into a stone covered area. There were barracks, training areas, trading squares of all types and roving bands of Dwarven warbands. It was the closest people got to the mountain without being a Dwarf, emissary, or well-trusted ally.

Another massive door—one that led into the mountain—greeted them.

One of the three warbands that was spread in front of the gate stopped him. There needed to be three of them just so that they could cover the entire length of the massive door.

"State your business," the warband leader demanded.

"I am David Grahslagg. I am here to meet with Jesal. Kol sent me." Dave pulled out his necklace.

"Get Durn," the warband leader said to the shield bearers under his command.

One ran off. A few moments later, he came back with a Dwarven mage. He muttered, annoyed about being taken away from his chess game and grabbed Dave's necklace.

"Well, seems you've come to test your skill," Durn said. "Come with me."

Dave made to move forward.

The warband leader held up his hand to everyone else. "I am sorry, I cannot let you in."

Dave and Deia shared a look.

"We'll wait here. Just let us know what's going on once you talk to your new teacher," Deia said.

"Thanks, babe." Dave gave her a kiss and turned to follow Durn.

"Half-Dwarves and Elves, ehh? I'm just an old rock biter—don't mind me." Durn grinned.

The massive door opened enough to admit the two of them. The corridor was smooth as they walked through. The glow of the lights made the place seem warm instead of dark and gloomy, even as the door shut behind them, not letting any light in.

Dave looked over the walls. Not only were they shaped to a polished sheen twenty feet above his head, but they also had intricate carvings on them and several defensive runes designed to bolster friendly forces in the tunnel and weaken enemy forces, or add magical barriers or shoot down fire and spikes.

Dave nodded at it all before they reached another door. It opened for them and they passed through. They continued through two more doors.

Dave saw lights up ahead, as if instead of being greeted by another door, he was greeted with Benvari Mountain. Dave looked around and stopped in place.

Buildings seemed to almost grow from the walls. Houses were stacked on one another; roadways hung between them and hung over others. He could see dozens of levels, all open to the light of the hollowed-out mountain.

Mirrors directed light into a massive crystal in the roof directly over their heads and others that were spread throughout the massive space. They acted to illuminate the whole place. It didn't feel as though they were in a mountain, but rather in a city that had been folded together.

Light came in to feed the crops that were growing in malachite-formed greenhouses.

Nadorf had been large, but Dave couldn't even begin to understand the scale of what he was seeing.

The homes didn't look like slums of shacks, even if they might have been on top of one another. They were carefully crafted, made from metals that blended together, turning the city into a beautiful landscape. The light of the different mini-suns seemed to make the houses glow.

"Wow." Dave had never seen something that was so beautiful or technically challenging. His mind as an engineer and a romantic could only sit there, drinking in the sights.

"Welcome to Benvari Mountain, young one." Durn smiled and gave him some time to take it all in. "Now, Jesal is not the kind of person you want to keep waiting. Let's go find her."

Dave followed Durn in a daze. His Touch of the Land extended all out around him, studying the way that the homes had been formed, the architecture of the entire mountain. It was an engineering and artistic marvel the more he studied it, from the floating bridges to the wire suspension that held up some entire floors. Runes made the materials light and durable.

It was a maze to Dave, though, as Durn took elevators and a rail cart to get to their destination deep in the heart of the mountain.

It went from warm to hot as the city fell away and it was clear that they were in the industrial area of the mountain. Metal in all different states was being gathered, refined, and moved through massive machinery.

"How the hell haven't you mined everything in these mountains?" Dave asked.

"Well, they're massive and the materials keep on coming back—not in the same place but we have to keep constant surveys going as an old mine might have new materials in it well after it has dried up," Durn said.

Those must have been from those material-making things that Bob was talking about.

It got hotter as they passed through areas where massive items were being built to where ingots were being formed and past different smithies, where hundreds of Dwarves were working on different projects.

Dave's Touch spread out; he could sense multiple magical forges all around him. The sheer production power was astounding.

They moved past magical forges, which were increasingly stronger as more magical power had been unleashed upon them.

It was still getting hotter until Durn came to a room where there were seven people working on different projects. None looked up as they entered.

Dave looked at the forge. The heat coming from it was immense.

Holy shit, that isn't a damned forge—it's a magma flow being routed through this room and a dozen other forges!

Coal lay overtop what was a massive metal sheet as the lava flow below heated it. Air was forced into the lava chamber at points, coming out the other side, creating a blowtorch that could heat metals up in seconds.

Durn moved next to an anvil where a female Dwarf was working on an intricate staff. Her hands moved quickly and precisely.

It's like watching a CNC machine work. Dave was astounded at the quality of her work and the speed at which she worked.

She wove runes and art into the piece, making it appear as if it were a singular rose weaving its way all the way to the bloom at the top. There was a socket space there, waiting for an attuning gem that an enchanter might place within it.

She ignored Durn and Dave completely, at one with her work as she finished the last flourish. The runes looked to be complete as she pulled out a red gem that had been carved into rose petals. She placed it within the socket at the top of the staff. Using a small hammer and some other fine tools, she secured the central gem into the staff.

She pulled out a soul gem, muttering a few words as it seemed to leak light. The runes of the staff flared to light as the gem at its peak started to glow. More power filled the staff until the runes projected light and the gem was like a flashlight.

Then the soul gem was gone, turning to dust.

It was a work of art as beautiful as it was powerful. Dave could understand the majority of the runes that would enhance a mage's power. It was a destruction/restoration staff, helping to heal others while it gave a great boost to destruction spells and could pack a nice punch. Even if it wasn't charged, it would focus a person's attacks if they channeled their Mana through it.

Under the white outer material—which could only be Mithril—there was a core of ebony, the two materials working together with the silver-filled runes and detailing would mean that the item would only grow more powerful with continued use.

It truly was a masterpiece.

Jesal looked around, as if seeing Durn and Dave for the first time. "When the hell did you get in here, you ornery old bastard?" She looked at Durn, as she took the staff and chucked it on a table covered with weapons, armor, and all manner of items. Each of them gave off a sense of power.

"Got you a new student, you damned anvil hermit!" Durn said.

Jesal's irate glare turned into a snort as a grin spread across her face. Durn smiled likewise.

"So, who are you?" Jesal looked to Dave.

"I'm Dave. Kol sent me."

"Well then, I guess we better get started. Let's see your metals," Jesal said.

Dave pulled off his necklace and gave it to her.

She held each between her fingers, closing her eyes for a few moments before moving to the next. "What level is your skill in smithing?" Jesal handed him back the necklace.

"Master Level 1." Dave didn't need to look around the room as his Touch was already showing him all of the work that was going on around him.

Their work, the different techniques, the way that the metal changed: in his search to create more powerful conjurations, his study of smithing and the creation of different objects had gone well beyond what nearly all others saw.

Jesal's eyes thinned as she looked over Dave. "How long have you studied smithing?"

"Here? I guess, maybe nine months?" Dave replied, trying to pin it down.

"Show me your associated skills with smithing as well as your Affinities and your character sheet," Jesal asked.

Dave complied, checking out his stats and Affinities. It had been awhile since he had.

Character Sheet

Name: David Grahslagg Gender: Male

Level: 3 Class: -

Race: Human/Dwarf Alignment: Chaotic Neutral

Unspent points-285

Health: 2,600 Regen: 2.10/s

Mana: 1,350 Regen: 5.65/s

Stamina: 680 Regen: 3.40/s

Vitality: 26 Endurance: 105

Intelligence: 135 Willpower: 113

Strength: 68 Agility: 68

His Intelligence was a pain to get up but it was still increasing as he and Malsour had talked and he'd spent many hours to look into the various secrets that were hidden in the forums.

When I get to actually make something from all those ideas, my Intelligence will probably go up a few points.

Knowing something was good and all, but actually demonstrating it showed the difference between theoretical and possible. Unless he made it in Emerilia; then his level wouldn't increase. But like a good math question, he might get points for attempting something that could be possible. A scientist who had their theory proven wrong had still learned a lot going through the process of trying to confirm it.

His straight Strength and Agility training was slowing to a crawl. He'd upped the amount of weight that he'd been carrying, decreasing the weight toll on his armor.

Seems that my Agility grew by three points while Strength only went up once. I was doing a lot of tree tag, so maybe it's not just simple repetition but doing something new and working my way through it. Kind of like breaking through plateaus or constantly showing progress, like I do with inventions.

Dave bit his lip in thought as he turned to the Affinities.

Affinity Levels

Dark 58 Light 35

Air   39 Water 25

Earth 48 Fire   37

They were getting rather high, and the fact that there was only a difference of about twenty between his Affinities was probably why Jesal was frowning, as if not understanding what the heck she was seeing.

Most had one Affinity that far exceeded the others. Dave was 58 in Dark Affinity; it would make more sense if he was 5 in Light. The two competed yet, somehow, he was skilled in both. In the end, it came to his conjuration as he used all of the Affinities in order to conjure.

His Dark was higher as he *knew* the most about elements of the Dark items, such as metals. It also went back to what he knew of back on Earth: he'd tinkered with a few rockets here and there, but he also worked with forges and understood the different effects fire had on different objects. He knew the various states of water, how it could change the compositions of different things, but he didn't know it as intimately, which was why he didn't have such a high Affinity in it.

Air—well, his damned rockets had to make it out of Earth's atmosphere when he'd been on Earth. Applying that knowledge and showing his understanding of air had increased it.

His stats were a reflection of his knowledge and his capabilities.

Once I get them higher, then I can start to look at the real damned projects. He smiled, thinking to himself about the various drawings he'd made on his interface's notepad, completely secure and away from prying eyes.

"Soul manipulation?" Jesal asked.

"What about it?" Dave asked.

"It says that you have been dabbling in the Dark arts for building your weapons," Jesal said, not looking pleased. Durn started at Dave oddly.

"Well, you know how we enchant things with soul gems?" Dave asked.

Jesal nodded.

"Okay, well, I kind of went and looked into how to make soul gems. It meant I had to understand the very basics of soul gems, the Dark containers that Dark mages created, then into how it was used like a power source for those with limited understanding of magic. Well, I needed something a little better, so I went and started playing with soul gems, changing them around. Meant that I got to know the ways souls worked pretty well. Then I got to study some daggers that were big ole soul-powered nasties and, well, learned a bit more. Had to delve into the Xelur Demons' information. Then, when I was fighting at Boran-al's Citadel, I manipulated the souls of the cultists and the Undead Demon Lord to my use." Dave left out the fact that he had used the souls of the people on his side.

He thought that they might get all religious on him. Souls were simply energy here; through everything he looked, only the twisted people thought of souls as people. In reality, they were just a power vacuum. When the cultists had sealed their "souls" to their bodies, they'd sealed their consciousness. When a person died on Emerilia, they were gone but a "soul" of energy was left behind.

Players were different, as their consciousness was uploaded at the very moment of their death and this was then put into a new body.

It was just power for the using, but people got all freaked out because it was the Dark mages who found it first. They were just looking for another way to get a lot of power, save it up, and then use it when they needed it.

Dark mages, always looking to make the biggest and baddest impression.

"What did you use this on?" Jesal asked.

Dave scratched his head. "Can we go somewhere?"

Jesal tapped the hammer at her waist in thought. "Come. Durn, you might as well come—otherwise you'll be pestering me for decades."

Durn smiled as Jesal led them out of the smithies and into a break room. There was food, drink, and safety equipment around. A few people were talking; they waved and nodded to Durn and Jesal as they passed.

Jesal walked to a workshop that had seats and different furnaces and anvils around. It was a classroom, complete with a forge facing the others and a chalkboard.

Dave checked the windows and closed the door behind him. "Give me a sec." Dave opened his interface.

Jesal's hand lowered to her hammer.

"What kind of sensing ability do you have?" Dave asked using quick commands to change his outfit to preset leather pants and cotton shirt.

"What kind of question is that?"

"Well, I don't know if you'll be able to see through the different layers."

"Different layers of what?"

"The armor. Kind of made it so that it is pretty damned hard to see all the layers." Dave rolled up his sleeves revealing runes across his arms. Jesal's eyes went wide; Durn moved closer as they studied the runes across his arms and under the collar of his shirt.

At least they don't look too horrible for battlefield tattoos. Probably a good idea not telling them where I was when I added them to my body.

"I don't even know many of these runes." Durn looked at the markings.

"Nor I."

"Ahh, well, that's because I didn't use just the Dwarven lexicon of runes. I went and found a few different languages of them. It was a pain in the ass," Dave said.

"Why did you do this?" Jesal asked.

Dave smirked. "Check the armor."

Jesal took the armor and turned it over in her hands. "Simple steel armor. Rather thick. Trace elements of..." Jesal's eyes went distant as her face pinched together, as if finding something she wasn't expecting. "Ebony and silver sheets, very thin, turned into a composite magical rune." Her face opened up as she shook her head, her eyes still unfocused as her hand moved over the armor.

"Damn, that is fucking complex. Multiple three-dimensional circuits and formations that can create multiple variations of Magical Circuits. There are a few complete circuits for power draw and release as well as passive defenses, though the majority of the formations and circuits aren't complete—as if they're missing a few runes here and there. I don't understand all of the runes and the way that they've been put together. Though I can *feel* their disjointed Man... Holy fucking tin men." Jesal's eyes focused on Dave.

"Do you want to blow the mountain up with that kind of soul gem! How the fuck did you even find it!?" Jesal demanded.

"Ahh, well, that whole soul manipulation thing was so that I could better link to the armor, for the power source. What I had found wasn't good enough for my needs, so I had to go and make a new one. Thus, what you've got in your hands."

"You made a soul gem?" Durn asked.

"No!" Jesal cut off Dave before he could explain. "He took the idea of a soul gem, tipped it on its head, pounded it apart with a damned power hammer, and then reformed it together into something that might kind of, barely, be related to what we know of soul gems." Jesal's serious face turned into a grin and then a smile. "It's fucking awesome!"

That more than anything made Durn look scared as Jesal started to mutter to herself and looked over the armor again.

Dave pulled on his shirt again, waiting a few minutes.

"Jesal," Durn said.

"What?" she asked, going back to muttering. "Those layers—might need some alterations. Maybe his own forging techniques might help him. If not, need to get Horkum to mess with it. Horkum would ruin this little beauty."

"Will you take me on?" Dave asked, trying to disturb her muttering.

"Huh? Oh, you're still here? Well, yeah, I'll take you on. Even with your limited understanding, you went to the damned limits, boyo. Never thought of anything like this in all my years. No wonder Kol was going nut-bag about making you a Dwarven smith. This thing is—well, fuck, it might be better than some of the sex I've had." Jesal looked up to the ceiling as Durn held his head in his hands, shaking it.

"Nope, take that back—better than *most* of the sex I've had." She nodded as if agreeing with the statement and stroked the armor.

"Can I get that back?" Dave pointed to it.

Jesal turned it away from him, waging an inner battle before turning back and giving it to him. "Okay, well, I'll teach you how to really forge. Then you're telling me about how you made that damned thing. I've seen a few Legendary weapons, but that is clearly one of them. Damned thing is a piece of art—want to mount it to my wall!" Jesal laughed.

"Uhh, thanks?" Dave said.

"So, we'll work together. First, we meet in here, talk about what we've figured out, and I give you some goals. We go into the smithy and you work your heart out. At the end of the day, we come back here, talk about it all and then go our separate ways. Room and board will be provided to you for your stay. Got any questions?" Jesal thundered on.

"Uhh, well, I have a few friends who are here. I was wondering what I could do for them," Dave said.

"We could get them a place within the keep, but while you're here, I don't want you distracted. Focus on training. I don't know how long it might take." Jesal's voice became serious.

"Yes, ma'am."

"Very well. Go tell them about it and get ready for tomorrow. Be here at the fifth bell. We'll begin early and work through the day. Tomorrow your true training to be called a Dwarven Master Smith starts."

Quest: Of Anvil and Fire

After meeting with Jesal, she has decided to accept you as a candidate to be a Dwarven Master Smith.

You will need to:

Master the material Stone

Master the material Malachite

Master the material Gold

Master the material Mithril

Find your Smithing Art

Reward: Title of Dwarven Master Smith

Do you accept?

Y/N

Chapter 20: Path of a Dwarven Smith

Deia watched Dave as he stood up from the bed, moving to the bath-tub to wash himself. She pulled the sheets around her, making a dress out of them as she traced the tattoos that covered his back.

He now stood at around six-foot tall, just a half foot shorter than her, but nearly twice as wide. His dense muscles rippled as he cleaned his face and chest. Deia rubbed his back and he turned around.

"I'll be back soon enough," he reassured her.

"I know, and I understand it. Just, my damned emotions are getting the best of me." Deia gave him a small smile.

Dave smiled, pulling her close to him, and kissed her.

It was over too soon as he pulled on his different clothes and grabbed his bag of holding. His armor was stored in the bag; now, he just wore simple but hardy clothes.

"Hurry up becoming a Dwarven smith. When you come out, we're going to need to make up for your lack of training for Agility," Deia said.

"Training, training, training," Dave complained.

Deia silenced him with a kiss.

He grinned. "I look forward to learning from you, master." He bowed his head and gave her a sweeping bow.

Deia laughed and shook her head.

"Thank you for letting me do this." Dave's arms wrapped around her.

"I'm old enough that I know that it is better to let you do the things that you want to than try to hold you back." She pouted and looked up at him. "Though I can't help but wish I did."

Dave laughed. "Well, thank you for supporting me. If you ever want to go off and train with some master on some remote mountaintop, let me know."

Deia snorted. "I think Induca will be able to teach me a good number of things. Mixing her teachings with what I'm learning from Earth, you might see a whole new kind of magic by the time you see me again."

"I look forward to it, my smart, brilliant, and pretty firecracker."

She rolled her eyes again, kissing him. "Now get out of here, and hurry back to me!"

"Yes, ma'am." Dave turned and walked out of the door, turning back. "I love you."

"I love you too." Her emotions wanted to grab him and hold him back, but she knew that as she wouldn't want him to do that to her, she didn't do it to him.

His smile made her blush and feel butterflies in her stomach before the door closed behind him and he was gone.

Deia sat on the bed, trying to get her emotions under control. She moved to the bathroom, where there was a thing called a "shower." Dave had jumped into it as soon as he saw it. It had led to him pulling her into it.

A smile passed over her face as she opened the valve for the warm water. She showered, thinking of her own goals. As Dave was working on his smithing, she and the others would work on their various skills. Already, Malsour had talked to a few Dwarves about growing his skills with his Dark Affinity. Deia and Induca were going to train with each other at an outside training ground that the Dwarves ran. Suzy and Anna would work on Suzy's summoning. Deia had also mandated that they get together in the afternoons and work on their melee fighting techniques.

Deia was wondering what kind of damage they would be capable of once they left the mountain. Boran-al's Citadel had served to show her just how weak she was. She might be over three hundred years old, but she had been happy with her skills, thinking of herself highly. The time that she had spent with the Stone Raiders showed her that she needed to improve in all aspects.

Even Malsour seemed to grab this concept as he was throwing himself into learning how to fight. He was a decently high level and he knew a lot of information, but he had never put that information to use, so Emerilia had not rewarded him with higher stats. Now he was applying those theories.

Armed with the knowledge of the Emerilia forums, both Suzy and Deia were becoming founts of knowledge to improve the others' skills.

While Dave was working on becoming a Dwarven Master Smith, the rest could finally take their ideas and test them out. Before Boran-al's Citadel, they had only been testing out different ideas that might give them an edge in that fight. Now, well, they had no pressing concerns so they were free to experiment.

Next time those Affinity lords and ladies show up, they better damned well watch out.

***

Dave walked into the classroom.

"All right, get your kit on and store your bag in that locker there." Jesal pointed to a bunch of lockers. Dave equipped his smithing gear and Jesal led him out to the smithy.

"Okay, so first of all, we're going to need to get you up to speed on gold and stone. First we'll work with stone." Jesal pointed to a big piece of stone that was sitting on a workbench at the side of the smithy. "Turn that into something."

"Anything in particular?" Dave asked.

"Whatever comes to your mind."

Dave nodded and walked over to the stone. He used his sense, closing his eyes and passing his hand over the stone. It wasn't like metals; veins ran through the rock. It would be hard to form something from the block with hammering; it would just crack and break.

Going to have to carve the damned thing out.

Dave grabbed a piece of sharpened coal and worked on a piece of paper, making a simple sketch of what he wanted to make. He opened his Internet browser, checking out different images and practices that people used to shape stone.

This is going to be interesting. He continued to browse. People went for lunch; he just ate a snack bar he'd made.

***

Jesal was impressed. Dave was taking his time to plan out what he wanted to make. Most people felt as if they had to prove themselves right away. This was only increased if someone got to this stage and didn't know how to use all of the materials.

Malachite was a normal one to not know. Only the Elves on the Ashal Islands knew how to make the best malachite weapons and they weren't telling anyone their secrets.

The Dwarves were good with it, but they couldn't create the flowing creations that the Elves were able to make. Their malachite was prized around the world in the halls of kings and the richest of nobles.

Every smith knew how to carve stone and gold was necessary to add flair to many different pieces, and it was a great conductor of Mana.

Though why that boy used silver instead of gold on his armor interests me. It might be worth trying out a few experiments of my own. I should ask him after today's work.

Jesal's mind was off somewhere else as she walked into the shop again.

Dave was hammering away at his block of stone.

Jesal looked over, trying to not distract. She snorted, looking at his face. *Seems that this one also knows how to get into his smithing fugue.* She smiled.

A smithing fugue to Dwarves was as close as smiths got to meditation unless they were mages as well. It was when a Dwarf was so in tune with their work that everything else seemed to fade away. It was just them and their work. People who were in a fugue were rarely interrupted, the others knowing that they were deep into their work.

She looked at his work, knowing that he didn't even care she was there.

He had various pieces clamped down, a half-dozen arrowheads to the side. They had a gleam to them.

She picked one up. It nicked her tough skin. "Damn." A normal smith might have thought that they were formed with Earth or Dark magic but she knew that Earth and Dark magic left a certain residue on their works and they weren't as strong as items that had been made in a smithy.

She looked at the work table. A piece of parchment appeared in Dave's hands and he used it to rub back and forth on the knife he was making. The parchment had a rough look to it as the roughly carved knife was smoothed out.

Jesal studied the arrowhead again and placed it back down.

Impressive. Kol was right about how he mixes techniques from his land with our own. I've never seen anything like that rough parchment. Using a file might make the stone crack and break but using this applies less pressure and friction, allowing for a finer finish without the strain of a file. I wonder if it would work well on smoothing out other items?

Jesal moved back to her work. She didn't feel as if it would take long for Dave to attain his stone ring on his necklace.

***

With Dave already attaining the first rank of Master Smith, he had worked with different materials, many of them a lot more difficult to form and change, as those higher materials needed strength and power of will. Stone needed a person to understand the material that they were working with and understand that they could only cut once. It was the easiest material to form, but it was also the most challenging.

If he didn't use the right chisel, hit the wrong place, or used too much force, then he would ruin what he was working on. He'd made the arrowheads as practice. It was hard to make the bottom without cracking the stone.

He'd broken ten or so arrowheads just because of that.

After he'd made a half-dozen or so, he'd gotten used to the material. He'd started understanding the faults in the stone. They were harder to find as it was a more organic material than metal. Still, he worked through.

He stopped, realizing that he was tired. He stood and rubbed his eyes, cracking his back that was strained from leaning over to study his work.

"Was wondering when you might come out of your fugue. Let's go grab a beer and have a talk. You've got all week to work on that stone," Jesal said.

"Sure." Dave put his tools away and cleaned his area.

Jesal led him toward an elevator. They rode it upward to the more inhabited sections of the mountain. "You don't seem at all alarmed by our lifts."

"Well, we have something similar back on Earth, not all that different. We just use electricity instead of magma tunnels to power ours."

"Electricity?"

"Think of it as a poor man's magic." The mixture of mental fatigue from working hard for nearly a day straight and the strain of working in the smithy made Dave think of Earth.

He felt proud. He knew that he was probably some kind of test-tube creation but he was proud of his race. They had done so many interesting and great things. They'd come out and challenged a massive power in the universe.

They'd built machines that he couldn't even comprehend and they'd survived and thrived on a planet that was meant to train them to fight aggressive species that the most powerful empire in the known universe didn't want to deal with.

At times, we might be a bunch of idiots, but together, not even the most powerful empire in the universe was able to completely wipe us out.

Dave's thoughts returned to what was around him as he realized that they had walked through a few streets and now found themselves at a tavern.

Jesal walked through the door. Laughter, the sound of drinks coming together, conversation, and a band working away registered in the background.

Dave looked at the two-storied tavern. Dwarves were everywhere and anywhere; waiters and waitresses moved through tables, picking up empties and dropping off food and new drinks.

It was a brisk business.

Jesal took a table with Dave and ordered by catching a waiter's eye and holding up two fingers.

The waiter nodded and disappeared.

"So, it seems that you're getting the hang of stone working."

"It takes longer to work with, but once you get the hang of it, it's easy enough." Dave shrugged.

"I saw that you were using some kind of parchment on the blade to sharpen it instead of using files."

"Sandpaper?" Dave watched Jesal's confused look. "Guess you don't have it here. It's like a tough sheet with sand on it to grind down burrs and expose the material underneath. Takes a hell of a lot of work without a sander but gives a better edge and shine to a piece."

"Where did you get it from?"

"Oh, I uhh, made it," Dave said, not wanting to admit that he had just conjured it. *Need to be more careful about what I make.*

"Does it work on metals?"

"Yes, but you need to make one that is more durable."

Jesal looked to be caught in thought as the waiter returned with two meals and tankards of ale. "Thanks, Sean," Jesal said.

"No worries, Jesal." Sean grinned and left quickly to deal with other tables.

"So, why didn't you learn to work with gold?"

Dave took a bite of the meat pie that was in front of him. Gravy and juices poured out as he took a big bite. He chewed his food, savoring it and thinking of the question.

"Damn, that's good." Dave took a drink.

Jesal nodded in pride, also digging into her meal.

"Well, I didn't really need it. Sure, it looks pretty but it doesn't have much more use."

"It's the strongest conductor of power, though."

"Actually, that's wrong." Dave grimaced.

"What?" Jesal drank from her tankard.

"Many people, even on Earth, thought that gold was the best conductor. In reality, silver is better. Gold is useful in certain circuits, yes, but it's thirty percent or so weaker than silver at conducting energy."

"I'm going to have to check that out." Jesal dove back into her meat pie again.

Dave smiled and dug into his pie as well. He knew that tomorrow would come soon and he still had a lot of work to do with carving out the stone weapons. It was tedious work and easy to screw up, but he hoped to finish off his last three materials quickly and get onto working with Mithril.

Chapter 21: Stone Work

Dave rubbed his eyes. It had been a week and a half since he had stepped into the forge to start learning. After the fourth day, Jesal had given him a block of rock and told him to make something to display his talents.

"So, what is it?" Jesal looked at what looked to be an octagon with magical runes sorted into circuits around its surface.

"Well, I don't know what you would call it but I'm going to call it a core," Dave said.

"A core?"

Even Gorrund, the other Master Smith who came around every so often and was teaching four other apprentices, stared at it in curiosity. "What does it do?" Gorrund asked, his voice gruff.

"Well, my friend is a summoner. She is working on her creator class right now. When I saw this rock, I couldn't help but think of the really creepy-ass creatures that she'd been making with her magic. When I left her, she was rather weak, but with time she will grow. As I watched her making her creatures, I realized that if the thing she creates is stronger, then she won't need as much Mana to make something that works. Then, I moved into how about if she just stored Mana inside her creations to keep it going. You'd need some kind of container that could hold a lot of power, then make a decent creature that didn't make me think of some B-class horror movie and needs to have the ability to be turned on and off. Oh, and it needed to be connected to the element she is creating them from."

"Sounds all rather simple," Jesal drawled. She and Gorrund shared a look.

"So, what does this do?" Gorrund asked more forcefully.

"You place this on the ground, then you channel your power into it as if you were a summoner. I made it multi-faced so that each face could hold a different Earth element. Make a rock snake, or a tentacle thing, or a golem. The summoner thinks of the shape and the core molds to it. They have to apply starting power to it but then it should be good for about a day or two until it falls apart if just relying on its power. You can feed it your own Mana and it keeps going, or use a soul gem."

Jesal and Gorrund looked at each other.

"How did you know what a summoner might need for this?" Gorrund asked.

"Well, I've been talking to my friend the entire journey here, wrote down her issues and then referenced what other Players have done to come up with solutions. Some used more powerfully linked soul gems to Earth materials. I was thinking that while working with the most Earth akin element that a smith gets, that it might be an idea to mess around with it." Dave realized that it didn't sound at all very technical or as if he wasn't taking the whole smithing thing very seriously.

Jesal's expression was unreadable as she placed her hand on the core. After a minute, her eyes widened as she looked up at Dave. "There is silver and ebony weaved into this rock."

"Yeah, that was difficult. I wanted the core to grow with the abilities of my friend, so I had to find rifts within the core and insert ebony and silver." Dave shook his head. "That was a fucking pain in the ass."

He'd had to talk to Malsour. He'd been able to move the metals in a large fashion; moving them in just minimal ways meant he had to heat the metal up to make it more pliable but then keep certain areas cold on both the rock and the metal so that the whole thing didn't just explode.

"I guess we know what happened with the first rock," Jesal said.

"Yeah." Dave scratched his head. "I cut it all out. Then, as I was putting metals into the structure, it turned into a bit of a bomb."

"What did you change the second time?" Gorrund asked.

"I put the metals in before I formed the core. It was stronger in its larger form and capable of more heat changes without turning into a big bomb. Once I was done, I just cut it out and then did the engraving, whipped up the runes and magical circles and here you go."

Gorrund turned to Jesal. "I don't know enough about summoners to know if this would work."

"Well, I was going to give it to my friend. She can try it out and we'll see if it works. I'm kind of interested myself."

"You didn't tell me that there's something growing in it," Jesal said.

"What would you say if I said it was a trade secret?"

"I'd say it feels like a damn soul gem."

"Exactly." Dave gave her a sly smile.

"Holy shit." Her eyes widened as she ran her fingers over her tied-back hair.

Gorrund placed his hand on the core for a few moments. A grin spread across his face, turning into a laugh. "Well, Kol knows how to pick 'em, I'll tell you that. I say we go and see what this thing is capable of."

"You've got four apprentices working away," Jesal said.

"They got to this stage—they don't need me standing over them while they pound metal. We both know this is more about pushing people in the right direction than instructing them." Gorrund shrugged.

"You just want to see if it works or blows up," Jesal said.

"Maybe." Gorrund laughed.

"Fine, grab your big block of rock. Let's go see if we can't put a hole in the keep's floor," Jesal said.

Dave put his bag of holding around the soccer ball-sized piece of rock, causing it to disappear.

The three of them headed for the elevators. Dave saw the reverence and respect in everyone's eyes as they nodded and waved to Gorrund and Jesal.

The Dwarves weren't big on the whole bowing thing. They saw one another on a level playing field. Bowing was the highest form of respect that a Dwarf could give another. If it was done without reason, though, it was seen as a great insult.

People cleared out of the way as they walked. Gorrund and Jesal seemed different up here, as if their masks had descended. Dave remembered it from his time as Austin Zane. They were no more or less than the Dwarves around them. Yet, because of their achievements, people thought that they were something else.

Dave pulled up his interface.

Party Chat

Dave > Hey, Suzy, I've got something that I want to test out. Can you meet me at the keep in the Dwarves' training area?

Suzy > Sure. Might take me a bit to get there.

Dave > Yeah, that's fine.

***

Suzy looked to Anna and then looked at the mountain wall that they were climbing. Going up was okay; going back down was the part that she hated. It became clear that her Intelligence was going up in leaps and bounds but a strong summoner needed the Willpower to control their various beasts and call upon more. So, Anna had taken it upon herself to ask Suzy when she was a few drinks in what her greatest fears were. From spiders to heights, Anna had started to go through them all. Suzy *hated* it and even putting on the climbing harness she'd copied from her interface's Internet made her Willpower go up a point. She hated heights more than anything. Now, she was about a hundred meters up as she looked at the drop below her.

Cold fear gripped her as she pulled herself closer to the wall of the mountain.

She had demanded that grommets and other climbing equipment be made. Even though she would come back after dying, she did not want to die from falling off a mountain. *I already had nightmares as a kid. I don't need to do it for real and know how much it's going to suck.*

"Okay, now we just work our way down, nice and easy," Anna said.

"Fuck, fuckety fuck fucker fuckington FUCK!" Suzy said into the rock.

Anna climbed down to her as if going up and down mountains was as easy as walking. "Are you okay?"

"Are you a fucking mountain goat?" Suzy shot back, staring at the wall and holding on to the line around her like the lifeline it was.

"Nervous?" Anna asked.

"'Bout near shit myself."

Anna laughed.

"Shut up."

"Sorry. Just didn't expect that from you!" Anna continued to laugh and not even Suzy could keep a smile from her face.

"Okay, now you watched those videos on how you get down. Just tilt back and grab that line running down parallel with you. Pull it back behind you to add friction and stop you; otherwise, just hop down the wall," Anna said, as if it was the easiest thing in the world.

"For fuck's sakes, why couldn't we have done something, *anything* other than confront my worst fears?"

"It's said that some of the Demons that a summoner calls on will use their fears against them to test their master. If the master fails, then the summoner can expect to be eaten by them."

"Great, fall down by gravity or get eaten by a fucking Demon." Suzy sighed. "Why the fuck did I come to this goddamn fucking planet?"

"Bit more lively than the office, no?"

"Not helping, Anna."

"Come on, let's do this nice and slow. The first time is the hardest. Remember how we tried this out at ten meters up? This is the same thing."

"The fact that we're going all over this mountain and I'm relying on a fucking magic rope is just skeeving me the fuck out."

"Come on, what's the worst that could happen?"

"I never stop having nightmares of falling a hundred meters and making a small crater in the ground?"

"See, not that bad. Now come on."

Suzy glared at her teacher but started to tilt backward so that she stood on it. She started to move her feet down the mountain's face slowly, letting out her rope bit by nervous bit. "I fucking hate this shit."

"Come on, you're a big girl now. Let out some more. Stop trying to imitate my tail," Anna said.

Fuuuck fuck fuck fuckfuck FUCK fuck. Slowly, Suzy started to descend a bit faster, getting used to it as Anna continued her mountain goat routine.

"Try that jumping thing," Anna said.

"Shut up, will you?"

"What, never wanted to live on the edge?"

"No, I'd rather keep the fuck away from edges and live in a nice padded goddamn cell where there are lollipops and unicorns farting rainbows."

"Wow, that's pretty graphic."

"I'm pretty much shitting myself."

"Oh, come on, just a bit of a hop," Anna said.

Suzy didn't want to, but she had seen the videos. She knew how much faster it was to do the jumping thing instead of just walking down. She pushed off the mountain wall, letting out as much rope as possible. She came back in about five feet lower than Anna, the mountain goat. Suzy did it again before she had time to think about what she'd just done. She jumped, five feet at a time, and quickly dropped down the mountain.

She looked down and there was just ten meters to go to the ground. She sped up, dropping and collapsing on the ground. Her legs shook from the rappel.

"Suzy, you okay?" Dave moved to help her.

"Yeah, in a minute."

"The hell made you want to go up a mountain? You *hate* heights."

"Increase my Willpower. Tell Demons to go fuck themselves." Suzy pulled herself together and stood. "Anna's training."

"Okay," Dave said.

"Is this your fiancée?" one of the Dwarves who was following Dave asked.

"Nope." There was a resounding boom as flames appeared over the wall of the Dwarven training ground that was tucked against the mountain and away from passing travelers' wandering eyes. "That is." He grinned.

"Hurry up, Anna, you old cat!" Dave yelled up to Anna, who was quickly descending.

"Shut up, you damned mole!"

Dave just grinned and looked to Suzy. "So, how did the training go?"

"Uhh…" Suzy opened up her blinking notifications.

Stat Increase

+3 Strength

+1 Intelligence

+7 Willpower

+1 Endurance

+2 Agility

"Wow, pretty good, I guess."

Seems that this conquering fears thing might have some validity to it. Though, fuck if I'm going to tell Anna that!

Dave smiled knowingly as Anna finally joined them.

"Well, what did you want us for?"

"Well, let's go to the training ground, then I can get Suzy to show you all," Dave said, being as mysterious as ever.

Anna tried to get more out of him but he deflected it. Suzy just waited; she knew how Dave was when he wanted to make something a surprise.

They entered the practice area to find Malsour and Induca going at it with fire, fighting inanimate objects and shadows. Induca was having to stay aloft with her fire in her hands and shoot at the same time while Malsour was throwing up shields for her fiery hits and sending errant spikes and weapons at her, making her fight to stay aloft.

Deia walked over to Dave, grinning like an idiot as they got close. They kissed briefly.

"You must be Jesal and Gorrund." Deia looked to the two Dwarves.

Suzy analyzed them.

Jesal

Level 179

Dwarf

Gorrund

Level 161

Dwarf

"Good to meet you." Jesal focused her eyes before they went wide. "Oson? Do you know a Oson'Mal?"

"I feel like that is becoming an all too common question," Dave muttered.

"Yes, he is my father," Deia said.

"I am sorry that we left you out here. If I knew that you were his daughter, I would have invited you in right away!"

"Don't worry. I know how Dave needs to focus on his work and it's best if I do my training out here in the large open area than in somewhere where we can do damage," Deia said.

Induca got too close to the ground; a shadow jumped up and grabbed her one foot as a pillar of metal rose out of the ground, trapping her.

"Aww shit!" Induca said.

Malsour let Induca drop to the ground. The rest of the area returned to normal, rough but flat.

"So, what is this that you want to show us?" Malsour looked at Dave.

"Anything with runes or magical tech and you go full nerd fest." Suzy looked at the two of them, drawing too many parallels between how Dave interacted with engineers back on Earth.

The two just shrugged, not denying the accusation.

Dave reached into his bag and pulled out what looked to be a soccer ball. "This is for you, Suz." Dave held out the ball to her.

Suzy took it, almost falling over. "How heavy is this thing?" She got some support on it so it didn't drop to the ground.

"Not that heavy," Dave said.

"Seems we have a new weight with which to train you with," Anna said.

"Hey! Don't go throwing around my core!" Dave said.

"Core?" Suzy asked.

"Think of this like the engine for the car. Everything else comes from it." Dave seemed to disregard Anna's words instantly as he turned to Suzy. "Just like we talked about how you think of a shape and then it forms—think of a shape and imbue it with your Mana and soul."

"Fine." Suzy started the process.

"Put it on the ground. It uses the materials around it to grow into what you're thinking. A golem might be nice." Dave winked.

"Suave, boss." Suzy smiled, putting the "core" down on the ground.

She thought of a rock golem, just a really big damned Human made out of rocks. Her power moved into the core and it reacted to her thoughts and energies. She felt as if she were putting it into one of her previous creations but it was completely malleable. There was no definite shape. She could expand the size freely without needing to make multiple dolls or call different elements to come together into a creation.

An image developed in her mind. She imbued it with her soul, her consciousness and Willpower, and sent it toward the core. She opened her eyes. Nothing had happened other than the runes glowed silver. "Well, did it work?"

"Might want to take a step back," Dave said, doing so.

Suzy took a half-dozen.

Not a moment too soon as a rock seemed to encase the core. Rocks in the rough shape of a Human's back took shape for the legs, arms, and head as a stone golem raised itself out of the training square's ground. It slowly rose to its full height, rocks forming into crude hands. There were no facial features, only smaller rocks around where the golem's joints were. It stood at two meters tall and half a meter wide. It turned, facing Suzy before it lowered itself to one knee.

"I am yours to command." Its voice passed through her mind.

"Holy crap," Suzy said.

"What?" Anna looked from the golem to Suzy.

"It just talked to me, in my mind." Suzy looked at Anna, shocked.

"It is indeed a powerful golem. Few are able to talk to their masters. Doing so shows that you are an expert, or at the very least a high-classed Journeyman."

"What level are you in creation summoning?" Jesal asked.

"Apprentice 8," Suzy said.

"Well, see, told you I make good stuff—bumped you up an entire category. Going to have to work on making smaller ones. With time and use, this one's going to get pretty darned powerful though. I'd suggest training with it from now on." Dave looked to Anna, who nodded.

"Very well." Jesal threw Dave a stone ring. "I believe you have earned this. I think it's time that we moved on to malachite. Take the night off. We'll talk more tomorrow," Jesal said.

"Thanks." Dave waved to her and Gorrund as they turned and left.

Quest: Of Anvil and Fire

After meeting with Jesal, she has decided to accept you as a candidate to be a Dwarven Master Smith.

You will need to:

~~Master the material Stone~~

Master the material Malachite

Master the material Gold

Master the material Mithril

Find your Smithing Art

Reward: Title of Dwarven Master Smith

Do you accept?

Y/N

***

"I didn't know such things were even possible," Jesal said to Gorrund.

"Nor I." Gorrund shook his head.

"An aide for a summoner? I thought that there was nothing to do but to make stronger bodies but he went right to the focal point. He might be my student but I will admit to being the one taught something more than once."

"I am interested what his smithing art will take the form of." Gorrund looked to her.

"I'm almost scared to know. If he has something similar to Quino's internal cutting skill, he could add multiple layers of runes to items without them ever being visible to his opponents." Jesal shook her head. "Quino's going to freak if he hears about this and Dave's understanding of runes. That old codger is always trying to figure out something new to use his techniques on."

"Two more materials and then we will find out his true smithing art." Gorrund broke into a grin. "You'd better invite me!"

Chapter 22: Train Like You Mean It

Suzy looked at the others in her party angrily. There was Malsour and Induca, who were talking about their last fight. Deia was also talking with Anna; it seemed that she wanted to get some sparring in later. Deia's two-handed weapons against Anna's one was one hell of a show.

It wasn't the fact that they were walking without her. It was the fact that they were all chatting away as if it was damned Sunday brunch! *Climbing a damn mountain and they make it seem like they're going for a damned hike!*

With her were also two summoned creations. They were nothing as complicated as what her core could create, but they were slowly draining her of Mana as Anna hadn't allowed her to use her core or any soul gems to do anything but create their forms.

Then, out of nowhere, Malsour climbed over a lip of the mountain. The others followed, with Suzy behind them.

"I heard you lot were climbing the walls. Is it really that boring outside?" a Dwarven guard stood next to what looked like massive artillery tubes, the kind that Suzy expected to see on a naval warship back on Earth. Except these ones were much bigger.

"Hi. Just came for the climb. We'll be going back down soon enough," Deia said, greeting the Dwarf.

"No worries. As long as you're staying outside, we're fine with it." The Dwarf grinned. "Got to say, it's one of the strangest things I've ever heard of but have fun!" The Dwarf went back to his post, scanning the next area with a set of large binoculars.

How paranoid are these Dwarves? At a time of peace and one of the major suppliers of metals and metal products in the country, yet they're always looking for a threat. I would think that they were overdoing it if it wasn't for what the others told me about the Earth Lord and Dark Lord. Always good to be wary.

"All right, let's break for lunch and then we're going right back down," Anna said. The others agreed.

Suzy tried to not think about it. She was slowly getting to grips with her fear, understanding her limits and not over-thinking things, and it was still upping her Willpower stat nicely.

If they're going to give me more training, then I'm going to take it and ask for more. Dave needs me in this world; my skills as a secretary are going to be of little help. I need to be able to fight.

***

Deia experimented with her fire again. She was still trying to stabilize her three-part cannon and the concentration she needed for the concussive wave created by burning up a large volume of air was still a pain in the ass.

She saw Anna watching her, leaning against a post. Deia gave up on her failed attempt and looked to Anna.

"So, you still want to have a fight?" Anna asked.

"I'd be interested." Deia checked the twin blades that lay along the top of her back.

Anna grinned and pulled her great sword from her back with one hand.

"Do you use any magic?" Deia asked.

"Yes. My Affinity is with Air."

"Interesting." Deia pulled her blades free as Anna came to join her in the sparring grounds. Malsour was teaching Suzy about different creations that she could make and forming them for the best effect. Induca was off somewhere, probably sleeping or in the town that surrounded the mouth of the Benvari Mountains.

Deia spun her blades. The two of them sized the other up as they walked around, watching the other's body and remembering the fights that they had been in: their reactions, the way that they feinted and connected with their attack.

Deia moved in. Her blades moved quickly as Anna deflected the hits or turned them aside with her great sword. Deia's fighting style led to more elegant twists and turns, using the additional power for the movements to get in close with her attacks.

Anna's attack was brutal and efficient. It took a lot of strength to keep it going but her defenses were like a stone wall. She might be using a great sword but it moved with the grace of a rapier, yet still hit like a damned mule.

They traded attacks, moving faster, slower, feinting and crashing into each other. A whistling filled the air as Anna twirled her blade and brought it down on Deia's. Deia moved to stab Anna, only to be greeted by Anna's blade sliding down and turning the blade away.

Deia grinned as she moved in closer, turning around Anna to try to get even closer and pin the big blade to Anna. Anna threw the blade, turning with Deia. She kicked out, catching Deia in the shoulder.

If this was real, she would have kicked me in the head.

Anna's sword hit the ground.

"Nice hit," Deia said as Anna retrieved her blade.

"Too many people think that weapons are the only way to fight a battle and don't think of their actual body."

"What was that whistling sound?" Deia asked as they squared off again.

"You heard that, huh? Well, usually that doesn't come out nearly ever. If it does, it means that someone is about to have a very bad day."

Deia believed her as she lowered herself to the ground, one blade along her leg and the other pointed toward Anna.

Anna moved in this time—no yelling or wild running, just swiftly pressing forward.

Deia was there to greet her as the sound of metal on metal once again rang out. The two warbands that had been training in the square watched as the two clashed.

***

"Have you used fire to augment your attacks?" Anna asked as she and Deia sat down at one of the benches in the square. A number of warbands were practicing in the training square. The sound of metal filled the air.

"What do you mean?" Deia asked.

"I'll take that for a no." Anna smiled and nibbled on some cheese. "A sword is a great weapon, but it limits you, especially when you have just one sword. It's hard to defend against multiple attackers or get pesky archers who are far away. The first thing to do is get good with a blade to make sure that you can beat most of the people who come at you. Though you can also cheat a little bit. That whistling you heard was part of how my blade is made." Anna pulled out her sword and showed Deia the fine holes that went through the ebony piece that went up the blade's large fuller.

"I use these holes to control the wind, so that I am able to make wind blades. With the aid of the wind, I can move my blade faster and I can hit people who are farther away. My blade cuts through the air and I propagate that cutting air to my target." Anna flicked her blade quickly; her Mana responded on an instinctual level as a wooden training figure lost its head some ten meters away.

"Wow. I've heard of Air dancing blade style but I thought it was just a rumor," Deia said.

"I don't know if there are any around who know it anymore." Anna ate her food numbly, memories of a time long past floating through her mind. "Though I think that you will be able to use the modified Fire blade dance."

"Fire blade dance?"

"Combining your skills with weapons and your ability with Fire to meld the two into a form that complements each other and compounds the damage done by both. Do you know what Fire magic really is?"

"The control of flame and heat."

"Someone has been reading the mages college's works." Anna smiled. "But it isn't correct. See, Fire mages like yourself control the fuel of fire. Fire comes from three things: heat, oxygen, and fuel. When you make a fire, you are vibrating that fuel so fast that it generates the heat. As long as you have air around, then you've got a flame."

"So, wait, what is the fuel made of?"

"Well, the compounds can vary by person. What you have is Dragon flame, the same stuff that Induca keeps in her gut."

"Lovely." Deia rolled her eyes.

"Dragon flame is the most powerful kind of fuel in known existence, though you can also create other types of fuels for low burning or high heat and so on," Anna said.

"How do you know all of this?"

"Dear, I've been around this planet before the Elves were even a glimmer in my father's eye. I've learned a few things." Anna grinned.

"Okay, so how can I use this Dragon flame to augment my melee fighting?"

"Using the blade to cut through the wind, you can direct fire exactly. You can use it around your blade to control air currents, speeding up your movements. It is a materialization to a certain degree, yet once its effects are out in the real world, you can will the fire to respond to you. If you stick baleful fire on someone, then it will only go out if you command it or someone of a higher skill in Fire does so."

"All right, well, I've got some free time. I'm interested to learn more about this Fire blade dancing." Deia grinned.

"It would be a pleasure." Anna smiled. *Two daughters of gods—who would've thought that I would have gotten a cousin after all this time?* Anna finished off their quick meal. *When did I think there*

*would be a time that not just one but two bleeders would be making
waves in Emerilia?*

Anna shook her head thinking of the progress that Dave and
Suzy were making in their respective fields. She couldn't deny that a
bit of their drive had rubbed off on her and the others.

Chapter 23: Glass Blows

Jesal showed Dave how malachite was treated and formed. They created warm forms for the mixture of silicate and malachite to go into and then cooled it slowly, creating thick and cloudy windows. Later they used cold metal tools to shape the glass compound.

"All right, any questions?" Jesal looked to Dave.

"Okay, so what about just silicate? Like for glass, will I learn that?" Dave asked.

"Silicate?" Jesal asked, looking genuinely confused.

"Uh, the sand that forms with the Malachite," Dave said.

"We call it all Malachite, when you find one aspect you find the other, though at different densities and purities," Jesal said.

"Okay, so Silicate can be used by itself to make glass, while Malchite can be added to silicate to make it a stronger and different colored compound. What you call Malachite are two very different substances," Dave said.

"Well the analyzing system tells us that they're the same thing so we never really looked into it," Jesal said, Dave could see that she was understanding what he was saying as she hit herself in the head.

"Okay so since you know about these two compounds. Do you know if there's anything that we can use them for, apart with one another?"

"Well we could make much clearer glass as well as cups and other items like that. Though I'll need some time with the material."

"Okay, well show me that you can make a few of these window forms and then I'll let you experiment with it,"

"Can do!" Dave smiled

She left Dave with his materials, forms, and tools, muttering about how the damned Elves of Markolm probably made their glass with silicate instead of combining silicate and malachite.

Dave heated up the forms, mixing in the malachite crystals that had been already harvested from magma chambers and deep mines. He had to work quickly, pouring the malachite into the forms and heating up the malachite in between to keep it in its viscous, pliable form.

Two forms cooled too fast, making the malachite form oddly. He was about to return them to the melting bucket when Jesal called the work day. Dave checked the others, which seemed to be doing well, and followed Jesal to the classroom.

"So, what did you learn?" Jesal asked.

"I have to pour fast, but not rush it once it's in liquid form. Malachite is thick and in the quantities used, it will quickly cool down and become less pliable. I did multiple forms in a go and realized that the third one had odd layers in it due to the glass cooling at different times—had to redo them all. Then the forms, once filled, need to cool at a slow rate or else the temperature differences can mess the glass up again."

"Good. You're learning." Jesal grinned. "Now, let's go get something to eat. I'm interested to hear about that rune layering. I was reading your book on runes. Not really a rune nerd like some, but I have to say, it will make my enchantments a lot easier in the future!" Jesal clapped him on the back as they left.

"I know you need those forms for something but I was wondering if I might be able to do some experimenting with a few ideas I've got from Earth."

"You get me thirty-five panes of glass and one malachite sculpture, then you can experiment as you desire. The sculpture has to be detailed, though!"

"Deal." Dave held his hand out to her. She nodded and shook it. "Never really been an artsy kind of person, though." Dave scratched his head.

"Ahh, when needs must, you'll learn." Jesal laughed.

***

Dave watched as his sculpture solidified.

"Impressive." Jesal looked at it. "What is it?"

"It's Benvari Mountain." Dave showed it in all its detailed glory before he turned it onto its side and ignited a flame near the peak of the mountain. On the dark wall, a picture appeared of Benvari Mountain from the Nadorf side.

"Impressive. You carved an image in the bottom, using the glass's ability to allow light through to make a projection. Okay, fine, you get to do your experimenting. Let me know when you have your final project in mind," Jesal said.

"Thanks, Jesal," Dave said. He had a lot of work to do.

***

It took him three days to get the supplies he needed, watch as many videos as possible, and start to attempt to work on blowing glass.

"Oh, come on! Damn marble!" The marble Dave was working on was getting warped as he hadn't turned the glass fast enough. He didn't even want to try true glassblowing yet, so he was still trying to figure out how to roll things into shape.

He took the malachite and went back to the furnace. His marble deformed under the heat as he returned it to a block. He rolled and turned it into a cylinder, pulling it back out and getting to work on it once again.

"What the heck is he doing now?" Jasper, one of the other smiths who showed promise of becoming a Master Smith, asked.

"I have no idea. I wonder why he needed that hollow piece of metal. Hasn't even used it yet." Gorrund stroked his beard in deep thought of the mysteries that Dave had created and brought into his and Jesal's forge.

"You sure he's a Dwarf-Halfling? With all of his crazy ideas, he seems at least three-quarters to me." Jasper grinned.

Gorrund let out a rumbling laugh and slapped Jasper's back. "Mighty tall three-quarter, and three-quarter just sounds weird. Now go and check out factory three. Check to make sure their rolled support beams are up for holding the new floor coming in." Gorrund opened his interface, sending the information on the cable's needs.

"On it." Jasper opened his interface and walked out of the shop.

"I've been thinking about those cables. What if we were to put a thin cord of ebony through them and add in strengthening and anti-corrosion circuits?" Jesal asked, moving from where she had been standing, trying to get another view of Dave's work.

"Hmm, ebony would be a good conductor—would also make it stronger over time—though how are you going to power it? Get under the houses and put a soul gem to it every time?"

"Well, maybe Dave has a fix for that. He's the rune dude," Jesal said.

Gorrund stroked his beard. Replacing cabling was one hell of a chore. With time, metal fatigue and corrosion set in and the cabling fell apart. Having cables that would never fall apart would put a lot of people at ease and ease up on the mandatory checks that ran throughout the year to make sure that a housing district didn't drop ten feet onto the floor below it.

***

It was another six days until he finally went for his exam.

Dave used tongs to turn the hot metal, spraying it with a blast of fire before blowing on the tube again. He checked his work, moving the glass once more. He moved to the end of the pipe. He pulled out a piece of hot malachite with his tongs, attaching it to the side of his creation.

He pressed it into the rapidly cooling first part. He'd been rolling, using various tools to open it up and give it an edge. Finally, he took his cutting tool to cut the finished product free from the malachite still attached to the blowing rod.

It dropped into a cushioned box, already pretty cool from all of his work.

"So, what is it?" Jesal asked as Gorrund looked over her shoulder.

Dave didn't answer as he grabbed gloves and held his creation.

Gorrund laughed as they found themselves looking at a large tankard.

"Pretty." Jesal took off her goggles and looked over the tankard.

"I colored different shards of malachite to add some color to the thing. It should keep your beer nice and cold without having to be made from wood." Dave grinned, still wearing his goggles and covered in dirt.

"It's nowhere close to as beautiful as the things that the Ashal Islands can make, but damn if it ain't functional!" Jesal grinned.

"Well, I say that we go try it out!" Gorrund agreed.

The other Dwarves looked over from their work, checking out the glass tankard Dave had formed with his odd techniques.

"I'll agree to that!" Dave said.

His notifications were blinking at him once again.

Active Skill: Builder

Level: Expert Level 1

Effect: 65% speed and efficiency.

Required: Tools

New Active Skill: Alchemy

Level: Expert Level 5

Effect: Combine multiple ingredients together. Creations gain a 73% boost in effectiveness

Required: Alchemy tools

Active Skill: Smithing

Level: Master Level 2

Effect: 87% improved quality of smithing creation. 10% Chance to imbue metal with skill. Able to analyze items made of Stone, Iron, Steel, Malachite and Silver.

Active Skill: Soul Manipulation

Level: Expert Level 7

Effect: You understand Soul Manipulation 77% better. Tools you make to manipulate souls and their energy are 77% stronger.

Cost: Dependent on creation.

Active Skill: Magical Circuits

Level: Master Level 5

Effect: 93% chance of creating better Magical Circuits and understanding them. 20% Reduction of cost.

Cost: Dependent

Level 60

You have reached Level 60; you have **285** stat points to use.

Stat Increase

+2 Strength

+7 Intelligence

+1 Willpower

+1 Endurance

With all of these new techniques and ways that I'm using, it makes sense that my Intelligence is still increasing. I have a feeling that it's going to be my largest category by far.

As he swiped away the notification, he could almost feel as if the world weighed less on him and that he was able to think clearer. At the lower levels, there had still been large changes but it was only now that Dave was truly paying attention to them.

At higher stat levels, when he gained a level, it was easier to see what the difference was. At a lower level, his stats went up so fast that it was hard to figure out which was doing what to his body.

Character Sheet

Name:	David Grahslagg	Gender:	Male
Level:	3	Class:	-
Race:	Human/Dwarf	Alignment:	Chaotic Neutral

Unspent points-285

Health:	2,600	Regen:	2.12/s
Mana:	1,390	Regen:	5.70/s
Stamina:	690	Regen:	3.25/s
Vitality:	26	Endurance:	106
Intelligence:	139	Willpower:	114
Strength:	69	Agility:	65

With a grin, he followed Gorrund and Jesal, who studied the glass tankard with interest, talking about different temperatures and about using glass for more things. Having something that was see-through and could be shaped to contain items was useful indeed.

Chapter 24: Creatures of Metal and Malice

Boran-al looked up as his lord entered. He bowed deeply as the figure, vaguely Humanoid and wreathed in shadows, glided into his area.

"My lord, I was not expecting you," Boran-al said to the floor, remembering his own cultists' losses all too soon.

"It is no worry, Boran-al. I have come to see how our Creatures of Power fare," the Dark one said.

Boran-al nodded and bowed. They had recently found that the balancer had his vision lessened. The Dark Lord had never before seen Boran-al's experiments as the balancer was sure to see them if he went into the unknown area. With the creature's vision limited, the Dark Lord was checking over his various projects that he had started.

"We have created a number of Demon classes, based off different iterations we have had in the past as well as creatures that the People of Emerilia have encountered. We were also finally able to complete the Lich Lords and Banshees," Boran-al said into the floor, not daring to come out of his bow.

"Rise. Show me," the Dark Lord said.

Boran-al raised himself and moved between the various altars and Magical Circuits that lay around them. They came to a table with what looked like a skeletal creature wearing a crown upon its head and almost ethereal shadows clinging to its form.

"Rise," Boran-al said.

The Lich Lord floated from its position, grabbing a staff of darkness with red runes written down its length. It was hunched over, as if its body had given up trying to support its mass.

Boran-al could feel the power that emanated from the being. He had been experimenting on creations for thousands of years. Although the Undead Demon Lord was one of his creations, he had not powered it and it was only made up of the combination of things that people could find on Emerilia. It was because of this that it was not classified as a Creature of Power. The cultists had attained the body and then proceeded to animate its undead flesh with their own powers, firmly making it a creation under their power.

With so much time on his hands, the ability to change and form creatures as he wanted and with his lord's permission, Boran-al had spent centuries playing with different forms of monsters and listening to the Players who talked of great dark and powerful beasts.

The Dark Lord walked around the Lich. The Lich bowed its head, understanding the power that the Dark Lord wielded.

"Very well. Begin seeding them across Emerilia. For now, they are to lie in wait and build their strength."

"Yes, my lord." Boran-al's voice caught as he bowed.

"Speak," the Dark Lord said, sensing that he had something new to say.

"We worked with the Demons a lot and we started a breeding program for them. Using my own power, as you instructed, I created a place for them to study their habits. It was an experiment but there have been a number of interesting results and their population is rather large."

"Show me." The Dark Lord's voice was hungry and cold.

"Yes, my lord." Boran-al guided him between the various creatures that he had spent hundreds of years creating. They moved to an area where a magical crystal looked over a large town of Demons. There were all kinds, from those that flew to those massive ones that stood at twelve-foot-tall or quicker ones that stood at just five feet.

The Dark Lord's aura seeped out as a hand of shadow manipulated the controls. Different scenes were shown as Demons ripped apart one another with a viciousness few other monsters would show.

"I adapted them from the Demons of Xelur. They have the symptoms of the same Demons—an unending hunger that twists and warps their mind with hunger for more. Unlike the Xelur, they gain little respite for killing their prey. They cannot absorb souls. At a later stage, if they teach themselves, then smarter ones might rise to power. Those that advance the furthest are those that dabble in magics to feed or curb their insatiable hunger for souls."

"I am impressed, Boran-al. Make sure that these creatures understand who their ruler is. I do not want to destroy them all over again," the Dark Lord said.

"Thank you, my lord." Boran-al bowed, shivering slightly at the aura the Dark Lord emanated.

The Dark Lord's hands stretched and contracted in anger.

I knew that the Demon princes angered the Dark Lord. I forgot how angry he was when his incarnated Creatures of Power turned against their master, attempting to kill him.

He had delved into the death magic and manipulation magic born of the Dark Affinity but the Dark Lord's aura made him feel insignificant, as if an ant looking at a magnifying glass.

"Get the Dark Elves to prepare for them. It is time that they once again marched across Emerilia." The Dark Lord left the room.

"Yes, my lord," Boran-al said with a hungry voice. His people had long ago looked into the darker arts; their Elven brethren had discarded them and turned to attacking them as the Elves delved deeper into the magic of the Dark.

Dark magic had turned to death magic with curses, hexes, and necromancers as the Elves continued to attack their cast-out brethren. It had grown a hatred within the Dark Elves that led them to allying themselves completely to the Dark Lord.

Boran-al was one of them. His parents had died on the run and he had been raised by his uncle, a man who had fully turned to the dark and deadly side of magic. His uncle had died later on, sowing the darkness deep in Boran-al's soul.

While the Elves had lived their lives ignoring the things that they had done to their brethren who were interested in Dark magic, the Dark Elves had worked and studied to become masters of death and Dark. They no longer just tried to understand the inanimate of Emerilia. Now they lived to cause others pain and sow destruction across the land so that only the inanimate remained.

"I wonder what a reunion it will be as we meet with our long-lost cousins." Boran-al sighed softly, his face warped into a cold and twisted smile that made even the Lich Lord back away in fear.

***

Suzy looked at the small metal figures that moved across the training square.

"Well done," Malsour said, looking over the different creatures.

Suzy smiled. Malsour might love to nerd out over magic but he was also a really good teacher. He had certainly taught her a lot about creations made from metal. She could create and control two Human-sized golems and had quickly moved on to metal. It was harder to make creatures of metal and the Mana cost was many times that of the golems.

The metal figures were a hand tall but there were only four of them. They needed Mana to not only transfer her presence into them, but to keep them moving. Earth creations would fall apart if they were not powered by Mana.

The metal creations would stop moving, needing the Mana to heat up their bodies so that the metal was supple. They were also surprisingly interchangeable. With the metal, it took a decent amount of Mana but Suzy could turn them from people-looking models, to roaming squids and anything in between.

With Earth, it was easier to create one doll and then imbue it with energy. Moving earth, rocks, and sticks around was much harder than melting metal and shifting it around.

"Now try to hit that target with one of them." Malsour pointed to a target ten feet away.

Suzy sent a command to one of her servants and it sent out a lance of metal. She frowned as the lance failed to reach the target and it rebounded back into the model.

"Now try that again and detach the metal from the model."

The model sent out a lance of metal again, but this time the end disconnected before it ran out and sped out to slam into the target.

"Good. Now why weren't you able to hit it the first time?"

"I wasn't close enough."

"That is one factor. The other is because you didn't have enough metal. When you are fighting with your metal figures, it is most likely that they will transform their bodies into weapons. The more metal they have, the more damage they can do as they can hit targets farther away. With metal, you need to move away from the melee aspect that you would get with your Earth creations and toward the weapons based."

"How do you mean?" Suzy asked.

"There are the six different creations based off the different Affinities. Earth is good at close combat; they are usually heavy and not all that mobile but their hits are extremely powerful. Air is created from different types of gaseous chemicals that can be used to create area effect damage with either their stored gasses or the air blades they have. Water is much the same. Fire is good at close combat but they are more agile than strong. Dark is good at range; give them a supply of metal and they will be the best archers you know, hurling metal spears into battle. Light has a greater range and they can hit faster, but their hitting power is greatly decreased. They are the hardest to create and least versatile as you need to have a supply of

Light to keep them active and replenished. Dark creations can fight no matter the time."

"So how strong are the Light creations?"

"It reflects on a person's ability with Light Affinity and their ability with summoning. They are the hardest to make, but in no way impossible. Right now, you don't have a grasp of them." Malsour shrugged. "But in a few months, who knows?"

Suzy nodded, taking it in.

"Now, another thing that metal creatures are good for is providing reconnaissance. If a place you are attacking has good air defenses, they'll pick up the disturbances that an air servant makes. If their ground defenses aren't as good—and they rarely are—then you can get your servants inside to create havoc."

"How?"

"You send them underneath." Malsour gave a devious smile. "Send them through sewers, through the water pipes and the cracks of the walls in your way. With enough stored Mana, metal creations can condense themselves and get through the smallest of gaps, or force their way through. Light can as well, but metal is dark and using different metals can make it simulate the look of the area around it."

"Wow, I knew that they were capable of changing forms easily, but I didn't think of that." Suzy gave her four metal figures a thoughtful look.

"One's magic is only contained by a person's imagination and their will to push the limits."

"Well then, I say we push some more of these limits." Suzy grinned as an explosion rippled through the courtyard, the air rushing toward them.

"The hell?" Suzy yelled. Deia and Anna, who had been sparring, and the Dwarves in the courtyard looked over to Induca, who was jumping and dancing around in victory.

The wind calmed down and the dust and dirt from the surrounding area settled back down.

"I did it!" Induca cried out, running to Deia.

"How? What was your area pressure and what form of fuel were you using? And the dispersion pattern?" Deia asked.

"Well, it looks like we're not the only ones pushing boundaries." Malsour rubbed his forehead.

Suzy laughed. Malsour and Induca's reactions to each other always made her grin.

***

"This is gold, the second most expensive material in all of Emerilia. Once you've got this one in the bag, then you will be qualified on all materials except Mithril." Jesal passed Dave a green-looking piece of ore shaped into a ring.

Dave nodded, taking his necklace off and putting the ore on the necklace, showing the first material to the last that he had mastered.

Quest: Of Anvil and Fire

After meeting with Jesal, she has decided to accept you as a candidate to be a Dwarven Master Smith.

You will need to:

~~Master the material Stone~~

~~Master the material Malachite~~

Master the material Gold

Master the material Mithril

Find your Smithing Art

Reward: Title of Dwarven Master Smith

Do you accept?

Y/N

They sat in a classroom; Jesal had a case with different gold items. "Gold is pretty damned heavy as well as soft." She pushed a chisel into the gold, making an indent. "It doesn't rust like other metals but it'll scratch easy. It can hold some higher-level enchantments that lesser materials would break from. Unlike ebony, it does not absorb part of the Mana that might be flowing through or around it. Its lack of reactivity makes it good for using on high-level Magical Circuits."

Dave's jaw worked in thought as he stroked his beard.

"Well, at least we figured they did. I had to do some tests to confirm but it does look like silver, although not able to hold the higher-level Magical Circuits that gold can—is actually better for filling in the runes of a Magical Circuit."

"Told you." Dave grinned.

"No one likes a smart arse," she shot back, making Dave chuckle. "And it won't be enough to get you out of learning about working with gold.

"Gold is primarily used for three things: Money." She pulled out a few gold coins from different places. "Rings." The rings were high quality, with details on them that made them seem as if they were small, curled up animals, or golden flowers and trees. A few of them had different gems mounted in them. A few of the gems glowed and Dave could sense Magical Circuits in them. "And presentation, though before your little epiphany, it was used for runes." She pulled out an ornate dagger with a simple steel blade. Ebony, gold, and silver accents melded together to turn the weapon into something of beauty and power. It was a well-made blade that looked capable of cutting through a quarter-inch steel plate. Its sharp edges and strength was only emphasized by the workmanship that had gone into making the blade so beautiful.

"Personally, I only use the first two unless I've got some major piece. Even then, it's rare." Jesal picked up the rings. "These are the most useful things in here, so I will be teaching you the most about these."

Dave peered closer at the rings, using all of his senses and his Touch to check out the finer details of the items. They had powerful Magical Circuits hidden in them. They might be fashion items but they were also highly protective and powerful. "Damn."

"Indeed. We ain't making no knockoff crap here." Jesal grinned. "I want you to go from ore to ingot to different forms and then to rings. Once you get to rings, we'll get to working with some of these gems. For the most part, I think you've got this covered after your work with your own armor."

"Thanks, boss," Dave said.

Jesal shook her head at him. "While we're working with gold, we can go into the different kind of gems that you can use. From diamonds to rubies and everything in between. Unlike those Human and Elven smiths, when a Dwarf smith makes something with gems, you better take it damned seriously. Depending on the gem, it can augment your enchantments, store some energy, and can even be engraved with magical formations or entire circuits, if done properly."

Jesal had Dave's complete attention as he looked at the rings with a new interest. "They are just like a chipset—put in the right formation, plug it into the Magical Circuit, bingo." He shook his head, thinking about the possibilities.

"Chipset?"

"Something from back on Earth."

"Well, I look forward to seeing what this chipset is capable of doing." Jesal smiled.

"Not sure if it will work, but if it does, then it could change more than a few things." Dave rubbed his head, thinking seriously.

He didn't catch Jesal's growing smile. She'd learned a lot over the past couple of weeks. Whenever Dave talked about something that was from Earth, it nearly always meant that he was going to make something interesting.

"Jesal, I was wondering if you would be able to look at two weapons for me? They're pretty damaged but I was wondering if you would be able to repair them," Dave said.

"Well, let's see them."

Dave pulled out the Daggers of Demons Ruin from his bag and handed them to her. Josh had given them to Dave in order for him to see whether there was anyone able to fix the blades. Dave had forgotten about them as he had bent to the task of getting his final materials before being allowed to touch Mithril. The thoughts of runes and circuits had made him think of the complicated daggers.

"Where did you get these from?" Jesal's voice was almost reverent as she studied the daggers, turning them over in her hands and admiring them.

"My friend gave them to me. He wanted to see if there was any way to get them repaired."

"They're in bad condition but they show that they've actually been used. These things are not supposed to be out in the world. They're Weapons of Power. Where did he get them from?"

"A raid against an Xelur Demon Lord?" Dave said, hoping to get some more information out of her.

Jesal put the blades down, her face pale. "Then it may be time to open the vaults." Her voice quivered slightly.

"Vaults?"

"We Dwarves were given a sacred duty: to protect and hold the Weapons of Power. They are not all weapons like this, but might be something similar to your armor. We have made a great number of items ourselves that rest in those vaults. We believe a creature calling itself Lo'kal created the duty, giving us special vaults which hid the weapons from the outside world and then contained their power, not allowing them to be transported to a new location to be found by a new wielder. If this was found in Emerilia, then it might be possible that other weapons of great power will return."

Jesal looked at the ceiling in thought, not seeing Dave's wide eyes or the cold sweat that fell from his brow.

What the hell have you been up to, Bob?

"I can have a look at the blades, but I don't think that I have the necessary skills to look after this blade. I know of one who might be able to. We will wait until we find out your smithing art before doing so."

"You keep on saying smithing art. What does it mean?"

"You'll find out soon enough. Now put these away and get working on those rings!" Jesal said, trying to put some emphasis on her words. But the recent revelations made her feel distant.

***

Making the ingots wasn't too hard; it was a matter of smelting the gold down, getting rid of the impurities, and then placing it into a form.

It might have been difficult for someone who hadn't been doing it for months already. Dave had worked with multiple metals that were formed into ingots before being used. Working with stone and glass had been difficult but not impossible.

He'd had to adapt what he knew and what he could find out to get his previous results. Even with the gold, he spent time looking up different facts. He didn't want to mess up what was about a thousand gold coins' worth of solid gold.

Dave grunted as he moved the gold ingots around. They might be soft but they were heavy as all hell.

"Now time to turn you into something useful." He grabbed different tools, working on cutting a sliver of the gold from the ingot to reheat it and pour it into a ring form.

He looked around after a few minutes, forming a dagger in his hands and slicing through the gold easily. His conjuration ability had increased in leaps and bounds. He was not only making items down to the molecular level—his creations could have different aspects augmented to make them better. Combining his knowledge of builder, smithing, and maintainer, he could easily make a blade that cut clean through gold.

The blade disappeared as he moved the refined gold to a crucible that he'd been heating up. He put it in, adding a bit of fire to the base and increasing the melting heat. He moved to the forms, using what he had learned from other metals and the malachite. In fluid motions, he poured the gold in—not too much or too little—moving to the next easily. There was no time for hesitation. Waiting or pausing could mean that he messed up the entire thing.

Dave watched the crucible. By the time that it would cool in the crucible, the poured gold would be sorted.

As he waited, he played with his magic. No one was around, so he worked with making different things. They weren't anything crazy, just a few tools here and there. He started making things and added runes into their creation.

Simple items he could make not only identical to their physical counterparts, but he could change their very makeup so that they were actually better than the normal item. At this stage, he only thought that he could eke out maybe a ten percent improvement.

With enough time and more knowledge, I can hopefully improve that.

He knew that he couldn't even make a perfect copy of more complicated things, like Cassie's longsword. Josh's daggers, he couldn't even make half as good as the originals. They were just so powerful and well-made that they were leagues ahead. He might be able to repair them marginally but the skill needed to recreate that through his mind was not his yet.

Dave moved the crucible around. The gold inside didn't move as it was now hard. He moved to the form, cracking it open.

"Well, let's see if we can't make a damned ring."

Chapter 25: Private Discussions and Public Promises

Jesal pressed her hand against the magical mirror, getting transported to the meeting room of the Dwarven Master Smiths.

"How goes the new student?" Quino asked as she appeared.

"Wouldn't you like to know?" Jesal grinned.

"Well, I got a chance to check out those runes that he told you about. Ingenious! I never thought to go in that direction. Here I was, trying to imbue spells with more power and try different metal permutations and instead he was developing a condensed inter-layers runic platform! I am making plans to come visit. The boy interests me greatly."

"Well, he will probably be interested in your assistance. He just showed me the Daggers of Demons Ruin."

Quino's exuberant energy seemed to fall away as if his entire reality took pause to understand those words. "I will be there on the first teleport pad!" Quino practically exploded.

"Wait. First, we have a good many things to discuss, then you can head to Benvari," Sola, the Dwarf who had been picked by random to be this month's mediator, said.

Quino looked as if he were about to argue as several other masters looked at him, forcing the old Dwarf to sit down, muttering to himself about meetings and old codgers keeping him from his work.

"Hey, you're one of the oldest here!" Endur said.

"Well, it's not my fault I have more spirit than some of you darned rocks! Damn rock pounder!" Quino accused but there was a grin to his face. He had been Endur's teacher, after all.

Such an odd combination: a Dwarven master with Hammer Blows and another with Mind's Razor. Jesal grinned to herself as the two of them bickered about the other smithing methods.

"Damned metal punching ape! No class—just beating up your metal!"

"Better than staring so hard at the metal that I get hemorrhoids!"

"You couldn't even think your way out of a form!"

"Shows how much I didn't learn from my *teacher*."

"Why, you ungrateful sprite!"

"Who's the sprite, you damned wisp?"

Jesal tuned it out after a while, moving to Kol.

The others were still gathering for the bi-weekly meeting. Although Endur and Quino would yell at each other for a few hours, it was a way of them affirming their old relationship and new as fellow Master Smiths.

"Master Kol," Jesal said in greeting. They might all be Master Smiths in this room but Kol was one of the most powerful, having forged several Weapons of Power by himself, destroying them as soon as they were completed, as if they were misshapen nails.

"How is my errant smith doing?"

"Well, he seems to have made some more breakthroughs that I'll be revealing. He is an interesting smith to work with."

Kol grunted but Jesal thought that she might have seen the hint of a smile on his ruined features.

"How did his tests go?"

"So far, he has blown them out of the water, using new or different techniques to combine knowledge in different ways." Jesal shook her head.

"He truly is a man of great drive and different ideas," Kol said as Sola hit the table with a hammer.

The master Dwarves took their seats as Sola looked out among them. "Does anyone have any issues that they wish to bring to the attention of this meeting?"

Jesal raised her hand. "I do not have an issue but some new techniques and discoveries to be entered into the records."

"Do you have the information copied down?"

"I do."

"Very well. Give it to me at the end of the meeting and I will have it passed out to everyone by the next meeting. Anyone else?" Sola looked around, nodding to herself as no one indicated they had anything to say.

"Very well, to the issues at hand. The dragons have indeed reappeared on Emerilia. We have had a number of them come to our different mountains. Most have moved to their old homes. Others have created new ones. We have communicated with Denur and she will look to deal with any issues that our people or the dragons have with this council," Sola said.

There were nods of agreement and deep grunts of respect. Having a good relationship with the dragons was good for everyone involved. The Dwarves had kept their secrets for lifetimes and would look after the dragons' homes, even if they left and went traveling the world in their different forms.

"We have also received a message from Lo'kal," Sola said. The previous ease turned to tension.

"He sends word that the lords and ladies are able to not only take paladins but also Creatures of Power." Sola looked around the table. "We all know that neither the lords of Dark or Earth are too happy because we told them to fuck off after attacking our people. I ask that everyone keep an eye out and look for any sign of these Creatures of Power or new paladins. We need to know what the powers of these creatures are and where they will appear. As we are connected to the Dark and Earth by where we live, we must be watchful for things that lurk in the depths of our mountains."

"Did he say anything about the Weapons of Power?" Jesal asked.

"He did not. Why do you ask?"

"I was asked to repair two Weapons of Power—the Daggers of Demons Ruin. They were found during a raid by one of the Player groups."

"I have also seen a number of Weapons of Power. It seemed that the Lady of Light got them into the hands of those who were considered her followers so that she could have them open the portal to the Alturaran lands," Kol said.

"You say they were considered her followers. What of them now?" Sola asked.

"After the fighting at the citadel, the guild known as the Golden Sabres has started to integrate themselves with the People of Emerilia. It seems that the events affected their view on the world greatly. The Stone Raiders guild has actually bonded to them in such a degree that I think the two guilds might merge at one point."

This sent a ripple of mutterings and whispers through the gathered Dwarves. It was early days of this generation of Players, but the two guilds had already shown their strength by taking on Boran-al Citadel, even with their low levels. They had been around long enough to see a few iterations of Players as they rose and fell. Few felt that the Stone Raiders and Golden Sabres were weak.

"They did have an issue with people from other Affinities in their ranks betraying them. As the Pantheon's abilities increase and they are able to reach more of their followers, then the Golden Sabres would become weakened. If they are to join the Stone Raiders, then it would strengthen both groups." Sola voiced the thoughts of the other Dwarves in the room.

"Have the Chosen Warriors ready. We are walking into an unsure time. If Weapons of Power once again wander our lands, then a time of change is upon us. The lords and ladies of the Affinities are not to be underestimated. They are as powerful as they are conniving. We have already made our play to weaken them from the start. Does anyone have thoughts on this subject?"

Quino was acknowledged. "I say that we create some contacts with the various guilds and Players. The more we can connect ourselves to them, then the more people we might be able to call on in our times of need. It might also be an idea to give them bounties for the different Creatures of Power. Use them to find out what these creatures are capable of."

"Use them as bait to find out everything so that we can use their teachings to train our own people?" Endur said, nodding in respect and understanding to his master.

Wouldn't think that they were arguing with each other like two children just a few minutes ago.

"Agreed. We have been slow to interact with the Players. It will be good if we extend some relations with them. We must be sure to vet those we do come to trust. We do not need to accept an agent of the Affinities into our home." Sola's voice was cold and hard.

Jesal shivered with the thought, imagining if Dave or any of his friends thought to try to fight the Dwarves. At their current levels, they would do a decent amount of damage but be stopped. Yet Dave, even though he was ranked as a level 3, showed that he had the skill and abilities of someone with much more skill points than that.

We aren't the only ones with secrets.

***

Dave had finished early and Jesal was off at some meetings. Dave practically skipped through the mountain as he made his way outside. He found Deia and Induca fighting each other as Malsour read a book and Anna taught Suzy a few sparring techniques. With their time in the training area, they had become a common sight, the Dwarves caring little as they greeted and waved to them, or watched in interest.

Dave waited, watching them all. He could sense the power coming off them all now. They were much stronger than when they had first come to the mountains. Suzy walked with a confidence and will that Dave had always hoped to see in her. It wasn't just skin-deep, where she locked away her fears. She seemed to have faced her fears, baring all to the world and not caring what it thought about it.

I wonder how soon it will be before she starts to try to summon creatures to challenge them in a battle of wills. She had been working with her creation magic but she had talked to Dave multiple times about how to make a portal to these other realms to summon a creature that she might be able to tame and bend to her will.

Dave was still working with the basics of what he could understand about portals. Right now, he was focused on attaining the rank of Dwarven Master Smith. Once he did, then he would start to look into the information about portals, teleport spells, and teleport pads.

In a way, it was cheating: a summoner who used a soul binding on creatures was supposed to study how to open portals to different realms throughout their life. If Dave could create a portal capable of doing that, or use one of the ones hiding in the seeder, then all Suzy had to worry about was making the creature bow to her will.

Soul binding was just a part of the whole process and one that she was being taught by Anna. Without having to split her mind between two paths of study, she could get stronger as a creator summoner while also reaping the benefits of a soul binder.

Ahh, it is good to have friends. Dave watched them all, just taking the moment in. For years, it had just been him and Suzy. Even then, they couldn't really hang out and have a beer all that often as people would say that they were dating or report that they were doing something weird. Dave didn't want to show that he was giving Suzy preferential treatment as he knew that she wanted to make it or fail by her own efforts. Yet, it had left them both feeling lonely.

I'm happy that she was actually real and not another part of that simulation. Dave looked at her as she practiced. Her brow was

creased in concentration and she was as driven as ever as she and Anna traded blows.

Leaving her alone in Earth's simulation, he wouldn't have been
able to take it. Yet, he hadn't wanted to go into the simulation only
to find out that she was just part of the simulation, knowing that he
had not had a single person back on Earth. It might not be his home
anymore, but the thought made him sad.

*Now, I've got a new purpose, people who are more interested in my
skills than my money, no fucking reports and friends who are eager to go
into battle with me. I don't know if the last part is that healthy. Though,
I'll take it happily.* He chuckled to himself.

Malsour noticed him, smiling, and waved him over.

"Hey, Malsour. What you reading about?"

"Some interesting insight into the different Mana densities of
different metals that are mined all over the world. If we are to go to
other lands, then I am interested to know what kind of materials I
will be working with."

"Anything interesting?" Dave leaned in closer.

Malsour grinned, knowing that Dave would of course be interested in special metals. "Well, in Ashal, because it is such a high-level
area for monsters, there are some veins of ore that have been naturally imbued with Mana. In areas where the Mana lines of the planet are
closer to the surface, this happens more, but it is still something that
occurs all across the land. Say there's a place where there are great enemies that take a lot of power to kill. If there are metals in that area,
then it seems that they are imbued with some of that Mana force. For
Mithril and ebony, it takes them from Rare and Legendary ores to
mythical and deity proportions. If you can get some ore from those
areas, then you would be a rich man indeed."

"I'm more interested in seeing what you could make with it."
Dave grinned.

"As am I," Malsour said with a conspiratorial grin.

They laughed as Malsour marked his page and closed the book.

"What about lower grade materials like iron and silver?" Dave asked.

"Well, some of them can start to form Mana crystals within their metals; others will be attuned to a certain Affinity. If they are then enchanted with runes that evoke that same Affinity, then the strength of that enchantment can be greatly increased."

"How can you tell?" Dave asked.

"Well, either you have some kind of magical testing apparatus—the Dwarves would probably know—or you have someone who is highly skilled with identification magic or skill."

"Magic or skill? I thought you could only have one or the other?"

"Well, in most cases that is true. With identification, there are several factors that come into play. With the skill, it connects to how much knowledge you have of various items. Someone who has studied different items from all over the world or a singular realm of items has a large information base to draw from. When they see items and they have enough knowledge on the item or the subjects around it, they can guess or tell you what its properties might be."

"Kind of like how a merchant with more knowledge will be able to give you a better estimate of a good's value. If they don't know what the item is, they can use other things as reference to come up with a decent idea," Dave clarified.

"Right, and the Identification spell, although it might be complex and take a lot of Mana depending on what kind of spell you use, can tell you what you're looking at to a high degree of certainty. The stronger the spell, the more items you can identify and the more certain you can be of something's properties."

"Hmm, well, that is interesting." Dave tapped his chin in thought. "Not going to deny that I'm interested in checking out these ores and materials in Ashal. We've got some good stuff here but higher-level areas mean better stuff."

"I only request that we get to Per'ush and have a look at any mages colleges we might pass," Malsour requested.

"Well, we passed the one in Nadorf."

"Yes, but I have already looked over their books. Although there were a few interesting tomes, they were not high enough that I see them as a great loss."

"Book snob." Dave smiled.

"An educated mind is a man's greatest weapon." Malsour laughed.

"Or Dragon's."

Malsour's smile only grew.

"So, what are you two up to?" Induca asked, from behind.

"Nothing much." Dave's eyes went to Deia. She wore her Abscondita armor and her brown hair was tinted red and pulled back in a braid to keep it out of her face when fighting.

She was breathing a bit heavily, her face open in a large smile as she walked toward Dave.

His own smile widened and his heart beat faster as his hand snuck into his pocket.

Anna and Suzy, noticing that the others had finished their training and that Dave was there, made their way over to the group.

Dave took a knee in front of Deia.

"What are you doing?" she asked the man on one knee.

"Well, where I'm from, we've got this kind of tradition. I know that for the last couple of months we've been engaged, as weird as your Elven ways are." Dave grinned at Deia's "Oh, really now?" body language as she crossed her arms and leaned back. "So, on Earth, we make a show of telling the world that two people are connected and looking to come together to face the rest of the world." Dave pulled out a ring from his pocket.

Deia wasn't one for expensive gifts or jewelry but Dave had spent two weeks learning the ways of gold to make this one item. A red diamond, said to be pure fire dragons' blood hardened by the Earth, rested in the center, glittering with light. On either side, rubies and yellow topaz formed flames that seemed to lick at the red diamond.

Suzy let out a squeal at seeing it all and rushed over.

Anna picked up her pace, interested in what was going on.

"So, Oson'Deia, think you can take this Dave Grahslagg and evaluate him to the best of your abilities to see if he's the man you want to marry?" Dave's face was split in a massive grin. The world faded away as Deia's look of shock turned into realization as she looked to him and then the ring.

Her face and posture melted as her eyes watered. "I'll think about it," she said with a teary laugh.

Dave's heart jumped for joy as he held out his hand; she gave hers as he placed the ring on her finger. The engravings on the inside of the ring glowed as Deia's red eyes seemed to flash with power.

Engagement Ring

Formed by David Grahslagg for Oson'Deia the woman he loves and wishes to stay with for the rest of his days.

Quality: AA

Abilities:

Increase user's intelligence by 8%

Ability to resize

Soul Bound (not currently bound)

Charge: 70,810/70,810 (15 weeks)

Durability: 20/20

She laughed as Dave stood up, finding his face firmly planted into her breastplate.

"My head isn't that hard!" he yelled to the others' laughter.

Deia tilted her head down; Dave kissed her. They pulled apart, their eyes dancing as they looked at each other. It felt as if Dave's body burst with heat, the nerves of earlier turning into relief and happiness.

"Well, here's to many more adventures to come," Dave said.

Deia beamed as they kissed each other.

Suzy was making odd noises, jumping and clapping for joy. The others seemed to understand that something big had happened. Yet, on Emerilia, it was the woman's choice as to who she would check to see whether they were worthy to be the father of her children. It was only nobles and people of standing where marriages were made to increase strength when a woman didn't really get a say.

Dave was acknowledging that she was testing him to see whether he was a good mate. Then, the betrothal would come and finally marriage in order to support the children. In Emerilia, where the future was unknown, marriage was a sacred contract and vow to look after each other and their family.

"Woo-hoo! Let's go to the tavern, you two love birds! This needs to be celebrated," Suzy said, still excited.

The other three smiled. They hadn't been around when Deia had told Dave that she wanted them to be betrothed. Now they got to enjoy it.

"I'm buying," Malsour announced to the grins of the others.

Chapter 26: Practical Training

"Lady Deia! What can I help you with this morning?" Lovan, the warclan leader of all Dwarven shield bearers along the western entrance to Benvari, said.

"I'm as much a lady as you are a lord." Deia grinned and took a seat in front of the man's desk.

Lovan chuckled. "Be that as it may, your father did us a great service helping us with our troubles in the past. A Dwarf always remembers their debts and there is no debt greater than one where our family was defended." His voice turned serious.

Deia tilted her head in thanks on her father's behalf. "I am sure that my father would only tell you that he was doing what he felt to be right."

"Pah! You damned Elves!" Lovan waved with a smile.

Deia returned it.

"So, what reason do you have to meet with this old man?"

"I was wondering if you might know of any good areas nearby to train?"

"What kind of training?"

"Combat."

"Looking to move outside of the training square?"

"We both know that the training square is no substitute for a real fight," Deia said.

"A good place to develop techniques but lack of practical training. So, what are you looking for from me?"

"Are there any dungeons, caves, or areas where mobs or particularly nasty races might be holed up?"

"Hmm. What level creatures are you looking for?" Lovan moved a few objects around to get out a map that had different markings across it.

"One or two places with level 10 to get Suzy some confidence and then some higher level 50 to 90 areas to try out different techniques."

"This is a map that my scouts have made while looking over the nearby hiding areas for potential troublemakers." Lovan passed it to Deia.

She saw a number of caves and valleys, as well as a few dungeons listed. The map was highly detailed, showing a good few miles on either side of the western entrance.

"May I keep this?" Deia asked.

"Sure. Let me know which places you are going to and I'll let other patrols know about your whereabouts to check in. We'll be happy to give you supplies to help clearing out the nearby rabble."

"Thank you. I'll go talk with the rest of my party and we'll let you know which ones we'll be visiting."

"I should be the one thanking you. With you taking care of those ones, I can pool my warbands together and send them into some really nasty caves and dungeons." Lovan rubbed his hands together.

***

The classroom was empty; only Dave sat at a workbench as Jesal walked in with a sturdy steel box.

Before he'd given the ring to Deia Jesal had looked over it, but kept her judgement to herself.

"The gold ring was interesting, it looked pretty and it had hidden attributes, getting more than a five percent increase to ones attributes is hard. The way that you integrated, the gems and the coding, it was a neat and simple solution to a complex issue. That said I think if you devoted your talents to making just a functional ring over one with form you could easily increase the power of your magical coding."

She shut the door before she tossed Dave a gold ring for his necklace.

"Thanks Jesal, thought you might not like it because I went overboard with its appearance," Dave said, adding the ring to his necklace.

"You're a brilliant magical coder, but the form of a piece the way it works with different metals creating something beautiful in abilities and form is a hard balance to find. Not everyone can make magical circuits, or your more advanced Magical Coding. I was afraid that you would be all function with no form. Making a sword that can break armor is great, but if it doesn't have a proper blade on it, then you're just going to have to beat them to death," Jesal grunted and dropped the steel box onto the workbench.

"Now its time for your last lesson," Jesal said.

Quest: Of Anvil and Fire

After meeting with Jesal, she has decided to accept you as a candidate to be a Dwarven Master Smith.

You will need to:

~~Master the material Stone~~

~~Master the material Malachite~~

~~Master the material Gold~~

Master the material Mithril

Find your Smithing Art

Reward: Title of Dwarven Master Smith

Do you accept?

Y/N

It took a lot of power but Dave was able to see through the box and the runes that lay on the inside protecting the contents.

Jesal took a stone and pressed it to the steel box. It clicked before she opened the top to show the inside. Jesal pulled out an arm bracer. It was intricately designed, with runes glowing across it. It was in the realm of Legendary from its quality and the material it was made from.

"Mithril," Dave whispered, holding the metal. It was the first time that he had been able to touch it. The other times he had seen Mithril, they had been used as parts of different Player's gear.

This—well, it was made from a single sheet of Mithril. It seemed to glow and almost be blinding. It was silver but it gave off an almost white aura. Dave could see the work that had gone in to craft such an object. It truly was a piece made by someone of a master's reputation.

Dave sent his Touch into the Mithril. It was hard to get a deeper image and understanding of the metal and its contents. Before he had even gotten through the surface, Jesal pulled it away.

"Now before we get into you messing with Mithril, which I am *very* interested in seeing, we need to talk about your smithing art," Jesal said seriously.

Dave leaned forward. They had been talking about smithing art for nearly two months now.

"I see I have your attention." She chuckled and took a seat.

"Well, you and Gorrund have been talking about it for a while now. Can't say that I'm not curious." Dave smiled.

"Well, smithing art refers to a smith's personal skills and way of smithing. It is when you have evolved beyond the forge by looking back at your most basic instincts. Personally, I have the smithing art of Nature's Guide. When I am making pieces, it is easier for me if they are formed into pieces of nature. It probably comes from me being a child and spending my days in the greenhouses with my father and then the smithy with my mother. I would always try to make metal flowers and carve out nature reliefs onto metal.

"I moved past that and went on to work with all kinds of smithing. Then, when it came time for me to learn my smithing art, I was stumped. It took me five months and came to me when I hadn't slept for a week.

"I was working on a blade when my mind wandered to the gardens that I still visit. They bring me a sort of calm. I thought that

I was already messing up trying to find my smithing art, so it was worth just messing around and carving out something that reminded me of nature, something to calm me.

"I worked for three days and nights until I created a blade that looked like a blade of grass with scenes of gardens across its polished blade. My smithing art made the blade and the enchantments much more powerful. Now, this is one kind of smithing art, but there are as many smithing arts as there are people in the world. Another Master Smith called Endur uses his fists to form the metal."

"His fists?" Dave asked in alarm.

"Yeah. He was a soldier for a long time before an injury made him turn toward smithing. When he makes his blades, he punches the hot metal into form, imbuing it with different Affinities. His weapons and armor might be large, but they have passive bonuses to Affinities that would take an enchanter months to create runes for, leaving no room for any other bonuses," Jesal said.

Dave whistled at that news.

"So now, we need to discuss why you got into smithing and your different techniques when working with the metal."

"Okay," Dave said. *How the hell am I going to avoid telling her about shadow conjuring?*

"So why did you get into smithing?" Jesal started.

"Well, uhh..." *THINK OF SOMETHING, DAMMIT!* "I guess it would be to gain a better understanding of materials and different objects' makeup."

"Why?"

With that, there was a rush of air as the room seemed to cool a bit.

"Bob, what the fuck are you doing here?" Dave looked at the gnome who appeared. He wore a floral shirt and shorts, and had what looked like a damn coconut with a straw.

"What! I thought that it would be better if I was here—you know, so you could tell her the actual reason." Bob took a loud slurp from his coconut.

Jesal looked at the gnome in shock, quickly recovering. "Who are you?" She put the Mithril armor back in the box and sealed it.

"Wow, what a greeting. Should just go back to Markolm," Bob muttered. "Don't even get a hi, how are you doing? Sorry, I've been in a mountain this entire time so we couldn't hang out!"

"Bob," Dave said as Jesal looked as though she were going to do something any minute.

"Hiya. Jesal, right?" Bob must've seen something as he grinned. "Good! My name is Bob the Gnome. Great, huh? Though, you Dwarves might know me as Lo'kal. How are those vaults doing?" Bob took a seat as Jesal's eyes looked as if they were about to pop out of her skull.

Dave promptly facepalmed.

"So, how are things?" Bob asked, like a long-lost friend catching up on the latest gossip.

Dave sighed but he couldn't resist a smile. "Not bad. Hitting metal and stuff."

"Heard you made some ripples with that glass stuff," Bob said proudly.

"Y-you're Lo'kal?" Jesal stuttered, getting over her shock.

"Yep, though I'm rather liking this body. Pretty fun being Bob the Gnome. Felt like it was a good change from being a walking, talking furry frog." Bob took another noisy drink from his coconut. "So, what's Anna been up to?"

"You haven't been watching?"

"Jukal are being a bunch of a-holes. Cut my damned TVO-Emerilia—dicks."

"Can you prove it?" Jesal interrupted.

"Hmm." Lo'kal tapped his chin. "A Dwarven Master Smith does not forge weapons and armor, but forges a path for their entire race. By their creations, Emerilia itself may change. They are the protectors, the unknown crucible that refines and assists the Dwarven lords in their actions." Bob looked straight at Jesal, who looked pale, her mouth slightly open. "As long as you keep your faith in one another, I will keep my faith in you. With your words, you bind yourself to the Dwarven laws and the laws of the Master Smiths; protect, teach, and push your race forward. Use your actions to change the world, not your weapons. For my name is Lo'kal, and I entrust you with the protection of these vaults. Keep them secured and safe for a time when these weapons might be needed to protect this land."

Dave didn't say anything as he looked between Jesal and Bob.

Jesal looked as if she were still in shock but recovering quickly. "I never thought that I would meet the great balancer." She started to bow, a sign of great and true respect.

"Stop that, lass. I'm in a damned floral shirt—you know how ridiculous that would look! Oh, and next time you're in Markolm, you've got to taste out these pena-dri, so tasty!" Bob took another drink from his coconut thing, grinning as Jesal stopped her bow.

"Master Lo'kal, are the vaults to be opened?" Jesal asked.

"Master—that does have a nice ring to it. You should try it out, Dave."

"In your dreams." Dave sat back in his seat.

Bob chuckled. "Jesal, I gave the protection of those vaults to the Dwarven Master Smiths. This is your home and your planet. I may have made it but you have long since come to turn it into your home. I would not give you commands in your own home. Do what you feel is right. That said" —Bob's face turned serious— "there are things coming that will make the stories of the dark ages look like fairy tales. Creatures of Power and paladins of all Affinities will walk Emerilia once again. Skill should not be replaced by the Weapons of

Power and nor should only the Dwarves have all of them. It would make others jealous and for more power, many races are willing to go to extremes. It might be an idea to call a seasonal tournament hosted by the Dwarves for all races."

Jesal had a serious expression as Bob put his coconut down.

"Now that wasn't the reason that I'm here and why your guards are going to run in here after sensing me. The real reason is because of this handsome bastard right here." Bob gestured to Dave.

Jesal's eyebrow rose. She had picked up the easy way in which Dave and Bob talked to each other.

"Dave, you can tell her about everything if you so desire. I have been watching and I know that you haven't revealed your gifts to anyone openly but I feel that it might be indeed connected to your smithing art—" Bob turned his head to the side as if hearing something. "Well, I've got to go. I'll see you later. Watch out. The other Affinities are gearing up for a large power grab here."

Dave nodded and Bob disappeared.

Just moments later, the door opened, showing an armored warband looking around the room.

"Sorry, Master Jesal. The runes picked up an anomaly in this room," the leader said.

"No worries. It was just a new rune that my student and I were trying out," Jesal said.

"Ah, sorry, Master." The warband leader turned, waving at the rest of his warband to exit the room.

"How the hell do you know Lo'kal?" Jesal demanded after the warband leader closed the door.

"It's a long story." Dave rubbed his head. Some tension left him as he could now tell Jesal the whole truth about his interest in smithing.

"I've got some time." Jesal moved the steel box away. Even Mithril paled in comparison to learning more about the mysterious creature that was Lo'kal.

"Well, I guess it started when he told me that I was a bleeder between Earth and Emerilia," Dave started.

***

As Dave's tale had gone on, he had created a great number of things with his shadow conjuring ability. Calling it a spell at this stage felt as if that somehow cheapened it. Dave altered and change the parameters of what he conjured so completely.

Others might think of just making weapons and armor, but he has gone onto a whole different level. She drank from the glass; both the glass and the beer had been conjured from Mana.

As long as he could get close enough to analyze something, he could create a decent copy, though the power it took to create something was not small. Also, conjured items were unstable. There was a time limit on them, usually because their structure was unstable and as more time went on, their weak formation fell apart.

Dave's growing knowledge of weapons and items allowed him to take items and copy them up to a certain level. Not just because he had come to see the object. He knew the processes that the items had gone through to reach the final state. Conjuring was not just recreating an object. It was using a different object as a blueprint and imbuing it with Mana to make it reality. Dave had complete control over whatever he conjured. He had control down to what he called the molecular level, building blocks of different elements that made up the materials he was working with.

"So, you started smithing as you were looking to reduce the cost of Mana to conjure. Then, you kind of got swept up in the spirit of creativity and looking to augment your abilities with different items to increase that power's strength, like your armor. Now, it makes sense why you have so many empty spaces between different layers of your Magical Circuits. With your ability to conjure, you are able to insert the right runes, changing the circuits within to give you a level of control I have never seen before." Jesal sighed and rubbed her face. They had been in the workshop all day, eating Dave's rations as they talked.

The other facts, like him being a bleeder and Lo'kal, almost seemed trivial with all of the things that he showed off. There was no denying that his power was a strong one, with time and more understanding of smithing, building, enchanting and soul manipulation. Jesal shook her head at it all.

"So, do you have any idea of what my smithing art might be?" Dave asked.

"Not a damned clue. Like me, you're going to have to figure that out. Before we do, I'll teach you the secrets of Mithril, the last metal." Jesal checked the time on her interface.

"That is a lesson for tomorrow. Right now, I need some damned sleep and a good meal before we get into that." She rose from her chair, cracking and stretching her joints that had become stiff from sitting for so long. She laughed at the eager look in his eyes, which drifted to the steel box holding the Mithril bracer.

27: Holy Metal

"Okay, Mithril is no ordinary metal." Jesal pulled out a thin sheet of metal. She'd spent the night thinking about what Dave had told her and relaying what Lo'kal had said to her to the other masters. Still, there was an energy in her as she moved the Mithril sheet around in her hand and passed it to Dave.

"Wow. It's so light, and strong." Dave studied the metal, biting it and trying to bend it before flicking it and listening to it.

"Mithril armor is the thinnest and strongest armor in the known world. Two millimeters of this stuff is equivalent to two inches of the finest steel."

Dave whistled and rubbed his hand over the metal. "There's a grid form to it." His eyes unfocused as he used his Touch of the Land.

"Good, and yes, there is. When Mithril is put into its final state, then it creates a grid pattern naturally, aligning itself to its new creation. No matter what form you put it in, the Mithril will settle into a pattern that is the strongest for that shape."

"That's incredible," Dave whispered.

"It is, but it also makes refining and changing Mithril a right stone cold bitch." Jesal smiled.

Dave's eye twitched before he let out a laugh. "Well, I didn't think that it was going to be easy! What do I need to know?"

There were no manuals or information on the forums about how he could change and form Mithril. No Player had been able to smith Mithril before. This was one of the greatest kept secrets of the Dwarves. One that gained them fame and the world's interest.

I wonder just how many secrets these Dwarves have? If Bob knows them enough to give their Master Smiths advice, I think that there is a lot more than meets the eyes with this bunch!

Dave smiled. No matter their secrets, he felt at home with the Dwarves. They showed respect to one another for their different skills and the Master Smiths were idolized.

Yet, people didn't avoid them and the Dwarves were as happy to teach anyone anything. All were valued equally and people were allowed to do as they desire. Other races and groups might make it mandatory for people to be in the military. For the Dwarves, it was completely free. Their mindset was much that of the Stone Raiders: they could do whatever they desired; no matter what, the Dwarves would treat one another as if long-lost family.

I'm not entering into a trade—I'm entering into a family. That thought struck him more than the Mithril. He felt a smile spread across his face in joy.

"Well, first of all, the way that you get Mithril to move is you need to imbue part of your soul into it. Mana doesn't work, but your soul—well, it has much more raw energy and a higher degree of control."

"How the hell do I use my soul?" Dave frowned at Jesal.

"Well, that is where things get fun." Jesal's grin was hungry, making Dave quiver.

She pulled out what looked like a piece of shaped malachite. Taking it, she placed it on the Mithril and closed her eyes. Her face turned into one of concentration as a thin sheen of sweat was visible on her face. Dave saw and felt the bonds that had been made slowly changing, allowing the metal to be moved easier. It would still need someone to pound on it with some damned strong tools but it was now possible to forge the metal into something else.

Jesal wiped her brow, grinning, and handed Dave the rounded glass.

"That is a gem that allows someone to use their soul energy on another object. Your soul's energy is much more refined than your

Mana. As you expend your soul energy, then your Mana will fill the void and become refined by your soul."

"Okay, this soul stuff is all really confusing," Dave said.

"Think of soul energy as your hand and Mana energy as a river. With the Mana, you need to make contraptions in order to change the direction of the river, using its power for different things. Those contraptions are Magical Circuits. Soul energy moves with the user's mind. It exercises power over the natural order, but it doesn't need runes, formations, or circuits to control it. It has been imprinted with your very consciousness. You think of something and it will react *exactly* the way you're thinking.

"Mana is easy to think of as infinite as with enough time it will always come back; so will soul energy. The difference is the toll on the body and the mind. Using soul energy is a hard task. The more you use, the closer you become to a vegetative state, with your mind incapable of making connections or even talking in proper sentences. With Mana overuse, you get headaches and pain, but you don't lose your mental faculties."

"So, why do I need to use soul manipulation tools?" Dave asked.

"They direct your power and amplify it. Your soul energy is more refined and powerful compared to Mana energy. Using tools instead of just our minds allows us to leave less of an imprint on the energy and thus retain more of our mental faculties for longer."

"So, I don't have to concentrate as long, which will keep me from going wide-eyed and stupid?"

"Well, pretty sure you got that part down easy enough." The corner of Jesal's mouth turned up into a smile. "What you've got to look out for is draining yourself. With time, one can grow their Willpower; becoming more sure in their person, facing more fears, using their focused soul energy and so on. Though it is not an easy task, as it grows, you will have more energy to use on this kind of finer magical alterations."

"So, the soul contains an imprint of our consciousness and is formed from energy. We're using this refined energy that the soul produces on the Mithril to break down the complicated bonds that hold it in place."

"Correct. As one's Willpower stat increases, the power that you can draw from your soul and the rate at which it can be refined increases. With your friend, the summoner, she is able to call more creatures as she is able to make an imprint of her soul's energy onto different creatures with a higher Willpower. That said, she is storing it in another creation and while her soul's total energy will refill with time, it is only until she destroys the creation that she can use the Willpower controlling the creature. With too many copies floating around, it weakens the imprint on the creation."

"Okay." Dave nodded. "Then, when we are using these tools, how is that energy being used?"

"When using this and other soul extending tools on Mithril, you are not passing on a part of your consciousness onto anything. Think of your own conjured blades. The reason you can't make so many is because your Willpower is low. Now, you're not putting your consciousness into them as much as your summoner friend does with her different creations. Yet, the plans—the thoughts and the ideas of what you want your conjured blades to be—are used as a template, waiting to be imbued with Mana to turn it into reality. Your Willpower creates a blueprint and your Mana empowers it. At least that is my running theory." Jesal shrugged.

"Interesting. So, how much power does it take to shift Mithril?" Dave asked.

"Quite a bit, especially if it is refined. It is not abnormal to find people who store up their soul's energy in soul gems for weeks before starting a Mithril project. Heat, special forges—all of it is needed to not only purify Mithril but to turn it into a piece of armor.

"Once it is made pliable, one has to be careful about how they work the metal. One must be aware that once the Mithril bonds are broken and it is being changed into a new form, it sucks up Mana like a damned sponge. Weapons of Power were usually created when a great number of powerful individuals gave their power to the Mithril, increasing its initial growth potential. Some even say that strong enough blades gain sentience due to the magical imbuement."

Dave's eyes widened, looking at the metal on the desk and the crystal lump in his hand. "It's that strong?"

"With great work comes a few rewards," Jesal said.

"Damn." Dave knew it would not be easy to work with the Mithril but its potential was great enough to make ideas begin sprouting up, hinting at new ideas, methods, and possible ways to enhance the armor's effectiveness even more.

"At more advanced stages, you can imbue a piece of armor with not only Mana, but Affinities. These do not count as enchantments but base attributes. Passive abilities that the metal will bestow onto those using it without runes or enchantments." Jesal shifted, her face thoughtful. "With you, I don't honestly know what will happen with any Mithril you craft. It might have a number of the Affinities within it. Or it might have all of them. Or it might have none."

Dave sighed and rubbed his face. The path ahead of him would not be easy but it would be well worth the effort.

"Before we go through all of that, time to check up on those stats!"

Dave checked his interface. If he didn't think about it, it kind of faded into the background. As he looked around, he found his notification bar blinking.

Active Skill: Maintainer

Level: Expert Level 5

Effect: 73% chance to restore durability, at higher levels possible to increase durability, quality and gain 4% Sharpen bonus to items that have been cared for.

Required: Dependent on gear; sharpening stone, hammer, anvil. Better maintainers tool leads to higher chance of increasing stats.

Active Skill: Builder

Level: Expert Level 9

Effect: 69% speed and efficiency.

Required: Tools

Active Skill: Smithing

Level: Master Level 3

Effect: 89% improved quality of smithing creation. 15% Chance to imbue metal with skill. Able to analyze items made of Stone, Iron, Steel, Malachite, Gold and Silver.

He'd finished off two new materials and done a number of different techniques that had changed his abilities as a smith.

Getting his Master levels was like getting twenty or thirty Beginner levels.

Still feels good to just get up a single level.

Active Skill: Magical Circuits

Level: Master Level 6

Effect: 95% chance of creating better Magical Circuits and understanding them. 25% Reduction of cost.

Cost: Dependent

It does seem that my Magical Circuits are racing ahead. Must be due to the large amount of information I have and the different things that I've tried out. It is a lot easier to make a number of runes in the right format than beat the hell out of Mithril with my soul powering my tools. Well, I would guess, at least.

Stat Increase

+2 Strength

+4 Intelligence

New Active Skill: Glassblower

Look at you go, just putting that pole right to your lips and givin' it your all. Damn, you could probably blow a golf ball through a garden hose with them lungs! Ah, sometimes I crack myself up. Get it? Glass, cracking? Ah, go touch yourself! I didn't put my lips to a big tube and start blowing!

Level: Journeyman Level 4

Effect: 51% chance of creating better glass-blown products

Cost: Dependent

The fuck is with these damned skill descriptions? Dave shook his head, continuing through the remaining prompts.

Level 61

You have reached Level 61; you have **290** stat points to use.

He skipped over to the character sheet.

Character Sheet

Name:	David Grahslagg	Gender:	Male
Level:	3	Class:	-
Race:	Human/Dwarf	Alignment:	Chaotic Neutral

Unspent points-290

Health:	2,600	Regen:	2.12/s
Mana:	1,430	Regen:	5.70/s
Stamina:	710	Regen:	3.25/s
Vitality:	26	Endurance:	106
Intelligence:	143	Willpower:	114
Strength:	71	Agility:	65

With a flick of his hand, he sent it to Jesal. No one except him could see that he had nearly three hundred experience points stored away.

"I still don't get why your rank is so low. Your other stats are all quite impressive," Jesal said.

"Ahh, a man has to have his secrets—maybe later. It really is a pain in the ass to try to explain it."

"How do I think it's more of the latter than the former?" Jesal drawled.

"Because then you would be right; takes like *days* for people to get it." Dave shuddered as Jesal rolled her eyes.

"Fine, keep your secrets. In the meantime, let's get working on that Willpower of yours. Use that disrupting stone in your hand and break this Mithril's bonds apart. Do it three times and we'll be done for the day." She stood and wandered away.

"Why do I feel like it's going to be hard as hell to do it even once?" Dave said to her as she got to the door.

"Ahh, I wondered when you were going to learn." She smiled and walked out of the workshop.

"Fuck." Dave looked at the stone in his hand and then back at the Mithril in front of him. "First, let's see if anyone else uses tools like this—might be able to help me out a bit. Just forcing my soul through it sounds like a bad idea, however you want to phrase it."

Dave twirled the stone around in his hands, sitting back in his chair. He scrolled through messages, replying to them, and then moved on to his research.

"I never thought that smithing would make me look into such strange things." Dave snorted as he got to a forum post about people using soul gems for a whole bunch of different things, from clothes to alchemy. Smithing took time and patience. It seemed that few had gone beyond even ebony. Few had varied away from the forms that Emerilia automatically gave a person. So, there was little help there.

Using the disruptor sounded pretty easy. The problem was managing your soul power. As time went on, then the soul power would increase in amount and how long it could regenerate.

Power that came from the soul was greatly condensed and powerful. It was ten times more powerful than normal Mana, and at least that much more controllable. Having his consciousness imprinted onto the very energy that made up his soul power meant that even his faint ideas would be easily communicated into a spell or whatever he was using his soul power for.

Smiths were never taught to use their soul power, but creation summoners did it a ton.

Dave looked through different parts of the forums, sending messages to Malsour, Anna, and Suzy to ask about different aspects of using one's soul to imbue an item with power.

Party Chat

Anna > The first thing you need to find is your soul power. Once you have that, then you can proceed to try to move it around.

Suzy > Why the heck do you even want to know?

Dave > Just looking into something. Saying you don't want me to keep on making more cores?

Suzy > No! I was wondering if you might be able to make me one from metal.

Dave > What kind of metal?

Suzy > I don't know.

Malsour > Well, I think I know what our next lesson will be about.

Suzy > Fuck. More books.

Dave laughed in the workshop; a few walking past sent interested glances into the room, where Dave looked to be playing with a piece of glass in his hands.

Party Chat

Dave > How do I find my soul power? I feel like I should be in the 1970s, with an afro and bellbottom pants.

Suzy > No one else is going to get that, genius.

Dave > You did.

Suzy > Metal core—make it!

Anna > It is connected to your Mana, siphoning off a very small but constant amount to keep it sustained.

Dave > What would happen if I don't have Mana for days?

Anna > Nothing. Your soul also uses the natural energy of your body and your environment.

Dave > All right, thanks. Going to do some soul searching!

Suzy > *Double facepalm*

Dave snorted and pushed the interface away. It would be a distraction for what he needed to do next.

Dave searched inside himself, looking at his Mana circulating around his body, and then looking at the soul power; it had a constant but minimal drain on his Mana, so that it was like looking for a raindrop in an ocean.

"Man, it would be nice if all of my Mana was more dense and easier to control." Dave sighed. His eyes widened as he sat up slightly. "No, there's no way, right? Surely? Right?" Dave's mind whirled.

"I've been thinking of Mana like electricity, but what if I thought about it as food, or gasoline, or wood? That would make more sense, because how else would my soul have that much energy? Simply having a better storage is one way, but if it was, then the information would be lost. My consciousness would be fluid. Instead, it's solid. The fact that my Willpower has a numerical system makes me think that it might be packets of power. Maybe it isn't but my soul power shows that somehow you can condense Mana into the refined form of soul energy."

I've used soul energy before, and it just converted right into Mana. I must have been using soul energy to change those spells at Boran-al. I wasn't calling a spell, but rather willing my Mana to change the formula of the spell.

"I need to work on making the storage I have of my soul energy larger. Going to need to tamper with my soul gem and see if there is a way to convert Mana. Could store a lot more power in there—maybe ten times more? Will increasing the amount of soul energy I store increase my Willpower?"

Dave sat there, talking and thinking to himself for some time, as a plan formed in his mind.

"Well, I've got nothing but time on my side." Dave smiled to himself. Eternity was a long time, or even the few centuries that would go on in Emerilia before the Jukal Empire cleared out the Players and reset the world, ready for the next batch of Players they had grown.

***

Suzy's eyes went wide as her rock golems mowed through the underground henir.

Henir looked like a cross between an armadillo and a mole. They were blind as shit but they used their earth sense to traverse the area. They had small and loud mouths; they could form drills of earth in front of them to cut through rock. They had sharp teeth and claws and hard armor plates that covered their bodies.

Her rock golems acted as her shields while her metal creatures threw metal spears into the midst of the creatures.

"Metal, get into their middle!" she called out, reading the battle.

Her metal creatures, a part of her will turned animate, stuck out their arms and reached into the middle of the battlefield. Instead of letting go of their metal, they seemed to flow into the spear. Their extended arms acted as a focal point as they transferred their bodies, moving from the edge of battle into the middle.

The henir screeched, their voices imbued with Earth magic and making the cave they were in shudder. Even as the metal creations were starting to fight in their midst, the creatures charged forward against the golems. Their claws were small but sharp, taking chunks out of the Human-sized golems.

"Earth, trip them up!" Suzy said, playing one of her hidden tricks: simple squid creatures that cost one Willpower to make. Two stretched out of the ground, their tentacles latching onto the henir with spikes.

Need to work on arming them with some kind of poison.

The henir, even at their low level, were able to tear through the Earth-formed tentacles after a few hits. They weren't really harming the henir, but they slowed their progress, allowing the golems to smash the henir's sides and turn their innards to pulp with heavy smashes.

Suzy looked back to find Anna and Malsour watching and talking to each other. Deia and Induca were stretched out, with a fire going in between them, talking as if they were on a camping trip and Suzy wasn't fighting a horde of henir by herself.

She made an annoyed noise and looked back at the fight. "Metal spin!" Suzy pushed Mana into her creations. She checked her character sheet quickly.

Character Sheet

Name:	Suzy Markell	Gender:	Female
Level:	1	Class:	-
Race:	High Elf	Alignment:	Chaotic Neutral

Unspent points-60

Health:	1,100	Regen:	0.24/s
Mana:	430	Regen:	3.35/s
Stamina:	270	Regen:	1.55/s
Vitality:	11	Endurance:	12
Intelligence:	43	Willpower:	67
Strength:	27	Agility:	31

Her Mana reserve had increased to over four hundred. She'd prepared her creations beforehand, powering them with soul gems that Dave had given her. It had meant she had a greater Mana pool to pull from for this fight.

She wasn't allowed to use the vault-classed soul gem that held a good chunk of the party's unused Mana for the last few months.

Best to know how to fight with the bare minimum than all of the extras. She watched as her Mana started to plummet.

Her metal creatures stood about four feet tall. With her command, they flattened themselves to about two-foot-tall, their metal turning into whirling blades as they spun. The Mana it took to make them transform and be able to move that fast was no small thing.

Henir watched as metal blades cut them apart from within their center. They tried to fight the metal creatures but they spun too fast for the henir to get close.

"Golems, forward," Suzy commanded. They marched forward, hammering henir or tossing them into the metal blenders.

Suzy had to stop the metal creatures that were doing the least damage. She didn't want to waste the power from the soul gems as they were just simple ones, not the rechargeable kind. Another hindrance Anna had added to her training.

"Solidify. Use sword arm." Suzy felt lightheaded for the Willpower she was using. The longer she used a large amount of her Willpower, the more confused she could get. With just fifty percent of her Willpower being used, she was slower to react and think of complex ideas. It was as if her mind had been starved of oxygen.

She pulled her consciousness from her unused Earth tentacles. Her mind became sharper as she surveyed the battle.

The metal creatures pulled back into their original shapes, the metal slowing their spins.

Suzy could see statuses over all of them, color-coded to state their condition:

Metal Summoned Creature
Durability: 89/125
Charge: 471/1000
Metal Summoned Creature
Durability: 41/125
Charge: 817/1000
Metal Summoned Creature
Durability: 84/125
Charge: 587/1000
Metal Summoned Creature
Durability: 17/125
Charge: 119/1000

Metal Summoned Creature

Durability: 39/125
Charge: 315/1000

There were a good number of the golems in the yellows, with a few red. Three of the five metal creations were yellow, with one green and one red.

If the creatures' charge or Health was low, then it would change status. On the right side of Suzy's screen, she had her creatures color-coded from green down to red, knowing which of her forces could be used easily and those that would have to be changed out or sacrificed to keep other units alive.

One of the larger henir let out a screech as the others seemed to pause in their battle before trying to flee.

"Oh no, you don't," Suzy muttered. "Metal, transfer in front of the henir. Spinning blades—make a line and cut them down."

The metal creatures that were fighting the henir with their arms turned into blades now shot out a length of metal, reforming before the retreating henir. They formed a line across the cave, cutting and slashing the henir that got close before they turned into spinning cyclones once again.

"Golems, push them into the metals." Suzy lent her strength to the metal creatures so their soul gems wouldn't be drained too quickly.

The six golems advanced, four of their comrades already down over the course of the fight. They harried the henir, who turned toward the walls when they realized they were getting hit from both sides. Earthen drills made from green Mana formed in front of them as they started to escape into the walls.

Shit, hopefully I've scared them away enough that they won't think about doubling back. Suzy watched as the last henir was kicked by a golem into a metal creature's spinning blades. Suzy didn't have to say anything as the metals stopped spinning and the golems stopped moving, conserving their power while still holding their form. Suzy rubbed her forehead, drained from powering the metal creatures.

A henir jumped out from the ceiling, aiming right for Suzy, and let out a high-pitched squeal imbued with Earth Mana to push her to the ground.

She grunted, falling to her knee, seeing her oncoming death before a firebolt tore it apart.

"T-Thanks," Suzy said. The pressure released, her heart racing from the near-death experience.

"I trained you to use your sword better than that. Next time I won't save your ass," Deia said with a hard look.

"Yes, Deia," Suzy said, angry with herself for letting her guard down. *I didn't even have my sword out.* She mentally chastised herself, thinking that she would fight everything at arm's reach.

"Remember, you might be a mage, but when someone gets within blade distance, you need to be able to defend yourself. Mages are glass cannons; once your Mana is out or your enemy is close by you, you need to know how to defend yourself and be ready for that," Deia said.

"Yes, sorry. It won't happen again." Suzy's hand was on the hilt of her sword as she looked down in shame.

"Good, because Anna and I are going to make sure you remember that when we get back to the western gate."

Suzy winced, but she knew that Deia was doing it for her own good. Her stats were higher than she had thought possible in just a few short months. The party might train like monsters but it showed in not only their stats but the ways that they held themselves. Their harsh words would help to make Suzy stronger and for that she was grateful.

"Otherwise, that was very well done." Malsour looked to Suzy.

"Thank you. The Earth tentacles weren't much help but I think with some poisons for their thorns, I might be able to make them a lot more effective."

"Good. Not only taking a victory but learning from it is how you will grow. Never think that your strategy is perfect. That said, you did make good use of the terrain and pulled the henir right into a trap. Studying and knowing your enemy led to a decisive victory," Anna said in approval.

Suzy smiled, still irked about her screw-up at the end and a few other things she thought that she could improve on.

"With that, I think that we should move on and continue to clear this place up. Should be some higher-level creatures farther in and some kind of cavern big enough for us to try out some bigger techniques." Deia smiled.

"Well, what are we waiting for?" Induca jumped up and stretched.

I might be surrounded by monsters, but one day I'll stand shoulder to shoulder with them. For now, I can just enjoy the show. Suzy smiled, excited to see what their new techniques would do. She had yet to see them in a full-on battle but she knew it would be something she didn't want to miss.

Chapter 27: Testing

They had left the henir burrows and the cavern that it was attached to a few weeks ago, moving to bigger and stronger areas where different creatures were resting, from rock snakes to goblins and wild wolves.

They had each taken a cave and worked their way through it, taking frequent breaks to critique one another and talk of improvement.

Even though their overall levels weren't that high after using Dave's strategy and working on their stats rather than the levels to get stat points every level, their stats were enough to turn it into a difficult fight against level 50s but not impossible. Well, for everyone except Anna, who could breeze through them easily as she had been using Dave's method for hundreds of years. Her father had limited her stats when she had come back but she was still really damned powerful.

It was now Deia's turn as they entered a cave system that should have level 60 to 80 residents.

Suzy sent out her different groups, using her metal creatures as scouts to check out the area. As they found new targets, a red silhouette would appear through the rock, showing the position of the various creatures. Most of them faded as their positions were only updated if Suzy's creatures remained in their vicinity.

A few dozen showed up before the metal scouts entered a larger room, moving around the edges. The interface's map showed the different rooms' layouts, which would be saved to their maps.

A large creature was revealed, creating a red cloud. Before the silhouette could be completed, it started moving.

"Ah shit, it saw my scouts," Suzy said. The map stopped expanding as the creature destroyed the different metal creations.

"Well, looks like this one will be interesting," Malsour said.

"One can only hope." Deia laughed and pulled her compound bow down. She needed a new one. With her strength and spell-imbued arrows, she was close to ripping the bow apart at just half her power. She moved the black helmet on her head, which looked to have two crystals on its front, like eyes.

This was linked to Suzy, who could look through the gems to tell the others what she saw. Most had gone on ahead, the others too slow or trying to move in stealth that Suzy had come up with the idea from something she called a camera.

Deia moved into the cave system. The mid-morning light faded behind her as the deep gloom of the cave system awaited her. She closed her eyes, listening for anything that might be near, and let her eyes adjust to the newfound darkness. She opened her eyes, finding the cave system's darkness easy to see through. She maintained a hold on her strung arrow, moving forward quickly, her shoes not making a sound.

You did make this armor well, my little smith. A smile formed on her face as she thought of her armor like one of Dave's hugs, his large arms protecting her from the world even though he wasn't there.

It didn't make a noise as she moved through the area.

Rock Troll

Level 54

Deia breathed deeply and pulled back on her bow. She released, just using her strength without any special skills. The arrow flew true, catching the troll in the throat before it knew what was going on. Deia grabbed another arrow, moving into the area the troll had been living in.

It smelled like decay and death, but there was nothing else other than animal bones and a few trinkets. The troll lay on its back, struggling for a minute as blood pumped out of its wounds. Slowly it stopped moving, staring upwards with lifeless eyes.

Deia moved forward, her eyes and ears open as she released the tension on her bow. She heard two creatures grunting at each other before there was a metallic ring of combat. She shifted her shoulders, keeping her body relaxed as she moved forward.

Steel Tusked War Hogs

Level 61

Steel Tusked War Hogs

Level 63

How the hell did two war hogs get down here? The Dwarves should keep a better eye on their steeds.

The two war hogs clashed with each other; their horns smashed into the other's as they pushed each other up so they stood on their hind legs. They jerked their muscled necks, trying to free their tusks and bring them down on their opponent's flesh, grunting and bellowing as they fought.

As their names suggested, their tusks were not made from bone but rather steel. They were the favored rides of the Dwarves. They were smaller than horses, heavily built, loyal to a fault, and hard as hell to train. Although the warclans were usually made up of shield bearers, a number of special mounted units used the war hogs with devastating results.

War hogs would challenge one another and their riders constantly. Once they were shown that they were weaker, they would follow for a time, testing their strength every few years.

These two looked as though they had matured under harsh conditions, shown by their scarred fur and tusks. It seemed that they were fighting for dominance.

Deia watched with interest. She wasn't about to run in and get herself between these two. If they injured each other or grew tired, then she could use that to her advantage. *Well, this is exhilarating, seeing two muscled creatures beating the crap out of each other.*

She stopped herself from sighing, not sure how good the war hogs' senses were at finding danger. If they could keep the rock troll at bay, then they must've been decent fighters.

They came apart for a second before they slammed into each other again, using their entire bodies and head to try to get some kind of edge over the other. Their strength and muscles made Deia happy that they were fighting each other instead of her.

She studied their bodies, looking for weaknesses and a way to get a clean shot into their chests. *I just hope the bow has enough strength to handle it all.* Deia watched and waited for an hour.

Both of the war hogs had deep slashes in their hides from one or the other hit. Finally, they disengaged, walking around each other before the level 61 turned to its side, showing off its unprotected side as a sign of submission to the other.

Deia pulled back her arrow at the opportunity.

The level 63 beast roared, raising itself up onto two feet in victory.

Deia was unfazed by the beast's war cry, letting loose with her arrow. The air cracked at the passage of what looked like a lance of fire. Without waiting to see it land, she grabbed her second arrow, changing her aim and letting loose.

The 61 was startled and tried to raise itself up as the first arrow slammed into the upraised 63, catching it full in the chest, making it scream out as the arrow got past its strong hide and into its vital organs. It howled in pain but it still had life in it. Until the arrow exploded outwards, tearing its chest apart. The 61 had turned enough to make the second arrow hit its side instead of through its softer stomach. It exploded as well, burning it badly and making it roar in pain.

Deia cursed; she grabbed another arrow and let loose.

The level 61 turned its face, only to get an arrow in the eye. It howled, followed by a muffled explosion that tore the war hog's head apart.

Both creatures stopped moving. Not a sound came from any of the caves.

"I'm leaving this to you lot," Deia said, knowing the camera would pick it up as she grabbed a new arrow and put it on her bow.

The war hogs' pelts, meat, and fur would go for a good cost. They had not been lacking for money so far, but all of them were looking forward to a bit of coin in their pocket to get items that would help their advancement.

Deia had been raised in the way of a Wood Elf and wasn't willing to leave anything useful behind. She would kill to grow stronger but she wouldn't let it go to waste afterwards.

She advanced, moving through a long tunnel that dipped down. She came to an open area with a slight slant to the ground. Deia was about to walk forward when she heard a grating noise. She spread out her Earth sense, her bow low and ready as she crouched slowly.

Rock snakes.

The metal creatures were decent at finding most enemies but they were still limited due to Suzy's knowledge of different animals. As she knew more, her imprints on her creations would know more about different enemies.

Well, this is a fine mess. Deia realized she was just a few feet from a large rock snake mating pit, filled with tens of snakes that were between her and her destination.

Deia moved backward to the safety of the corridor. She put her bow away in her bag of holding and spread her hands out, remembering what she had learned over the last couple of weeks. She used her fire Mana, changing the chemical compounds in the air around her, and turned them into a combustible substance. Her Mana converted more of the mass around her into fiery fuel. She directed the compounds toward the snake pit. Clear liquid raced away from her, making wet trails toward the snakes.

Now she had the knowledge of what Fire Mana really was. It had led to her making a number of discoveries. Before, she had been ruled by emotions; now she had buried her head in books about chemical compounds.

Her Fire Affinity combined chemical compounds in the air into fuel. Drops formed out of the air, creating a light mist over the rock snakes' pit. A few shifted around, their rock bodies scraping on the ground.

Deia gave a grim smile as she commanded the substances around the snakes to vibrate.

The snakes looked up in alarm at the mist that had settled over them and was now shaking. Now alert, they looked toward the oddity in their domain. Dozens of heads looked toward Deia.

"Soul trap." Deia cast the spell as many times as possible, knowing she had just seconds.

The room turned into a furnace; the chemicals erupted into the fire they were meant to be. It was hotter than a plasma torch as Deia fed Mana into the fire, keeping it alive as the rock snakes simply exploded.

The heat around them combined with their hard bodies' inability to contract or expand much; the water inside them turned to gas in seconds and turned the rock snakes into exploding firecrackers.

She cut off the fire as the popping stopped.

"Well, I think they know that I'm here." She pulled out a soul gem and a red gem that seemed to swirl with Fire Mana. She placed the gems together and the soul gem turned to dust as its energy was absorbed by the Fire Mana.

After seeing Suzy's core, Deia had her own idea of how to make summoning her Fire atronach easier. If she was to hold it in a ready state without the activation power in a gem, she could have an atronach ready to go for a week. It lessened the amount of Willpower that she could use on other things as it was constantly devoted to the atronach gem.

But right now, it meant it only needed a few seconds and no additional Mana from her as an apprentice-stage Fire atronach appeared. It looked like a forest sprite with ague Human features formed from living flame as it looked to Deia, ready to carry out her bidding.

"Well, let's go on a walk. You stay back so nothing can see you," Deia said.

The atronach didn't say anything but she felt it understood. She grabbed her twin blades and advanced farther down the cave. Her blades, like her bow, could barely hold her new techniques. They were fine weapons but she had long outgrown their abilities.

With enough coin, I can replace these with some blades better suited to my level. Dave was a great smith, but she knew he had his own thing and didn't want to trouble him when she could get another weapon off a Dwarven vendor. All of their wares were of the highest quality.

Though, he will no doubt find a fault with it in trying to protect me.

She smiled, shaking her head slightly as she advanced through the oven she had just made. Her armor pulled in any residual Mana and souls in the area. Her soul trap had done well as she'd targeted the highest-level rock snakes she could see.

Abscondita Armor
Forged by Dave Grahslagg, this armor is more than meets the eye.
Quality: B

Defense: 527 (Magical shield with enough power)

Abilities: Magical shield

Automated Mana Siphon

Automated Soul Siphon

Automated Self-Heal

Increased Agility and Strength (base 10%)

Increased Fire Affinity (3%)

Grows in strength with user

Manipulation possible (Associated values liable to change due to creator's changes and level of charge.)

Armor Link (Users of this armor can share their power and link capabilities. If one armor is fully charged, then it will feed power to the other to charge it.)

Charge: 24,3973/2,000,000 (Linked Armor within range 0/0)

Durability: 231/259

Because she was too far away from Dave, she was no longer able to use his Mana reserves, just as he could no longer use hers.

Her armor was different from Dave's in one large way. His didn't give any bonuses to magic; hers gave her a 3% increase in Fire Affinity. That 3% might not sound much but most armors just gave a few points boost. Having a percent instead of an additional number of Affinity points would allow Deia to find the armor useful for a much longer time. It would also give her a lot more with her current Affinity levels.

Affinity Levels

Dark 27 Light 40

Air 82 Water 10

Earth 47 Fire 232

She gained 6 points to her Fire Affinity, making it not only stronger, but also easier to control and increasing her resistance to Fire-based attacks. Those 6 points didn't seem like much but at her high levels, those few points were a lot more potent and harder to come by.

She continued on her path, checking her own power reserves.

Character Sheet

Name:	Oson'Deia	Gender:	Female
Level:	66	Class:	Rogue/Mage
Race:	-/Elf	Alignment:	Chaotic Neutral

Unspent points-10

Health:	5,900	Regen:	1.78/s
Mana:	2,713/3,250	Regen:	5.20/s
Stamina:	1,290	Regen:	4.05/s
Vitality:	59	Endurance:	89
Intelligence:	325	Willpower:	104
Strength:	129	Agility:	81

Deia felt a change in the air; her instincts told her to move.

She jumped onto a wall as four Earth wolves pounced where she had been. She saw several more advancing down the corridor at incredible speed. Deia saw the green Mana surrounding their bodies. Some animals with a high enough level could build up an affinity to a certain kind of magic. These cave wolves had imbued their bodies with Earth Mana. They used it on an instinctual level, augmenting themselves.

As they looked around for their prey, the green glow fell away. Deia didn't give them the time to find her themselves. She rolled to the ground. Her twin blades moved through the air as she infused her attacks with Air and Fire Mana.

Cuts appeared in the cave's rocks and across the bodies of the wolves. They cried out in pain and anger as the fire reached them, burning their hides. Their prey now found, they rushed toward Deia.

Deia's blades didn't stop moving. *Damn, they're strong!*
Cave Wolf
Level 71
All of them were at least four levels above Deia's own, yet her stats gave her a slight edge. That and her own techniques were her only strengths.

She smiled. Her blades moved as she poured more Strength and Mana into her attacks. She sent a wave of Air, cutting one wolf in half and cutting the eyes of the wolf behind it. She sent a wave of heat at another group of wolves, twisting and kicking, as she sent a fireball into their midst.

The wave of fire burned three wolves as the fireball went off like a grenade. Then, they were upon her. While most were damaged and hurt in some manner, there were still eight left. They tried to race past to wound her and get clear of her blades.

She didn't let them as she flowed through their awkward attacks. Fighting with Anna had improved her Agility and ability to dodge and attack greatly.

Outstretched paws were turned into stumps.

She dropped low and pushed her Fire blade out, cutting through a wolf racing past. It didn't even have time to howl as it tore itself apart on her blade, coming to a smoking ruin behind her as she sent a fist of Air into a wolf's open mouth.

The wolf reeled back on his hind legs. Deia jumped forward, bringing her Fire blade across its neck, and tore it open as the wolf fell over.

Two wolves remained, looking at Deia and then each other before they ran away.

"No, you don't." Deia fired twin Fire lances from her hands. They hit the wolves, making them yelp in pain before the lances broke through their weak Mana barrier and through their bodies.

"Well then, time to keep moving." Deia moved through the cut and charred bodies of the wolves, flicking her blades to clean them of blood.

"There's one room area and then that hall-looking place where the metal creatures didn't advance through. I wonder what's in there?" Her smile turned hungry as she advanced, her two blades out and ready for anything that might come her way. Behind her, the atronach followed its master, ready to be called upon at a moment's notice.

Deia entered the room—what was really a series of burrows that had been cut into the rock by the wolves. It went on for some time. Other than the smell of wet fur, she didn't encounter anything else. She kept moving forward, her steps silent as she moved toward the mysterious room and its occupant. She lowered herself down, looking around the room for something.

"Come out, creature. Hiding in the darkness will not keep you from my eyes," a deep voice rolled out. It sounded as ancient and tired as time.

Deia held her breath, waiting.

"Fine, stay there," it said, as if it mattered not what Deia did. "How long has it been since the Dark Lord last used his Creatures of Power?"

Again, Deia said nothing.

The last time he had Creatures of Power? The Demon race's rebellion where they fought the control of the Dark Lord? The reign of the Dark Princes as they united their people together to fight the Dark Lord?

All of the gods except Fire aided in suppressing the Demons of northern Ashal.

"Come, Elf, I may have been idle for a long time but I have still not learned patience."

"Who are you?" Deia moved forward so that she brought the creature into sight. Deia's voice caught in her throat as her eyes widened in shock.

Sitting on a rock was a man with obsidian eyes, horns down the side of his head, and rippling muscles. His skin looked like dried blood and his nails were as dark as his eyes. He wore a simple loincloth with bones and small skulls on it.

"I am Demon Prince Alkao, first of my name and reign, commander of the Third Demon Horde and leader of the Xerzit lands. Now tell me, how long has it been since the Dark Lord has had Creatures of Power on this plane?"

Alkao Travezar

Level 238

Aerial Demon

His name didn't show in red, showing that he was at least not hostile toward her.

"That was four or five hundred years ago—twelve or so generations of Players at least," Deia said.

The Demon let out a breath that would have been angry if not for the tired way he looked at the room around him. "Where am I?"

"You are in the Benvari Mountains on the Opheir continent."

"Do any of my race still live on?"

"Not that I know of," Deia said.

Alkao nodded, as if he was expecting this. "So, why have you come to kill me?"

"I came here to train. I thought that there was just some beasts in here to clear out. Didn't think that you would be here," Deia said.

"So, you wish to train on me?" Alkao rose as if he was pushing up the very mountain.

"That wasn't my aim."

"Lies. Just scared after looking at my level, aren't you, little one?" He snorted and distorted, racing at Deia.

She dodged to the side as his fist passed her face. A cut formed on her cheek as the air cracked and slammed into the wall behind her.

It was all Deia could to dodge and throw attacks meant to slow Alkao. *What the hell is he like with a weapon?* She dodged his attacks, which seemed to be better suited to blades and shields than fists and feet.

"ALKAO!" Anna barked from the cave, followed by a stream of words in Abyssal.

Alkao stopped and turned. His eyes thinned as a frown formed. He yelled back in Abyssal. After a few minutes, he moved out of a fighting stance.

Deia stayed low and ready, waiting for Alkao to make another move.

Finally, Alkao said something and it was Anna's turn to look angry.

"Shit."

"Anna?"

"Oh, don't worry about Alkao. He knows that if he tries anything that you'll come back and beat his ass down now. We need to get back to Benvari, and I need to send a message to my father."

"What's up?" Deia asked, slowly coming out of her stance.

"The Creatures of Power are being released back onto Emerilia, bit by bit. The thing is that many Creatures of Power were sealed away for being overpowered, being held in reserve, or in Alkao's case—to protect them. Now with the rules lifted, they're all coming back. From the Dragon Kinal, to the water snake Melhoun." Anna talked to herself, walking back through the cave system. "Shit! Why didn't I think of that sooner? It also means that brother and sister are going to be pissed! Uggh, not going to be happy to find I wasn't there when they came back."

Deia looked to Alkao, still not trusting to leave him alone.

"I am sorry, Oson'Deia. It seems that even at my age, my emotions lead me faster than my mind." He bowed deeply in respect.

"Then, you won't mind if you go ahead of me?"

Alkao snorted and the corners of his mouth lifted slightly. "That would be fine." He turned and walked through the caves.

Deia couldn't help but notice the ragged scars on his back—two large ones that seemed to flow into his shoulder blades and others that just seemed painful from looking at them.

Deia thought of his classification that put him as an Aerial Demon, remembering the stories of winged creations that flew in Emerilia's skies. *He had wings but they were torn off. Who would do such a thing?* She could only imagine the pain that had come with the act.

Chapter 28: Revelation

Dave looked at the thin piece of Mithril. With the current power of his soul energy, he was only able to break its bonds once a day. He'd been researching and looking through different information, going into all the information he could find on the Xelur Demons and making his way to one of the three massive smithing libraries in Benvari.

He pocketed the piece of Mithril and went back to studying. It took months for smiths to train themselves to use the disruptor gem. Dave didn't want to wait that long.

"Smarter, not harder, kids." Dave looked at the book in front of him. It was an expert-classed book on different weapons and tools the Xelur used. *Not the lightest reading, but they were masters of soul energy manipulation.*

"What the hell is a Halfling doing in here?" a Dwarf with a group of his friends said, loud enough for Dave to hear.

"Probably got lost on his way out of here. Half-blood." Another spit on the floor.

Dave rolled his eyes and kept reading, making notes on special paper that would add the information to his interface's notepad.

"He's reading an expert-level book on the Xelur."

"What kind of twisted bastard does that?" A red-bearded Dwarf growled. "It ain't right."

"There's no way a Halfling is even allowed in the smithy." The apparent leader stood. "We'll sort him out."

Dave found a part about how the Xelur fed their own souls with energy with something that they called a soul shunt. He started reading, writing notes as the group approached.

The leader put his hand on the book, forcing it onto Dave's table.

"Excuse me—do you mind?" Dave looked up at the leader.

"Sorry, I need to read this book," the Dwarf said. It was clearly a lie.

"We can share but I *need* this," Dave said.

"I ain't sharing nothing with a half-blood piece of shit like you." The Dwarf's lip curled as the others moved up around him.

"Wow, racial slurs. Bunch of freaking Einsteins." Dave shook his head. "Fine. Piss off, because I need this book."

"What did you say, fucking dirt breed?" The leader's hand went to the hammer at his hip.

"Do you have anything better to do than bully someone else because they look a bit different from you? Are you Dwarves?" Dave shook his head, going back to reading his book.

The Dwarf's hammer came out and he swung for Dave's head.

Dave used his hotkey action, armoring up in seconds.

The hammer hit his Mana barrier and careened off into a bookshelf.

The others looked at the hammer and then Dave as he looked up from his book.

"Your mommas never teach you manners? I guess I'll have to." Dave's arm shot out, grabbed the leader's shirt, and pulled him forward before he slammed his forehead down on the leader's face. Blood gushed from his broken nose as he fell to his knees.

Dave jumped from his desk as the other three made to attack him.

"Kill him!" The leader held his face. It looked as if he'd had his nose broken a few times, so he was quickly recovering.

The other Dwarves charged.

A shield appeared on Dave's arm, identical to the one he had forged at Cliff-Hill. He stopped the ginger Dwarf's fist, breaking it before he slammed his shield into his face. The Dwarf went down in a howl of pain as Dave turned and swung, smashing a brown-haired Dwarf's arm. There was an audible crack as they howled out in pain.

The last, seeing his friends down, made to run.

Dave destroyed the arm bracers on the inside of his shield, throwing it and catching the fleeing Dwarf in the back.

The leader moved around the desk, ready to attack Dave.

"What the hell is going on here?" Jesal stormed into the library.

"This half-blood shit was reading materials for an expert Master Smith. I asked him to put it away as it is restricted reading material but then he started fighting my friends and broke my nose," the leader said.

Jesal looked to Dave. "Well, Dave?"

The leader's face split into a grin, taunting Dave.

"I was reading up on the Xelur Demons, wanted to see if I could speed things up. These weirdos started calling me a half-blood and some other racial shit and then took it upon themselves to police me, by demanding me to give them a book that they are not qualified to read." Dave stored his armor and his clothes reappeared.

Jesal looked over the whimpering Dwarves on the ground and the one Dave had knocked out with his shield. Jesal moved to the Xelur book and checked its cover. "What is your smithing level?" Jesal asked the Dwarf leader.

"Journeyman, Master Smith," the Dwarf said proudly.

"So, you took it upon yourself to police a Master Smith-leveled Dwarf under my personal tutelage to become one of the council, who was reading an Expert-level book which you are not yet allowed to read?" Jesal said calmly.

The Dwarf leader's face paled as Dave pulled out his piece of Mithril and moved it between his fingers, grinning at the other Dwarf.

Dave noticed that several other Dwarves who had heard the commotion were listening in and watched a number of them whispering to one another.

The lead Dwarf didn't say anything and seemed to be visibly shaking.

"Tell me how that works out?" Jesal asked, still waiting for an answer to her question.

"Master Smith, I did not know." The leader bowed.

"Next time, use your head, not your brawn. If you had talked to Dave instead of assuming several things, then you and your friends could have avoided this. Smiths need to know when to hit hard and fast, when to stop, and when to tap lightly and carefully.

"It seems that you lot missed those lessons, so here is another. I'm going to give this to Gorrund and he can decide your punishment. We are the protectors and smiths of Emerilia. We strive for acceptance, and here you have gone against that ethos," Jesal said gravely.

"Yes, Master Smith." The Dwarven leader looked at his feet. Dave kind of felt sorry for the guy.

Dwarves didn't punish others with anger and force unless they needed to. First, they would do their best to teach them the error of their ways. Dave hoped that the gang of Dwarves would learn something from this.

"Very well. Dave, get your books and come with me. And you're paying for the hammer that's stuck in the wall!" Jesal said.

Dave winced. "Why do I have to pay for it?"

"It's your mana shield, right? Your fault for using the full strength!"

"It was only quarter," Dave grumbled. He picked up his books and grabbed a few others and tossed them into his bag, catching up with Jesal.

"Well, don't tell others that. The Weapons of Power are supposed to be secured away, not on a Master Smith wannabe." Jesal's voice was low so only he could hear.

"So now I'm a wannabe now? Is that some kind of weird groupie?"

"More like some bat-crazy lunatic who builds too many things that should simply be impossible."

Dave snorted.

"What?" Jesal asked as they left the library and the people who were already talking about what had happened and the new Halfling who was training to be a Master Smith.

"Back on Earth, many people told me that the things I was doing were impossible." It was a rare good memory from Earth.

"Oh?"

"I would tell them it's only impossible because someone smart or dumb enough hasn't tried it out yet and, fuck it, I'm still not sure which kind I am."

Jesal couldn't help but chuckle. "So, find anything interesting?" She'd given him all that she knew on expanding one's soul energy to be able to use the disruptor better, but she'd given him leave to look into whatever he felt like. His research had already come up with more than one kind of abstract idea.

"I think I will soon enough. People have used soul energy for every discipline. It's strange: with soul energy, Intelligence and Willpower stats are flipped. Straight up increasing my Willpower is one way to increase the volume of soul energy I can retain. The amount of Mana I have feeds into how much I can regenerate at a time. I think that I might have to do some of the training that Suzy did to increase her Willpower, though I think there must be another way to grow it. I've been channeling some of my soul power into my armor and I've increased a few points. Once it's stored in the armor, then the Willpower regenerates nearly instantly as my Mana reserves dip. It's as if the Mana is a raging river and my soul is a dam. As soon as the dam is opened, then the Mana rushes through, refilling my Willpower and turning into soul energy."

Jesal looked as if she were about to say something before she tilted her head to the side, getting a message on her interface. Her face paled. She turned toward the western entrance and broke out into a jog.

"Jesal?" Dave asked, jogging with her easily, his longer legs eating up the distance.

"Seems your friends found something—something that shouldn't be alive," Jesal said, her face hard as she used her interface to send messages out.

***

Deia sat in what had been the Dwarves' food hall. Now it was cleared as she and her party ate food with two warbands and Lovan himself, all watching the eight-foot-tall Demon Prince, who had been eating non-stop for the last twenty minutes.

The door opened; the warbands split, letting Jesal and Dave pass.

"Master Smith." Lavon bowed.

"Lavon, how many times must I say it's Jesal?"

"At least a few more." He grinned. Some of the tension in the room died down now that she was here and cracking jokes.

"Damned rank-loving weirdo!" Jesal rolled her eyes and continued into the room.

Dave looked over everyone, relaxing when he saw they were all okay.

Deia smiled upon seeing him, playing with the ring that he had given her.

"So, you must be Demon Prince Alkao. Well, where the hell have you been?" Jesal asked.

"Frozen." He looked to Anna.

"Well, he couldn't very well let you go roaming around to try to get a way to fight the Dark Lord *again*," Anna said.

Alkao let out a hot breath, sounding like a horse because of his lungs' sheer size.

"You two have a history?" Jesal sat down at the table, directly opposite Alkao.

Dave moved to Deia and the others, squeezing her hand as they got close. "Good to see you're all right."

"Worried?" Deia asked.

"Petrified," Dave said.

Deia smiled and squeezed his hand.

"So, what's going on? Who is he?"

"You'll find out soon enough." Deia hadn't really believed the story at first, but now, there was no denying it after Anna confirmed it.

"You could say that," Anna said.

Alkao made an annoyed noise and continued to eat.

Unlike when Deia had first seen him, his eyes were no longer pure black. They looked like a cat's but instead of a yellow pigment, they had a red pigment around their slit pupil.

"Oh, shut up, you big lummox. My father and I were around at the time of the Demon uprising. The Demons—no longer caring for their Dark Lord's orders, which placed them into many battles and killed many of their own—rebelled against their lord.

"It took all of the power of the Pantheon to put the uprising down. My father and I balanced out the scales and might have made a few careful moves. Like rescuing a few of the Demon Princes who were fighting for their people and those Demons who were fighting for their homes, lives, and families but were in a hopeless position. We saved thousands, and hid them away, saving the Demon race, quickening the end of the rebellion."

"Your father?" Jesal asked.

"The Grey God." Alkao's deep voice filled the room with little effort.

Deia didn't doubt that it could fill the skies if he yelled.

Jesal's eyes widened as she looked to Dave.

"I have some interesting companions." He shrugged.

Deia elbowed him.

"What? That was a compliment, right?" Dave grinned, avoiding her second elbow.

"Okay, so why is Alkao here?"

"To prepare," Anna said.

This seemed to interest Alkao as well, as everyone listened.

"My father, since he is classified as a lord of the Pantheon, is unable to kill creatures or have a direct influence on the way things are done. He can give orders, requests and guidance, but he cannot purposefully kill a creature with his own power. Imprison them? Sure. Kill? Never."

"And what does that have to do with this situation? He didn't kill Alkao, but shouldn't he be somewhere else?"

"As you know, the Pantheon are now allowed to have Creatures of Power and paladins at the same time, as long as they are made of their energies. That means *all* Creatures of Power, if they are animated by one of the Pantheon, must be returned to Emerilia if they are alive."

Jesal's face paled.

"By Anvil and Fire, how many of the creatures that were excommunicated does he have?"

Anna held her eyes. "All of them."

A chill ran down Deia's spine. She remembered the stories and books she had read about the monsters that had at one time or another wandered Emerilia.

Chapter 29: Shockwaves, Aftermath and Climbing

"All of them?" Jesal asked, clearly shocked, her mind reeling from that. She couldn't even start to imagine or think what that was.

"From the primordial monsters that the Pantheon messed with to the Angels that wanted to wipe out all of those who did not believe in their Lady of Light," Anna confirmed.

"So why is he here?" Jesal pointed to Alkao.

"My father is taking his time, as much as possible, in releasing his power over the creatures. He's sending all that might be potential allies to the People of Emerilia first. Alkao is the first of his race who has been returned. He's putting them down quietly so that they don't cause a big stir. He wants them to be as ready as possible for what is coming."

"How long do we have?" Jesal asked.

"In a year, all of the races that my father captured will start to return."

"Why didn't he simply leave them alone so that they might die in a different plane?" Malsour asked.

"He was scared that if they found a way to keep themselves alive that they might find a way to escape or do something that would endanger Emerilia," Anna said.

Malsour shook his head. "I will tell Mother."

"Good. Father is telling the first arrivals what is going on. He is trying his best to place them near cities that might accept them instead of kill them. He's also working on drafting up 'events' that will be centered around destroying the worst creatures that will make it out of storage. Creatures like Wokui, the Water Dragon." Anna looked to Malsour and Induca, who then looked to each other before they pulled up their interfaces.

"So, you're saying that all of the species that your father saved from annihilation are coming back to try to help us against all of the creatures that Emerilia and the Pantheon couldn't control. All of the fucked-up creatures are then going to come in waves of events, starting next year?"

"Pretty much."

No wonder he didn't seem all that fazed about deciding whether we should release those Weapons of Power from the vaults. Doomsday is coming.

"I need to go and talk to some people. Dave, get working on that Mithril!" Jesal rose from her seat. "If you need anything here, let me know." Jesal turned and moved from the room. "Treat them well, Lavon. They're our guests now, and make sure your clan is ready for a battle."

"Yes, Master Smith," Lavon said, with none of the playful tone from earlier.

***

It had been three days since the revelation was made. Everyone in the party was training. Anna was off with Dave, making him face his fears to increase his Willpower.

Suzy walked through the food hall, seeing Alkao consuming more food. She gathered her food up and went to go sit at his empty table. Others watched her; no one wanted to get close to someone of his level.

"So, you have the courage to sit with me, little one?" The Demon lord's eyes flicked to her.

"Going to have to try a lot better than that to annoy me or make me scared." She ate a mouthful of meat, gravy, and potatoes.

Alkao gave out a rumbling laugh that never made it past his lips. "Do you not know that I could kill you with a single swipe of my fist? I could kill everyone in here in minutes if I wanted to."

"Brother, get over yourself. So what, you kill us? Then what? People go and start attacking Demons because when we showed their leader hospitality, he went and killed those giving him shelter and food. Then, there's the little fact that I can't die, numb nuts. I'll keep on coming back, whether you're sleeping, taking a dump, or eating. Might not kill you, but I bet a dagger in your kidney will hurt a bit. Think I haven't dealt with threats before? I'm a summoner, dipshit. My aim is to bind big dumb brutes like you to my will. So, unless you want me to soul bind the shit out of you and make you wear a pink fucking tutu for the rest of your miserable life, shut up and be civil, ya goddamned stop sign!"

Alkao blinked at her as she ate another spoonful of food.

"Now that's a threat. Now we going to have a conversation or a dick measuring contest?" Suzy looked up at Alkao. She'd dealt with people of his kind. Either he would rise to the challenge over honor or some useless sense of pride, or they could actually work together.

The entire food hall was quiet as she continued to eat her food.

Alkao's face split into a genuine smile as he laughed. "You should've been born a Demon! None of that High Elf pretty girl crap!" He continued to laugh. "Very well, let us talk. It has been awhile since I have done so. Longer still when it was someone who did not fear my presence."

"So, how much food are you going to eat?" Suzy asked.

"As much as I can until I'm satisfied."

"So, do you hate Angels?"

"That is a hard question to answer." Alkao grabbed a chicken leg and ate it absently. "Demons and Angels fought one another constantly. We were always at one another's throats. When the Demons decided that they didn't care to be thrown into battle with the Angels anymore, we retreated to our own lands and started building our strength. The Pantheon, scared that we would be successful in our growing rebellion against the Dark Lord, banded together and sent everything they had at us, with the Angels in the lead.

"Fortresses that spanned across Ashal were torn down, villages were put to the torch and my people were beaten back. The forces attacking us didn't care who they killed. Anything that had Demon blood was thought to be a taint. Even after my people's rebellion, the Angels continued to hunt down and kill anyone who had a hint of Demon blood." His words were hot and angry as he bit through the chicken, crushing bone and flesh.

"I did not hate them before, seeing them as the slaves that they were. Now I cannot do anything but hate them for their blind devotion to the Lady of Light. The rebellion changed them. There was no power to withstand them and there was no one left for them to fight.

"I have read the histories, of how they went on a holy crusade for their Lady of Light. How they moved through Emerilia, killing anyone they believed to follow another lord or lady and destroyed the other temples and places of worship." Alkao looked almost sad as he lowered what was left of the chicken leg. "There was a time when they had a code of honor, but power, greed, and their own short-sightedness turned them into fanatics and zealots. Who was to question them? The rightful heirs of Emerilia that their own god had blessed?"

The food hall was once again quiet.

"So, I guess I did not hate the Angels that I fought. Before the rebellion, they had honor and integrity. After, with all that the Pantheon was doing to show that no one could raise a fist at them? I'll slaughter every single one of them who raises a sword in anger." His pupils expanded, turning his eyes to obsidian spheres.

A chill ran down Suzy's spine at the sight, but she forced herself to eat. She hadn't gotten over her fears, but she now knew how to confront them and keep a level head. *Who would know that Angels were a bunch of assholes?* "So, what are you going to do?" Suzy asked.

"I will find my people and return to our land."

"What about your fight with the Pantheon?"

"I have learned that it is better to build our power in secret than out in the open as we did with the rebellion. I have asked around and few if any people travel to the northern areas of Ashal. We will train and become stronger before bringing the Pantheon down to Emerilia for what they have done."

It would definitely be useful to have him as an ally later on. Suzy thought the scenario through with the mind that had made her an asset to Dave. "What weapons do you use?"

"Why do you want to know? Do you wish to fight me?"

"No. I was asking because I know someone who will be able to make you some weapons if you need some. Our priorities are similar." Suzy's eyes hardened.

Dave wanted to look after his friends and that meant becoming stronger and fighting the Pantheon that was gunning for them.

Suzy—her reasons were simple. She wanted to destroy the people who had created a life for her that would ridicule her and drive her away from the things that she enjoyed, just to get her to play Emerilia. She didn't care about what the Jukal Empire had done to the Human race. She cared what they had done to her life, how they had put her on the cusp of more than one emotional breakdown by forming her environment to make her depressed. Emerilia now gave her the strength to break free from that horror that people called normality and hit back at the bastards who had directly affected her.

She cared for those around her and their goals aligned with hers, but anger and hatred drove her.

"I see that we are more alike than I thought." Alkao's calm voice was almost sad. "Hatred is a powerful motivator. Make sure that it does not warp your mind into something that you cannot tame."

Suzy nodded sharply, using her coping strategies to push the pain of those memories—and the anger that welled up from them—away.

"I fight with a shield and a longsword. My Affinity is Earth."

"Well, I'll see what he can come up with, though it might take him awhile, if you are interested in waiting?" Suzy asked.

"My people are still coming to this land and it will take time for them to group together and reach our lands. I will use the time to train. Even for your low levels, your party is stronger than I thought it would be."

"Yeah, we're full of surprises." Suzy smirked.

"I am seeing that the more I look," Alkao said.

The two of them ate in companionable silence, an alliance growing between them.

***

Dave finally touched the ground. His legs shook as he lowered himself into a sitting position. "Let's never do that again."

"You did better than Suzy. I am surprised that the two of you are so scared of heights." Anna wasn't even using lines to support herself.

"It's a natural reaction," Dave said.

"Well, now you know how to fight it." She smiled.

Dave rolled his eyes before he focused on his notifications.

New Active Skill: Climber

Well, look at you go, regular spider monkey you are! Thought that rope was going to snap and you would just plummet all the way down. Also, bet you'd cry—nearly had you on that one!

Level: Novice Level 7

Effect: You can climb 17% faster, footholds and handholds are 10% easier to see (stacks with perception at 50% strength).

Cost: 25 Stamina/s

Stat Increase

+1 Strength

+1 Intelligence

+12 Willpower

+1 Endurance

+3 Agility

After a day of facing his fears, his stats had increased nicely.

Character Sheet

Name:	David Grahslagg	Gender:	Male
Level:	3	Class:	-
Race:	Human/Dwarf	Alignment:	Chaotic Neutral

Unspent points-290

Health:	2,600	Regen:	2.14/s
Mana:	1,430	Regen:	6.30/s
Stamina:	720	Regen:	3.40/s
Vitality:	26	Endurance:	107
Intelligence:	143	Willpower:	126
Strength:	72	Agility:	68

He leaned against the mountain's rock face and focused his attention inward. His Touch of the Land let him see the Mana and soul energy floating through his body. His soul energy had been the size of a pea before; now it was the size of a bottle cap. It didn't sound like much, but due to the condensed nature of soul energy, it was.

He pulled out the piece of Mithril he'd been given and his disruptor. He'd already destroyed the bonds twice today. He extended his soul energy through the disruptor, willing it to break the bonds of the Mithril.

Light descended from the disruptor, falling on the Mithril. The faint checkered pattern seemed to shake before cracks formed where the lines connected. The Mithril's lines faded away as Dave smiled.

"So, I guess we won't be seeing you for a while." Deia looked at the Mithril.

"I'll be back faster than you know. Then, we can go and meet up with the rest of the Stone Raiders." Dave stood up to meet her.

Deia smiled, pulling him close and kissing him. "Better make this up to me."

"I got you that." Dave pointed to her ring.

"That's more of a deposit." She grinned.

Dave made an annoyed noise. "I should have never told you about the forums!"

"Ah, she'd learn enough from just talking to Suzy," Anna said, heading for the practice square.

"I'll be done as fast as I can. Mithril is a right pain in the ass to forge, but once you can, the items it makes are impressive. I never saw any kind of material like it on Earth," Dave said as they looked at the flat sheet of Mithril.

"Well, I will be here when you get back," Deia said.

"I love you." He leaned upward.

"I love you too." She leaned in for the kiss. It was longer and more heated than most, as Dave pulled her tight to his muscled body.

"Can you stop trying to do mouth-to-mouth out in the open?" Suzy smiled.

Dave just gave her the middle finger, holding Deia close to him as he kept kissing her.

Deia laughed and pulled away after a few seconds. "Damned horny Dwarf," she said, low enough for only him to hear.

"I'm not the only one." Dave raised an eyebrow and pulled her against him.

"Better hurry back so we can both relieve some *tension*." Her eyes flickered to his body and then back to his eyes.

"You two done?" Suzy sounded amused.

"For now, you cock block." Dave looked to Suzy but didn't let go of Deia. "Whaddya want?"

"Could you make Alkao a shield and a sword?"

"Why?" Dave asked, curious as to Suzy's interest in the Demon.

"He is a good ally to have and fighting alongside him would be beneficial for both parties. Giving him a shield and sword that he can use to protect his people is not something that he is likely to forget in the near future," Suzy said.

"When did you get so good at making alliances? Okay, I'll make it, though I'm going to need some sizing done. I'll send you a list," Dave said.

"Fine," Suzy said, trying to sound like a pouty teenager forced to do something they didn't want to.

"I'll walk you back to the gate," Deia said.

"Okay." Dave smiled.

"Good luck," Suzy said.

"Thanks, Suz." Dave grinned.

"So, how long do I have to wait till you're back?" Deia asked as Suzy headed off toward the training square.

"I honestly don't know. Once I can forge Mithril—I've just got through the first stage—then I have to figure out what the hell my smithing art is and there isn't really any other way to find out what it is other than just keep on making things." The world was moving by fast. Learning about smithing was fun and Dave knew it would be useful, but it was slow.

Emerilia seemed to be calling out to him.

Deia and Dave walked hand and hand toward the gate.

I wonder if I'll look back on this moment and wonder how everything could have been so peaceful?

"If you're making a shield and sword for Alkao, could you make me two new blades and a compound bow? The ones I have now can't handle my Strength or Mana."

"Send me your character sheet, your Affinity levels and I'll see what I can do," Dave said.

"Thanks, babe!" She kissed his cheek.

"My fiancée is a weapon freak," Dave muttered.

"I heard that," Deia said, bumping him slightly.

"Well, it's true." Dave grinned.

"So?" Deia smiled.

Chapter 30: The Last Metal

Once Dave had shown Jesal the piece of Mithril and told her that he had broken its bonds three times, she took him to a different area.

"Now, turn that nugget into pure Mithril and then something we can use."

"Are you kidding me? That's like seventy percent stone!" Dave looked at the amalgamation of Mithril ore and stone that stood around three square meters.

"Well, you should hurry up about it, then." She left him to his ore.

That was three days ago. He had worked with different tools to break off as much of the stone as possible. He knew hitting the Mithril with his tools wouldn't break it. There were a few gems and other materials but he didn't care for them as he whittled it down so that he could actually see all the Mithril.

"Damn chunk of rock and crap," Dave muttered to himself. Even though the other materials had been useful, getting in his way meant he had a new hatred toward them.

He looked at the rock, pulling out the soul tools that he had been given to use on the Mithril. He started using it on the big rock and breaking the bonds in places, making it possible for him to cut away sections. Using a crucible and constantly applying soul energy, he was able to remove most of the impurities before he pulled out the re-fined Mithril and put it to the side. He moved quickly, removing sections as fast as possible and melting them down to take out impurities.

"A full day and I've barely got three pounds of material to work with." He shook his head at his luck, letting his Willpower recharge before going in again.

***

"Four fucking days to get it all refined." Dave looked at the Mithril laid out around his workstation. He had only moved to eat, drink, and go to the bathroom.

Now with the first part done, he laid out on his workbench and went to sleep, not caring where he was as long as he got some rest. No one disturbed him, most of them sharing impressed looks as he quietly snored.

On the sixth day, he woke up and ate some rations from his bag. "Okay, well, time to work with some Mithril."

It had not been an easy or quick path to get to this stage. Dave had developed a lot faster than any other Dwarf. Even with this, he was excited to get started on his work. He pulled out a piece of parchment with different measurements. He grabbed the disruptor and focused his energy on two decent-sized ingots of Mithril, breaking its bonds and putting it into the furnace. Now the real work would begin.

***

Deia hadn't seen Dave in two weeks. Alkao had finally left the food hall to do some training. His skills were incredible. Anna could only barely hold him off, even with her swords. Deia had tried but he had easily beaten her.

Now, she and Induca were once again working on different spells.

"So, what do you think of Suzy?" Induca asked.

"She's had some impressive growth. If I didn't know Dave's own ability to jump up stats like he has, I would think that she was some kind of glitch in Emerilia."

"Yeah, she has worked hard for her position, there is no doubting that. I'm interested in what kind of creature she will summon and soul bind to," Induca said.

"Why the sudden interest?" Deia asked.

"I'm always interested in how everyone is doing. We are a party, after all. The weakest of us all shows our strength." Induca looked a little flustered.

Deia nodded and decided to not prod anymore into the subject. "So how did your tests with the cannon go?"

"Well, I took what you and Anna were saying. I don't know if you would be able to do it as it takes a level of control that is damn hard." Induca put out her hands in front of her as fiery tubes of different colors appeared.

A cyan capsule of fire appeared in the middle of the tubes. It started through the cylinders, picking up speed faster than Deia could track, and let out an ear-shattering *boom* as it left the cylinders, which recoiled from the force of the barrels' acceleration.

The barrels disappeared as the cyan capsule disappeared from the sky.

"Wow." Deia could only imagine the destructive force that had been imparted on the plasma round.

"Yeah, that shit is scary. In close combat, you'd need to make it a lot smaller. In large-scale combat, you'd need to refine the spells a bit but it would be damned powerful support weapon. Though, that's why you're engaged to Dave." Induca grinned.

Deia rolled her eyes and smiled. Dave could not only tear apart spells to use as power, he could also strengthen them to increase their effectiveness. With him supporting Deia and Induca, their Plasma Cannon spells could be truly terrifying.

***

Dave sat in the magical forge, at a workbench, and stared at the Mithril in front of him. He had forged it three times, taking four days the first time and two days for his latest one. It still wasn't how he wanted it to be.

He rubbed his tired eyes, conjuring blades within his right hand and destroying them in a few moments. He conjured Mithril, taking a good few seconds even for a square inch and a good third of his personal Mana stores.

He collapsed it, getting back half of his power, and repeated the process over again. He could conjure most things on a whim now. Legendary and above items at higher than D class quality were a lot harder to do, but anything less he could do with barely a thought.

His smithing and understanding of different materials had changed everything.

He held up a new piece of Mithril he'd conjured.

Party Chat

Dave > Malsour, how do you move metal with magic?

Malsour > I use a spell called Metal Bending. I can send you a book that will teach it to you, if you're interested?

Dave > If you could, that would be awesome. While I can conjure things, once I have it in its final form, I have to destroy it again before I change it. I want to see if I could alter it once it's conjured using Metal Bending.

Malsour > Sending Trade request

Trade Request: Malsour

Malsour would like to trade:

1x Spellbook – Metal Bending

For: -

Do you accept?

Y/N

"Yes." The spell book transferred into his inventory. Dave looked to the inventory bar at the bottom of his interface and selected it.

The spell book floated in mid-air. Dave grabbed it and read the first page. The pages moved faster and faster and he *knew* how to cast Metal Bending.

The book turned to dust and floated away.

New Spell: Metal Bending
Effect: Bend metal to your will.
Cost: 10 Mana/s
Affinity: Earth 5, Dark 5, Fire 5

"Wow, that's quite a few Affinities it needs in order to work. Going to need to figure out how to use it with Touch first before I can cast it at a distance." Dave conjured a piece of iron and focused on turning the sheet into a ball.

"Well, I'll be damned." Dave smiled as the sheet bent inward on itself, forming a ball and sealing together. It was hard to control and it would be some time until he could get it to be as fine as he wanted it to be.

Maybe it will work better if I use soul energy?

Dave concentrated on his soul energy, forcing it into the spell. Runes started to form on the ball. They were small and detailed on the inside and outside of the ball.

"Hmm, well, it's a bit rough, rougher than what I would be willing to accept, but it is much more detailed than I would get with just using my regular Mana." Dave rolled the ball around in his hand as he collapsed it and then started on a piece of steel, replicating what he had done with the iron.

"It seems my knowledge of the different materials has an effect on the quality of my metal bending." He used soul energy to bend the steel, turning it into a perfect ball as runes formed on the inside and outside of the metal.

For hours, he sat there, using his soul energy and adapting his knowledge of smithing to metal bending. It was like conjuring but with the ability to alter the creation. He still needed to work on the Mithril, but after so many failures, he was taking a day to relax to think things over.

***

Jesal looked in on Dave, watching him forming swords out of nothing.

That boy has some incredible gifts. She shook her head. She was about to walk away as she saw runes form on the outside of the sword with silver metal that Dave had conjured, moving as if it were living and filling the engravings.

Jesal's eyes went wide as she extended her senses into the room using Aura sense. She saw Mana as a silvery color when being used, but the sword and the silver wasn't silver; it was gold.

"He's using soul energy to form it," she whispered to herself, squinting at the blade in his hand.

Steel Sabre

Quality: B

Damage: 68

Abilities: Soul Trap

Charge: 10/120

Durability: 29/29

Materials: Ebony, Steel, Silver, Gold

As Jesal had come to know weapons more, her appraisal skill had allowed her to not only see the information on a weapon without a person's permission, but she also knew what materials went into forging the material.

That is rather complex. She didn't see the ebony on the outside of the blade, meaning that it must've been hidden in the center. The runes on the outside were not perfect—there were a few mistakes here and there—but for being formed without tools, they were excellent.

The kind of mental control it takes to get soul energy to form runes of that quality—I doubt many others could replicate it. It probably has to do with how he conjures items. He needs to memorize so much information that now it's much easier for him to think of all of those details.

The silver finished filling the sword's runes.

Dave looked it over and spun the blade in his hand as if checking out his work.

It evaporated into thin air as a piece of silver appeared a few moments later. It turned into what looked like a tower with a flat bottom. There were words and letters on the side with windows at the top of the tower.

Jesal would never know that she was looking at a model space rocket, though she could see the detail and skill that it took to form such a thing, gold and steel being added in to represent different contours and lines.

"Using his understanding of the material in combination with his ability to imagine—is this his smithing art?" Jesal stood there, watching as he made a half-dozen different things before he looked up and noticed that she was there.

"Sorry. Was just trying something new out. Haven't been having much luck with the Mithril." Dave looked sheepish.

"Don't be. A smith needs to know when to work and when to take a break to collect their thoughts. You won't make your best blade when you're half asleep and brain dead from working for seven days straight." Jesal walked into the smithy.

"Thanks. It's just that it's being such a pain. I know what I need but it forms its bonds so quickly that I don't have the time to keep it in a bendable state." Dave sighed.

Jesal had a thoughtful look on her face as she looked at Dave. "How long have you been playing with that alteration spell?"

"The metal bending?" Dave asked.

"Yeah."

"A few hours. I realized that only having the ability to form something without being able to modify that form afterwards would make it a pain in battle. Having to form and reform blades just because I want an extra few inches of metal? Kind of annoying."

"I want you to try something new. Do you have a spell that deals with heat?" Jesal asked.

"Deals with heat in what way?"

"Makes it so that you can put your hand into something really hot, or to touch something really hot."

It was Dave's turn to look thoughtful as he scratched his beard. "Well, I could use the Fire ability and make a kind of glove that would allow me to push heat away from my hand. I don't know how good it would be for touching, though. Don't really have something that would keep the heat from my fingers."

"What if you conjured a piece of bonded Mithril onto your finger?"

"That would work." Dave nodded. "Why?"

"I want you to try to use Metal Bending on Mithril."

"I was just playing around with it. I don't know how good it would be with that," Dave said.

"Who's the teacher here? Try it out."

Dave didn't say anything for a few moments before he shrugged. "Fine, might as well give it a go." Dave pulled out his distortion gem and focused his soul energy through it.

Soul energy was hard to deplete as long as you had big stores of normal Mana and a high Willpower, though its toll on the mind was heavier as you were using power from what held your consciousness together. Using too much could lead to headaches. In extreme cases, people had passed out and others had gone into coma states for a few days to recover from the overuse of their soul energy. Dave had been training his soul energy and keeping away from spending too much of it in one go, building up his tolerance and allowing him to use more and more.

It took a few minutes before the bonds were destroyed.

Dave quickly put the rough breastplate and unformed ingot into the forge. He had about five minutes before it started to re-bond.

With the added heat, it would become as pliable as heated steel and increase the time he could form it from five minutes to ten. Dave shifted the breastplate and rough ingot around in the forge, making sure it heated evenly.

"Now, don't pull it out. Instead, I want you to reach in there and touch it, using your Metal Bending. With it in the forge, you should get a few extra minutes before you need to break the bonds once again," Jesal yelled over the forge's noise.

"Okay!" Dave yelled back, clearly doubtful.

They waited a few more minutes as the Mithril went from silvery white to gray.

Flames sprouted around Dave's hand, a piece of conjured Mithril on his forefinger. The flames around his hand made a channel of cool air, cycling it through while keeping the other flames at bay. Dave closed his eyes as he placed his finger on the rough Mithril breast-plate.

Jesal felt the hair on the back of her neck rise as Dave's aura went from blinking silver to glowing silver, channeling Mana to make the rough changes on the Mithril. In the forge, the Mithril twisted and formed.

His silver aura showed gold flecks in it as he started to use soul energy for some of the finer details.

Standing next to Dave was like standing next to a magical furnace with all of the energy that was pouring off him.

"Abscondita."

Jesal barely heard the words as Dave's armor appeared over his clothes.

The room seemed to shake with the magical and soul energy that he expended now. The Abscondita did a good job of hiding it but there was too much for even it to hide.

Dave looked like a new star being formed. Gold outlined his body, with a silver shadow around it. His tattoos lit up with the mix of soul and Mana energies.

Jesal saw them through his shirt and lighting up his neck from underneath his armor. They were brightest down the length of his arm and into the furnace.

Dave's eyes snapped open, twin glowing silver orbs as he looked at the transforming Mithril that was trying to fight him and reform its bonds. "Form." The single word was quiet, but the power behind it felt as if it could shift mountains and divide seas.

Jesal watched as the Mithril obeyed Dave's commands.

The aura around Dave slackened as Dave pulled his finger off the thin sheets of Mithril. He stepped back from the forge, his legs shaking before he fell to his knees.

"I think...I'm going to... take... a nap." With that, Dave's eyes rolled back and he fell to his side.

Jesal caught him before he fell all the way.

"Heavy bastard!" she complained, holding him by the collar of his breastplate as she lowered him slowly to the smithy's floor.

"Well, aren't one to do things by half-measures. Let's see what you've done." She moved to the forge, blinking to try to clear her eyes of the silver and gold outlines in her vision. Her eyes widened in shock as she blinked a few more times, as if trying to understand what she was seeing.

She quickly grabbed two tongs and stuck them in the forge, pulling out four connected pieces of Mithril. She pulled them out, the Mithril already cooling now that it had re-bonded. Not even the hottest fires could get it to melt without breaking those grid-shaped bonds first.

She held them all up. There were two back and breast plates. Each one looked as though it were form-fitted. She glanced from the largest breastplate over to Dave's chest.

"Well, I think that we've found your smithing art." She smiled, turning the breastplates over, and looked at the fine runes that had been carved into the Mithril. They were written out in boxes instead of circular formations, lining up with the grid format of the Mithril.

She might not understand it, but to a coder on Earth, it might look oddly familiar but with different characters than they were used to.

Jesal put the Mithril down on the bench. "Gorrund!" she yelled through the smithy, toward where Gorrund was working with one of the Dwarven master hopefuls.

He finished talking with them as Jesal traced over the runes. The Mithril was just five millimeters thick.

"By Anvil and Fire." Gorrund moved around Jesal and looked at the front and back pieces of armor.

"He found his smithing art." Jesal looked to Gorrund. "He's a Soul Smith."

Gorrund looked at the cuirasses' interiors, flipping them over. It looked simple on the outside, smooth and well formed. Only the well-trained eye could see it was not simple, but exquisite. The metal had been spread out perfectly, no area with more or less; it was even brighter than other pieces as it was as smooth as malachite.

"I've seen Mithril not this well formed after months of work," Gorrund said.

The soul energy and limited amount of time that a smith could work with the material meant that it was hard to not only make Mithril into a shape, but to give it a quality finish. Even roughly formed Mithril was worth five times its weight in gold simply because it could beat nearly any other weapon.

For a while, they just simply looked over the four pieces in front of them. Smithing was a passion and a way of life to them. When seeing the piece that Dave had created, they didn't feel jealousy—they felt pride in Dave's accomplishments and excited to try to beat his efforts.

"Well, I think when he gets up, it'll be time to give him his last metal and his invitation," Gorrund said after a few minutes.

"Couldn't agree more," Jesal said proudly.

"Loren, Mox—come pick Dave up and take him to his room!" Gorrund bellowed.

The two hopefuls wandered over. Their eyes widened as they looked at the Mithril pieces on the workbench.

"Get him checked out by the healers and in bed. Make sure you do it right and I might even let you have a look at his final exam piece," Gorrund said.

"Yes, Master," Loren said.

"Get his legs!" Mox quickly moved to grab Dave by the shoulders.

"Be gentle!" Jesal warned. She turned to Gorrund. "Well, it looks like we have a ceremony to prepare." Jesal grinned.

"'Bout time we had some new blood in the council."

Chapter 31: A Quest of Anvil and Fire

Dave woke up and looked around his quarters.

"Shit, I must have passed out. Knew I was using too much soul energy, even when I was drawing from Abscondita. Hopefully the armor was a bit better than the last three times." Dave sighed and looked at the ceiling.

His notifications were blinking, so he opened them.

Active Skill: Builder

Level: Master Level 1

Effect: 85% speed and efficiency. Creations' material cost is reduced by 5%.

Required: Tools

Active Skill: Smithing

Level: Master Level 3

Effect: 91% improved quality of smithing creation. 15% Chance to imbue metal with skill. Able to analyze items made of Stone, Iron, Steel, Silver, Malachite, Gold, Ebony, and Mithril.

Active Skill: Soul Manipulation

Level: Master Level 1

Effect: Tools you make to manipulate souls and their energy are 85% stronger. Able to use Soul energy to fuel spells. 5% increase to soul energies' reserves (can only be used for spells, does not act as extra Willpower points).

Cost: Dependent on creation.

Level 62

You have reached Level 62; you have **295** stat points to use.

Stat Increase

+3 Intelligence

+5 Willpower

+3 Endurance

He was impressed with the different notifications. His eyes lingered on the Building skill notification the longest.

"I wonder if that will carry over to conjured items?"

Even with these thoughts, he didn't want to get out of bed, knowing that he would have to come face to face with his latest Mithril failure. *Not going to do anything just lying here and looking at the ceiling.* He pushed off the bed and got to his feet.

"Shower and then down to the smithy to see what the hell I made." Dave wandered into the shower and washed off the grime. For the last couple of weeks, he had practically lived in the smithy. He pulled on new clothes and tossed the old ones into a garbage chute that the Dwarves used throughout the mountain. He numbly ate some jerky as he headed out into the mountain.

"I really hope that I get to show Deia inside one of these places once." Dave looked at the different levels as Dwarves moved around everywhere, going about their day as trains, carts, and elevators moved constantly, shifting people throughout the mountain.

As he walked, he studied his character sheet.

Character Sheet

Name:	David Grahslagg	Gender:	Male
Level:	3	Class:	-
Race:	Human/Dwarf	Alignment:	Chaotic Neutral

Unspent points-290

Health:	2,600	Regen:	2.20/s
Mana:	1,460	Regen:	6.55/s
Stamina:	720	Regen:	3.40/s
Vitality:	26	Endurance:	110
Intelligence:	146	Willpower:	131
Strength:	72	Agility:	68

After some mental math, if he was to convert the stat points to the equivalent he would have got for straight level grinding, he was the equivalent of a level 98.

"Come a long way since starting." He still felt gloomy about his latest mess-up. Mithril was a lot harder than he'd thought. He knew that his friends were willing to wait for him to become a master, but he couldn't fight the feeling that he was holding them back from so many adventures they could be having.

I just need to work harder to get this done so we can go and work on their abilities. I owe them big time. Players would have just left me alone to myself to grind out mobs and other creatures. I'm a lucky dude to have friends willing to hang around for me.

It didn't take him long to get to the smithy, using trains and elevators to reach his destination. He checked his interface. It was afternoon, so he went straight to the smithy to find Jesal instead of the classrooms.

She wasn't in the smithy when he got there, but he saw a long row of Mithril on one of the workbenches, surrounded by Gorrund's four understudies.

"Dave!" Mox noticed Dave there.

"Hey, Mox." Dave walked into the room toward them. "How bad is it?"

"Bad?" Mox looked confused as the others tore their eyes from the Mithril.

"If you mean that it is some of the finest smithing I have ever seen? Then yeah, you'd be right," Loren said.

"What?"

They moved out of his way as he looked at four pieces of metal.

He finally used his Touch of the Land, having held back on it as he hadn't wanted to know how bad his mess-up had gone. "Holy fucking shit." It was exactly as he had thought of it within his mind. He was completely absorbed in looking over every inch of the armor.

"Runes are a bit fucked up in places, but shit, it actually worked?"

"That it did. Seems that we found your smithing art," Jesal said from the entrance to the smithy.

"You're a Soul Smith." She tossed him a white ring.

Dave caught it and looked at the last metal he needed to finish his necklace.

A new popup appeared.

Quest: Of Anvil and Fire

After meeting with Jesal, she has decided to accept you as a candidate to be a Dwarven Master Smith.

You will need to:

~~Master the material Stone~~

~~Master the material Malachite~~

~~Master the material Gold~~

~~Master the material Mithril~~

~~Find your Smithing Art~~

You have completed the necessary requirements of a Dwarven Smith. You have been named: Soul Smith, a Smith that uses their very soul's energy to form and change the material they work with. It is one of the hardest practices to conquer.

Reward: You have been named a Dwarven Master Smith

New Active Skill: Soul Smith

You're all about the soul, huh? Should start a record label named after you. Well, anyway, you're a special kind of weirdo who likes to use your very consciousness to change the things you're working on. If that ain't freaky, well, I'm not sure what else is.

Level: Apprentice Level 5

Effect: 15% less soul energy necessary for crafting with Soul Smith.

Cost: Dependent on creation.

"Huh. Only get a one percent bonus per level instead of the two percent of other levels."

"It's rated as a rare Action skill, so it only gives a little boost, though no one can see it unless you show them, unlike your basic skills where certain people can figure it out," Jesal warned.

"Well, that is kind of weird as hell." Dave looked back to the armor, still not understanding how the hell he had finished it.

The other Dwarves moved out of the way as Jesal held out a simple stone badge of a hammer striking an anvil with a fire behind it.

"David Grahslagg, you have completed the challenges of smithing and shown yourself to be a dedicated man to Anvil and Fire. I now ask you if you desire to become known as a Dwarven Master Smith?" Jesal asked, none of her usual joking in her voice as she offered the badge to Dave.

"What do I have to do?" Dave asked.

"Bring your creation showing your abilities to a meeting of the Master Smiths and make a binding oath to the Council of Anvil and Fire."

The other Dwarves looked between Dave and Jesal. Smithing was an almost holy act to them. Seeing someone become a Master Smith was a rare occurrence. Seeing the first-ever Halfling become accepted into the Council of Anvil and Fire—none of those there would forget this day for the rest of their lives.

"Well, as long as you give me some time to finish this up, then I'd be happy to." Dave smiled.

"What the heck are you going to do now?" she asked.

"A few tweaks." Dave smiled.

She shook her head and gave him the badge.

Dave put it into his bag of holding and looked back at the Mithril again. "Well, I did it once, let's see if I can do it again." He pulled out Abscondita from his bag of holding.

***

Kol looked around the council's table. There were more Dwarves around than normal. They all wanted to see the Halfling who had progressed faster through the stages of smiths, faster than any before him, and was supposed to have the rare skill of Soul Smithing. It was so rare that there was no other Master Smith recorded as having the same smithing art.

It had been four days since Dave had been given an invitation to join the Council of Anvil and Fire.

Kol knew as soon as he had entered through the Benvari Mirror of Communication.

"Well, that is certainly different—didn't think it was capable of that. Will have to think of that later when talking to the rebels," Dave muttered to himself.

Kol's ear easily picked it up as his sense found Dave wearing a familiar set of armor.

"What has he done now?" Kol thought out loud as Dave was brought into the chamber.

"Dave Grahslagg, you have been given an invitation to join the Council of Anvil and Fire. Please present your final exam item," Sola said from the head of the table.

Dave's armor disappeared before he pulled it out of his bag of holding.

There were murmurs and whispers as Dave handed it to Jesal, who gave it to Sola.

Kol didn't need to hold the armor in order to understand it. He looked through the armor. He chuckled to himself, seeing Dave glance over and grin. Kol couldn't quite hide his own smile.

"It seems to be simple. Wait—" Sola put her hand to the metal and closed her eyes, looking past the surface. After a few moments, her eyes snapped open as she looked from the armor to Dave. "How?"

"Well, I needed some time to integrate the parts together. I had the Mithril done but it wasn't meant to stay on its own. With the ebony that I got from Boran-al's Citadel, I made a new interior. Using Soul Smithing, it was quicker than I dared hope."

"These runes—they are incredible. I can feel their potential but understanding them is complex. You are even using a different way of making Magical Circuits."

"Well, on Earth, we have this thing called coding. I kind of took that and adapted it over to Magical Circuits to make it easier. I didn't think it would work at first but I did some tinkering and it seemed to work fine." Dave shrugged, as if talking about different ways to grow crops.

He's going to turn smithing practices on its head. Once that whole factory thing he has going on at Cliff-Hill catches on to other Dwarven smiths, production is going to skyrocket.

"Well, pass it around, will you, Sola? I'm rather eager to have a look at it myself!" Quino said.

Sola handed it to her left. One by one, Dwarves looked over the armor, asking different questions.

"Why the Boran-al ebony?" Gorpal asked.

"Well, in the time that the cultists spent in the citadel, they did nothing but practice magic all the time. It's some of the highest Mana-charged ebony I have ever seen or heard of in my research," Dave answered.

"This central layer—it seems that it is growing. What is it?" Helick asked.

"That is a vault-classed soul gem—was a pain in the ass to figure that thing out. It will take a few weeks until it is fully formed."

"You have two sets of runes here—runes on the ebony sheets stacked on one another and then the Mithril sheets. Why?" Quino asked as the armor got to him.

"The soul gem is the power source; the ebony is the detailed processes and set commands. The Mithril should be thought of as a control panel. I input different runes and it connects to the layers of ebony and performs a task."

"Why hide the Mithril under a layer of steel?" Endur asked.

"If people see someone wearing Mithril armor, then they're going to come at me with everything they have to steal it from me. Abscondita is more than meets the eye. While on the outside it looks like well-made steel armor, underneath there is Mithril plating for defense, engraved ebony plating for augments, and a soul gem of my own creation powering the runes carved into the ebony." Dave shrugged. "The Mithril is just one piece of it, as you know. The runes in it are more powerful than the Mithril, in my opinion."

"Why do you have pieces of wood between the layers?" Kol asked. Everyone looked between the two of them with shock.

"You noticed that, huh?" Dave smiled. "It was a pain in the ass finding some Elven wood. I used it because if you get hit, metal can take an impact and stop it from getting through, mitigating the puncture effect. It does nothing to try to stop the blunt impact of being hit. Having the wood in place allows the armor to compress slightly and spread out the impact force more."

"Why Elven wood?" Jesal asked.

"Most woods don't allow the transmission of magic through them. I needed to have that ability so that the Magical Circuits could continue to work," Dave said.

"Well, I think that I will be getting a few pieces of wood to try out different things," Quino said.

"Be useful for Dwarven shields. Having your arm numb from a nasty impact is a pain in the arse," Endur agreed. "Should have thought of it sooner. Too stuck on just ores to think of wood."

"There is always more to learn." Sola smiled and looked to Dave. "Well, I say we put it to a vote. All those in acceptance of David

Grahslagg' s application to be a Dwarven Master Smith, raise your hands."

Kol smiled as every Dwarf's hand climbed into the sky. "Welcome to the club, boy. Now get a damn seat."

The other Dwarves chuckled and laughed as Dwarves moved to make room for him. Those nearest patted him on the back, accepting him into their world as one of their peers.

"Now we've dealt with the good stuff, we need to deal with the issues of the time," Sola said. The armor continued to make its run, with more than a few of the Dwarves making notes on paper that would save it to their interface's notepad.

"Lo'kal has made it clear that we are allowed to do with the Weapons of Power as we see fit. It also seems that he is releasing all of the creatures that he has captured and held away from Emerilia since its beginning. Right now, he is letting out those that he saved from death and persecution. Within Benvari Mountain, the Demon Prince Alkao is training and gathering strength. We have had reports of other Demons surfacing across Ashal. New water creatures roam our seas and there are Aerial species that have not been seen in millennia. Dave, we have heard a lot about Lo'kal, but we do not know him. What do you think of his character?"

"Well, I know him as Bob the Gnome, and well—he cares deeply for the People of Emerilia. He cannot directly act here but he has moved more than one group of people and used them as instruments in order to keep the balance on Emerilia. Wait—why haven't you talked to him?" Dave asked.

"Well, he is an almighty being. Would he not find us?" Sola said.

"One second." Dave opened up his interface and typed out a message.

When did Dave come to know Lo'kal? Kol wondered.

"What is our conference room code and password? He needs it to get in," Dave said.

Sola opened up her interface, sending Dave a message back.

There was a light at one of the room's entrances. Out walked a Gnome, lighting a pipe. "Well, this is where you've all been? Lost the last password a few centuries ago. Hey, Dave, how's everything going? Seems like you're doing well." The Gnome leaned against one of the pillars around the room and puffed on his pipe.

"Bob, this is Sola. Sola, this is Bob, or Lo'kal, or balancer, or gray weirdo, or the seventh strangeling."

"We're going to have to work on your presentation." Bob puffed on his pipe absently. "So, everyone, what's going on?"

"He's Lo'kal? The administrator and creator of Emerilia?" Endur said.

"Hey! It was a lot of work making this place, I'll let you know. None of that seven days shit. More like two decades, what with the change in the atmosphere and then the seeders and lack of funding. Jukal cheapskates always giving you a tenth of what you need and still expecting you to be on time and happy with their *generosity*." Bob sighed.

***

Dave conjured a beer in his hands; everyone in the room could be trusted. He conjured a table for Bob with a single Scotch on it.

The other Dwarves had looks of shock, to confusion and amusement.

"I knew I picked the right guy for the job!" Bob took the Scotch, taking a sip and making a silent cheers with Dave.

"Well looks like you've been keeping a few things close to the chest," Sola said, looking at the conjured items and then Bob, leaving Dave and his secrets alone.

"With regards to all the creatures that you pulled off Emerilia, is it true that they are coming back in a few year's time in some kind of event basis?"

"Unfortunately, yes. I tricked the system somewhat, turning it into an event instead of just having it full-out. That said, it's not going to be pretty. Some of the races I had to move in groups, or in the middle of a ceremony. They're going to appear in large numbers and sometimes, right before casting one hell of a shitty spell. Some will be weak. I can let you lot and some other groups who hold conferences like this know. I cannot appear on Emerilia for more than five minutes of time."

"Why?" Dave asked.

"I have lost my ability to see the other lords and ladies of the Pantheon. After five minutes of being on Emerilia, if they have a scrying spell, they can see where I am and what I am doing. Whoever I am talking to will be of interest to them and in grave danger. Lucky thing that I have friends and the interface's chat is perfectly secure." Bob smiled and looked to Kol. "Dwarven Master Kol, would you like to be my friend? It makes sense that the two people who taught this bozo to make things get acquainted."

"I will," Kol said.

"Regular charismatic guy, I am!"

"He has to or else the only other person is me or my party," Dave said.

"Yeah, which reminds me—I need you to go and meet up with the Stone Raiders. Even if the rankings don't show it, they're one of the most powerful guilds, not for their equipment or levels, but due to their stats and their determination. Never seen a group get killed so many times and then go right back into battle. You Humans are weird."

"Sir, we are Dwarves," Quino said.

"I know what you are—I made you. Was really messy, all kinds of subsets, the gene splicing and making you people stable. Took me an entire century!"

"Bob..." Dave's warning tone got him back on track.

"Yeah, so I need you to go and meet up with them. Need someone influencing them. That way, got more chances for the People of Emerilia and the Players to work together for the common good. Look at me, making alliances and shit."

"You sure that he's a lord of the Pantheon?" Gorpal asked.

"Gorpal Dunsk, lives in the Akrimon Mountains, southeastern Ashal, creator of three Weapons of Power: Mace of Fury, Treanar tower Shield, and Boots of Smash. Dude, seriously, Boots of Smash? Well, yeah umm, smithing art—Paint Copy. Oh, that's cool—whatever you paint, you can then replicate completely. Kind of go into a fugue state. Props, dude. Call a pendant the Pendant of Shiny for all I care—that's cool as fuck. Hmm, never been an Affinity dude—agree with you there, they don't deserve any of your power. Umm, you've got what, like eight Weapons of Power in Akrimon? Wow, got the Staff of Growing. Trust me, Arch-mage Jekoni was not a pervert—just, well, you know, names shit weird stuff. Plus, he bound his soul to it. You are keeping up with having someone from the mages guild talking to his bored ass, right?"

Dave rubbed his face as the Dwarves seemed shocked and unsure of what they wanted to say.

"Yeah, we do. He really wants to get out. Nearly started hopping his stick ass across the vault when we said that the dragons had returned." Gorpal shook his head.

"Might be like what, five hundred years old, but he's always been a spritely fellow. So annoying when he actually had legs." Bob shook his head and finished off his Scotch.

The Dwarves chuckled and snorted.

"In light of the upcoming arrival of some rather nasty people who will wish us and the People of Emerilia harm, we are debating whether or not to have a tournament for new owners of the Weapons of Power," Sola said.

"I like your style, Sola. I'll do my best to hide the Weapons of Power. Most of the Players are too low of a level to attract attention with the Weapons of Power as they can't use their full strength. The People of Emerilia, on the other hand, you've got quite a few high-leveled people. Might be an idea to brief them and make them sign a contract that they use the weapons under certain conditions and then another one that they can't use it against the People of Emerilia. Going to be a pain to write up those contract runes, but thankfully that guy right there has been messing around with a *ton* of runes." Bob pointed right at Dave.

"Do you have anything else for us?" Sola said.

"I can't see what the others of the Pantheon are doing. I know that they will be working to make their own Weapons of Power, Creatures of Power, and swaying people to be their paladins. The Dwarves and a good amount of the Elves have stopped worshiping them and that is going to lead to quite a few problems. I will help as much as possible but I am trying to look after *all* of Emerilia. Now is not the time to start fights with your neighbors. You're going to need one another more than ever. Remind the lords of this." Bob's voice was serious for the first time; all of the Dwarves listened to him as it turned cold. "If they don't listen, then tell them that *I* will visit them. Do not abuse your power but look out for Emerilia. You have been secluded in your mountains for generations. That separation has created walls, both physical and societal. Send out your people more. Get those smithies working and ready yourselves for war. Meet and greet your allies. Broker peace in readiness of war."

The room was quiet as the reality of what was coming started to settle in. Here the creature who had created Emerilia was telling them that a war was coming.

I wonder how the hell it's going to change Emerilia? Dave thought.

Chapter 32: Tools and A Mission

Deia heard someone entering her room. She quickly got out of the shower, grabbing her dagger as she moved to the door and wrapping a towel around her as she went.

"Don't stab me," Dave said through the bathroom door.

Deia pulled it open. Dave stood in her room, with a tired smile on his face and all of his gear.

"Dave!" She ran and jumped, colliding with him and wrapping her legs around him. He staggered back; his arms wrapped around her as she kissed him hungrily. She hadn't seen him in weeks and it had weighed on her heavily. "How did it go?" She pulled away.

Dave grinned and pulled out his necklace. On it there were eight different materials, including Mithril.

"Babe, that's great!" She kissed him again as he pulled something else out. She looked at it, confused by the badge. "What is it?"

"It's the sigil of Anvil and Fire, showing that I am a Dwarven Master Smith." Dave smiled, clearly proud.

"I knew you could do it." Deia smiled, joining in on his moment, proud and happy for him.

"Now, it doesn't look like you finished showering." Dave walked toward the shower, which was still running.

"What are you doing?" She laughed as he dropped his bag of holding and pulled her towel off. She didn't have time to do anything but pout as he walked straight into the shower, getting soaked in his clothes, still carrying her. She laughed, happy to have him back.

"Do you need to do anything else?" she asked as he pressed her up against the wall of the shower.

"Nope. I am free and clear. We can go and join up with the Stone Raiders whenever we want." Dave smiled.

"Good. Then we need to make up for lost time." She kissed him and drew him closer to her. His beard brushed her skin as she pulled his clothes off and her fingers ran over his tattoos and runes.

***

"Suz, catch!"

Suzy looked around at the familiar tone as a black core flew in the air toward her.

"*Oof!* Dammit, Dave! It's heavy as hell!" she complained, putting the metal core down.

"Good thing I made three more of them." Dave walked into the training square. Deia gave him a kiss on the cheek and moved toward Induca and Anna, pulling her new blades out to show them.

Suzy studied the core as Alkao moved over in interest.

"You must be Alkao. Good to meet you." Dave held out his hand for the Demon Prince.

"You must be the smith," Alkao said, not moving to shake Dave's hand.

"Ye-up." Dave pulled his hand back.

"Do you have my weapons?" Alkao demanded.

Dave frowned as Suzy stood up.

"Alkao, why you being such a prick?" Suzy asked.

"He is no warrior. Smiths just sit in the rear, making weapons so that others can kill one another. They profit from war while others give their lives to defend their people." Alkao sneered at Dave.

Dave turned to Suzy, as if leaving Alkao out of the conversation. "I do have something for you, bit of a second-hand—"

"I'm talking to you, Smith. You better go in there and make me some weapons or else I will personally start—"

It was Dave's turn to interrupt Alkao. "Abscondita." Dave's armor appeared over his body as he raised his hand toward Alkao.

"You dare to challenge—"

Metal erupted out of the ground and wrapped around Alkao in thick bands before he was able to do anything. Alkao pressed against it but the metal became tighter and thicker as runes appeared on its outside. A band of metal moved around his mouth.

"Is he always this rude?" Dave asked.

"Usually he's a decent enough sort, crude but honorable. Guess he doesn't act that way if he thinks anyone is less than him." Suzy shook her head. "Sorry about that, Dave. Thought that he would want to make allies instead of ostracize his people."

Dave took out a large shield and a blade from his pack, holding his hand to them before he tossed them at Alkao's feet.

"I added in runes that if you attack someone first with these, then they will backlash on you. Suzy convinced me to make these items so that you could help your people out. I don't want to deal with your rudeness. I might be a smith, but a smith is not all I am." Dave shook his head. "There are always arrogant pricks no matter where you go."

"Sorry, Dave. I didn't know that he was without honor. You think someone who strived to be something other than what they were created for wouldn't just attack someone for their profession—would stain my honor just fighting beside him." Suzy looked to Alkao. She respected Dave and he had gone to great lengths to make the shield and blade for Alkao.

Alkao looked away, as if trying to get away from the look of disdain in her eyes.

***

They were all sitting in a tavern at a table near the back, having beers and eating food as they planned out what they wanted to do.

"Okay, so there are three main options. One—we meet up with the Stone Raiders again, going full bore training, raiding and improving on our martial skills and such. Two—we go straight to

Per'ush or some of the reputable mages colleges to learn from them. Third—we adventure on our own to check out Emerilia." Deia looked to everyone.

"Well, the mages colleges can wait. With the creatures that are going to be released in a year, I think it would be best if we met up with the Stone Raiders again and get some training in," Malsour said.

Anna smiled to herself. She had come back to Emerilia with one purpose: to save her friends and her people from an oppression that they didn't even know. She had started off as an AI that ran Emerilia, but now—now she was a Person of Emerilia and she couldn't just sit back and see all of these things happen to those that she cared for.

"So, what does everyone say?" Deia looked around.

"I vote option numero uno," Dave said.

"I agree," Anna said, excited to use her training. They had been working on different skills for months now. She was eager to get into a big fight. From what she had seen and read, it looked as if the Stone Raiders were magnets for trouble.

"I want to see a plasma cannon in action." Induca smiled.

Deia rolled her eyes as Malsour sighed.

"I was told to watch out for my little sister, so I guess I agree," Malsour said. Over the months that they had been together, Malsour had really come out of his shell. Anna could see that he loved his books still and liked to have some peace from the world, though this little group had roped him in and drawn him out of his reclusive ways.

"I agree. Well then, I'll send a message to Josh and see where they are so we can meet up with them."

"I have one request," Dave said." If we go past the Zolu Mountains in Heval, there is someone I need to meet in order to get Josh's daggers fixed."

"And if we go past any places of magical interest that we stop, unless we're with the rest of the guild." Dave and Malsour shared a look.

Those two are magical book fiends.
"Fine, I think that is all reasonable," Deia agreed.

***

"Who the hell is messaging me now?" Josh yelled as he ducked out of the way of a norbu's spike. "Not going to get me this time!" Josh jumped onto one of the pillars in the room, flipping and pushing off it, out of the way of its Air-slash. He threw daggers as he passed over the norbu.

A group of tanks slammed into the side of the creature, getting its attentions as Josh's blades hit the lizard's skin. It looked like a big gecko but its tail was much more mobile and had spikes on it. More than one person had fallen victim to those spikes and the Air blades that they let loose with their attacks. They had a mane that popped up; heavy scales created a shield around their head to make them look larger and ward off predators.

There were twelve knight-classed norbu and one lord-classed. The lord was much larger and had an area attack ability that would throw people off their feet and stun anyone unlucky enough to hit the walls or floor too hard.

Right now, it paced around, trying to get past its knights that were fighting groups of Stone Raiders.

Their plan was a simple one: kill off the norbu knights, and then bring everything to bear on the norbu lord.

Josh landed, taking the battle in. Josh saw his buff timers increase as the support groups kept everyone safe and deadly as possible. *With all of these buffs, it's going to suck afterwards.* Unlike other games, buffs were like coffee in Emerilia. You could have some and it would greatly improve your performance, but the more you had for a longer time, you prolonged the crash. But when the crash came, it was a pain in the ass.

A bit of healing sorted this out but still, those who had been buffed were left feeling tired and hungry for all the work their avatars had gone through.

The norbu knight he had been fighting popped its mane up. In the area under its mane, there were a collection of veins and its windpipe. Usually it was protected by the mane's strong scales.

Josh saw an opportunity and went for it. "Step," Josh said, disappearing from where he was to a few feet above the back of the norbu.

It started turning as Josh drove his short sword through the soft scales that lay under where the mane rested. The norbu yelled out as Josh twisted and turned his blades, cutting for all he was worth.

"Step!" Josh yelled again as the norbu tried to roll over in order to kill him.

He appeared in front of the norbu as it moved around as if drunk. Blood came down from its neck.

The people who had been working on the norbu knight moved to assist other parties in fighting their opponents. Seven norbu knights were now three.

"'Bout time—took two hours." Josh looked at the battle and opened his messages quickly.

Private Message: Deia

Deia > Hey Josh, Dave has finished off his training at Benvari. Wondering when and where we can meet up?

Josh let out an excited whoop and pushed the message away.

"Just deal with these norbu here and then get back to them. Be good to have them along. Having Dave around to fix our weapons instead of getting gouged by the damned smithies we go through will be nice." He moved toward his next target.

"Clear, artillery!" Kim barked.

Josh and the other Stone Raiders turned and ran.

"Fucking hell, Kim! More bloody warning!" he yelled as they rushed away from the norbu that looked at the incoming magical artillery spell, spreading its mane to take it straight on. The spell hit, making the cave system shake as the front half of the norbu knight disappeared.

"And then there were two knights and one lord," Dwayne said.

"Dwayne, stop trying to make bloody songs up and get that lord pinned down. Lucy, support him. Kim, well, whatever—come on, Stone Raiders! I'm looking forward to some norbu stew tonight!" Josh ran toward the two remaining norbu. One had been flipped over by the blast. It had crushed two Stone Raiders, who were being group healed by Lucy's supporting group.

Josh's heavy hitters were like piranhas, jumping in and cutting the norbu's soft stomach open until its Health points hit zero.

"Party three, four, and seven onto the last knight. Rest of you, take that fucking lord out!" Josh said.

The lord jumped on the ground, letting out his AOE spell. People were thrown in every direction and it even deflected a few spells.

"Rotating tanks!" Dwayne yelled.

Tanks that had been rushing over formed into two groups, one inside and one outside the AOE of the lord. That way, if one force was knocked down, then the second could rush in before the norbu lord started snacking on people or tearing them apart.

Josh moved to the final knight, knowing that Dwayne had a good grip of the norbu lord situation.

The knight was letting out its own AOE spell but it was less than five feet instead of the lord's twenty feet.

"AOE! AOE!" Everyone jumped out of the way as air rushed away from the norbu knight.

"Get it!" Josh said as soon as the attack wore off. A few had been blown back but the mages were already going to town with their healing spells.

The norbu lashed out, catching a hunter who was moving in behind it. They cried out but three others made it past the norbu's defenses. The tanks once again moved into position to shield bash and taunt the norbu.

Josh ran in, cutting deep with his short sword and dagger combo, and gained a sneak attack bonus as he came in behind the creature. Combined with his Ignore Armor spell, he took a good ten percent of its Health off before it turned to try to hunt him down. "Step!" He vanished.

People called out all kinds of information, from what the norbu was doing, to the best attacks to hit the creatures with.

Josh didn't even get in for another hit as the final knight fell. Someone ran up and planted a blade in its eye to make sure it was really dead. There had been a few times when a creature with no HP had enough energy to snap out and kill a few people. With the POE who had joined the Stone Raiders, everyone was taking precautions to keep them alive and active.

"To the lord!" Josh yelled. Everyone shifted from the norbu knight to the lord.

It didn't seem to like this as it raised its mane, letting out a cone of slashing wind that opened up a space ahead of its large head. Casters, archers, and hunters fired spells in toward the unprotected neck.

The norbu that had been leaning down to chew on two Stone Raiders howled as it tilted back from the pain of the spells.

Rogues, thieves, and fighters ran in, their weapons cutting under the norbu's neck as its mane came to rest back on its neck.

"Pull back!" Josh said as the norbu shifted and started to twirl.

"Tail AOE!" Kim called out.

Josh felt as if he needed to jump and roll. He had long ago started to follow these instincts, recognizing it for his Dodge skill. He came under the massive tail that slammed through anything in its path.

People called out in pain as they were thrown or the spikes found them.

"Second line!" Dwayne yelled. A number of their tactics had been pulled from the Dwarves now that they were teaching all of their tanks and frontline fighters how to fight.

The second line rushed up and over their friends, most of which had escaped the norbu lord's tail. Others weren't so lucky and had their first-line friends pulling them out of danger as they were fed Health potions. Lucy's support mages and healers rushed over the field, looking after people.

"Come on, you ugly bastard! Right here! Yeah, you want to get all pissed at me and open that mane—I know it!" Esa yelled at the creature. She had become one of Dwayne's tank commanders.

Now she was taunting the creature, slapping and slamming it.

It turned around with a speed that belied its size, using its Air Affinity to give it a burst of speed as it slammed its head into Esa.

She braced her shield, digging grooves into the floor with her boots.

"Bastard! I just bought these boots!" she yelled. A red aura came around her as she activated her berserker state. She slammed his head away, yelling out her anger to the universe and stabbing her blade into its eye.

It screamed out in pain, trying to get away.

Josh's group moved in. They might not be the most heavily armored, but they were the people who could get in close and lay the most damage per second into something.

If they were out in a larger area, then he might have used the mages to hammer the creature from multiple directions while he used his high Damage Per Second Agility and taunts to kite the big bastard. That would keep it looking somewhere else as the tanks gave the mages protection from anything the norbu sent at them.

Instead, the tanks were taunting and keeping the attention while the mages buffed them and the DPS fighters got in any attacks they could. But the main damage dealing was left to Josh and his people.

The DPS fighters were some of the riskier and ballsiest mother fuckers out there. They got in close, with little protection to connect their hits. They were also fast and agile, making it hard to land good healing spells on them.

The tanks, taking up Esa's roar, slammed and bashed the norbu lord. It tried to release its AOE spell but found a war hammer smashing one of its legs out from under it. It activated the spell by flexing and then releasing its stomach violently. As it screeched out in pain, trying everything it could in order to kill those that were around it, everyone who was close started slashing, cutting, and stabbing—lowering the lord's ridiculous Health pool down.

The Stone Raiders kept it pinned, not allowing it to get up.

The norbu lord couldn't do anything but try to get people with its tail and mouth, leaving its long sides completely open.

Everyone got into a rhythm, chipping through the norbu's Health pool as Lucy's supporters went around checking on people's Health, Mana, and Stamina, using spells and buffs to help where they could and giving out food and potions.

The norbu lord let out a screech before it fell to the ground, its Health pool finally at zero. Someone made sure it was dead.

Everyone relaxed, panting and recovering from the massive battle. It had taken five days just to reach the cliffs that they had fought in. Then, another three days to get to this point.

A notification appeared at the end of the raid area as several chests overflowing with loot appeared.

Norbu Infestation Raid

1. Stone Raiders

Josh's notifications bar blinked at him, demanding attention.

Norbu Infestation Raid

You and your Raid party are the first to finish this area. As such, you get a +10% modifier to XP and +40% increase to Raid's bounty!

Josh didn't know who started it but they started whooping and cheering, celebrating their victory and holding up their weapons, excited for the hard-won victory and the prizes that they had gained.

It took some time before it settled down.

"All right, well, I say that we camp here for tonight, see how this norbu tastes and then head back to Selhi tomorrow morning!" Josh yelled out.

Again, there were cheers and yells of agreement.

"Play hard, party harder?" Dwayne asked, a grin on his face and his helmet tucked under his arm.

"Stealing my words, mate?"

"Only when they aren't completely ridiculous." Dwayne smiled.

"I'll have my mages lay out tripwires and the like," Kim said, through their party chat that allowed them to hear one another at all times.

"Thanks. Don't want some other creatures smelling all this blood and thinking they can make a meal out of us." Josh felt as if he was forgetting to say something. "Oh, damn, my memory's going. Dave just finished with the Benvari Mountain's Dwarves. The party is looking to meet up with us as soon as possible."

"I'm interested to see how they've grown," Lucy said. "They certainly had a few interesting ideas of how to use their powers when they left."

"With that lot, expecting to be surprised is probably the best bet," Kim chipped in.

Chapter 33: Good-byes and Good Travels

Gorrund, Jesal, and Lovan saw them off as they headed away from Benvari and back up the path toward Nadorf.

Dave had made new and improved Abscondita armor for himself and Deia; the old armor he'd reformed to meet Anna and Suzy's sizes. Induca and Malsour still wore their matching cloaks with different interiors.

As they walked, two metal golems and one Earth golem wandered with them. Suzy's strength had increased in leaps and bounds at Benvari.

All of them had gotten much stronger with their stay. Now, they had some coin in their pocket and a destination.

"Suzy, let's see if your golems can keep up." Deia went from a walk to a jog and then a full-out run. Dave smiled as she jumped into the trees that were on either side of the road.

"Malsour, Induca, you're it!" Dave called out as they were the last two to make it into the trees.

The golems were too slow to keep up. The rock golem turned back into its core but the metal lost some weight and turned into drones that easily kept up with them.

Well, that could be very useful in the upcoming battles.

They came down out of the trees after a few games; Dave was the one winded first now.

"We're going to have to work on that Agility of yours. Your Endurance is high but even at the speeds we're going, your lack of Agility will weigh on your Endurance," Deia said.

Dave just nodded and agreed as they continued on at a run but not a full sprint so that he could recover his Stamina somewhat.

"Seems that my student has not been keeping up with his training. I will have to remedy that!" Deia yelled as Dave had half of his Stamina bar filled. She chased after Dave with her sword drawn.

"What are you doing!?" Dave jumped into the trees to get away from her.

"Training my student! 'Bout time you had some fighting practice. Best we learn just how rusty you've gotten spending all your time hammering metal into submission!"

Dave didn't have a good feeling about it as he started being attacked by Deia while running through trees. *Crap, I have gotten worse and she's gotten a lot better!* He fought her off as they continued on their journey.

None of them needed more than a few hours of sleep and they all had good night vision, so they continued running into the night. It took them just over a day and a half to get to Nadorf, instead of the two days it had taken to get to the Benvari Mountains.

They camped outside Nadorf, waiting for the gates to open in the morning.

"Well, either we wander around and check out Nadorf, or we go over to Selhi right now. Selhi is three hours behind us, so right now they're still asleep," Deia said.

"Well, I vote for checking out the town. There is a mages' guild here, after all," Suzy said.

"It has a respectable selection," Malsour said.

"And I already have a guide." Suzy smiled and tapped Malsour on the back.

"I'll come as well—interested what they've got on Fire magic," Induca said.

"I would only be too happy to help you both with your studies." Malsour led them into the town and off toward the mages college.

Dave made to follow them but found Deia's arm on his elbow.

"You've had enough time cooped up in dark and dingy places. We need to get you back into good shape. You got stronger but your Agility has had little to no improvement. You've been sitting still and not fighting. This will give you a chance to limber up. You are always on the front lines, so it's time we started getting you fighting ready."

Dave made to argue but Anna stepped in.

"Dave, you're the only other person who can fight at the front. Deia is better suited for hitting someone with her magic or from behind with one of her ranged attacks. Malsour and Induca are pure mages but their natural abilities make them deadly in a fight, if they're in their Dragon forms. Suzy doesn't have those capabilities.

"If either me or Deia go down, you are going to be the frontline fighter. You are a good fighter, but we're going to Heval. If Opheir is a level-one continent, then Heval is a level-four. You need to be ready for those kinds of threats."

"All right, well, let's start. I feel like I'm going to regret this all too soon," Dave said.

"Possibly." Deia smiled.

For the good of the party. I know they're looking out for me and the others. I really wanted to check out the mages college—maybe later?

The three of them went through exercises, and then through fighting. Dave didn't realize how sloppy he'd become after the months of smithing. His Strength was impressive but his Agility was indeed lacking. They moved him through different Agility training regimes to see what leveled up his Agility the fastest. In the end, they went with obstacle courses.

They were much harder than the forest as there was a set path that stretched a person's abilities to the limit. There weren't any branches to swing off of, or close-knit trees to jump from and to. Sure, there were obstacles like that. Though there were others like sand running, or cargo nets that you had to climb up. It didn't simply work on the speed at which you could do things; it worked on technique, thinking your actions through.

After four hours, Dave was panting, drinking from his waterskin, and regretting ever putting his Agility training on hold. He was certainly paying for it now.

They moved into more sparring.

Deia and Anna were a sight to behold. Many groups of Players and POE turned to watch their fights as their blades rang out through the air.

Dave watched them, studying their movements as well as their weapons.

Seems that those new blades can finally handle her full strength, Dave thought with a bit of pride as Deia kept pressuring Anna to make a mistake as Anna threw Deia's blades away and out of her way.

Deia took the blows, using them to pivot and drift out of the way.

Anna slammed into Deia; Deia danced. Their two ways of fighting were very different but their skill with each turned it into one hell of a show.

Anna put her foot in Deia's instep; she slammed her knee into Deia's, whirling out and around so that her big great sword rested next to her neck before Deia could even move.

Why is it that I have the feeling Anna is holding back? It was a scary thought but the burst of speed at the end made him doubtful that she had been using her full talents.

Being able to match someone for skill and only use the minimal amount of extra force to finish a match—that took a lot more work than someone who was just a few levels above.

That was the work of a master.

"Dave, your turn!" Anna said.

"Shit." Dave sighed and moved to take Deia's spot. She would be watching so that she could see his form. They both fought with dual weapons; seeing Dave's ability would allow her to understand where he was at.

"Don't beat me up too much because I didn't train," Dave asked as he lowered himself down. He turned off all the Abscondita's enhancements and pulled out his twin axes from his belt loop. He meant to do something about them, but making everyone else's weapons and gear had come first.

Dave moved the axes, feeling their balance once again as he automatically triggered Touch of the Land, creating a detailed picture of the area around him as well as Deia and Anna.

Anna's high levels and her magical abilities made it hard to see through her personal space. He increased the Mana use, seeing her heartbeat and the muscles that were held tense, ready to act.

"Just act and react," Dave said to himself, taking a deep breath.

Anna didn't say anything but moved forward to attack him. Dave saw it. Even though he wouldn't have been able to see her muscles through her armor, now he could see them contract and release, the flow of blood as she prepared a diagonal slash.

Dave jumped backward onto his right foot, before he rushed in and brought his left axe toward her head as her great sword cut through the space between them.

She dodged, bringing her sword up to deflect Dave's right axe; her great sword came across to collide with his left hand.

Dave brought his left axe in, slamming his axe head against her great sword; he had a few moments to slow her momentum and get clear of her reach. Dave was breathing heavy as he squared up with Anna again.

"Well, seems that not everything was lost on you," Deia said.

Anna came in again, this time faster. Dave's eyes picked up her actions and reactions. His perception was actually working with his Touch of the Land ability and letting him see Anna's actions as they were happening on a muscle level.

There was no room for conscious thought on Dave's part. Only his high Intelligence was allowing him to intercept her hits. His brain was firing fast enough to make up for his body's slow reaction speed.

She opened up his defense and slammed her shoulder into his chest. He lost his standing, toppling over to find her great sword near his groin.

"Watch out, he's rather useful down there," Deia said playfully.

"Ow." Dave dropped his head to the training area's dirt ground.

"You're not as fast as Deia, but you're not as rusty as I was scared of." Anna held out a hand to him.

"Thanks, I feel so much better." Dave took her help up to his feet.

"Your footwork is good, your speed is lacking, and your blows—you're fighting like you're beating your opponent into submission. Kind of like you think the air is the ore you're working with," Deia said.

"That doesn't sound good," Dave said.

"Thankfully, your fiancée and good friend Anna will endeavor to correct your problem areas." Deia's smile was like that of a hungry wolf.

Dave did not feel one bit safe after seeing that expression.

"We've got two more hours until we meet up at the teleport pad. Anna, you good for a few more rounds?"

"Yep." Anna jumped, her armor shifting around until she was comfortable.

"Well, let's get going. Less rest breaks should mean that your Agility increases a bit faster," Deia said.

"What the hell did I get myself into?" Dave asked as Anna came at him with her great sword. *With friends like this, who needs enemies!?*

***

Induca chuckled as Dave, Anna, and Deia made it to the transport pad.

Malsour found it hard to not grin at Dave's appearance. He looked as if he'd been training all day by the sweat and the way he was barely staying upright.

"Transport to Selhi capital," the transport hub's manager said in a bored tone as the transport hub glowed. People moved toward it and disappeared in one side as people from the Selhi capital departed out the other side of the transport pad, heading toward the guards who processed all new arrivals.

"Well, it sure as hell beats flying," Dave said.

"You look like crap," Suzy said.

"Find anything good in the mages college?" Dave asked, ignoring the statement.

"Not much—few things. Might find something interesting in Selhi," Malsour said as they walked with the line.

"You used one of these before?" Induca asked Suzy.

"Nope. Anything that I should be worried about?"

"Nah, you'll be fine unless you get motion sickness. You ready for this, bro?" Induca asked with a wicked gleam in her eye.

"No," Malsour said.

Damn unnatural looking things, swirling rainbows and lights. I'm a Dragon, but if I'm riding a carriage or a transport pad, I feel nauseous as all hell. He tried to not think of it as he kept walking.

"Does Selhi have a mages college?" Dave asked.

"It does."

"Ahh, it's good that we get to see the Mages College of Heval right away." Dave sounded relieved.

"There is more than one mages college in Heval. After all, Heval is controlled by four main groups separated by mountain ranges."

"I thought Heval is as big as Opheir."

"Did you never look at a map?" Deia asked.

"Well, no." Dave scratched his head.

Deia sighed, opening her interface and sending him something.

"Oh wow, okay. I did not think that Heval was that big. Opheir is tiny! Only Per'ush is smaller and they're technically floating city states."

"There are a number of mages' guilds on Heval. Per'ush still have the strongest, but Heval's mostly deal with nature and alchemy as they have a thriving economic situation," Malsour said.

"I would think that with all of those different kingdoms and such, it would make things complicated?" Suzy turned the statement into a question.

"Well, with Players being around, there are plenty of economic opportunities. There is also the threat of attacks. When there are no Players around, nations are known to fight—though in the last two hundred years, there has nearly always been an active cycle of Players.

"There are armies, but they usually work with one another to fight Players who are harming the People of Emerilia or they are looking to secure their own lands from mobs and the native aggressors of Emerilia. Politicians and royalty deal with alliances and trade agreements more than war and issues of violence, except in Ashal."

"Ashal?" Deia asked.

"You must've heard of their expansion wars," Anna said.

"Well, yes," Deia said as they continued on, getting closer to the transport pad.

"The Ashal continent is the only continent where the kingdoms, empires and whatever groups there are, actively try to increase their claim of the land, whether or not there are Players on Emerilia or not. It is the highest rate land mass at Level 5. They have the most Rare and Legendary class resources with more dungeons, higher-leveled enemies, and events nearly every month or more. People of Emerilia in Ashal usually range about level 100, with fighters around level 150. A rare few of them are even 200 and up," Malsour said.

"It is rare to see someone of that high of a level as other groups will make temporary alliances to deal with those higher-leveled people. They also actively look for Players to aid their wars." Induca frowned.

"It has calmed down in recent years as my father has limited the Jukal influences on the different leaders. It used to be that Jukal people could spend money to gain a position of power, becoming enlightened advisors to the leaders of Ashal groups. They would use their armies and forces like a chess set to try to win control of Ashal. Now, the wars have gone on for so long, few know why they are happening," Anna said.

"Well, Emerilia is certainly filled with surprises," Dave said.

Malsour looked up at the transport pad.

"I hate this bit," he muttered, before he stepped onto the transport pad. He focused on a point in the distance as he saw a swirl of colors all around him. His foot hit the ground and he was walking out of the transport pad and into Selhi's capital city.

He was a bit wobbly on his feet, better than Suzy who came through not realizing that she was still walking. Induca caught her before she fell over. Suzy went bright red for her near-accident.

Deia did the same for Dave as he came through and almost face-planted.

They all grouped together, heading for the line talking to guards.

"Shit, you've even got customs here," Dave said.

Emerilia will be continued in For The Guild.

As a self published author I live for reviews! If you've enjoyed Emerilia, please leave a review!

Hope you have a great Day! ☺

Want a bigger map of Emerilia and the continents? Check out http://theeternalwriter.deviantart.com/

You can check out my other books, what I'm working on and upcoming releases through the following means:

Website: **http://michaelchatfield.com/**
Twitter: **@chatfieldsbooks**[1]
Facebook: **Michael Chatfield**[2]
Goodreads: **Goodreads.com/michaelchatfield**[3]
Thanks again for reading! ☺

---

1.   https://twitter.com/chatfieldsbooks

2.   https://www.facebook.com/michaelchatfieldsbooks/?ref=hl

3.   https://www.goodreads.com/author/show/14055550.Michael_Chatfield

Interested in more LitRPG? Check out https://www.facebook.com/groups/LitRPGsociety/

Continue on for Character Sheet!

In Alphabetical order

Ankol

Dwarf

Dwarven Master Smith. Smithing Art: Metal Spinner. Lives in Grorart Mountain.

Boran-Al

Lich

One of the Dark Lord's Champions. Works directly under the Dark Lord. Creates Creatures of Power and carry's out the Dark Lord's orders. His Citadel was destroyed.

Cassie

Elf/Human Halfling

Holy warrior. Leader of the Golden Sabres. In a relationship with Josh Giles.

Dark Lord

God

Embodiment of the Dark affinity. Created Demons. Normally an ally with the Earth Lord. Always looking a way to tip the power balance of Emerilia in his favor.

Dasano

Dwarf

Dwarven Master Smith. Smithing Art: Metal Press. Lives in Grorart Mountain.

Akatol Dracul

Dragon

Water Mage. Was the second Dragon, Denur's husband. Went mad and started a genocide, disappeared.

Denur Dracul

Dragon

Fire Mage Hailed as 'Mother of Dragons'. First of her race, a creature of power created by the Lady of Fire. Seen as her daughter. Sister to Oson' Deia.

Gelimah Dracul

Dragon

Dark Mage. Brother to Induca, Louna and Malsour

Fornau Dracul

Dragon

Earth Mage. Quindar's mate Malsour and Induca's grand-nephew.

Induca Dracul

Dragon

Fire Mage. One of the youngest from the first generation of Dragons. Sister to Malsour, daughter of Denur, aunt to Quindar, great aunt to Fornau. Member of the Stone Raiders and Party Zero.

Kinal Dracul

Dragon

Louna Dracul

Dragon

Induca, Gelimah and Malsour's sister.

Malsour Dracul

Dragon

Dark Mage. One of the oldest Dragons in existence, first born of Denur. Deia and Induca's Guardian, Stone Raider and Party Zero member. Brother to Induca. Great Uncle to Fornau Dracul and Uncle to Quindar Dracul.

Quindar Dracul

Dragon

Wind Mage, wife to Fornau, Niece to Induca and Malsour.

Wokui Dracul

Dragon

Water Mage

Xednai Dracul

Dragon

One of the first Dragons, had several Dragons. Her son is Fornau.

Gorpal Dunsk

Dwarf

Dwarven Master Smith, lives in Aldamire Mountain, created 3 Weapons of Power - Mace of Fury, Tower Shield, Boots of Smash. Smithing Art: Paint Copy

Earth Lord

God

Embodiment of the Dark affinity. Created Earth Sprites.

Edmur

Dwarf

Dwarven Master Smith. Had been in the Dwarven War Bands as a Shield Bearer. Former pupil of Quino's Brother to Endur. Smithing Art: Metal's Song

Endur

Dwarf

Dwarven Master Smith. Had been in the Dwarven War Bands as a Shield Bearer. Former pupil of Quino's, brother to Edmur, lives in Zolu Mountain. Smithing Art Hammer Blows

Esa

Human

Melee fighter. Member of Mikal and Jule's party. Fought at Boranl-Al's Citadel.

Member of the Stone Raiders. Going out with Jules. Works under Dwayne as a fighter. Being trained for a leadership position under Dwayne.

Fend

Dwarf

Lord Under the Mithsia Mountains.

David Grahslagg

Dwarf/Human Halfling, in-game character of Austin Zane. Dwarven Master Smith, Resident of Cliff Hill, member of Party Zero and the Stone Raider's Guild. Other names: Austin Zane

Josh Giles

Human

Rogue. Leader of the Stone Raiders. Was a investment broker on Earth, became an E-head. In a relationship with Cassie from the Golden Sabres.

Gorrund

Dwarf

Dwarven Master Smith in Benvari Mountain with Jesal, teaching four apprentices. Smithing Art: Blood Bender.

Gurren

Dwarf

Shield bearer, member of Dwarven War Band under Lox's command, sent to guide people to Cliff-Hill. Friend of David Grahslagg, Kol's Grandson. Member of the Stone Raiders.

Helick

Dwarf

Dwarven Master Smith.

Kim Isdola

Human

Cleric/alchemist. Lieutenant in Stone Raiders.

Arch-Mage Jekoni

Human/item

Soul bound to Staff of Growing, over 2,000 years old; missing legs. Held within Dwarven Vaults with other Weapons of power.

Jesal

Dwarf

Dwarven Master Smith, Dave's master smith trainer. Smithing art: Nature's Guide

Jules

Human

Healer. Member of Mikal and Esa's party. Fought at Boranl-Al's Citadel.

Member of the Stone Raiders. Used to be an army medic, E-head without legs IRL. Going out with Esa. Works under Lucy as support, leads the healers of the Stone Raiders.

Joko

Dwarf

Shield bearer, member of Dwarven War Band under Lox's command, sent to guide people to Cliff-Hill. Friend and trainer of David Grahslagg.

Deceased.

Anna'Kal

Wolf Beast Kin/Administrator AI24681

Air mage. Originally a program meant to assist Lo'kal with the running of Emerilia. Anna was uploaded to a Player body and inserted into Emerilia. She became emotionally attached with her charges. When the Beast Kin people were wiped out from Emerilia she went into cold storage, waiting for her father to awake her when a chance came to fight against the prison they had created.

Member of the Stone Raiders and Party Zero. Daughter of Bob.

Lo'kal

Jukal

Scientist, created Emerilia. Awarded the position of the Gray God, maintains Emerilia, its people and Players. Other names: Bob, Bobby McMahnon, The Balancer, Gray God.

Kol

Dwarf

Dwarven Master Smith. Gurren's grandfather. Resides in Cliff-Hill. Taught Dave how to Smith. Runs his Smithies. Smithing art: Blind Man's Touch

Lady of Air

Goddess

Embodiment of the affinity Air. Known for causing mischief. Her Champions act as spies and information brokers, tilting the balance of Emerilia.

Lady of Fire

Goddess

Created Dragons, Mages Guild and College. Gave gift of 'knowledge' to the people of Emerilia. Mother to Deia, Lover of Oson'Mal and best friend with Bob.

Other Names: Ignil

Lady of Light

Goddess

Sent Players to kill/capture Dragons to make her own Creatures of Power. Created the race known as Angels. Large rivalry with the Dark Lord.

Lovan

Dwarf

Mithsia Mountain Warclan leader

Lox

Dwarf

Shield bearer. Was the commander of the War Band sent to guide people to Cliff-Hill. Friend of David Grahslagg. Member of the Stone Raiders.

Suzy Markell

Human (IRL)

High Elf (Emerilia)

Austin Zane's secretary and best friend. David Grahslagg's best friend and assistant with running Cliff Hill Smithy and Factory. Summoning Mage. Steven's contractor, member of Party Zero and the Stone Raiders.

Max

Dwarf

Shield bearer, member of Dwarven War Band under Lox's command, sent to guide people to Cliff-Hill. Friend of David Grahslagg. Deceased.

Melhoun

Water snake made by the Water Lord.

Sealed away.

Mikal

Human

Rogue. Jules and Esa's party member. Member of the Stone Raiders. Friends with Party Zero.

Oson'Deia

Elf/Demi God Halfling

Elven Ranger and Fire Mage. Daughter of Oson'Mal and Lady Fire of the Affinity Pantheon. Resident of Cliff Hill and member of the Stone Raider's Guild, Leader of Party Zero.

Other names: Ouluv'Deia

Quino

Dwarf

Dwarven Master Smith, lives in Zolu Mountain. Trained the brothers Endur and Edmur. Smithing Art: Internal cutting.

Tounk

Dwarf

Shield bearer, member of Dwarven War Band under Lox's command, sent to guide people to Cliff-Hill. Friend of David Grahslagg. **Deceased.**

Demon Prince Alkao/Alkao Travezar

Aerial Demon

Melee fighter. Commander of the Third Demon Horde and leader of Xerzit lands. Oldest of the five remaining Demon Prince's of Devil's Crater.

Dwayne Trebault

Human

Melee fighter. Lieutenant in Stone Raiders. Leads and trains the melee fighters in the Stone Raiders.

Lucy Vernia

Wood Elf/Human

Lieutenant in Stone Raiders. Spy master, deals with supporting the Stone Raiders and paperwork.

Water Lord

God

Embodiment of the Water Affinity. Created the Mer-People and water creatures. Created the Water Serpent Melhoun. Rival to the Lady of Fire.

Austin Zane

CEO of Rock Breaker's Corporation. Engineer specializing in space vehicles. Background in Astro physics. Other names: David Grahslagg

Wis'Zel

Wood Elf

Bard. Works for David Grahslagg, managing his Ceramics factories in Cliff Hill.